DEADLY CARE

DEADLY CARE

LEONARD S. GOLDBERG

A DUTTON BOOK

DUTTON
Published by the Penguin Group
Penguin Books USA Inc., 375 Hudson Street,
New York, New York 10014, U.S.A.
Penguin Books Ltd, 27 Wrights Lane,
London W8 5TZ, England
Penguin Books Australia Ltd, Ringwood,
Victoria, Australia
Penguin Books Canada Ltd, 10 Alcorn Avenue,
Toronto, Ontario, Canada M4V 3B2
Penguin Books (N.Z.) Ltd, 182–190 Wairau Road,
Auckland 10, New Zealand

Penguin Books Ltd, Registered Offices:
Harmondsworth, Middlesex, England

First published by Dutton, an imprint of Dutton Signet,
a division of Penguin Books USA Inc.
Distributed in Canada by McClelland & Stewart Inc.

First Printing, March, 1996
10 9 8 7 6 5 4 3 2

 REGISTERED TRADEMARK—MARCA REGISTRADA

LIBRARY OF CONGRESS CATALOGING-IN-PUBLICATION DATA
Goldberg, Leonard S.
    Deadly care / Leonard S. Goldberg.
        p.   cm.
    ISBN 0-525-94092-8
    1. Forensic pathologists—Fiction.   I. Title.
PS3557.O35775D43   1996
    813'.54—dc20   95-39816
                                                        CIP

Printed in the United States of America
Set in New Baskerville
Designed by Leonard Telesca

For I.M.

Love is stronger than death.

— *Yizkor*

Commit the oldest sins the newest kind of ways.

—SHAKESPEARE, *King Henry IV*

DEADLY CARE

Prologue

Someone had drowned.

The search-and-rescue helicopter skimmed over the shoreline looking for the body. Dusk was falling, daylight almost gone. There would not be time for another run.

Karl Rimer sauntered down the boardwalk with its tacky stores on one side, the beach on the other. He glanced up as the helicopter whizzed by, paying it scant attention. Rimer strolled on, a man at his leisure, but he was acutely aware of his surroundings. He saw everything without watching. A shopkeeper, closing his T-shirt store, nervously peeked over his shoulder looking for some hidden danger. This was a mean neighborhood, particularly at night. An old drunk, smelling of stale urine, weaved his way off the walk and into an alley. A scrawny dog followed him. Soon the boardwalk would be completely deserted.

Rimer was wearing a dark tan trench coat and floppy rain cap. It was an unusual outfit for most of Southern California, but not for the Venice–Santa Monica area. Here there were freaks in outrageous dress everywhere. Rimer would blend in, just like he wanted to.

In his peripheral vision, Rimer again counted the few people remaining on the beach. There were four. A young couple walking in the sand at the water's edge, a surfer hoping for one last perfect wave, and a man in a kayak paddling in the shallows against the current. Rimer concentrated on the kayaker. That was his target.

Rimer watched the kayaker without seeming to watch him. The man was now paddling out despite a rough sea. A big wave smashed down on the kayak and nearly flipped it over. With great effort, the kayaker managed to right the boat. Rimer hoped the man didn't get himself drowned and swept out to sea. He needed the man and his kayak intact, at least for a while.

Rimer glanced down the boardwalk and saw a cop on a bicycle coming toward him. Rimer was instantly on guard. He didn't see the cop's partner. Policemen—even those on bicycles—always worked in pairs. The cop got closer. An Oriental. Young. Beady-eyed. Rimer knew how to behave and not arouse suspicion. He didn't stare and he didn't look away. Rimer assumed a meek posture and waved slightly. He appeared to be a nobody, a nothing. The cop nodded importantly and Rimer nodded back. But he kept his head down, even when glancing up. All the cop saw was trench coat and cap.

The cop slowed his bicycle to a crawl, keeping it balanced but barely moving. He stared down at Rimer, his expression impassive. Rimer looked at the ground submissively, wondering if he was going to have to kill the cop. There was no way he would allow the cop to search him.

"Let's go, Paul," the cop called out over his shoulder. "Get a move on."

Rimer saw the second cop pedaling furiously down the board-walk, trying to catch up. Another Oriental. Shit! They were like ants.

Rimer walked on, keeping his pace even and unhurried. He let a full minute pass before bending over to retie a shoelace. He glanced quickly down the boardwalk. The cops were almost out of sight.

He turned his attention back to the beach. The young couple was gone. The surfer was dragging his board toward the pier where the parking lot was located. The kayaker was still paddling, but now very close to shore, just beyond the surf.

Rimer waited patiently, still walking. It wouldn't be long now. An offshore fog was starting to roll in, bringing with it a brisk wind that made the sea even rougher. Choppy waves battered against the kayak, making it difficult to control. The twilight was turning into darkness and Rimer had trouble seeing his target. For a moment Rimer lost sight of the man, then picked him up again. The kayaker had had enough. He was paddling in to shore.

Rimer took out two amphetamine pills and chewed them thoroughly before swallowing. The drug gave him the extra power and quickness he liked before he did a job. He also believed that amphetamines heightened his senses and enhanced his ability to respond to the unexpected.

Rimer unbuttoned his trench coat but kept it closed with his hands. He stepped off the boardwalk and trudged across the sand, his gaze fixed on the kayaker, who was pulling his boat out of the water and onto the beach.

Rimer looked away briefly. The boardwalk was deserted, its lights muted by the mist. He picked up his pace and headed toward the man leaning over the kayak. Rimer let his trench coat fall open.

"Hi," Rimer called out.

"Hey," the man said pleasantly as he glanced up.

Rimer swung the baseball bat with all of his might. A Louisville Slugger. Thirty-four ounce. The kayaker's hand came up. Too late. The bat hit the young man just over his eyes with a sickening thud. Rimer heard bones crack. The young man dropped to the sand like a deadweight.

Rimer searched the body quickly and thoroughly, looking for a strip of microfilm. He had been told that it would be small, probably the size of a postage stamp, but it might even be smaller— like a matchhead. It could be anywhere. In his watch, tucked away in his wallet, inside a hollowed-out ring. Anywhere. Rimer removed the man's watch and rings, then went through the kayaker's wet suit, looking for secret pockets or a belt that might hold his wallet or keys. Nothing. Maybe he'd hidden it in the kayak. Rimer tore the boat apart searching for the microfilm and finding nothing.

Rimer heard the helicopter coming back. In the distance he saw the copter's lights blinking. For a moment he felt panic, but he quickly pushed it aside. They didn't have their floodlights on, Rimer noted, which meant their search was over and they were returning to base. But still, if they were flying over the beach rather than the water they might see him. The helicopter came closer and closer and they *were* over the beach. Goddamn it!

Rimer quickly grabbed the kayak and, turning it upside down, covered the young man's body. Then he sat on the kayak and stared out to sea. A man alone, contemplating.

The helicopter passed over and Rimer was almost certain they hadn't seen him. Too dark, too misty. And the crew wasn't looking for anything. They just wanted to get home. Rimer knew all about copters from his tour in Vietnam. At night you couldn't see a damn thing unless the floodlights were on. No, they hadn't seen him. Not a chance. Rimer watched the helicopter's blinking lights fade into the night.

From beneath the kayak, the young man groaned weakly. Rimer looked down and saw the man's arm sticking out from under the boat. The fingers moved, clawing at the sand. The man groaned again. This time it sounded like a cry—a child's cry.

Rimer kicked the kayak aside and, picking up the baseball bat, went back to work.

1

Lucy O'Hara held on tightly to her father's arm and started up
the steps to Los Angeles Memorial Hospital. She tried to maintain
her composure and ignore the pain in her back and hips, but
walking up an incline made it worse. A dull ache was rapidly becoming a throbbing, stabbing pain. Quickly she reached down and
pressed on the morphine pump that was implanted beneath the
skin in her abdomen. Eight milligrams of morphine sulfate flowed
out into the subcutaneous tissue.

At the top of the steps, Lucy paused and leaned heavily against
her father, weak and exhausted by the short climb. She stared at
the black glass doors to the hospital and studied her reflection. A
young, attractive woman, tall and slender with a blond ponytail.
But she couldn't see the finer details of her face. The sunken eyes
and the pallor. The signs of life slipping away.

"Dad, suppose the transplant doesn't work?"

"Oh, it will work," he assured her. "Remember we have the
luck of the Irish. And we have a good Irish donor, too."

Her father held the door for her and Lucy entered the lobby,
wondering if she would be alive when she left the hospital. She
bit down on her lip, trying to hold her emotions in check. But
tears welled up in her eyes and she had to sniff them back. *Why
me, Lord? Why me?*

Lucy eased herself down on a couch outside the Admissions
Office and waited while her father went in to fill out the necessary

forms. Across from her was an obese Hispanic woman holding a crying child. The little boy had red sores on his arms and legs, some open and draining. Suddenly he coughed, sending a visible spray into the air. Lucy quickly raised a hand to protect herself against the virus-laden droplets. She knew that an infection now could be disastrous. A viral infection would make her very ill and the bone marrow transplant would have to be delayed indefinitely. A bacterial infection would be even worse. That could kill her.

Lucy sighed sadly, thinking how her disease had turned her life upside down. Until eight months ago she had been a happy, healthy twenty-four-year-old law student, never sick, rarely taking any medicine except for birth control pills and an occasional Tylenol. Then the weakness and bone pain had started and she was diagnosed as having acute myeloblastic leukemia.

The first cycle of chemotherapeutic agents induced a partial remission. Her blood counts rose and the normal cells returned. There was hope. Maybe she would be one of the few lucky ones to respond. But the leukemia recurred and a second course of chemotherapy had no effect at all. The disease progressed; the bone pain caused by proliferating leukemia cells became intolerable. The morphine pump helped, but the pain was always there, reminding her that a mass of tumor cells was growing inside her, expanding and crowding out the normal cells. Her white blood cell counts were always low, predisposing her to life-threatening infections. She had been hospitalized four times because of it.

And now there were very few normal cells left in her bone marrow. The leukemia tumor mass had destroyed everything. A bone marrow transplant was her last and only chance. Without it she would die.

"We're all set, Pumpkin," her father said, breaking into her thoughts.

Lucy looked up at her father and the orderly beside him who was positioning a wheelchair. She stood with her father's help and plopped down heavily in the wheelchair. "You don't have to come with me, Dad."

"Yes, I do," Michael O'Hara said firmly.

The orderly made certain Lucy was secure, then pushed the wheelchair in a wide semicircle, heading for the main corridor. Lucy stared down at the floor, hating the wheelchair. It made her feel helpless and dependent and self-conscious. She had to look up to see people who glanced down at her and tried to guess why such a young, attractive woman was in a wheelchair.

They came to the bank of elevators. The area was crowded with doctors, nurses and visitors, all talking at once and creating a hum of conversation. Lucy stared up at the floor indicator for the patients' elevator, disliking the crowd and feeling claustrophobic. But that wouldn't be a problem much longer, she thought grimly. In a matter of days she'd be in total isolation, separated from the world and all its bacteria and viruses while she waited to find out if the bone marrow transplant would take. And what if the transplant didn't take? Then there would be no hope, no chance of survival. She'd been told that straight out by the hematologist. For the hundredth time Lucy found herself wondering if there really was an afterlife.

The elevator door opened. Another patient in a wheelchair was in the car, so Lucy and her chair had to be backed in. Her father touched her shoulder and squeezed it reassuringly. Lucy glanced over at the other patient, wondering if it was a boy or girl. All of the patient's hair was gone and this accentuated the nose. It looked like a beak on a bird's head. Lucy gazed at the IV running into the patient's arm, and then she saw the patient's fingernails, painted a bright red. A girl, Lucy thought, no more than sixteen and trying desperately to hold on to some vestige of femininity. And then Lucy cringed, now realizing that soon she would look exactly like that young teenager. No hair. It would all fall out, the hematologist had carefully explained to her. To prepare her for the bone marrow transplant she would be given large doses of radiation and chemotherapy. These would destroy all of her leukemic cells. They would also cause her hair to drop out. But the hair would grow back. If she lived.

The elevator jolted to a stop and the door opened. As Lucy was wheeled out she smiled to the other patient. The teenager tried to smile back, but only one side of her face went up. The other side drooped down, paralyzed. She pursed her lips and with effort attempted to say "Bye," but only a high-pitched squeal came out. It sounded like a cry for help.

They went down a wide corridor and came to the nurses' station. A ward clerk seated behind a counter began asking her father questions and filling out forms. Lucy tilted her head back and tried to see the clerk, but all she saw was the top of the counter. From down the hall Lucy heard a cry of pain, shrill and piercing, as if it came from a woman. A door closed and Lucy heard a second cry, muffled this time. The ward clerk kept asking questions, ignoring the cries altogether. Lucy wondered if the screaming woman was having a bone marrow aspiration. That hurt like hell, Lucy knew from experience.

"You have to sign here," her father said, handing her a form and a ballpoint pen.

Lucy quickly scribbled her signature. She studied it for a moment before handing the form back. Even her handwriting had changed. Now it looked weak and uneven.

Lucy was wheeled into a private room that had the distinct scent of an air deodorizer. It was not a fresh aroma, but a sickly sweet one. Lucy sniffed the air, wondering what had made the smell that they were trying to cover up. A young nurse with cold hands came in and took Lucy's vital signs, then gave her hospital pajamas, a robe and a plastic identification bracelet. On the bracelet was her name, hospital number and date of birth. Her birthday was a month away. Lucy wondered if she would live to see it.

"I guess I'd better let you get settled in, huh?" her father asked as the nurse left.

"I guess," Lucy said.

"We're going to come through this okay, you know."

Lucy tried to nod and smile, but now she saw tears welling up in her father's eyes. "I'm going to be fine."

Her father hugged her tightly and quickly turned away.

She watched him hurry from the room, knowing that he didn't want her to see him crying. Lucy stared blankly at the door, her lower lip quivering as tears flowed down her cheeks. She had an almost irresistible urge to run away from the hospital and find a hiding place where there were no doctors and needles and nurses. But she quickly pushed the silly notion aside. She was not going to run away from her only chance to live.

Lucy reached for a Kleenex and blew her nose, sniffing back the last of the tears. She saw the mascara stain on the tissue and, muttering "Shit!" under her breath, went into the small bathroom.

The sickly sweet aroma was even stronger now and Lucy hoped the odor wouldn't permeate her clothes. She studied her face in the mirror and wiped away the green-black streaks, deciding not to add new mascara. But she did apply rouge to her cheeks, covering the marked pallor caused by the anemia. She also covered little, pinpoint red spots on her chin. Petechiae. They were small skin hemorrhages caused by low platelets. The disease was eating away at her, leaving its mark everywhere.

She walked over to the closet and undressed, then put on the hospital pajamas and robe. The pajamas were too big, the robe too small. Lying back on her pillow, she stared up at the television set that hung from the ceiling. It was nine-thirty a.m. and she didn't feel like watching game shows or talk shows. Maybe there was an old movie on. She reached for the *TV Guide*.

There was a knock on the door. Lucy looked over as Dr. Robert Mariner walked in.

"Good morning, Lucy," he said, his voice warm and friendly.

"Hey, Dr. Mariner."

"I just stopped by to make sure they're treating you well."

"So far, so good."

"Excellent! But if there's any problem, you let me know. We're going to make sure you receive the very best care possible." The beeper on his belt sounded and he reached down, pushing the button to silence it. "May I use your phone?"

"Of course."

Lucy watched him pick up the phone. She liked his voice and his bedside manner and his looks. He looked like a doctor and he sounded like one. Just over six feet tall, he was a well-built man in his early fifties with thick brown hair that was heavily grayed. His facial features were sharp with a jutting jaw and clear blue eyes.

Mariner placed his hand over the phone and smiled at Lucy. "Dr. Black told me to tell you that she'll be by to see you this evening."

Lucy nodded and smiled back as the doctor returned to his phone conversation. She continued to watch him, wishing that he was her doctor, the one looking after her at Memorial, the one doing the transplant. But he wasn't. He was the president of Health First, the HMO that Lucy's family belonged to.

They had not enrolled in the HMO for financial reasons but because their family doctor, Dr. Amanda Black, had given up her private practice and joined the staff at Health First. Dr. Black had seen the family through too many crises and illnesses for them not to follow her to the HMO. And it had worked out wonderfully well. They saw Dr. Black as often as needed with no delays, hassles or paperwork. When it was discovered that Lucy had leukemia, Health First was marvelous. She was treated by their staff hematologist, and when it was clear she needed a bone marrow transplant they referred her to Memorial with no hesitation.

Mariner put the phone down. "I've got to run. One of our patients is not doing as well as I'd like."

"Thanks for stopping by."

"No problem. Now remember, everything is going to go just great. The transplant people here are the best in the world."

"I'm going to get through this," Lucy vowed.

"With flying colors," Mariner added.

"And if everything goes well, I'll be able to go back to law school in September, right?"

"You can bank on it."

"I am," Lucy said softly.

She watched the door close, now feeling the fear creeping back. Suppose it doesn't work? Suppose the transplant doesn't take? Oh, Jesus! Get me through this. Be positive, she commanded herself, be optimistic. The transplant was going to be successful. No complications. Out of the hospital in a few weeks. Mustn't forget to send a thank-you card to her bone marrow donor, a big Irish cop who lived in San Diego. Then back to law school in September. In two years she'd have her law degree and she'd join her father's firm. O'Hara, O'Hara, Diamond and Stern. It sounded great.

"Lucy O'Hara?" a technician asked from the door. She was a stocky, middle-aged woman with a puffy face and very narrow eyes.

"Yes, I'm Lucy O'Hara."

"My name is Wendy Fujiama. I'm here to draw some blood."

"Not again!" Lucy protested. "I just had blood taken yesterday."

"Talk to your doctor about it," Wendy said tonelessly. "He's the one who ordered the test. Now, which arm do you want me to stick?"

"Why didn't they get all the blood they needed yesterday?" Lucy asked, hating to have another venipuncture done. Most of her veins were scarred and thrombosed from the numerous needle sticks she'd already had.

Wendy shrugged indifferently. "You'll have to ask your doctor. I'm just following his orders." She glanced at her watch, irritated by the delay. "Do you want me to draw your blood or not?"

Lucy stared up at the technician, disliking her and her abrupt manner. She wanted to tell the woman to leave and not come back. But she didn't have the strength, and sooner or later they'd have to draw her blood anyway. Lucy sighed resignedly and held out her arm.

The technician turned her back as she prepared her needle and syringe and test tubes. She held something up to the light briefly, but Lucy couldn't tell what it was.

Lucy closed her eyes and prayed again that the bone marrow transplant would work, that she'd never have another venipuncture, that she'd never be hospitalized again as long as she lived—except for childbirth.

Lucy felt the alcohol swab on her skin, then a quick stick. Then another stick, followed by a stinging sensation.

"Something is stinging me," Lucy said, concerned.

"It's just the alcohol around the venipuncture site," the technician said as she removed the needle and placed a wad of cotton over the area. "Press down on this."

Lucy pushed down on the cotton ball as the technician left. She hoped a little clot would form quickly at the site of the venipuncture. Otherwise it could ooze for hours because of her lack of platelets. She pressed down harder and began to count to a hundred, but her mind drifted back to her father's law firm, which she would one day join. O'Hara, O'Hara, Diamond and Stern. It had a nice ring to it.

Lucy felt a strange, deep burning in her abdomen. Then came a wave of nausea that she tried to swallow away. For a moment she was better, but the nausea and burning returned, now intensified. Suddenly her chest was tight and she couldn't catch her breath. Terrified, she reached for the nurse's buzzer. The room began to spin. The light dimmed. Lucy heard herself gasping, sucking for air, just before everything went silent and black.

2

Simon Murdock hurried down the corridor on the B level of the hospital, fuming over the phone conversation he'd just had. The county was going to pay Memorial five hundred dollars for each autopsy the hospital performed for them. An absurdly low price. Ridiculous. But one he had to accept because the county of Los Angeles was in big trouble. Its morgue had been closed because of an outbreak of Legionnaires' disease. All of the coroners and most of the staff had come down with the disease and the corpses were piling up. And Memorial was the only other facility in the Greater Los Angeles Area with a forensic pathologist. So when the county contacted Murdock a week ago, he'd agreed to perform the autopsies for them. It was the right thing to do. But Murdock hadn't expected the county to gouge the hospital and take advantage of his generosity. He should have known better.

Murdock went through a set of double doors with a sign that read POSITIVELY NO ADMITTANCE EXCEPT FOR AUTHORIZED PERSONNEL. A secretary talking on the phone looked up and, seeing who it was, went back to her conversation. Murdock pushed through another set of swinging doors and entered the autopsy room.

He quickly scanned the brightly lighted room with its eight stainless steel tables lined up in rows of twos. His gaze went to the tiled walls and floor—sparkling white—then to the individual refrigeration units in the wall where the corpses were kept. He thought back to how the autopsy room had looked when he became dean of the medical center twenty years ago. It had been like a museum, dark and dank, with cement floors and marble slab tables with bloodstains that would never come out. A two-million-dollar gift from a wealthy benefactor had transformed the room into a first-rate facility.

"Can I help you with something, Dr. Murdock?"

Murdock turned to a young pathologist, gloved, mask down on his neck, goggles pulled up to the top of his forehead. "Contaminated case, huh?" Murdock asked.

"A gay heroin addict," the pathologist said matter-of-factly.

Murdock nodded. The AIDS virus was everywhere, homosexuals and addicts the most likely to be infected. "I'm looking for Dr. Blalock."

The pathologist pointed to the rear. "Last table on the left."

Murdock walked around the periphery of the room and glanced down at the corpses in varying stages of dissection. They appeared so unreal, almost all of their humanness gone and the little that did remain now being chopped away.

He saw Joanna Blalock leaning over a corpse, magnifying glass in hand, as she explained a finding to a small group of residents. She still seemed so young to Murdock. Although she was nearly forty she could easily have passed for being in her early thirties. Murdock remembered the first time he saw Joanna, when she came to Memorial to be interviewed for the position of forensic pathologist—so young and attractive, with soft, patrician features and sandy blond hair that was severely pulled back and held in place by a simple barrette. He had thought she was an intern at first, but the moment they began to talk he knew she was someone special. The glowing letters from Johns Hopkins had not exaggerated her talents. She was sharp with a quick, penetrating mind. Still he had hesitated before offering her the position at Memorial, thinking she was far too pretty to have that much brain. He had been wrong. She had turned out to be a superb addition to the staff.

Murdock waited patiently off to the side and watched Joanna carefully examine the big toes of the corpse. A superb addition to the staff, he thought again, but she was not perfect. There were flaws. She was far too independent and ran the division of forensic pathology as if it were separate and distinct from the medical center. And she was too ambitious and self-centered and spent too much time away from the hospital serving as a forensic consultant for a fee of a thousand dollars a day. It made her seem mercenary and that was not the image he wanted his staff to project.

And there was one other problem. He didn't like her and she didn't like him. There was no reason for it. Just a natural, mutual dislike that had built up over time.

Murdock cleared his throat and approached the dissecting table.

Joanna looked up from the corpse. "Hello, Simon. What brings you down here?"

"A little business. Could I have a moment of your time?"

"Sure." She handed her magnifying glass to Emily Ryan, the chief resident in forensic pathology. "Study the body carefully and tell me where he'd been the day he died."

Murdock's curiosity got the better of him. The telltale signs had to be on the surface. But where? He quickly scanned the dead man's legs and trunk, seeing nothing unusual. Then he saw the head and looked away with revulsion. There was no face, no discernible facial features. The front of the head was mashed into red pulp, the eyes and nose gone, teeth knocked out, bones smashed into fragments. Murdock swallowed back his nausea. "What kind of accident caused this?"

"It was no accident."

Murdock winced. "Do we know who this fellow was?"

"Not yet."

"Maybe his fingerprints will help."

Joanna shook her head and lifted up one of the corpse's hands. The ends of all the fingers had been cut off.

"Jesus!" Murdock tasted bile coming into his throat.

They walked over to the X-ray viewboxes that were mounted on the wall. The sound of an electric saw cutting through bone filled the air. A high-pitched squeal, like a dentist's drill. They waited for the noise to stop.

Joanna glanced at the wall clock and wondered if she was ever going to catch up with her schedule. She had two more autopsies to do, a lecture to give, slides to review. And now she had to put up with Simon Murdock. She stifled a yawn and briefly studied him. He was a tall, slender man with sharp, chiseled features. His hair was snow-white and the lines and age spots on his face were more obvious than ever. He was aging very rapidly. But his narrow brown eyes were still clear and cold with not even a hint of warmth. The eyes pretty well summed up the man, Joanna thought.

Depending on whom one talked to, Simon Murdock was either Albert Schweitzer or Niccolò Machiavelli. To the outside world he was a devoted, tireless physician whose foresight and energy had transformed Memorial into a world-renowned medical center. To those on staff he was a cunning, manipulating administrator— tyrannical and ruthless at times—who would sacrifice anyone and anything for Memorial. So which one was he, Schweitzer or Machiavelli? Joanna wondered. Probably a mixture of both. He was good and bad, just like everyone else. But she still didn't like him, not even a little, and trusted him even less.

The noise from the electric saw stopped.

"How many of these coroner's autopsies have you done so far?" Murdock asked.

Joanna shrugged. "About ten."

"And you've been able to keep up with your other duties at Memorial?"

"Barely."

"Well, if the load becomes too heavy, you must let me know."

Joanna nodded, studying his face and wondering what Simon Murdock really wanted. He hadn't come all the way down to Pathology to talk about coroner cases. He could have handled that over the phone.

"I understand they've located the source of the Legionnaires' organism," Murdock went on. "It was in the air-conditioning unit. With a little luck the morgue will be functional again in a matter of days. A week at the most."

"Longer," Joanna said at once. "All of the medical examiners are still down with Legionnaires' disease and their recovery will be slow despite the use of antibiotics."

The electric saw went on again and Murdock began calculating numbers in his head. Ten autopsies a week at five hundred dollars each. That came to a total of five thousand dollars, and if Memorial did the autopsies for three weeks, the grand total would be fifteen thousand dollars. A pittance. A big nothing for a lot of work. Better not to accept it, Murdock thought. Better to be generous and call the county commissioner and tell him that Memorial would accept no money from the county for performing a civic duty. Yes, call it a civic duty. And make sure the news media learned of Memorial's generosity. The story would give them a million dollars worth of good publicity. And most important, the commissioner and the county would be indebted to Murdock. They would owe him.

The squealing noise from the saw stopped and Murdock came back to himself. "I'm going to need another favor from you, Joanna."

Joanna exhaled weakly. "I'm already being stretched to the limit."

"This is important," Murdock said gravely. "Very, very important."

"I'm not going to say yes until I know what the favor is."

"Yesterday a young girl with leukemia was admitted to Memorial and died suddenly. The family is demanding a complete investigation."

"Acute leukemia?"

Murdock nodded. "Yes, I think so."

"People with acute leukemia almost always die of their disease, Simon."

"Suddenly?"

"It can happen. Frequently their platelet counts are low and they can have a major hemorrhage." Joanna gestured with her hands. "It sounds routine to me. Why not let one of the other pathologists handle it?"

"Because the girl's family requested you specifically. You see, her father heads a very prestigious law firm here in Los Angeles. They handle the legal affairs of the Rhodes family. It was Mortimer Rhodes who recommended you to the family."

Joanna thought back to Mortimer Rhodes, whom she hadn't seen in years. The old man was a multimillionaire, rich in oil and real estate, politically very powerful. His granddaughter had been the victim of a serial killer Joanna had helped to track down. To show his appreciation, Rhodes had established the Karen Rhodes Forensic Laboratory at Memorial and funded it generously. "All right, I'll do it. Have her chart sent to my office so I can review it."

"There is no chart to speak of. She died suddenly, thirty minutes after reaching the ward. The doctors hadn't even examined her."

"Where would her medical records be?"

"With her private doctor, I would imagine. I'll find out for you." Murdock took an envelope from his coat pocket and quickly scribbled a note to himself. "I'd appreciate it if you'd phone me as soon as the postmortem examination is completed."

"It won't be until late tomorrow afternoon."

"That'll be fine," Murdock said gratefully. "Now, I'd better let you get back to your work."

Joanna watched him walk away and immediately regretted that she hadn't insisted that one of the other pathologists do the autopsy. Death from leukemia wasn't a forensic problem. Any member of the staff could have done the postmortem examination and she could have reviewed the findings. Damn it! Why hadn't she insisted? She was already so far behind and falling further behind by the hour. And she wanted to spend more time on the man with no face and no fingers.

Her gaze went to the X-ray viewbox on the wall. The film showed a lateral view of a skull, the bones anteriorly mashed almost beyond recognition. The chin was partially intact. One of the supraorbital arches still had some semblance of its former shape. What instrument was used to smash this man's face? Joanna asked herself. And why? Why was it so important to the killer that his victim not be identified?

Joanna stretched her back and neck, the vertebrae cracking pleasantly. She looked around the room, all tables filled and busy, all conversations muted by the noise of the power drill. Glancing down at her gloves, she spotted a small hole in one of them. Cursing under her breath, she stripped the latex gloves off and inspected her hands for any scratches or blood spots. Satisfied there weren't any, she snapped on a fresh pair of gloves and headed back to her table.

Emily Ryan looked up as Joanna approached, then went back to examining the corpse. She started at the feet and slowly worked her way up. The legs and thighs were unremarkable, the buttocks negative except for a tattoo of a small butterfly. His torso was well tanned with a small old appendectomy scar. Emily didn't re-examine the corpse's face. Once was more than enough. She stepped back and wondered what she'd missed. Blalock had said there was something that would tell them where the corpse was the day he was killed. Was it the tattoo? The tanned skin? No. It had to be something else.

"Tell me what you found," Joanna said.

"He has no face and his fingertips have been cut off. So who-ever killed him didn't want the victim's identity known."

Joanna glanced at the corpse's face, wondering again what type of weapon was used. "Were there any other positive findings?"

"Not really. He's got a pretty good tan and a tattoo of a small butterfly on his butt."

"Good," Joanna said approvingly. "That's two out of three."

"What's the third?"

"The most important. It will tell you where he was the day he died."

"Can you give me a clue?"

Joanna looked up at the wall clock. A lecture had to be given in an hour. Lunch would have to be skipped. "Let's start at the beginning of this fellow's story. Where was his body found?"

"In a shallow grave in the Angeles National Forest."

Joanna reached for her magnifying glass and went to the feet of the corpse, carefully examining the toes and the spaces between them. She picked up a few grains of sand and rubbed them be-tween her fingers. "Sand. White sand. Is there any white sand in the Angeles National Forest?"

"No," Emily said promptly.

"So . . . ?" Joanna said, dragging out her voice.

Emily squinted her eyes and concentrated.

"White sand," Joanna said again.

"The beach!" Emily blurted out.

"Exactly," Joanna said. "The beach. Now tell me which beach."

Emily's face went blank. She stared out into space, lips moving, as if the answer was on the tip of her tongue.

"Los Angeles has a number of beaches," Joanna went on, "and the chemical content of the sand varies from beach to beach. For example, in Huntington Beach the sand has a high concentration of oil. This is not present in the sand from Will Rogers Beach.''

"So an analysis of the sand will tell us where he was earlier,'' Emily said. "And it might also tell us where he lived.''

"Precisely. Now connect the sand to the man's tattoo.'' Joanna waited patiently for the resident to come up with the answer. Her gaze went to the wall clock again. She waited thirty seconds more before giving the next clue. "Where do all the young people go for tattoos?''

Silence.

"Which beach has the most tattoo shops?'' Joanna asked.

"Venice,'' Emily said at once.

"Right. And I'll be willing to bet you the sand on his toes came from Venice or a nearby beach.''

Emily nodded, thinking how easy it was to fit all the pieces together once someone pointed out all the clues. And the god-damn white sand between the toes. The most important clue. So stupid to miss it. Dummy! Next time be overly compulsive—like Joanna Blalock was.

"How old do you think this fellow was?'' Joanna asked, breaking into Emily's thoughts.

"It's hard to say, but I'd guess somewhere between twenty-five and thirty-five.''

"Can you narrow it down a little more?''

Emily shrugged. "Without a face, who knows?''

"Look at his skin,'' Joanna instructed her. "See how much elasticity there is. Search for lines and cracks that indicate aging.''

"But there's no face.''

Joanna pointed to the corpse's neck and upper chest. "Any loosening of the skin there, or is it taut?''

Emily pinched at the skin of his neck. "Kind of loose, and I see some early lines. I'd put him in his thirties.''

"And what about the deep freckling on his shoulders and upper back?''

"A lot of sun exposure.''

"Good,'' Joanna said. "So we've got a young man, in his early to mid-thirties, with light brown hair, who lives on or near the beach and has a tattoo of a butterfly on his buttock.''

"That's not a hell of a lot to go on,'' Emily said and sighed wearily. "If we only had a face or a part of a face.''

"We will," Joanna said.

"What!" Emily looked at her strangely. "You expect to get a face from this pulverized mess?"

"I do."

"How?"

"I'm going to reconstruct his face."

"That's going to be impossible."

Joanna reached down and picked up a fragment of a facial bone and held it up to the light. A part of the zygomatic arch, she guessed.

"How will you do it?" Emily asked softly.

"You'll see."

3

Jake Sinclair stared at the phone, not believing his ears. He took a deep drag on his cigarette before he spoke again. "Are you telling me that you're pissed because I didn't bring you with me to Greece for my ex-wife's funeral?"

"You could have asked me," Joanna said.

"Ask what?" Jake snapped. "To come to the funeral of a woman you didn't know? You would have been a stranger to Eleni's family, a total stranger."

"That's not the point," Joanna said, her voice crystal-clear despite the seven thousand miles separating them.

"What is the point?"

"That you shut me out and thought only about yourself. Did you ever consider that maybe I'd like to be by your side in Greece?"

"Jesus Christ," Jake groaned.

There was a long, awkward silence. A burst of static came and went.

"We'll talk about it when you get back," Joanna said evenly. "Take care of yourself."

Jake heard the phone click, then a loud dial tone. He crushed out his cigarette and thought about calling her back and trying to explain. Women! Who the hell could understand them? He reached for the phone and placed another call to Joanna in Los Angeles. Now her line was busy. Fuck it! Jake got to his feet and signaled to the bartender, who would call the operator and get the charges and add them to his bill.

Jake walked across the taverna that was located in Piraeus, just north of Athens. The room was crowded and noisy, the air thick with cigarette smoke. He motioned to the waiter for another round of drinks and sat down at a corner table. Across from him was Theo Papadakis, the husband of Eleni's oldest sister.

"Is everything all right?" Theo asked, trying to read Jake's face.

"Nothing is right," Jake growled.

Theo nodded. "It's always tragic when someone as young and beautiful as Eleni dies."

"All because some drunk bastard ran a red light and crashed into Eleni's car."

"The driver will be convicted of manslaughter." Theo was a thin, short man in his mid-fifties with hollow cheeks and gray-black hair. "He will spend time in jail."

"That won't bring Eleni back, will it?"

"No, my friend. That it will not do."

The waiter came, bringing their drinks. Jake poured his ouzo into water and watched it cloud up, his mind now on the church service for Eleni he'd just attended. A small chapel crowded with people dressed in black. At the front a closed coffin, closed because Eleni's car had been broadsided by a taxi going sixty miles an hour. She hadn't been wearing a safety belt and was thrown from the car. There was massive damage to her face and head. Even her parents hadn't been allowed to see her.

"How long ago were you and Eleni divorced?" Theo asked, breaking into Jake's thoughts.

"Six years."

"I'm surprised you haven't married again."

"I guess I'm not the marrying kind."

"Everybody is the marrying kind—when they meet the right person." Theo studied Jake briefly. The American detective was a big man, powerfully built, with high-set cheekbones, blue-gray eyes, and brown hair that was swept back and sprinkled with gray. There was a small scar across his chin that most people noticed, particularly women. Theo's wife thought that the scar made Jake look dangerous. "You shouldn't let one bad experience poison your life."

"Yeah, I guess," Jake said, but he was thinking that his whole life was filled with mostly bad experiences. He could barely remember his father, a policeman who had been killed in the line of duty when Jake was a boy. His mother had died just before his graduation from high school. Jake had to think hard to recall what she'd looked like or sounded like.

"A man shouldn't be alone," Theo said thoughtfully. "He is not complete that way."

Jake shrugged, not giving a damn. He had always been a loner, even as a cop, with few friends and no family. He figured that was the way it was and that was the way it would stay. Until he met Eleni, a striking Greek stewardess. God, she was beautiful! Tall and sensuous, with big, expressive eyes and brown hair that cascaded down to her shoulders. They married and life turned wonderful for Jake. He kept telling himself that it was too good to be true. And it was. The marriage lasted only two years and came apart when Eleni was having a miscarriage and they couldn't find Jake. He was on a stakeout somewhere.

Jake went back to being a loner and hated it. And again he resigned himself to it. Then he met Joanna. A young nurse at Memorial had been murdered and Jake was the detective assigned to the case. He needed Joanna's help and reluctantly asked for it. At the beginning they rubbed each other the wrong way. He was the tough, no-nonsense cop and she was the bright, refined forensic pathologist. There was real friction between them. And real sparks too. Jake remembered asking her out a half dozen times, but she always refused, wanting to keep her private life separate from her professional world. But he persisted, and over dinner in a Greek restaurant they fell madly in love with each other. Head over heels. Just like that. And at least for a while Jake was happy again. But that too was now coming apart and Jake knew he was on his way to becoming a loner again. All because he hadn't brought Joanna to Greece with him. Goddamn it! She had no place here. None at all.

"We should be going soon." Theo checked his watch. The church service for Eleni had been held that morning. Now the most immediate family members were meeting with the priest. Soon they would bury Eleni in a small cemetery just north of Piraeus.

"Do we have time for another drink?"

"If we hurry." Theo motioned to the waiter, then tilted back in his chair, rocking gently. "I hope I don't have to stand next to Eleni's fat pig of a husband in the funeral procession."

"He's kind of a horse's ass, isn't he?"

"Worse," Theo spat out. "Did you see him in the church this morning? Crying and wailing like some old woman. Disgusting!"

"I think he was hurting a lot."

"We all are hurting a lot. Probably more than that fat American cow. No offense meant."

"None taken."

"And the way he threw himself across the coffin and embraced it." Theo flicked his wrist disdainfully. "Did you know their marriage had turned into a nightmare and that Eleni was in the process of filing for divorce?"

Jake jerked his head around. "Who told you that?"

"Eleni told my wife the day before she died. Apparently her husband had turned into a mean, arrogant son of a bitch with two mistresses that he flaunted in public."

"Jesus," Jake said softly, wondering if there was any happiness anywhere in the world.

The waiter came with double brandies. The men gulped the drinks down and got to their feet.

"And Eleni told my wife something else."

"What?"

Theo hesitated. "My wife told me these things in strict confidence. I must have your word that you will never—"

"You have it. Now what else did Eleni say?"

"That she never stopped loving you."

Joanna punched the keyboard and a picture of a young woman appeared on the computer screen. She was beautiful, with a thin face, high-set cheekbones and doelike eyes. Her hair was short and light brown, her skin flawless. Joanna pushed another key and the computer began to peel back the layers of tissue on one side of the face. The skin and muscles were stripped away down to the bone. Now the woman's face was half skeleton, half beauty.

Joanna looked over at Scott Ballemore, chief of plastic surgery at Memorial. "How do I simulate a crush injury to her face?"

"Mild, moderate or severe?" Ballemore asked.

"Severe."

"Punch SEV."

Joanna typed in the code and the skeletal side of the face exploded into fragments and bone chips. The orbital bones disintegrated and the eye drooped out of its socket. There was a comminuted fracture of the mandible, its ends splintered. Some teeth were missing, others displaced.

"Can her face be surgically reconstructed?" Joanna asked.

"Punch in REP."

Joanna watched as the computer sorted out the bone fragments, arranging them and wiring them in a best-fit order. The gaps were filled in with implants and the bony structures contoured to match the uninjured side. The muscles and skin were put back in place. The face was whole again. And beautiful.

"Magic," Joanna said.

"Not really," Ballemore said, packing tobacco into a briar pipe. "It's just a computer giving us shapes and contours based on measurements from the uninjured side of the face. Keep in mind, the computer can't see. All it can do is take numbers and translate them into form."

"So, the computer can't reconstruct the face unless it's programmed with the measurements from the contralateral side."

"Exactly. It has to be told in numbers what the good side looks like. Or if we had detailed photographs of the injured side before the injury—the computer could work with that too."

Joanna sighed wearily. "My man downstairs has no face and we have no photographs. I don't think a computer is going to help me very much."

"Maybe, maybe not." Ballemore was a tall man, fair complected, with graying, sandy blond hair and sharp features. "How many bone fragments do you have from his face?"

"Forty or so."

"All crushed?"

"Some pieces are large enough to be recognized. A piece of the chin and a part of the zygomatic are the biggest fragments."

"How many pieces are as large as a quarter?"

"Maybe ten."

Ballemore lit his pipe, sending up a thick plume of smoke. "One of our staff is a consultant to a manufacturing corporation that makes silastic implants for most of the facial bones. As you know, bones from different parts of the face have different densities and widths and contours. The manufacturer would have to have those measurements to make the implants. That data might be available in a computer program."

Joanna nodded slowly. "And if it is, the computer might be able to tell me where those ten big pieces of bone fit into my man's face."

"But it will only give you part of a face at best," Ballemore cautioned.

"I'll take anything I can get."

"Let me see if Phil is in. He's just down the hall," Ballemore said and reached for the phone.

They were sitting in Ballemore's office on the eighth floor of

Memorial. The room was immense and Joanna thought it must have been at least two smaller offices in the past. In the center of the floor was a polished mahogany desk and behind it a bay window streaked with raindrops from an early afternoon shower. One wall was lined with bookshelves. The other was covered with watercolors and lithographs.

There were no diplomas or certificates or plaques. Ballemore didn't need to advertise. He was a world-renowned plastic surgeon, far and away the best in California. When someone famous or important needed reconstructive surgery, they didn't go to some Beverly Hills surgeon who spent his day doing tush tucks, boob jobs and liposuction. They came to Ballemore.

Joanna remembered a well-known actress who had fallen from a stepladder and smashed the left side of her face several years ago. When she arrived at the ER her face was lopsided, the cheek shattered, the nose and mouth off center. Her career in front of the camera seemed obviously over. Scott Ballemore spent ten hours in surgery reconstructing her face, and while he was at it he did a little tightening and contouring on the uninjured side. She ended up even more beautiful than before and appeared five years younger. Her career soared.

Joanna looked into the darkened computer screen and studied her reflection. She couldn't see the early lines at the corners of her eyes, but she knew they were there. Tilting her head back, she focused in on her neck. That was her main concern. The skin in front of her neck was no longer taut and was beginning to loosen. It was the first sign of real aging in the women in her family. It had happened to her mother and aunts and was now happening to her. She reached up and gently tugged at the skin of her neck, wondering if there were any exercises or creams that could prevent the loosening.

There was a brief knock on the door. Joanna looked over as a young surgeon dressed in a green scrub suit entered.

"Ah, thank you for coming, Phil," Ballemore said. "Do you know Joanna Blalock?"

"Only by reputation," the surgeon said.

"Phil Weideman, meet Joanna Blalock," Ballemore said.

"How do you do?" They spoke almost in unison, their voices very formal.

Ballemore waited for Weideman to take a seat. "Phil, Joanna has a unique problem we may be able to help her with. She has a man with no face and she wants us to help her in reconstructing his facial features."

"Give me the details." Weideman studied his nails, avoiding eye contact with Joanna.

Joanna shifted around in her chair and cleared her throat. "A young man in his thirties was found in a shallow grave. His face had been smashed in by a blunt instrument and virtually every bone was fractured and fragmented. There were no discernible facial features. We can't identify him by fingerprints because his fingertips were cut off. So I've got to try to reconstruct his face and Scott thought you might be able to help."

Ballemore said, "I was thinking of the corporation you act as consultant for, the one that makes facial silastic implants. They must have the average measurements for every facial bone. And if we were to measure all the bigger pieces of facial bone from Joanna's corpse—maybe, just maybe, a computer could compare the measurements and tell us which bone goes where."

Weideman slowly strummed his fingers on the arm of the chair, thinking, wondering if he wanted to get involved in the project. It would take up so much of his time. He glanced over at Joanna, studying her briefly. She was prettier than he'd heard. A lot prettier. She had a fresh type of beauty, the kind that appealed to him. His gaze went to her gracefully shaped legs and the outline of her thighs beneath her scrub suit. "Are the bones smashed or pulverized?"

"Mainly smashed into fragments," Joanna said promptly. "Ten pieces are decent sized. The rest are bits and chips."

"Have you left the pieces in place?" Weideman asked.

"Some of the larger pieces were loose, so I had to remove them. But I took multiple measurements as well as X rays and photographs to show their exact position."

Weideman nodded approvingly. She was smart and thorough. He'd heard that about her too. "I'll ask the people at Medical Products and Instruments if we can use their data. If they agree, you'll have to sign a form that forbids you from transferring or copying the MPI data. And you won't be able to discuss it at scientific meetings or publish it without their permission."

"I have no problem with that. But keep in mind this is a murder case and might come to trial. If that occurs, a lot of this information could become public knowledge."

Weideman hadn't thought of that possibility, but it didn't bother him. The publicity would be good for MPI. And most of the methods and technologies were already protected by patent anyhow. "I'll call the people at MPI today, and if they agree to let you use their data I'll stop down tomorrow and have a look at your corpse."

Weideman got to his feet and Joanna stood up with him. He extended his hand and she shook it firmly. He was tall and slender with tousled brown hair, a strong angular face and eyes so blue that they reminded Joanna of the Sea of Cortez. She thought he looked more like a cowboy than a doctor. "Thanks for your help," she said.

"I haven't done anything yet," Weideman said.

Joanna waved to Ballemore and left the office. As she closed the door she heard the men speaking in low, muffled tones.

Joanna walked away, thinking that she'd seen Phil Weideman somewhere in the distant past. Way, way back. For a moment she couldn't put her finger on it. Then it came back to her and she smiled to herself. He resembled Mark Elliot, a handsome football star she'd dated when she was a sophomore at the University of Colorado. An old flame who had broken her heart. How long ago was that? At least twenty years. God! Where does the time go?

Joanna dashed into the elevator just behind a group of interns. They nodded to her deferentially and went on with their discussion of a patient with hemochromatosis. Joanna glanced over at the interns. Two males and two females, all looking young enough to be college cheerleaders. Another sure sign of aging, she thought miserably, when the young look too young.

Joanna tuned out the interns' chatter and concentrated on the corpse with no face. There were only bits and pieces of his face left, but she was already beginning to form a vague image of what the corpse had once looked like. His hair was light brown, almost blond in places that had probably been bleached by the sun. She knew his eyes were deep brown because she'd found the iris from one eye embedded in the supraorbital ridge. And the top of his forehead seemed broad while the piece of chin Joanna had uncovered was narrow. A triangular face, she guessed, with brown hair and brown eyes. Not much. But it was a start.

Joanna left the elevator on the B level and hurried down a wide corridor, now recalling another feature of the faceless corpse. Although his mandible had been badly smashed, there were ten or so teeth still in place, some with fillings. She wondered if she should take dental X rays and mail them for possible identification to all the dentists who practiced in the cities along the beaches of Los Angeles County. A long shot, she decided. A very, very long shot. Hardly worth the time and effort. But then again, maybe she'd get lucky.

Joanna walked into her office and began to shrug out of her long white coat.

"Lucy O'Hara is set up and ready to go," said Virginia Hand, a middle-aged secretary with frizzy blond hair and designer glasses. "And Harry Crowe is bitching about Lucy being autopsied out of turn."

"Too bad," Joanna said tonelessly.

"And the police have a probable suicide in the mid-Wilshire area they'd like you to look at."

"No way. Too busy. Tell them to find somebody else to do it." Joanna went to a file cabinet and reached for a candy bar. Her stomach growled as she pulled the wrapper off.

"Is that lunch?"

"It is."

"Very nutritious."

"Better than no lunch at all." Joanna chewed into the almonds embedded in chocolate-covered coconut. "What else have you got?"

"Nothing that can't wait, except for . . ." The secretary's voice trailed off as she flipped through a stack of messages. "A phone call from Lieutenant Jake Sinclair in Athens."

Joanna stopped chewing. "When did he call?"

"About thirty minutes ago. He said to tell you he was fine and that he'll be back next week."

"Did he leave a number?"

"No. He said there was no need for you to call him back."

Joanna began to chew involuntarily on the candy bar as a picture of Jake Sinclair flashed into her mind. She could still see the deep pain in Jake's face when he got the phone call about Eleni's death. She had never seen him that way before. Sad and shocked, straining to keep it together. He made his plane reservations, dressed and left Joanna's apartment, hardly saying a word as he ran back to a memory, to a lost love that was now dead. Suddenly a dead ex-wife was the most important thing in the world to Jake. What bothered Joanna the most was that Jake had shut her out so completely and pushed her into the background as if she was a casual piece of nothingness. That hurt. That hurt like hell.

"I'd call him back," the secretary said, breaking into Joanna's thoughts.

"You said he didn't leave a number."

"Cops always leave numbers where they can be reached. With a little digging, I'll bet I reach him."

"Maybe later."

Joanna hurried out and down the hallway, still thinking about Jake. How long had they been together now? Three, almost four years. Off and on, mainly on. Good and bad, mainly good. The past year had been the best of all. At least that's what she had thought until he turned around and flew off to Greece for a former wife. A dead former wife. Jesus Christ! How could she depend on a man like that?

Joanna wondered if their relationship was just running its natural course and was now fading. She had always believed that in most relationships there comes a point where the couple either marry or go their separate ways. She and Jake had passed that point. Maybe it was time to move on.

But Joanna knew that it was a lot easier said than done. She still cared about Jake and liked to be with him. He was strong and bright with some rough edges he made no effort to hide. What you saw was what you got. And she felt comfortable with him. Joanna hated the thought of having to find another man. But she'd do it rather than stay in a relationship where she had to compete with the ghost of an ex-wife.

Joanna passed a group of surgery residents, all tall and attractive. Memorial was full of attractive men. Like Phil Weideman. Damn, he was good-looking—with those eyes so blue they seemed unreal. A woman could get lost in those eyes. Joanna smiled to herself. She wondered if Weideman was as he seemed. Cosmopolitan, confident, bright, refined—all features she admired in a man.

For a moment Joanna's mind flashed back to Jake and she felt a pang of guilt. But she quickly pushed it aside. He was the one who went to Greece without giving a second's thought to her or her feelings. Even during the phone call from Greece, all he talked about was Eleni and himself. Joanna decided not to make a final decision on their relationship until Jake returned and they had a chance to talk it out. But something had changed between them and Joanna felt they would never be the same again.

Joanna stopped at the water fountain and took a quick drink. She wetted her hands and rubbed them together absently, removing the last traces of chocolate candy. She wondered if she should return Jake's phone call. No, better to wait. Nothing would be settled over the phone. They would sort it out face-to-face. Her mind went back to Phil Weideman and his blue eyes. She wondered if he was married.

Joanna took another swig of water and cleared her mind, then pushed through a set of swinging doors and entered the autopsy room. She put on a black plastic apron and reached for a pair of latex gloves, then quickly scanned the area. It looked like a scene from *MASH*, except that the patients were all dead and the cutters were pathologists, not surgeons.

All of the stainless steel tables were filled and busy. Pathologists were dissecting corpses as quickly as they could, knowing there was no way they could keep up with the flow of bodies from the county morgue. Most of the cases were straightforward with the cause of death obvious—natural causes, gunshot, stabbing. But the majority of pathologists performing the autopsies were not trained in forensics and they were working at breakneck speed. Joanna couldn't help but wonder how much they were going to overlook.

Her gaze went to the rear of the room where Emily Ryan was leaning against the tiled wall, arms folded across her chest. Joanna walked over. Emily pushed herself off the wall.

"Are we all set?" Joanna asked.

"Just about," Emily said, motioning with her head. "Harry is waiting over there for your okay to open the skull."

Joanna glanced over at Harry Crowe, the diener of the morgue, the keeper of the corpses. He was a short, stocky man in his late fifties, balding, with a round face that had BBs for eyes. Joanna nodded to him and he nodded back, almost imperceptibly. They exchanged cold stares.

Joanna looked down at the corpse of Lucy O'Hara. Her skin was a ghostly gray-green color under the fluorescent light, her silky blond hair appearing much lighter than it was in life. Joanna leaned forward and examined the young woman's scalp. There were no cuts or lumps or abrasions, nothing to suggest any trauma. The hair smelled clean, as if it had just been shampooed. Across her lips and skin were scattered petechiae, little hemorrhages caused by a lack of platelets.

Joanna motioned with a finger to Harry Crowe. "Open her skull."

Harry walked over slowly and picked up a scalpel. He lifted the corpse's head and expertly made an incision across and through the scalp. Working his fingers between the scalp and bone, he pulled the scalp forward and off the bone, exposing the skull.

"It ain't right," Harry grumbled loudly, "and it ain't good to do autopsies out of order. It throws everything off schedule. We got a schedule to keep down here, you know."

"Well, she's an exception," Joanna said evenly.

"Why?" Harry snapped. "Because she's rich and her father is a big-time lawyer?"

Joanna narrowed her eyes, disliking him even more than usual. "Just open the head, Harry."

Harry turned on the electric saw, testing it, then turned it off. He touched the blade with a finger, measuring its sharpness, knowing he was taking up valuable time and irritating Joanna.

Emily watched the two, enjoying the tension between them. Harry Crowe had been at Memorial for over thirty years and was accustomed to having his own way and pushing others around, even the senior staff. But he was very careful around Joanna Blalock. She didn't tolerate his boorishness and arrogance, not even for a moment. And when he tried to push her in public, she pushed back. Harder.

Harry turned on the electric saw and carefully sawed through Lucy O'Hara's skull. When he was done, he slowly coiled the wire around the saw and walked away.

"Enough time wasted," Joanna said impatiently. "Are you ready to begin, Emily?"

"Yes."

"Give me a brief history."

"Lucy O'Hara was a twenty-four-year-old law student with acute myeloblastic leukemia that had become refractory to chemotherapy. She was admitted to Memorial for a bone marrow transplant and died suddenly thirty minutes after admission. She was found dead in bed."

"Was she infected or bleeding at the time of admission?"

"No. And her vital signs were all normal."

Joanna glanced down at the corpse's arm and saw venipuncture marks in the antecubital fossa. They were at least a week old. She gently palpated the area, feeling for thrombosed veins. There weren't any. Sudden death in a young leukemic, she was thinking. Sepsis and hemorrhage were far and away the most likely causes, but leukemics could die very quickly from a hundred other things, just like everyone else.

Joanna looked over at Emily. "I take it that you've examined her."

"I have."

"Tell me the positive findings."

Emily shrugged. "There weren't any."

Joanna groaned her disapproval. "There's no such thing as a corpse without a positive finding."

"Let me rephrase that," Emily said quickly. "There were no positive findings that could explain her death."

"Well, we'll see."

Joanna picked up her magnifying glass and began examining Lucy O'Hara's toes and feet. There were scattered calluses and a bunion from wearing pointed shoes. A large number of petechiae were present around the ankles, as would be expected. Hemorrhages into skin were most likely to occur in dependent parts of the body. The thighs and groin were clear. Joanna spotted the small abdominal incision and palpated the metal device that was implanted in the subcutaneous tissue.

"Is this a morphine pump?" Joanna asked.

"Right."

"Do we have any information on it?"

Emily reached for an index card. "I called her doctor at Health First, a Dr. Amanda Black. The pump was inserted several months ago because of bone pain. It holds ten doses of morphine sulfate—eight milligrams in each dose. The pump is refilled externally and this can easily be done by the patient."

"So the most she could give herself at once was eighty milligrams?"

"Correct."

"Not exactly a lethal dose." Joanna reached for a scalpel and cut through the skin. She extracted the pump device and examined it carefully. It was black and round, about the size and width of a woman's compact. Joanna pried it open and studied the calibration on the clear plastic holding vial. "It's still half filled, so the most she could have gotten just prior to death was forty milligrams."

"Enough to put her to sleep, but not enough to kill."

"Assuming it's morphine sulfate in the vial."

Emily's eyes widened. "You think she might have committed suicide?"

"I don't think anything. But I'm not going to exclude that possibility either. We'll analyze the contents of the holding vial and then we'll know for sure."

Joanna methodically examined the corpse's chest and neck and head and found only scattered petechiae and a small hemorrhage on the hard palate. Nothing else. Nothing to point to the cause of death.

Joanna stepped back. "Let's open her up."

She watched Emily make a long incision, sternum to pubis. The skin and muscles were folded back and the abdomen opened. Joanna took another step back and viewed the corpse as a whole, sensing that she'd overlooked something. Something simple. But what? Not the toes or feet or ankles or thighs or pubis. Not the arms where she'd seen the venipuncture marks from needle sticks—all fresh, no tracks or thrombosed veins, nothing to suggest she was shooting drugs intravenously. And the pump had been examined, its contents to be analyzed thoroughly.

Emily asked, "How is it going with the man with no face?"

"Slowly," Joanna said absently.

"I'd really like to work with you on that."

Joanna nodded and moved closer to the table. She reached into Lucy O'Hara's abdominal cavity and began studying the viscera, concentrating as she searched for clues to explain the girl's sudden death.

But she still had a gnawing sensation that she'd already overlooked something important.

5

"Sally Wheaton," said the voice over the public address system.

Sally didn't hear her name being called. She was lost in her own thoughts, remembering back to when the world was a better and kinder place. When kids didn't carry guns to school. When people didn't lock their front doors at night. When her children weren't grown and still at home and her husband was still alive. When she didn't have breast cancer. A thousand years ago, or so it seemed.

"Sally Wheaton!"

Sally came out of her reverie and pushed herself up from the chair. She walked slowly across the waiting room of the outpatient clinic, passing rows of women sitting quietly in uncomfortable Naugahyde-covered chairs. There was no idle chatter or laughter in the advanced breast cancer clinic at Memorial Hospital.

At the receptionist's window, Sally gave her name. The receptionist didn't even bother to look up. She reached for a thick chart and handed it to someone Sally couldn't see and the chart disappeared. The receptionist gestured to the left with her thumb.

Sally walked into the clinic. A young nurse's aide with very blond hair that still smelled of peroxide weighed Sally and commented, "Well, at least you're not losing weight."

Then the aide took Sally's temperature, pulse and blood pressure. She actually took the blood pressure recording twice. The second time the aide measured the blood pressure she wrinkled her brow up as if she didn't believe it.

"What's my blood pressure today?" Sally asked.

"You'll have to ask the doctor," the aide said.

But I'm asking you, Sally wanted to shout. And you should be able to tell me my blood pressure because it's not a national secret and it really doesn't matter a damn to anybody but me. And your hair smells awful, Sally wanted to add, and you don't know how to deal with patients because you're both young and stupid. Sally wanted to say all these things, but she didn't. She held her temper and her words because that was the way she'd been trained to behave. That was the way ladies behaved.

Sally was led into an examining room and told to undress, taking off everything except her panties, and to put on a paper gown. She waited for the door to close, then slowly disrobed, carefully folding sweater and skirt over the back of a chair. Compared to the stuffy waiting room, the examining room was cold and Sally felt goose bumps popping up as she removed her bra. She glanced into the mirror over the basin and briefly studied herself, now rubbing her shoulders with her hands and generating a little heat.

Not bad for sixty-four years of age, she told herself, but it wasn't good either. She had aged a lot over the past four years. There were plenty of lines around her eyes and mouth and they seemed more obvious than before. Her face was slender with soft features and pale blue eyes that still sparkled. But her hair was deeply grayed and looked almost white in the bright light. Her gaze went to her breasts and she saw the healed incision where the lumpectomy had been done. She touched it and felt for nodules and induration, but there weren't any. There was no cancer recurring at the site of the incision. None. But there was plenty elsewhere. In her liver and lungs. None in her brain—so far, thank God!

Sally put on the paper gown and it immediately tore along the side, exposing her thigh up to her waist. Why in the world don't they make them out of cloth like they used to? she wondered. Why does everything have to be made flimsy and disposable? Paper was something you wrote on, not something you made clothing out of. She was still cold and she covered her shoulders with her cashmere sweater. The sweater had been a gift from her husband, Jack, dead almost four years now. God! Four years! It seemed more like a lifetime. A picture of Jack flashed into her mind and she tried to remember what his voice sounded like, what his touch felt like. It was all so vague now.

Sally Wheaton could divide her life into thirty-year cycles. The first thirty years had been ordinary and unexciting. Born and raised just outside Bloomington, Indiana, she grew up in a middle-class setting. She went to Indiana University and lost her virginity to a boy named Bill who huffed and puffed and groaned and grunted. Sally hardly felt anything. She wondered why everyone made such a big fuss over sex.

She graduated with a degree in teaching and followed her best friend to California. But life didn't change very much for Sally. It was still ordinary and unexciting except she was in California rather than Indiana. When her roommate married, Sally was left all alone and things got worse. She gave serious thought to moving back to Indiana, where at least she'd be close to family. But then she met Jack Wheaton, a handsome, fun-loving aeronautical engineer, and life became wonderful. They married when she was thirty and the next thirty years were paradise. Children. Travel. Love. God, how that man could make love! The children grew up and left home and married. Jack moved up the ladder of success at Rocketdyne. He put men on the moon and sent spaceships to Mars and Venus before finally retiring as a senior vice president.

He assured her that the best part of life was now about to begin for them. And she believed him. If he had made the second thirty years of her life so wonderfully happy, surely he could do the same with the final thirty years. Then came the trip to Bermuda. Their last day together was spectacular. A bright, sunny day with not a cloud in the sky, she remembered. They went swimming in the morning, bicycled in the afternoon, made endless love in the early evening. Then, just before dinner, Jack became nauseated. Probably from something he'd eaten earlier. Maybe the clam chowder. Sally went to the pool area and bought a Coke from a machine to help settle Jack's stomach. When she returned he was lying perfectly still in bed, eyes staring up at the light. He was dead. A heart attack. Sally Wheaton's thirty years of happiness were over.

There was a sudden knock at the door. As Sally looked up, a team of physicians entered. The lead doctor was wearing a long white coat with a small bloodstain near the hem. He was short with a round face, curly blond hair and wire-rimmed glasses. He looked so young. Sally couldn't imagine him being over twenty-five.

"Mrs. Wheaton? I'm Dr. Hampton," he said, flipping through her chart.

Sally cleared her throat nervously. "Dr. Chandler is the doctor I've been seeing."

"Well, he's not here today," Hampton said, burying his face in the chart. He still hadn't made eye contact with her. "So I'll be looking after you."

"Is he ill?"

Hampton ignored the question. Something in the chart caught his attention and he used his finger to point at it.

Sally shifted around on the edge of the table and the paper gown tore a little more. She sighed resignedly, hating the sudden change in doctors but knowing she had no choice. At Memorial one was assigned a doctor, just like at Health First. Lord, she thought, the old days were so much better.

Shortly after Jack's death she was informed that Rocketdyne would no longer provide private medical insurance for their retirees and spouses. Instead she would be assigned to an HMO. Sally was very upset with the change, but because of financial constraints she had no choice and joined up. Her initial visit to Health First was awful. Her new physician, Dr. Arnold Kohler, didn't even look like a doctor. He was a little man, dark complected, with hollowed-out cheeks and narrow eyes. His clothes reeked of cigarette smoke and when he spoke he avoided all eye contact. Sally just didn't like him or his office with its worn furniture and potted plants that seemed more dead than alive. After her initial examination, Sally did not return to Health First until she felt a small lump in her breast. Dr. Kohler wasn't certain he could feel it, but Sally insisted on having a mammogram that confirmed its presence. Sally's breast cancer was treated aggressively, and when her tumor became refractory to chemotherapy she was referred to Memorial.

Sally reluctantly returned to see Dr. Kohler six months ago when she began having fainting spells. He wasn't overly concerned and told her it was probably due to anxiety. When she passed out in the lobby at Health First, an EKG clearly showed the presence of cardiac arrhythmia. Sally had a pacemaker inserted and the fainting spells stopped. She had written to Health First, asking that she be removed from Dr. Kohler's care and assigned to another physician. Health First had written back, telling her that the matter was under consideration.

Hampton glanced over his shoulder at the others in the group. "She has mets to the liver and lung. Her alkaline phosphatase is sky-high."

The other doctors nodded solemnly.

Hampton turned back to Sally. "Are you having any shortness of breath or abdominal pain?"

"No. Just fatigue. I'm tired all the time."

"That's to be expected."

Hampton closed the chart and looked over at the youngest-appearing member of the medical team. He was very slender with a scant beard and scattered pimples on his cheeks. "What are the therapeutic options available to this woman? Keep in mind that she has now received multiple courses of chemotherapy and her tumor has become drug resistant."

"Has she been tried on high-dose Adriamycin?" the young doctor asked.

Hampton nodded. "Last summer. Her response was not very good."

"Then we're left with autologous bone marrow transplant."

"Exactly," Hampton said, then turned to Sally. "I take it you are familiar with the bone marrow transplant procedure."

Sally nodded slowly. "Dr. Chandler and I discussed it at length several times. I think I know what it involves."

"Let's make certain you understand it in detail," Hampton said, again looking at the very young doctor. "Rick, explain the autologous bone marrow transplant procedure to Mrs. Wheaton."

The young doctor stepped forward and stood between Hampton and Sally, staring straight ahead, not looking at either. He cleared his throat like someone about to begin a long oration.

Sally studied him and noted that the name on his name tag was Richard Stone. There was no "M.D." after his name, no "Dr." before it. He was a medical student. Jesus Christ! she fumed. They're talking about a procedure that could save my life or kill me and they want a medical student to give me the particulars.

She felt like grabbing her clothes and running out of the room, but she forced herself to stay put.

The medical student cleared his throat again. "The autologous bone marrow transplant procedure consists of three parts. First, bone marrow is removed from the patient and is frozen and stored away. Secondly, the patient is given large doses of chemotherapeutic agents and radiation that should kill all of the breast cancer cells. Unfortunately, this also destroys the patient's bone marrow. In the final step, the patient's frozen bone marrow is thawed and returned to the patient. So, the patient ends up with good functioning bone marrow and no cancer."

Hampton nodded approvingly. "And what is the success rate of this procedure?"

The medical student hesitated and kicked at an imaginary object on the floor.

"The patient has got to know," Hampton said without emotion. "What are her chances of survival at a three-year follow-up?"

"Ten to twenty percent," the student said quietly.

"And what are her chances without the procedure?"

"Almost none."

"Exactly. That's why Mrs. Wheaton has decided to undergo the autologous bone marrow transplant." Hampton turned to Sally Wheaton. "Are you having any second thoughts?"

Sally shook her head, almost in slow motion. "I want to have the transplant done."

Hampton stepped up to the examining table and removed the sweater from Sally's shoulders, then pulled the paper gown down to expose her breasts. He quickly examined the nipple and surrounding area, the incision scar where the lumpectomy had been done, and finally her axilla, searching for enlarged lymph nodes.

Sally stared straight ahead, trying to avoid the stares from the other doctors and students. She hated this part of the examination, hated having total strangers peering at her breasts. They were nothing more than spectators. Professionals, yes. But still spectators. Her gaze went to the medical student who had just explained the transplant procedure. Their eyes met for a moment and then he looked away. A ten percent chance of survival, Sally was thinking, twenty percent at best. Such poor odds.

"Your exam is unchanged," Hampton said, gently pulling the

paper gown up to her shoulders. "We'll need a few more tubes of blood to complete your evaluation."

"More blood?" Sally asked weakly. Her arms already felt like pincushions.

"Just a little." Hampton handed the chart to the medical student and turned away, then turned back. "Oh, there's one other matter. I know you're scheduled to undergo the transplant in two weeks, but there's a good chance we can do it next week. The other patient who was scheduled has become quite ill."

Sally hesitated and nervously squeezed her hands. "Does it make any difference if I do it one week sooner or later?"

Hampton shrugged noncommittally. "Maybe, maybe not."

Sally watched his body language and got the unspoken message. Better do it sooner. Bad things can happen in a week. A lot of bad things. "I'll do it as soon as possible."

"A wise decision," Hampton said, nodding firmly. "The technician will be in shortly to get your blood."

"You'll notify me if—"

"Of course," Hampton said and left the room, his team a step behind him. The last one out, the slender medical student, closed the door.

Sally tore off the paper gown and quickly dressed. So the procedure was probably going to be done a week earlier, she thought. She'd have to tell her children and her best friend, meet with the lawyer to make certain everything was in order, get a housesitter, somebody to feed the cat and dog. A thousand things. But she'd do them all. If Sally Wheaton was anything, she was organized. And she thought again about the fact that she'd used up her thirty years of good luck. Maybe there was still a little left. Just a little. That's all she needed.

She heard a knock on the door and turned as a heavyset technician entered carrying a tray.

"I'm Wendy Fujiama and I need a little blood from you."

Sally pulled up her sleeve and exposed her antecubital fossa. She closed her eyes as the technician swabbed the area with alcohol. She felt a sharp stick, then a slight sting. When Sally opened her eyes, the technician was already filling the second tube.

"Just press down hard on the cotton," the technician said, removing the needle.

For a moment Sally felt light-headed, as if she was losing her balance. She grabbed for the technician's arm.

"Are you okay?" the technician asked.

"Just a little dizzy," Sally said, now feeling foolish. A simple needle stick and you make a major production out of it, she told herself.

"Are you sure?"

"Positive."

"Maybe you should lie down for a minute."

"No, no. I'll be fine." Sally managed to smile, but she still felt queasy.

Sally watched the technician leave the room. She rested her head on the examining table. It felt cool against her forehead and for a moment the light-headedness stopped. But then it returned and now she was experiencing a burning sensation in her chest and neck. *My heart! My heart! Something's wrong with the pacemaker!* Quickly, Sally reached for the carotid area and took her pulse. Nice and even and strong. Sixty, maybe seventy beats per minute.

The burning in her chest intensified and suddenly she couldn't catch her breath. She gasped, sucking for air. Panic flooded through her as she got to her feet and stumbled toward the door. The room was spinning faster and faster and Sally could no longer keep her balance. She lurched forward and slammed into a small writing desk. Desperately she tried to reach for the door.

Sally heard herself make a crying sound and then she lost consciousness and fell to the floor like a deadweight.

Dr. Amanda Black gestured with a hand to the skyline. "It's a beautiful view, isn't it?"

"Spectacular," Joanna said.

The women were standing in front of a huge window on the tenth floor of the Health First Tower. In the distance Joanna could clearly see Memorial Hospital and beyond that the snowcapped San Bernardino Mountains. To her immediate left she saw a second Health First Tower that was joined to the first by an enclosed bridge. It was a bright, cloudless day and the sun was reflecting off the glass-plated building, making it sparkle like a jewel.

"Would you care for coffee?" Amanda asked.

Joanna nodded. "With cream, please."

They turned away from the window and walked across the well-appointed library, past a rectangular conference table surrounded by leather-upholstered chairs and over to a small wet bar.

As Amanda poured coffee, Joanna's gaze went to a cluster of framed photographs that hung on a nearby wall. In one photo a former president of the United States had his arm around the shoulder of a tall man with tousled gray-brown hair and sharp features. An inscription read: "Bob—Thanks for helping us see the light." Another photo showed the same man arm in arm with the two senators from California, everyone smiling. A third photo was of the same man with the governor of California, both men dressed in tennis outfits. Joanna could see that these were not staged photographs. This man, whoever he was, really knew the people, probably on a first-name basis. She studied his face at length, now sensing that she'd seen the man before.

"Somebody has some powerful friends," Joanna commented.

Amanda handed her a steaming Styrofoam cup and glanced up at the photograph. "I think that's a fair statement."

"Who is he?"

"Bob Mariner."

Joanna instantly recognized the name and the face. Robert Mariner, one of the fathers of managed medical care in America. *Time* magazine had done a cover story on him the year before, detailing his meteoric career. Mariner had been a boy genius, graduating from Harvard Medical School on his twenty-first birthday. He became board certified in two subspecialties, oncology and immunology, and his research in cellular immunology was world-renowned. At thirty-five he became a full professor and was offered the presidency at Sloan-Kettering and later the directorship at the National Institutes of Health.

He turned down both offers. He was on track to become the youngest-ever chairman of medicine at Mass General. But at forty years of age, Robert Mariner stunned the academic world and resigned his position at Harvard. He became a visiting fellow at the Rand Corporation, where he studied and developed the concept of managed medical care in America. In 1985, he started Health First in a small two-story building in Santa Monica. Ten years later Health First was among the largest HMOs in America, a huge, smooth-running conglomerate, a model that everyone was now trying to copy. *Time* had said that Robert Mariner had again performed his magic. Everything he touched turned to excellence.

Joanna sipped her coffee, still studying the photographs. Mariner had charisma and confidence, a man sure of himself. It even came through in a photo. "Is it true that he still sees patients?"

"Twice a week," Amanda said. "But only the difficult cases, of course."

"Remarkable."

"And then some."

They went to the conference table and sat across from each other. Amanda took out a pack of cigarettes and lit one, inhaling deeply and savoring the taste. "I hope you don't mind the smoke.

It's one of my few vices and I limit myself to five cigarettes per day.''

Joanna nodded politely. She did mind the smoke and she also knew that Amanda Black was not telling the truth. People who inhaled that deeply weren't casual smokers. And Amanda's clothes smelled like stale smoke and her index finger had a nicotine stain. At least a pack a day, Joanna guessed.

"So your autopsy didn't show very much," Amanda said.

"She had the usual changes one sees in acute leukemia, but I found nothing to explain her sudden death. I was hoping you might know something in her past history that could give us a clue.''

Amanda took a deep drag on her cigarette, her mind now concentrating. She was a tall woman in her early forties with long black hair that hung loosely to her shoulders. Her face was angular and attractive with a slight overbite. She had very dark eyes that seemed to move constantly. "Except for her leukemia, she had no real medical problems. No cardiac difficulties, no arrhythmias. Nothing like that.''

"Was there any history of sudden death in the family?" Joanna asked.

Amanda reached for a chart atop the table, opened it and studied it briefly before shaking her head. "No. Her mother and father are still alive, as are two grandmothers. One grandfather died of cancer, the other from emphysema with right-sided heart failure.''

"Did she use drugs?''

Amanda's eyes narrowed. "Did you find something in her blood?''

"Just morphine.''

"I'm certain that came from her implanted morphine pump.'' Amanda took another deep drag on her cigarette and held the smoke down for a long time before exhaling. "In answer to your question—no, she didn't use recreational drugs. She didn't drink or smoke, and before her illness she jogged two miles a day.''

"Tell me about the pain she was having.''

"Lucy had a great deal of bone pain from her leukemia and that's why the pump was implanted.''

"Have you had a lot of experience with these pumps?''

Amanda thought for a moment. "I've had them implanted in a dozen or so patients. But if you're asking me if I know how they work, the answer is no. I'm not very mechanically minded."

"They're not that complicated." Joanna took out an index card and, holding it up, pointed to a hand-drawn diagram. "It's an interesting little device that allows patients to administer morphine parenterally to themselves. Each dose is limited to a given amount, usually eight milligrams. And there's a microchip of some sort that permits only so many doses over a given length of time."

Amanda studied the diagram and pointed to a small tube. "And the patient refills the device externally right here, huh?"

"Right."

"Can the patients put any type of drug they want into the device?"

"No. I think it has to be refilled with a special type of syringe that contains the morphine. As I understand it, if the system is tampered with in any way, it won't accept the refill. But there's really no such thing as a tamperproof system, is there?"

Amanda leaned across the table, her gaze fixed on Joanna. "Do you think she injected herself with something?"

Joanna shrugged. "I don't think anything. All I know is that she died very suddenly and I don't have a cause."

Amanda took a final drag on her cigarette and crushed it out. "Lucy was not the type to kill herself. And besides, you said that only morphine was found in her blood."

"So far. But that's based on our preliminary studies." Joanna reached into her purse for an index card and briefly studied it. "This morphine pump was manufactured by a company called MPI. Are you familiar with them?"

Amanda smiled thinly. "Of course. MPI stands for Medical Products and Instruments. They are a wholly-owned subsidiary of Health First."

"I'd like to talk with one of their scientists, if possible."

"How about the head of research and development?"

"Do you know him?"

"Intimately. He's my husband. Shall I see if he's in his office?"

"I'd appreciate that."

Joanna watched Amanda walk over to a phone near the wet bar, her mind now flashing back to the *Time* magazine article on Robert Mariner. A whole page had been covered with a complex diagram showing the various divisions that formed Health First. In the center of the diagram were the outpatient clinics and those were connected by spokes to hospitals, nursing and convalescent homes, laboratories and medical manufacturing facilities. Health First was a self-contained medical system, carefully managed in every aspect except for pharmaceuticals. They didn't manufacture their own drugs but rather bought in bulk from the pharmaceutical houses at huge discounts. Health First was believed to generate substantial profits, but no one knew for sure since the corporation was not publicly owned. It was a privately held corporation whose owners remained anonymous. The only known major stockholder was Robert Mariner.

"Alex will be over in a moment," Amanda said, sitting down. She started to reach for another cigarette but decided against it. "Can I ask you why the great interest in Lucy O'Hara? We've had other patients die unexpectedly at Memorial and they certainly weren't investigated to this extent. And not by a forensic pathologist."

Joanna hesitated, but saw no reason not to be totally honest. "Her father has some very powerful friends at Memorial."

Amanda sighed sadly. "I've known Michael O'Hara for a long time and this is going to destroy him. Lucy was his only child."

"You looked after the whole family?"

Amanda nodded. "Michael, Ann and Lucy. All of them. Can you imagine what it must be like to lose a child? An only child?"

"It must be the worst pain in the world," Joanna said softly.

"Yes. The worst." Amanda briefly thought about the stillborn child she'd had. A little boy. Had he lived he would have been eight years old now. She went for another cigarette and lit it, exhaling a lungful of blue smoke. The air-conditioning unit switched on and the smoke over the table quickly dispersed. "What percentage of your sudden death patients end up with no known cause or precipitating event?"

"Approximately twenty percent. Less in the younger people. Say five to ten percent."

"And what do you think is the cause of these sudden deaths?"

Joanna shrugged, not wanting to speculate or theorize.

"Maybe spasm of the coronary arteries?"

"Maybe. But very unlikely in a twenty-four-year-old girl."

Amanda puffed away, sending up another plume of smoke. "Maybe a small hemorrhage in a critical area of the brain. Like, say, a bleed into the vasomotor center of the medulla."

"We'd pick that up in the microscopic sections," Joanna said. She had also considered the possibility that a small arteriole to a crucial area in the brain had become blocked and caused vasomotor collapse. And if the arteriole was small enough it could be missed on routine microscopic section. For that reason Joanna had insisted that every millimeter of Lucy's medulla be sectioned and studied.

Joanna glanced over at a pile of hospital charts stacked up on the edge of the table. "Are those Lucy O'Hara's charts?"

Amanda nodded. "Her hospital records. She was admitted four times. Twice for rectal bleeding, twice for sepsis."

"What organisms was she infected with?"

"Staphylococcus the first time, a gram-negative bug the next," Amanda said and, anticipating the next question, she added, "There was never any evidence of septic shock."

Joanna stared at the stack of records, resisting the urge to just accept Amanda's quick summary of the hospitalizations. She planned to take the charts back to Memorial and study each and every page, looking for some clue to explain Lucy's sudden death. It was at least four hours' work, she thought dismally.

Amanda checked her watch. "I wonder what's keeping Alex. His office is just across the way in the adjoining tower."

Joanna's brow went up. "That entire tower is for research and development?"

"No, no. Most of that tower is a hospital with its own ICU and operating suites. Only the top two floors are reserved for R and D."

"And the actual manufacturing itself is contracted out?"

"No. We have our own plant in Chatsworth. And another one in Singapore."

Joanna reached for one of the hospital charts and flipped through it. The admission history and physical and the discharge summary were typed, but all of the doctor's progress notes and most of the consultations were handwritten scribble, difficult to read and at times impossible to decipher. A note written by a hematologist was sadly prophetic. It read: "This girl is doomed without a transplant."

The door to the conference room opened quietly and a young secretary looked in. She cleared her throat audibly. "Dr. Black, your husband just called to say he's tied up with an experiment. If possible, he'd like for you to meet him in the Electro-Cardiac Lab."

Amanda sighed wearily and glanced over at Joanna. "Do you mind?"

"Not at all."

"Let's take Lucy's records with us. That way you won't have to come all the way back for them."

They took the elevator down to the second floor and walked across the enclosed bridge into the adjoining tower. The second tower was newer and more expensively done. Its walls were covered with light gold-colored grasscloth and trimmed with deep brown mahogany. A huge painting by Joan Miró, protected by glass, hung next to the elevators. There were four elevators in all, three for the hospital, one marked R AND D PERSONNEL ONLY.

They stepped into the R and D elevator. The door closed instantly and the car zoomed up at a dizzying speed. It stopped so abruptly that for a moment Joanna felt weightless, as if the force of gravity had disappeared. She also felt as if her stomach was a floor beneath them.

The lobby on the ninth floor was circular in shape with only two doors, directly opposite each other. In the center of the lobby an armed security guard sat in a Plexiglas cage watching the women. Overhead surveillance cameras moved silently back and forth.

Amanda removed her ID badge and passed it under a window to the security guard. He studied the card carefully, then looked up at Amanda's face, then back down to the photograph on the card. Finally he inserted the card into a machine with a blinking red light atop it. The machine made a whirling sound as it checked ten different details making certain the card was not counterfeit. The light turned green and the card reappeared. The guard handed it back to Amanda.

"This is Dr. Joanna Blalock," Amanda told the guard. "She's a visiting scientist."

The guard punched Joanna's name into a keyboard and watched the computer screen, waiting for the machine to process her and clear her for entry. The guard squinted his eyes at the screen, then looked up at Joanna and studied her face. "Are you carrying a camera or any type of recording device?"

"No."

The guard nodded, but he reached beneath the desk and pushed a button. Joanna would be fluoroscoped as she walked through the door. Any hidden metallic object would be clearly seen. The guard passed a visitor's card to Joanna under the window.

"Please wear it at all times," he said.

Amanda helped her pin it on. "This card allows them to track you while you're inside the facility."

"What happens if I remove it?" Joanna asked.

"An alarm will sound."

They walked through a door only to find a second door. Amanda punched a set of five numbers into a panel on the wall. Above the panel an electronic sign flashed PLEASE INSERT ID CARD. Amanda inserted her card into a slot and waited. They heard a loud click and the second door hissed open automatically.

The women went down a long, wide corridor. There was no sound except for the click of their heels on the tiled floor. Joanna glanced up at the overhead surveillance cameras that were following her. She stopped to adjust her visitor's card and the cameras stopped with her.

"They've got heat sensors," Amanda explained. "They follow your body heat."

They walked on, passing a string of closed doors, each clearly marked. One sign read IMMUNO-TOXINS. HAZARDOUS BIOLOGIC MATERIALS. Across from it was RADIOACTIVE ISOTOPE STORAGE FACILITY and next to that BIO-SYNTHETICS. At the far end of the corridor they came to the ELECTRO-CARDIAC LABORATORY. Amanda opened the door.

The room looked more like Mission Control than a laboratory. The walls were covered with huge video screens. On the largest screen a beagle dog was playfully running around, stopping every few seconds as if stunned and puzzled, then quickly regaining his strength and playing some more. A smaller video screen was flashing up numbers that seemed to be constantly changing.

"That dog has two electrodes implanted in its heart," Amanda explained. "One induces ventricular fibrillation, the other defibrillates and returns the heart to a normal sinus rhythm."

Joanna shrugged, unimpressed. "Implantable defibrillators have been around for quite a while."

"But this one is the size of a quarter and has a specially designed battery that will last for ten years."

A voice called out, "If you must talk, go outside."

Joanna looked across the room to a slender man sitting in front of a console, now busily punching numbers into a keyboard. As she studied him she realized that he wasn't sitting, he was standing. The man couldn't have been more than five two. She moved in closer and saw that he was wearing a white laboratory coat that was far too big for him. Its sleeves were rolled up into cuffs, exposing small, delicate hands. The light on the video screen brightened and Joanna could see that the man had swarthy good looks with jet-black hair that was carefully groomed.

"Alex," Amanda said, "this is Dr. Joanna Blalock."

"Right," Alex Black mumbled, not bothering to look up. He punched in new numbers and watched the beagle suddenly drop to its knees. The dog barked loudly and Alex Black pushed another set of keys. Now the dog was up and running again.

"Dr. Blalock would like to speak with you," Amanda said to her husband.

Alex ignored her, his eyes darting back and forth across the console. He punched in a new code on the keyboard. The beagle on the screen kept running and playing. Then suddenly the dog stopped, frozen in its tracks. But only for a moment. Then he was off and running again. Alex studied the screen briefly, then reached for the keyboard again.

"Dr. Blalock is going to need a little of your time, Alex," Amanda said sharply.

"Shit," Alex grumbled under his breath, knowing that his voice was loud enough for the women to hear and not caring. He switched off the console and pushed his chair back. "We can talk in the conference room." He walked out quickly, not bothering to hold the door for the women.

Joanna followed him out of the laboratory, disliking him more with each passing moment. A little man, she thought, with a typical Napoleonic complex. She wondered if Amanda had to put up with that kind of rudeness on a daily basis.

They walked into a conference room that was much smaller than the one in the other tower. And it wasn't nearly as well appointed. A circular conference table, chairs upholstered with Naugahyde, no wet bar. There was a small cubicle with a Dictaphone and telephone near the door. The room had no windows.

Amanda took out a cigarette and lit it, inhaling deeply. She began coughing and exhaled the smoke in Alex Black's direction. He looked at his wife disapprovingly but said nothing.

Joanna watched the two taking their seats, sitting as far apart from each other as the circular table would allow. There were no nods, no smiles, no touches. Almost strangers. Joanna wondered what their home life was like.

"Dr. Blalock needs some information on the morphine pump," Amanda said, breaking the silence.

"Why?" Alex asked defensively. "Is something wrong with it?"

Joanna shook her head. "No. It's just that one of our patients, who had the pump implanted, died suddenly."

"It isn't the pump's fault," Alex said at once.

"I didn't say it was," Joanna said evenly.

Alex leaned forward, his forehead knitted in intensity. "Did you find high levels of morphine in the patient's blood?"

"No."

Alex leaned back and nodded. "Like I said, it wasn't the pump's fault."

"Does the pump work by a spring device or does it have a power source?" Joanna asked.

Alex hesitated. "Maybe you should sign a nondisclosure form."

"Jesus Christ," Amanda hissed impatiently, "the goddamn pump is covered by a pending patent. Just answer her question."

Alex nervously fingered the reading glasses hanging from a cord around his neck. "It's run by a battery and programmed by a microchip."

"What's the maximum dose it can discharge?" Joanna asked.

"The microchip dictates the frequency of the injection—that is, how often the patient can administer the morphine. But the actual volume or dose is preset. For example, each dose is eight milligrams. The microchip allows two doses within a half hour. But the dose following that can't be given for another hour.''

Joanna quickly calculated in her mind. "So the most the patient can receive in an hour and a half is twenty-four milligrams.''

"Correct.''

"And the patient can reload the pump, right?''

"Right,'' Alex said and took a small, dark syringe from the pocket of his lab coat. It had a needle that was shaped like a screw except that it had a squared-off end. "The pump can only be reloaded with this special syringe.''

"Can anything be added to that syringe?''

"Nope. It's got a vacuum seal. If that's broken the pump will not accept new fluids.'' Alex pocketed the peculiar syringe. "It's foolproof.''

Nothing is foolproof, Joanna thought, least of all some battery-operated pump. But there was really no evidence that connected the pump to Lucy's death. It was just that Joanna didn't know everything there was to know about the pump, and until she did she couldn't completely exclude the possibility.

Amanda said, "If you'd like, Alex could examine the pump that was implanted in Lucy O'Hara. You know, just to make certain everything was working as it should.''

Alex gave his wife an icy stare. "We've made thousands and thousands of these pumps and never once has there been a problem. Never once.''

"Nothing is perfect, Alex,'' Amanda said hoarsely.

Alex said nothing, but his face colored and the veins in his forehead bulged.

Joanna wondered again what the Blacks' home life was like. "You said you've made thousands and thousands of these morphine pumps. Why would Health First need so many of them?''

Alex smiled for the first time. "We sell them to others as well. As a matter of fact, we're the third largest producer of implantable pumps in the world.''

The door opened as Robert Mariner backed his way into the conference room. He was carrying stacks of charts under his arms and a small Dictaphone was tucked between his chin and his neck. As he turned around, he saw the doctors sitting at the conference table. "Oh, I'm sorry. I didn't know the room was being used. I can come back later."

"We're almost done," Amanda said. Some of the charts under Mariner's arms began to slip out and Amanda hurried over to catch them and put them on the table. "Bob Mariner, meet Joanna Blalock."

Mariner extended a huge hand and shook Joanna's hand firmly. "I've heard a lot about you. And everything I hear is good."

Joanna felt her cheeks blushing. "Thank you."

"It's difficult being very bright and very young-looking, isn't it?"

"At times."

"I know. I once had the same problem." Mariner was a big man and, although he had tousled gray-brown hair, he still had a youthful appearance. His lopsided grin had a boyish quality to it. "I graduated from medical school when I was twenty-one and became chief resident at Mass General when I was twenty-five. I looked so young that patients thought I was a student. I couldn't wait to get older and now I'd like to somehow be young again." He grinned widely, laughing at himself. "But you haven't reached the older-looking stage yet, have you?"

Joanna smiled back at him, liking him instantly. He had charm and charisma and confidence—just like in his photos—and he seemed to fill up the room, although he didn't try to. Joanna glanced over at Amanda and Alex Black and tried to read their body language. Amanda was alert, sparkling, her eyes fixed on Mariner. Alex was slumped down in his chair, studying his fingers and working on an imaginary hangnail.

"Bob," Amanda said, her voice throaty, "Joanna is here regarding Lucy O'Hara."

Mariner's expression became solemn. "Dreadful! Dreadful business. The poor girl was all set for her transplant. We had a very good donor, too." He looked over at Joanna, his eyes narrowing slightly. "Was something unusual found at autopsy?"

"Nothing," Joanna said. "We couldn't come up with a cause for her sudden death."

Mariner leaned back in his chair, hands clasped behind his head. "It's either a bleed or an arrhythmia. I'd bet on a hemorrhage, probably small but into a vital area."

"We've looked," Joanna said promptly. "Her brain was sectioned millimeter by millimeter."

"Then it's the heart," Mariner went on, unfazed. "A little hemorrhage into the atrioventricular node or the Purkinje system could induce a sudden, fatal arrhythmia. I saw it once in a young basketball player."

Joanna made a mental note to double-check Lucy's heart and its conduction system. She doubted she'd find anything, but she'd look anyway.

Joanna watched Mariner as he glanced over at Alex, then at Amanda. He kept his eyes on her for only a second, but some silent message must have passed between them because Amanda quickly spoke. "Joanna wanted to know about the morphine pump that was implanted in Lucy. Alex was good enough to supply her with all the details."

"Was there any evidence for malfunction of the pump?" Mariner asked, concerned.

"None at all," Joanna assured him. "I was just covering all the bases."

"We've had no problems with that pump," Mariner went on, "absolutely none. It's been one of our very best products."

"So I was told," Joanna said. "I had no idea that your company was the world's third largest producer of those pumps."

Mariner was instantly on guard, but he kept his expression even. "Who told you that?"

"Alex mentioned it," Amanda said promptly.

Mariner looked over at Alex with stone-cold eyes. So smart in the laboratory, Mariner thought, and so stupid in the outside world. So dumb to tell outsiders about your business and dumber yet to brag about your best sellers and profit makers. The Japanese would love to know the profit margin on the implantable pump so they could copy it and mass-produce it at some factory in Thailand and then dump it on the American market at absurdly low prices until they captured the market. "That's a bit of an exaggeration," Mariner said easily, but he continued to stare at Alex.

Alex slumped down farther in his chair, his head bent low submissively. Amanda watched the men intently, her eyes darting back and forth between them. She briefly ran her tongue over her lips.

"Well, I've already taken up too much of your time," Joanna

said, wanting to get out of the room and away from the awkward situation.

"Not at all," Mariner said. "You take as much time as you need." He turned to Amanda. "Make certain she has all of our records on Lucy O'Hara."

"I already have." Amanda got to her feet and, motioning to Joanna, walked over to the charts they'd brought from the other tower. "Let me show you how our hospital charts are arranged. It's a little different than what you're accustomed to at Memorial."

Mariner tuned out the women's conversation and kept his gaze on Alex Black. Black finally looked up and Mariner nodded benignly. A reprieve. Black nodded back, relieved.

Mariner busied himself with a stack of correspondence, but his mind was still on Alex Black. So naive and so bright at the same time. Mariner remembered when he had first found Alex working as a research fellow at MIT ten years ago. He was brilliant, absolutely brilliant. And everything Black invented was immediately taken over by his professor, who claimed all the credit and got it. Black was a genius working for twenty thousand dollars a year. He jumped at Mariner's offer; his own research laboratory, seventy-five thousand dollars a year, and a thousand shares of Health First. The board of directors at Health First had thought Mariner's offer to Black exorbitant. But Mariner convinced them otherwise. And he was right. Alex Black had turned out to be an intellectual gold mine.

Mariner studied a letter from a United States congressman who wanted all the details on how Health First was run. Mariner knew the man. A diehard conservative who opposed every aspect of managed medical care and was rewarded with huge campaign contributions from the AMA. Over a hundred thousand dollars per year and probably more under the table.

The phone rang and Mariner quickly hurried over to answer it. He was expecting a call from an undersecretary of Health and Human Services. For a moment, Mariner forgot the man's nickname. Charlie? Chucky? Chuck! Yes, Chuck. Mariner picked up the phone, spoke briefly and replaced the receiver. Slowly he walked back to the table.

Amanda looked up and saw the stunned expression on Mariner's face. "What's wrong, Bob?"

"It's Sally Wheaton."

Amanda hesitated, thinking for a moment. "The lady scheduled for an autologous bone marrow transplant?"

"Yes."

"What about her?"

"She just dropped dead at Memorial."

7

The nurse looked up from the reception desk. "Are you a patient of Dr. Kohler's?"

"No, I'm a business acquaintance," Karl Rimer said.

"I'm afraid it won't be possible for you to see him this morning. He's got a very full schedule."

"I'm also a former patient of his," Rimer said, thinking quickly. "I've been out of town for a while and I need to talk with him about my medical records."

"Are you currently enrolled in Health First?"

"No, but I wanted to talk with him about that too."

The nurse hesitated, studying the tall man with a trench coat folded over his arm. "Let me see if he can squeeze you in."

The nurse walked away from the reception desk and disappeared down a corridor.

Rimer stood off to the side and looked out at the patients in the waiting room. Mostly senior citizens, mostly Caucasians, a few Hispanics, no blacks. The room was large and colorless with cheap, worn furniture and a linoleum floor. On the wall was a framed photograph of Health First's gleaming twin towers. The photo didn't show the old stucco annex that housed Arnold Kohler's office. Rimer turned as another patient was wheeled into the reception room. An old man with tubes in his nose, an oxygen tank strapped to his wheelchair. He looked more dead than alive.

"Dr. Kohler can see you briefly, Mr. Rimer," the nurse said and pointed the way. "He's in room six."

Rimer walked down a corridor with a blinking fluorescent light overhead. The walls were plain plaster, painted in light green. There were no pictures, no artwork. He heard a toilet flush, pipes rattle.

Rimer came to room 6 and entered without knocking.

Arnold Kohler was at his desk busily writing in a chart. Without looking up, he motioned Rimer to a vinyl-covered chair.

Rimer sat down heavily and glanced around the room. Like the rest of the annex, it was worn and antiquated. Against the wall was a wooden examining table with a flat mattress and no movable parts. What seemed to be leather straps hung down from the sides, but Rimer couldn't be sure because they were partially covered by a sheet. A nearby potted tree was more yellow than green.

Kohler put his pen down. "You should join Health First. It would make things a lot easier."

"I'm not joining any HMO."

"Why not? It's not that expensive."

"It's not the money. It's all the information they want. They want to know all about your life, and I'd rather they didn't."

"Your records would be kept confidential."

"Ha!" Rimer forced a laugh. "Once they put all your shit into a computer anybody can get to it."

"It's not quite that easy." Kohler rocked back in his small swivel chair and studied the man across from him. Rimer was a tall, lanky man with thinning red hair and gray-green eyes. "You just can't continue to come in this way."

Rimer shrugged, unconcerned. He straightened his back and slowly rotated his neck, stretching tight muscles.

"Is your back bothering you?"

"Naw. Just a little tightness."

The intercom on Kohler's desk buzzed. "Dr. Kohler, Dr. Mariner is on line two for you."

Kohler hesitated, staring at the phone before picking it up. "Yes, Dr. Mariner."

"What the hell is going on down there?" Mariner demanded.

"What . . . what are you talking about?" Kohler asked, caught off guard.

"We've just received another letter of complaint from one of your patients."

"I'm sure there's an explanation."

"Oh, sure!" Mariner said sarcastically. "Just like your explanation in the Sally Wheaton case. Remember? You told the poor woman her syncopal episodes were due to anxiety and she turned out to have a serious cardiac arrhythmia."

"An honest mistake."

"No! Sloppy medicine. Anxiety doesn't cause syncope. Even interns know that."

"Now, you look," Kohler said, raising his voice, "I'm a well-trained physician. I'm a board-eligible—"

"Board eligible, but not board certified," Mariner snapped. "Because you took the boards three times and failed them every time—a fact you neglected to mention when you applied for a position at Health First."

Kohler remained silent. Small beads of perspiration popped out on his forehead.

"And then there was that malpractice suit against you two years ago. I just found out about that."

"That case was settled out of court," Kohler said defensively. "I was never proven guilty."

"Or innocent, for that matter. Now I'm sending you that letter of complaint and I want your response on my desk by tomorrow morning."

"Why don't I come up and—"

"I want it written," Mariner said, cutting him off. "And I also want you to know that you're on notice. One more mistake and you're gone."

"But I have a contract with Health First."

"Contracts can be broken."

"I'd better talk with my wife about this." Kohler's wife was an associate in a large law firm downtown. She was an expert in labor negotiations and was tough as nails.

"Talk with whomever you want. But keep in mind, you're on notice."

Kohler put the phone down and took out a handkerchief to mop his brow. The last thing he wanted was to go back to private practice, where he'd had nothing but problems and had never really made a decent income. Yes, he'd be very careful with his patients from now on, but he'd also discuss the matter with his wife. She'd know how to deal with Mariner. Kohler wondered which of his patients had complained. "Goddamn patients," he grumbled.

"If you don't like it here, why don't you leave?"

"Because it suits me to stay." And it's none of your damn business, Kohler wanted to say, but he held his tongue.

The nurse knocked briefly on the door and looked into the room. "The patients are really piling up and Mr. Sims is starting to wheeze badly."

"All right," Kohler said, then looked over at Rimer. "So your back is still bothering you, huh?"

Rimer nodded, wondering what Kohler was getting at.

"And the pills I gave you last time helped a lot, huh?"

"Oh, yeah." Rimer smiled to himself. "They helped a lot."

Kohler reached for his prescription pad and pen. "Let's hope they work again."

Rimer stood and kept his back to the nurse so she couldn't see him taking the prescription slip. She also couldn't see the thick manila envelopes the men exchanged.

8

The cast was an exact replica of the dead man's head. Joanna reached out and touched the light brown hair atop the cast. It was soft and smooth and, although it was a wig, it felt real. She ran her fingers over the facial area. There was no face, only indentations where the eyes and mouth and nostrils should have been.

"I'd start with the pieces of bone that you are absolutely certain you can identify," Phil Weideman said. He was sitting on a bench-top in the forensic laboratory. The front of his scrub suit was soaked with perspiration, his surgical mask pulled down to his neck.

Joanna picked up the two largest fragments. "I've got a fair-sized chunk of chin and a smaller bit of his right supraorbital ridge."

"Then stick them on in place."

Joanna hesitated, studying the bones. "Let's see how good your computer program is first." She handed the fragments to Emily Ryan, who was sitting at a nearby desk. "Measure these carefully and don't tell me which numbers belong to which pieces."

Emily reached for a pair of calipers and measured the fragments, then measured them again, making certain her numbers were correct. She jotted down the information on a slip of paper and handed it to Joanna.

Joanna bent over the keyboard and punched in the measurements. Instantly a face appeared on the computer screen. It was an outline with no distinct features. Four slits for the eyes and mouth and nose. Then two pieces of bone came up on the screen and moved onto the face. The first fragment went to the chin and the words "MENTAL BONE" flashed up. Then the second fragment moved into position just above the right eye. "SUPRAORBITAL RIDGE, RIGHT, FRONTAL BONE," the computer noted.

"Fantastic!" Joanna beamed.

"Don't get carried away," Weideman cautioned her. "The smaller the pieces, the tougher it's going to get."

Joanna took the bone fragments and carefully placed them on the cast of the dead man's face. The facial area of the cast was glazed with an adhesive coat so that anything would stick to it, but not too firmly. The dead man's face now had a definite chin and part of an ocular orbit.

Joanna picked up the next largest piece of bone and felt its edges. It was triangular shaped, at least two centimeters in length, and thick, very thick. She couldn't be sure where it came from. Maybe it was frontal or temporal bone or maybe part of a smashed mandible. Joanna handed the fragment to Emily.

"What do you think that bone is?" Weideman asked.

Joanna shrugged. "It's impossible to tell."

"Then guess."

"In forensics, guesses will get you into all sorts of trouble. I don't like guesses."

"It's not a matter of what you like or don't like," Weideman said impatiently. "If you want to put this man's face back together, then do what I tell you to do. Now, take your best guess."

Joanna's face began to color. She felt as if she was being lectured to and she wanted to tell Weideman to go take a flying leap, but she held her tongue because he was Memorial's expert on facial reconstruction and she needed him. "Why is guessing so important?"

"Because the computer alone can't do it all. There'll be more than a few fragments it can't identify." Weideman scratched absently at his ear. "You're going to have to guess where those pieces of bone go. And the more you do it, the better you'll do it. Eventually you'll get a feel for this man's face. You'll get to the point where you'll start to look for pieces of bone with certain shapes because you know they'll fit into a given place. It's kind of like putting together a jigsaw puzzle.''

With one exception, Joanna thought. With a jigsaw puzzle you know the end result before you start. They show you a picture on the box cover. But she knew what Weideman was driving at. There would be plenty of missing pieces of bone, where the killer had smashed the fragments into powder. Here, Joanna would have to guess, and in order to guess correctly she'd have to have a feel for what the face should look like.

Emily handed Joanna the measurements for the fragment and Joanna quickly punched the information into the keyboard. Numbers flashed up on the computer screen and kept on flashing faster and faster. The computer was having trouble making a decision.

"Something's wrong," Joanna said.

Weideman hopped off the benchtop and came over to the computer. Numbers were still flashing on the screen. Names of various bones appeared, only to disappear instantly and be replaced by more numbers. Weideman punched in a new code and the screen went blank. Then the measurements Joanna had entered into the computer came up. "W—4 mm. L—32 cm. D—2 cm."

"I think you forgot a decimal point," Weideman said. "There is no cranial bone with a length of thirty-two centimeters."

"Jesus," Joanna groaned, embarrassed by her mistake. She punched in the correct measurements.

In a split second the computer identified the bone. "SUPERIOR FRONTAL." Then another possibility flashed up. "OR ANTERIOR TEMPORAL." Joanna cleared the screen and entered the numbers again. The results were the same. Two different bones. Two different possibilities.

Weideman tapped a finger on the desktop. "You're going to have to make a choice here."

Joanna hesitated. "But it doesn't tell me whether it's on the right or left side."

"That doesn't matter. In close calls, the computer assumes that both sides of the face are identical. And for all intents and purposes they are."

"Maybe," Joanna said with uncertainty. "But let's say the law of averages takes effect and I put every other piece on the wrong side of the face. It would end up a distorted mess. There's no way a computer could sort through that."

"Oh, sure it could." Weideman reached down and punched another code into the keyboard. A face appeared with a chin and part of a supraorbital arch in place. Then the new bone was added to the forehead. Suddenly four faces came up on the screen, showing the new bone in its four possible locations: "LEFT FRONTAL," "RIGHT FRONTAL," "LEFT TEMPORAL," "RIGHT TEMPORAL." "The computer will keep all the possibilities in its memory bank."

Joanna sighed wearily. "At this rate we could end up with a hundred faces."

"I don't think so," Weideman said, unconcerned. "The computer will sort through all the faces and give you the best fit analysis. In the end there won't be more than fifteen or twenty possibilities."

"Too many," Joanna said, almost whispering. "Way too many."

"Better than none at all," Weideman reminded her.

Joanna picked up the piece of bone under question and carefully palpated it. She closed her eyes, trying to envision where the bone belonged. It seemed to fit better in the middle of the forehead. On the left side. "Left frontal," she said aloud.

"Good. Then put it there."

Joanna walked over to the cast of the dead man's head and placed the piece of bone high up on the left forehead. She studied its position for a moment and then, not satisfied, she moved it down an inch and slightly more medial. Now it seemed right.

"I think you're beginning to understand the value of having a feel for the man's face," Weideman said. "And keep remembering that the computer can't see it, it can only interpret numbers. You can see and you can envision and in the end the face you construct will probably be closer to the truth than most of the images the computer draws up."

"And the face I make will match up with only a limited number of the faces in the computer, right?"

"Right."

"How many do you think it will match up with?"

"Probably ten or so."

"Still too many," Joanna winced.

"Life is hard," Weideman said lightly and grinned.

Joanna nodded and smiled back. He did look like a cowboy, she thought, with his thick brown hair and deep blue eyes. So blue. She wondered if they were real or the result of colored contact lenses.

Weideman went back to the benchtop and sat on it, propping his feet on the back of a chair. His legs were tired and aching from the long procedure he'd done earlier that morning. A young girl thrown from a bicycle with badly lacerated lips and nose and a huge forehead gash near the hairline. Weideman and another plastic surgeon had spent six hours putting the girl's face back together. A mess, a real mess. But the end result would be good, the scars barely noticeable—and with lipstick and makeup, not noticeable at all.

Weideman shifted around in his seat, now watching Joanna as she picked up another bone fragment and carefully examined it, first with her eyes closed and then with them opened. She was obviously inexperienced in facial reconstruction and Weideman could tell she hadn't spent a lot of time in front of a computer. But she jumped right into the project without hesitation, undaunted by the obstacles that made the task so difficult.

There was something adventurous and bold about her. It was a quality Weideman admired greatly in women. His wife had it when they first met, but ten years of marriage and two kids had changed that. Now she was cautious, careful, overly conservative in everything. And boring. Their marriage was coming apart and both of them knew it. They still shared the same house but slept in different bedrooms. And Weideman knew it was only a matter of time before he moved out.

His gaze went over to Joanna, now putting another piece of bone on the head. So damn pretty and so bright and still unmarried. God! Why? He scanned her body, focusing in on her firm buttocks and thighs. He envisioned her nude in bed and felt himself begin to stir.

"That's four pieces in place," Joanna said, breaking into Weideman's thoughts. "It's a start."

"A good start."

"I really appreciate your helping me out," Joanna said sincerely. "I know how busy you are."

"Not at all. It gives me a chance to get away from patients for a while. And besides, this project is beginning to fascinate the hell out of me."

That's not the only thing fascinating you, Emily Ryan thought, smiling to herself. She had noticed the attention he was giving Joanna and she had also noticed how Joanna seemed to be warming to him. Something was going to happen between these two, she decided.

"And thank the corporation you consult for, for allowing us to use their program. I'd be glad to write them a testimonial."

"For what?"

"For how their program could be used in criminal cases, such as this one."

"I'll tell them," Weideman said evenly, but his mind was racing ahead with the idea of making the program available to police units on a wide scale. He hadn't thought of that possibility. Nor had anyone at Bio-Syn. He wondered how many cases of faceless victims there were in this country. Or worldwide, for that matter. It was of more than passing interest to him because his consultant fee of twenty-five thousand dollars per year was paid to him in stock that went directly into his pension plan, so he paid no taxes on it. And anything he did to enhance the profits of the corporation would enhance the value of his shares, already worth over eighty thousand dollars.

"Dr. Blalock," Emily said excitedly, "I think these two pieces here fit together. If they do, we've got ourselves a very large, nice-sized chunk of bone to deal with."

Weideman came over to take a look. As the women tried to determine how good a fit there was between the two pieces, Weideman's mind went back to the value of the computer program in criminal investigations. A program like that could be marketed for at least five thousand dollars, probably more. It would depend on the volume.

Joanna studied the two pieces and tried to match them together. "It's a partial fit at best. We should probably treat them as separate pieces. What do you think, Phil?"

"I agree," he said, warmed by Joanna's calling him by his first name for the first time.

"Measure the pieces separately," Joanna instructed Emily.

Weideman waited for Emily to begin measuring, then said to Joanna, "Regarding that testimonial you mentioned, I'll ask Bio-Syn if they're interested in one."

"Just let me know."

"How many cases of faceless victims that need to be identified are there in America each year?"

Joanna shrugged. "I don't have an exact number, but conservatively it's in the hundreds."

"And worldwide?"

"Thousands. Why?"

Weideman quickly multiplied a thousand times the five-thousand-dollar cost of each program. Five million dollars! At a minimum. Jesus! "Just curious," he said.

Joanna looked over her shoulder as the door opened and Simon Murdock walked in. She could instantly tell that something was wrong. He had a frozen half smile on his face. That always meant trouble.

"Joanna, I'm going to need—" Murdock now saw that Joanna wasn't alone. He stared for a moment at Phil Weideman, the half smile still on his face. "Well, what's a plastic surgeon doing in a forensics laboratory?"

"Just helping Joanna reconstruct a dead man's face," Weideman said.

Murdock nodded, surprised by the tone of Weideman's voice when he spoke Joanna's name. There was a warmth and familiarity to it, something he hadn't expected. "Are you making any progress?"

"Some." Weideman pointed to the replica of the dead man's head.

Murdock walked over to the cast and studied it at length, mesmerized by its ghastliness. He reached out and very carefully touched an attached fragment of bone. The bone seemed to glisten in the light. "Is the bone real?"

"Absolutely," Joanna assured him.

"Why is it so white?"

Joanna explained that the facial bones had been treated with dilute acid to remove all tissue and debris. The end result was very white bones with smooth surfaces that reflected light brightly. Initially, Joanna had resisted the idea of treating the bones with acid, but an expert from the FBI told her that dead tissue hanging from bones may look realistic but adds nothing except distortion. It was better to start with a smooth skeletal base and build on it.

Murdock was still studying the head with scattered pieces of bone attached. It reminded him of a man who had cut himself in multiple places while shaving and had stemmed the bleeding with pieces of tissue paper. "Even with the facial bones in place, I still can't envision you making a face out of this. I mean, what about the details? What about the color of his eyes, for example?"

"They're brown. I found a piece of iris embedded in orbital bone."

"And his mouth?"

"We're working on it. I showed a portion of his maxilla and hard palate to one of our oral surgeons. He thinks the man had a small mouth with a noticeable overbite."

Murdock nodded, impressed, but he still wasn't at all certain that the man would end up with a face. "You've heard that the coroner's office and county morgue will be reopened this coming Monday?"

"I heard."

"So all the bodies and all the parts should be returned to them," Murdock went on, "including your dead man with no face."

"They can have his body, but I'm still going to work on his face."

Murdock shook his head. "No. It's better, I think, to let them take over the case entirely. It's their case, their problem."

"I will continue to work on this man," Joanna said firmly, "and when I'm done he'll have a face."

Murdock stared at Joanna, trying to keep his composure, but his jaws began to tighten noticeably. "Then make sure you do it on your own time, and don't use any of Memorial's resources to do it."

Joanna was taken aback by the dictatorial tone of Murdock's voice. "Is that an order?"

"Those are my instructions, yes."

Joanna glared at him defiantly, her face coloring, the veins in her neck now bulging.

Emily Ryan quickly got to her feet and checked her watch. She wanted to get out of the laboratory before the fireworks really started. "I've got to go to a lecture," she said and hurried from the room.

Weideman slowly stood, a knee popping loudly. "And I've got a rhinoplasty waiting for me." He walked over to Murdock and extended a hand. "It was nice to see you again, Simon."

"Same here," Murdock said, shaking the other man's hand.

Weideman glanced over at the head, studying it briefly, then looked back at Murdock. "Nobody else can put this man's face back together, Simon. Nobody but us. If you send this head back to the coroner's office it will just lie there and gather dust and no one will ever know who the dead man was."

Murdock shrugged, not caring if the dead man ever got a face. That was the coroner's business.

Weideman touched Joanna's shoulder with his index finger. "When you're ready to work on the face again, give me a call. Late afternoons are best for me."

Joanna waited for Weideman to close the door behind himself. Then she turned to Murdock and moved in closer, almost face-to-face. "Don't you ever give me orders again," she snapped. "Never. Because if you do I'm going to tell you what you can do with those orders."

"Now you look here. I'm—"

"No, *you* look here," Joanna cut him off abruptly. "I've done you more favors than I care to think about. Every time you've made a request, I've come through for you. Whether it was doing autopsies for the county or the postmortem examination on the O'Hara girl. And what's my reward for working my buns off? I'm given the pleasure of being embarrassed by you in front of my colleagues." She turned away, mumbling curses under her breath. "I'm not going to stand for that, Simon. Not from you or anybody else."

"It was not my intention to embarrass you."

"It may not have been your intention but you did a pretty good job of it."

Murdock sighed wearily. "I may have been too blunt," he conceded, "and for that I apologize."

"Your apology is accepted."

"Good," Murdock said, still not liking her and wishing there was some way he could force her out of Memorial, but knowing there wasn't. "I've come to ask for another favor."

"What?"

"You've heard about the sudden death of yet another Health First patient at Memorial?"

Joanna nodded. "I was in the Health First Tower with Dr. Mariner when he got the news."

Murdock's eyes narrowed. "Why were you meeting with him?"

"I was in a conference with Mariner and some other physicians who were involved in the care of Lucy O'Hara. I was hoping they could add something that might help us find out why she died suddenly."

"And did they?"

"No."

Murdock began to pace the floor, now circling the head, which stood on a small pedestal. "This is the second patient from Health First who has died suddenly at Memorial. And both in less than a week's time."

"I hope it wasn't another young girl."

"No. She was a sixty-four-year-old woman with metastatic breast cancer awaiting autologous bone marrow transplantation. And she had a pacemaker. So, with a little luck we'll find out she died a cardiac death. That's the most likely cause, right?"

"Maybe." And maybe not. Joanna thought about other causes of sudden death in a patient with widespread malignancy. Massive hemorrhage caused by the tumor's eroding into a big artery. Pulmonary embolism. A dozen possibilities. "We'll look and see."

"It's crucial that we find a cause for her death," Murdock said, still pacing. "We have a very lucrative contract with Health First. They send us their very sickest patients and we treat them and we're handsomely paid for doing so. If their patients are going to die suddenly at Memorial, then they're going to send them to other medical centers. And if that happens, Memorial Hospital can close its doors."

Joanna looked at him strangely. "I'm not sure I follow you."

"All of medicine is becoming managed care. The days of fee for service and simple private health insurance are coming to an end. Instead of private practices, medicine will consist of giant HMOs, like Health First. And medical centers, like Memorial, will depend on contracts with these giant HMOs for their income. Health First is a model HMO in California and everybody is rushing to copy it. We were lucky enough to get the Health First contract. And because of that we've gotten contracts with other large HMOs. Those contracts now account for twenty-five percent of our business, and within a few years it will be over fifty percent. If we lose the Health First contract for any reason and other HMOs walk out along with them . . ." Murdock's voice trailed off. "Well, as I said, we can close our doors."

"When would you like the autopsy done?" Joanna asked.

"As soon as possible."

"I'll set it up for tomorrow."

"I hope you won't mind if Dr. Mariner and one of his associates are present at the postmortem examination. He called and asked if they could attend."

"I'll notify him as soon as I set a time."

The intercom on a nearby phone buzzed loudly. Joanna reached over and pressed a button. "What?"

"It's the television people from Channel Two," her secretary said. "They want to know if they can start a little earlier. Say three-thirty p.m."

"What's my schedule look like?"

"Busy. You're supposed to be reading slides with the chief resident at three-thirty p.m. But I can switch that around."

"Good. Do it." Joanna released the intercom button and turned to Murdock. "Sorry about the interruption."

"No problem," Murdock said, straightening his tie in a nervous gesture. "What do the—ah—the television people want?"

"The Channel Two news department wants to do a segment on forensic pathology. They're interested in our difficult cases."

Murdock glanced over at the head. "And of course you'll present the man with no face."

"Of course."

Now Murdock understood why Joanna wanted so desperately to continue working on the faceless man. It wasn't just the challenge of identifying the victim. That was secondary. She wanted to be in the spotlight again. She needed the limelight and publicity, just like some insecure Hollywood actress. Maybe even more so. Fame was like a disease, Murdock thought. No, more like an addiction. At length he said, "It's a rather gruesome thing to present, don't you think?"

"Murder is gruesome business, Simon."

"It smacks of sensationalism to me."

Joanna took a deep breath, trying to remain patient. "It's not a matter of sensationalism. That's not the purpose of presenting the faceless man."

"Then what is?"

"We've got a corpse we can't identify because he has no face and no fingers. We know he's white, in his thirties, with brown eyes and light brown hair. And he probably had friends, acquaintances, a job, maybe even family in Southern California. In all likelihood our faceless man is being missed by somebody. Somebody is wondering where he is and what happened to him."

Joanna walked over to the head. Its wig was askew. She straightened it. "Now, the news program I'll be appearing on is seen by a million people nightly. Maybe—just maybe—someone will be watching and will say, "Hey, that could be Charlie or Mike or Rudy or whoever. Maybe we'll get lucky. Maybe somebody will identify him for us. That's the purpose of presenting him on television."

"I see," Murdock said, not believing her entirely, now wondering if she was going to receive a fee for her appearance. He glanced up at the wall clock. "I must run. I'm already late for an executive committee meeting. Please don't forget to notify Dr. Mariner when you've set a time for the autopsy on his patient."

"I'll call him within an hour."

Murdock nodded appreciatively and walked to the door. He turned and held up a hand, palm out. A peace sign. Joanna returned it. They both knew the problem between them. They simply rubbed each other the wrong way. But at least they could be civil. That they agreed on.

Joanna sat down heavily in a swivel chair in front of the computer. She leaned back and stretched her neck. Her gaze drifted over to the benchtop where Phil Weideman had been sitting. He had left a patient's chart behind. Wearily, Joanna stood and walked over to the chart and quickly flipped through it. She came to a page with a photograph of a young child, maybe four or five, glued to it. The girl had a huge cleft palate. The harelip gave the child a terrible disfigurement. Joanna could only imagine the sadness and anguish the little girl must have felt every time she looked in the mirror. Joanna turned to another page and saw a second photograph of the same child postoperatively. The defect was gone, the harelip replaced by a very faint white scar. The little girl was all smiles.

Joanna closed the chart, now thinking about Phil Weideman. She had expected to dislike him, to somehow tolerate him because she needed him to reconstruct the dead man's face. But it hadn't turned out that way. She liked him, more than she wanted to admit. She liked his mannerisms and his looks and the way he backed her up in her argument with Murdock. He could have easily done what Emily Ryan did—split and run. But he didn't. And where did he get those blue eyes from? They were too blue to be real.

She shook her head and tried to get rid of her foolish thoughts. And besides, he was married. Or at least she thought he was. Damn it, Jake, she grumbled to herself, now thinking about Jake Sinclair, the big cop who was the main man in her life. Come back from Greece already. You've spent enough time mourning over your dead ex-wife, Eleni. "Damn," Joanna whispered softly under her breath. Things had been going so well before Jake got the phone call from Athens. So well. A month ago they were in Hawaii and had the best time ever together. Warm, wonderful days and even better nights. They were finally finding the closeness that had been missing from both of their lives for so long. Then the phone call came. The past had come back to haunt them again. And now she was thinking about some surgeon's blue eyes, like a stupid teenager. Come on, Jake! Get back here and we'll go on with our lives together. We'll pick up exactly where we left off. But deep down, Joanna had an uneasy feeling they wouldn't.

Joanna went over to the computer and sat down heavily. She studied the images on the screen. There were six faces displayed with the bone fragments arranged in various combinations. There was not even a hint of what the facial features really looked like. But at least the frontal area—the forehead—had two large pieces of bone in place. Joanna punched in a code, asking the computer to project what the forehead would look like based on the two fragments already in place. Probably a hundred possibilities, she guessed.

Numbers flashed up on the screen, then facial outlines. Then numbers again. Finally the computer made its decision. "DATA INSUFFICIENT TO PROJECT IMAGE."

"No kidding," Joanna said and switched the computer off.

Theo Papadakis pulled up to the curb at Athens International Airport. He took a cigarette from his pack and offered one to Jake, then lit both carefully.

"So, my friend," Theo said, "we will never see you again, will we?"

"You never know," Jake said, but he knew that Theo was right.

"Regardless of where you are or what happens, you will always be a part of this family."

Jake nodded, his mind going back to the small cemetery where they had buried Eleni. He could still see the funeral procession led by a Greek Orthodox priest, Eleni's casket on the shoulders of her six brothers. "It's hard to believe she's dead."

"But she is, and now we must all go on with our lives. Right?"

"I guess."

Theo took a deep drag on his cigarette and flicked it out the window. His eyes suddenly narrowed and he quickly slouched behind the steering wheel. "Get down and don't look over at the terminal—unless you want Eleni's fat pig of a husband to see you."

Jake glanced over at Frank Stamos, a swarthy, obese man who had probably been very handsome fifty pounds ago. Porters carrying trunks and suitcases followed Stamos into the terminal.

"I'll bet he's on the same flight as you. You'd better pray he doesn't sit next to you."

"Don't worry about it. Chances are he'll be in first class."

"Yes, of course. That way he can eat during the entire flight."

"You really don't like him, do you?"

"No, I don't," Theo said at once. "But he did do one decent thing while he was here."

"What?"

"He arranged to have a special caretaker look after Eleni's grave. You know, to make certain weeds don't grow and to place flowers throughout the year."

"So he's got a little bit of good in him, huh?"

"Just a little," Theo said grudgingly.

Moments later Jake was inside the terminal and walking toward the TWA counter. The building was crowded and noisy, the air stuffy and stale. He almost bumped into a stewardess for Olympic Airlines. She was wearing the same type of uniform Eleni had on when Jake first met her. The stewardess smiled at Jake and he managed to smile back. Maybe if I get the hell out of Greece I can leave some of these memories behind, he told himself, not really believing it. Eleni's memory might fade, but there would always be something to bring it back. Always. On his right Jake saw a bank of phones, all occupied except for one. He headed for it. Jake put his suitcase down and lit a cigarette, then placed a call to Los Angeles.

"Hello." Joanna's voice sounded sleepy.

"This is Jake. I'm calling to let you know I'm on my way back."

"Where are you?"

"At the airport in Athens."

"Are you okay?"

"I think so." Jake drew heavily on his cigarette. "Are you still mad at me?"

"Not mad, Jake. Just hurt and disappointed."

"Because I went to a funeral, huh?"

"Because you dropped me like a hot piece of coal, like I really didn't matter a damn."

"I had other things on my mind."

"I know—like a dead ex-wife who was more important than me."

"Shit," Jake growled. "Can't you understand that when someone who was once close to you dies it still hurts like hell? Can't you just give a little bit?''

"I gave plenty and wanted to give more, but you pushed me away. You couldn't think of anybody or anything except your ex-wife."

"Are you that goddamned insecure?"

"Insecure? Over what?"

"Over me thinking about Eleni—a girl I once loved."

Joanna took a deep breath and exhaled loudly. "I don't give a damn what you think about. What I care about is how you treat me."

"That's not it," Jake said bluntly. "And you know it."

"I'm trying to hold my temper, Jake."

"I'd rather you tell the truth."

"Goddamn it! Goddamn it!" Joanna blurted out. "You can take your entire past and your present and your future and stick it! You can weep and mourn over your ex-wife all you want. I just don't want to be part of it."

"Don't worry, you won't," Jake snapped.

There was a long, strained silence.

"Maybe it's best for us to be apart for a while," Joanna said.

"Maybe."

"And I think it's time we started seeing other people."

"Seeing!" Jake yelled. "What the hell does that mean?"

"Dating other people."

Jake threw his cigarette to the floor and angrily crushed it out. "Who is he?"

"Who are you talking about?"

"The guy you're seeing or thinking about seeing." Jake could tell from the awkward silence that he'd guessed right. "Are you sleeping with him?"

"You can go to hell!"

"And you can go screw yourself!"

Joanna slammed the receiver back onto the phone so hard that the whole phone jumped off the night table. She quickly disconnected it, just in case Jake tried to call back. Goddamn you, Jake, she seethed, you always thought about yourself first, even when we first started going together. But I turned a blind eye to it because I thought you were so special. But you're not. And if I want to date Phil Weideman, I will. And if I want to sleep with him, I'll do that too.

Joanna went into the kitchen and poured herself a glass of cold chardonnay. She sipped the wine, trying to calm herself, but still furious with Jake. Now her stomach began rumbling. It always did that when she was upset. In the refrigerator she found the makings of a salad and a small block of cheddar cheese. The freezer was filled with unappetizing frozen dinners. She settled for a stalk of celery dipped in blue cheese dressing.

Her gaze went to the calendar on the refrigerator door. Tuesday. Always a bad day for her. And this Tuesday was no different. Her work at the hospital had not gone well. Things had been forgotten. Things had been left undone or not done as she would have liked. Not a good day except for the television interview. That went well. Or at least she thought it had. Joanna checked the kitchen clock. She'd know for certain how well she'd done in a few minutes. She went into the bedroom and switched on the television set.

Joanna sat on the edge of the bed and waited for the evening news. She thought about Jake again and wondered if he was as upset as she was. But it really didn't matter. It was over and done. Their relationship was now irreparably damaged and Joanna doubted they could put it back together even if they both tried. She should have been able to predict they wouldn't have lasted. They were too different, their worlds galaxies apart. Yes, it was time to move on, she thought.

On the television screen she watched an attractive blond co-anchor introducing herself.

"Good evening, I'm Cathy Harrelson. Our top story tonight is another tragic drive-by shooting that left a six-year-old girl seriously wounded. We have two reporters standing by. First, in Inglewood we go to . . ."

Joanna tuned out the anchor's nasal voice and carefully studied Cathy Harrelson's face. The transformation was amazing. When Cathy had interviewed her earlier, Joanna was struck by the anchor's hard looks and horsey face. But the television camera somehow muted those qualities. She actually had a soft attractiveness on TV. But Joanna kept remembering the woman's incredible coarseness when informed that the patient they'd be discussing had no face.

"He has no fucking face?" Cathy Harrelson had blurted out. "What the hell kind of story is that going to be?"

"We're going to give him a face," Joanna had told her.

"How?"

"With a computer and a lot of hard work."

"We're going to break for a few commercials," Cathy Harrelson was saying on the screen, "and when we return we'll be delving into one of medicine's most mysterious subspecialties, forensic pathology. And folks, let me tell you up front, this segment will be graphic. So, if you're squeamish—well, use your own judgment."

Joanna cringed, hating the sensationalism. Horror story to follow. Don't miss this. It'll scare the hell out of you. Why do they have to sensationalize everything? She knew it was meant to tantalize, but all it really did was to detract and cheapen. But that wasn't her biggest concern. What worried her most was the editing. The interview had lasted for over twenty minutes and there was no way she was going to get all that time on the screen. She'd be lucky to get more than a few minutes. She could only hope they wouldn't remove the most important segments, particularly the portion that dealt with the general description of the dead man.

"And now our special feature, 'Insights into Medicine,' " Cathy Harrelson said, her face very serious. "Tonight we delve into the area of forensic pathology. Earlier I had a chance to interview Dr. Joanna Blalock, who is the director of forensic pathology at Memorial Hospital. She is currently helping the police with one of their most difficult cases. We call it 'The Case of the Man with No Face.' In just a moment, you'll see why. Again let me warn you: this is graphic material."

Joanna leaned forward as she saw herself on the screen. She seemed older on television. There were no noticeable facial lines. The makeup artist had taken care of these with a layer of powder. But her eyes looked tired and heavy with dark circles beginning to form. Her hair was just a little disheveled and that added to her fatigued appearance. That's what you get from fourteen-hour workdays, she thought miserably.

"So he was brought in with no face?" Cathy Harrelson was asking her on television.

"No face at all. It was virtually destroyed by some blunt instrument. He remains unidentified," Joanna said.

"Weren't his fingerprints of any help?"

"His fingertips were cut off."

The camera moved to the replica of the dead man's head. In the bright light, the attached pieces of bone glistened.

"And this is a cast of his head, right?"

"Correct."

"And how do you plan to reconstruct his face?"

Joanna explained how she had harvested as many pieces of remaining facial bones as possible and how she was using a computer to find the correct position for each piece.

"Fascinating," Cathy Harrelson said breathlessly. "Just fascinating. What are your chances of coming up with a recognizable face?"

"Pretty fair, I'd say."

"Are there any features of his body that might help in identifying this man? You know, like scars or tattoos that somebody in our viewing audience might recognize?"

"He has an unusual tattoo on his buttocks."

"Can you describe it?"

"Not at this time, no."

"Can we say that the police didn't want its characteristics revealed?"

"You can say that, yes."

"Did they give you a reason?"

"No, they didn't," Joanna lied easily. The police had specifically asked her not to describe the tattoo because that would have caused a flood of phone calls from all the nuts and psychotics in Los Angeles, either confessing to the crime or claiming they knew the person who did it. And of course every phone call had to be checked out, resulting in a monumental waste of time. No. Better just to tell them he had a tattoo on his buttocks. If the victim was being missed by someone who really knew him, then the fact that he had a tattoo on his buttocks plus his other general characteristics would be enough.

Joanna turned her attention back to the television set.

"Absolutely fascinating," the male co-anchor was saying, "you did a superb job, Cathy."

Cathy Harrelson beamed. "Thanks, Bill. I wish I could take the credit, but to be honest the story literally told itself."

"Indeed," the co-anchor agreed. "Do you really think they'll come up with a face for their faceless victim?"

"I'd bet on it," Cathy said with certainty. "Joanna Blalock is one of the very best in the science of forensic pathology. Yes, this man will have a face. And soon."

"I hope you'll give us a follow-up story on this."

"Absolutely."

In a small motel room on Pico Boulevard in West Los Angeles, Karl Rimer switched off the television set and went back to cleaning his Beretta. He checked and double-checked the semiautomatic mechanism, making certain it was functioning properly. He liked the weapon. He liked its weight and feel and balance and, most of all, the caliber of its bullets. Nine millimeters. Exactly the right size. Big enough to do a lot of damage, but not messy. Not like the magnums. Their bullets went right through people and sometimes through the wall and into the next room. And magnums were noisy too. They sounded like cannons.

Rimer continued cleaning his weapon, but his mind drifted back to the program he'd just seen. Goddamn it! There was going to be trouble. He knew it. He felt it in his bones. His phone would ring shortly and he'd have to calm them down, soothe them, let them know that everything was going to be fine. And it *was* going to be fine. It was just a pain in the ass to have to go back and make certain. Double certain this time.

The phone rang. He picked it up on the fourth ring.

"Yes," Rimer said.

"Did you see the television program?"

"I saw it."

"I thought he was supposed to be dead and unrecognizable."

"He *is* dead and unrecognizable."

"But will he stay that way?"

"I'll take care of it."

"You'd better."

Rimer put the phone down and went back to cleaning his weapon. The barrel of the pistol glistened in the light and he stared at it, concentrating, trying to remember the name of the forensic pathologist he'd seen on the news program. What the hell was her name? He thought about it for a few moments until it came to him. Blalock. Joanna Blalock.

10

Emily Ryan looked down at the face of Sally Wheaton, then quickly turned away. The resemblance between Sally Wheaton and Emily's mother was striking. Both had small noses, generous mouths, dimpled cheeks, and blue eyes. And both had cancer of the breast. Except that the disease in Emily's mother had been detected early and was said to be cured. Stage I. Localized. No metastases. But with cancer of the breast one could never tell for sure. All it took was one malignant cell to break loose, travel to some other part of the body and begin to multiply, and then the disease category would change from curable to nightmare.

"What do you think these are?" Joanna Blalock asked, holding up the liver that had been removed en bloc. The liver's surface was dotted with white nodules.

Emily reached over and palpated the nodules. They were very firm and fixed in place. "Probably metastatic lesions."

"Probably," Joanna agreed. "Was the patient's liver clinically enlarged?"

"No."

"What about the liver function tests?"

Emily hesitated, thinking back. "There were no spectacular abnormalities. Some of the hepatic enzymes were modestly elevated."

"And what does that tell you?"

"That clinically we miss a lot." A whole lot, Emily thought, despite our elaborate blood tests and CAT scans and MRIs.

Joanna was now working on the corpse's chest. She had removed the pacemaker and was holding it up to the light. Its wires dangled down like tentacles. Using a magnifying glass, she read the information engraved on its surface. CARDIAC PACEMAKER. NUMBER 1408B. MPI, LOS ANGELES, CA. USA.

Joanna placed the pacemaker on a side table, then removed the heart and lungs. The pleura were studded with metastatic nodules and as a consequence there were small effusions bilaterally. The heart was normal sized with no thickening or scarring of the ventricular walls. Even the coronary arteries looked good. "Were you able to learn anything new about her cardiac disease?"

"Not much. I talked with the resident who evaluated her and he said she had an arrhythmia that sounded like atrioventricular block, but he wasn't sure. They're waiting for her records from her outside cardiologist to arrive."

The door to the special autopsy room opened and Simon Murdock led the way in, followed by Robert Mariner and Arnold Kohler. All were dressed in green scrub suits. Joanna stared at Murdock briefly. He looked so peculiar in the surgical garb, particularly with his undershirt still on and a latex glove covering his five-thousand-dollar gold Rolex.

Murdock approached the autopsy table and glanced down at the partially dissected corpse. "I thought you were going to wait for us before beginning."

Joanna pointed to the wall clock. It read twelve noon. "I did wait. Everyone was notified that the autopsy would start at eleven a.m. Nobody showed. We waited another half hour and still nobody showed, so we started."

"Couldn't you have waited a bit longer?" Murdock made no effort to cover his irritation.

"We're already behind," Joanna told him, "way behind. All of our regular autopsy tables are filled, so we had to use this special autopsy room, which is supposed to be reserved for contaminated cases."

Murdock was about to say something, but the ventilation system overhead turned on loudly. The system with its unique ducts was designed to push the air across the room in one direction, and when it reached the opposite wall the air was sucked out rather than recirculated. It was believed that this system would prevent the microorganisms from remaining in the room, thus lessening the chance that personnel would become infected. It was a belief based more on wishful thinking than scientific fact.

Murdock turned to Mariner as the noise from the ventilation fan diminished. "I apologize for our not being able to coordinate our times better."

Mariner nodded ever so slightly. "I would have preferred to be present at the start."

Then you should have been on time, Joanna wanted to say, but she held her tongue, knowing how important the Health First contract was to Memorial. "Perhaps I can go over our positive findings thus far."

"Yes," Murdock said quickly, "that would be very helpful."

Arnold Kohler smiled to himself, watching Simon Murdock bend over backwards trying to accommodate and soothe Robert Mariner. All because of money. All because of the multimillion-dollar arrangement between Health First and Memorial.

Joanna reached for the pan holding Sally Wheaton's liver. "The external features were unremarkable. We found her primary lesion in the left breast with obvious metastases to the pleura, lungs and liver. Her heart showed no abnormalities on gross examination. Certainly nothing to suggest a recent or old infarct. The cardiac pacemaker was in place with its wires intact."

"What about her brain?" Mariner asked.

"Normal. Nothing. No evidence for hemorrhage or thrombosis."

Mariner snapped on a pair of latex gloves and quickly examined the liver and lungs. He paid particular attention to the heart, checking its valves and the great vessels. He picked up a ruler and measured the width of the left ventricular wall, then inspected the coronary arteries inch by inch.

Joanna watched him, impressed by his thoroughness. He was no novice when it came to autopsies and he seemed particularly knowledgeable when it came to the heart and its coronary arteries. She wondered if he'd been trained in cardiology.

Mariner dropped the heart back into an aluminum pan. It hit with a soggy thud. "So what's the cause of death?"

Joanna shrugged. "I'm not sure."

"That means you don't know."

"Not yet."

Mariner turned to Murdock. "This is the second patient of ours that has died suddenly at Memorial, and nobody can give me a reason why."

"I'm certain it's just a matter of time before—"

"You've had plenty of time on Lucy O'Hara," Mariner said sharply, "and you still don't have an answer. Now we don't send our patients over here so they can die suddenly. But that seems to be happening, doesn't it?"

"Well, these things do occasionally happen. After all, these were terribly ill patients."

Mariner stripped off his gloves and dropped them into a wastebasket. "They were ill, but their illnesses don't explain their deaths."

There was an awkward silence. The ventilation fan switched on loudly, but only for a few seconds, then quieted.

Mariner said, "Would you object if we brought in an outside pathologist for a second opinion?"

"Not at all," Murdock said immediately. "We always welcome second opinions."

Joanna felt her face coloring with embarrassment. She stared down at the floor, but she could feel the others' eyes on her.

Mariner looked over at Joanna. "What about you? Do you have any objections?"

"You can bring in whomever you like," Joanna said curtly.

"Nothing personal," Mariner said. "I just want to get to the bottom of this."

"As we all do," Murdock said, his voice dripping with sincerity.

"Jesus Christ," Emily groaned, and it came out louder than she had intended.

Mariner jerked his head around to Emily. "You wanted to say something?"

"Yeah, I guess I do," Emily said, a slight quiver in her voice. "This woman had a pacemaker in her chest. Do you think it's possible—just remotely possible—that she died from a cardiac arrhythmia?''

If Mariner was affected by Emily's low-key sarcasm, he didn't show it. "Are you talking about pacemaker failure?"

"Right."

"That's a very, very rare event."

Joanna said, "But it certainly happens."

"Really?" Mariner asked derisively. "Are you an expert on pacemakers?"

"No. But I am an expert on death," Joanna snapped back.

"Then find out why my patients died suddenly."

"I plan to."

"Don't plan to. Just do it."

Joanna glared up at him, disliking his bullying tactics and quickly deciding not to put up with them any further. "I think you're giving orders to the wrong person."

The veins in Mariner's neck bulged. He took a deep breath and tried to calm himself. "I get the feeling that this is being treated like some sort of academic exercise. And I'm not going to stand for that. Now, let me make myself absolutely clear. Again. Two of my patients have died suddenly with no cause uncovered. They stepped into this hospital and dropped dead. I want you to find out why my patients died, what killed them. And if you can't, then I'm going to find somebody who can. And if that means bringing in another pathologist, then I'm going to do it. Am I clear on this? Crystal clear?"

"Yes, you are," Joanna said, watching Simon Murdock nodding in agreement and wondering where the man's spine was. "And I would also like to make myself and my position crystal clear."

"Great," Mariner droned.

Joanna tried to keep her composure but knew she was going to lose it. "All I've heard from you since you walked in here has been *I, me,* and *mine. My* patients this and *my* patients that. And *I'm* going to do this and *I'm* going to do that. Now I want you to listen very carefully to what I'm about to tell you because it's going to be a bit of a comedown. You're not going to do anything in here except watch and observe because these aren't your patients anymore. And I'll tell you why. These patients died suddenly and without apparent cause, so they in fact belong to the state and become coroner's cases. We're doing the autopsies because the coroner's office allows us to. You have no say in the matter, none at all. And as far as bringing in another pathologist, the final decision on that is ours, not yours. You can ask. You cannot order. Am I clear on this? Crystal clear?"

Mariner stared back, keeping his expression even, but he felt like wringing her arrogant neck. "Just find out why my patients died."

"That's what I plan to do."

"Now, we all want to find an answer," Murdock said in a conciliatory tone. "And we'll do everything possible to that end. And in the event we draw a blank we'll obtain a second opinion, and a third if necessary."

"Good," Mariner said, partially appeased.

"And you can choose the consultant."

"Let's hope it doesn't come to that." Mariner decided to back off a little and give everyone a way out of the argument. He didn't want to push too far because he needed Memorial every bit as much as they needed him. He needed their expertise, their name, their reputation. Prospective patients were delighted to learn of the close association between Memorial and Health First. It was a major selling point in convincing patients to join the HMO.

Mariner turned to Joanna, his expression softer now. "But there was one thing you were wrong about. Death does not end my commitment to my patients. I looked after them in life and I'll look after them in death. It's my final obligation to them to find out why they died. It's an obligation to them and their families."

"We'll do our best," Joanna said.

"If you need any additional information on their medical histories, just let us know and we'll be glad to furnish them."

Joanna was taken aback by the sudden change in Mariner's demeanor. One moment he was demanding and overbearing, the next he was concerned and accommodating. She wondered what he was really like deep down in his heart of hearts. "We would like to know more about Sally Wheaton's cardiac status."

Mariner gestured with a hand to Arnold Kohler. "Dr. Kohler was her primary physician at Health First. I'm certain he can fill you—" Mariner stopped in mid-sentence and sighed deeply. "I neglected to introduce you. Please forgive me. Arnold Kohler meet Joanna Blalock."

Joanna nodded, briefly studying Kohler. He was short and dark complected and his forehead glistened with perspiration although the temperature was a comfortable seventy degrees Fahrenheit. "Tell me about the arrhythmia Mrs. Wheaton had."

"Well, I—I don't have her chart with me," Kohler stammered, "but as I remember she had premature ventricular contractions."

Joanna squinted an eye skeptically. "Simple PVCs don't require a pacemaker."

"Well, that's what the cardiologist told me," Kohler said defensively.

Joanna shook her head. "Can't be. Not for simple PVCs."

Kohler shrugged and looked down at the floor.

"Mrs. Wheaton did have PVCs," Mariner said evenly, backing Kohler up. "They were present on all of her electrocardiograms. But she also had an intermittent type of atrioventricular dissociation. And when it occurred her blood pressure would drop precipitously."

Joanna turned to Kohler. "When was the pacemaker inserted?"

Kohler thought back. "About six months ago."

"I assume it's a demand-type pacemaker."

"A what?" Kohler's brow suddenly wrinkled.

"A demand pacemaker," Joanna repeated, articulating each word. "It's the type that's only activated when it's needed."

"Well," Kohler said hesitantly, "it might have been that type."

Joanna gave Kohler a long look. "I thought you said you spoke with the cardiologist before they inserted the pacemaker."

"I did, but they never mentioned—"

"It's a recently developed pacemaker," Mariner interceded smoothly. "It works on demand, but it can also be programmed to give out continuous impulses. It did wonders for Mrs. Wheaton."

"All of her symptoms disappeared," Kohler added.

"Maybe they recurred," Joanna said. "Perhaps a new arrhythmia occurred, say ventricular tachycardia, and the pacemaker couldn't deal with it. Or perhaps the pacemaker malfunctioned."

"I can check out the latter possibility easily enough," Mariner offered. "I can have the people at MPI go over it with a fine-tooth comb if you like."

"Once the autopsy findings are completed, I'll send it over," Joanna said, but she was thinking that first she'd have the pacemaker checked out by the division of cardiology at Memorial. Unbiased opinions were always the best, she told herself, remembering that MPI was a wholly-owned subsidiary of Health First.

Murdock asked, "Do arrhythmias cause any changes in the heart that can be seen under a microscope?"

"No," Joanna said at once. "The only way to document an arrhythmia is to record it on an EKG or by Holter monitor."

Murdock sighed wearily. "So if her death was caused by an arrhythmia, we'll never be able to prove it."

Mariner's eyes suddenly narrowed. He reached for the pacemaker and held it up to the light, trying to read its serial number. "I can make out one-four-oh-eight, but I can't tell if the letter following it is an *A* or *B.*"

"It's a *B,*" Joanna said, taking the pacemaker and double-checking it with a magnifying glass. "It's a *B.* Is there some significance to that?"

"There might be," Mariner said carefully. "Some of our later model pacemakers have a built-in monitor. It's like a miniature Holter monitor that records each heartbeat and then transmits that recording to a central computer network at Health First."

"Was it a continuous recording?" Joanna asked.

"Yes. But only on alternate days and only with certain of the pacemakers. Otherwise the volume of the recordings would have been immense and unmanageable."

Joanna slowly nodded, wondering if she was going to have a sudden change of luck. "So it's possible that her cardiac rhythm may have been recorded on the day she died."

"It's possible."

"How can we find out?"

"By checking the computers in the Electro-Cardiology Lab."

"How long will that take?"

"A few hours."

Mariner led the way out of the special autopsy room, Kohler a step behind. Murdock lagged back and waited for them to get beyond earshot.

Murdock turned to Joanna, keeping his voice low. "Do you have anything new on Lucy O'Hara? Anything that might explain her death?"

Joanna shook her head. "Nothing. Not even a clue."

Murdock uttered a rare obscenity and left the room.

Joanna turned back to the eviscerated corpse. She went over a mental checklist, making certain all the necessary tests on fluids and tissues had been ordered. She had already taken the precaution of quick-freezing some of the specimens without preservative in case additional studies were needed later on. And now that another forensic pathologist was likely to be called in, Joanna would have to be sure that adequate quantities of all specimens were available for restudy. She had the feeling that the consultant had already been selected. She could tell that from Mariner's tone and manner when the subject was discussed. Joanna took a deep breath, bristling at Murdock, peeved at him for caving in so easily. She glanced over at Emily Ryan, who was busily placing the dissected organs into separate containers. "Don't forget to freeze away generous amounts of the patient's blood and urine."

"Will do."

"And pleural fluid as well."

Emily took a giant syringe and, reaching into the pleural cavity, began to aspirate the fluid. It was thick and yellow and heavily tinged with blood. A malignant effusion, Emily thought, and her mind went back to her mother, who had breast cancer, and to her grandmother, who had died from the disease after it had spread to her lungs and caused massive pleural effusions. Inherited breast cancer. And Emily was next in line. Recently scientists had uncovered the gene on chromosome 17 that was responsible for the disorder. Emily had decided to have herself tested for the presence of the gene. She just hadn't decided when. Emily sucked out the last of the pleural fluid and leaned across the body for a sterile bottle. Her waist brushed against the corpse and one of Sally Wheaton's arms dropped off the table, dangling in the air.

Joanna came over and put the arm back in place. She moved away, then suddenly turned back, her gaze now on the venipuncture marks in Sally Wheaton's arm. "The patient had blood drawn just before she died, didn't she?"

Emily thought for a moment. "I think so."

"Check the chart."

Emily walked over to a side table and flipped through pages in Sally Wheaton's chart until she got to the nurses' notes. "Here it is. The patient's blood was drawn in the clinic by a venipuncturist named Wendy Fujiama."

"And I think Lucy O'Hara also had her blood drawn just before she died," Joanna said, more to herself than to Emily.

"I can check it out. I've got her records right here." Emily reached for a thick chart and quickly thumbed through it. On the last page she found what she was looking for. "Lucy had her blood drawn ten minutes before they found her body."

"Who was the venipuncturist?"

"Wendy Fujiama."

"Tell me the exact procedure you go through when you draw blood," Joanna said.

Wendy Fujiama hesitated briefly, thinking. She stared down at the floor, her eyes avoiding Joanna. "Well, first I clean the area with alcohol and—"

"Start at the very beginning," Joanna told her. "Start from the moment you enter the patient's room."

"I introduce myself and tell the patient I'm there to draw blood."

"Is your tray all set up beforehand?"

"Of course. Otherwise I'd waste a lot of—" Wendy stopped abruptly and looked across at Joanna, her narrow eyes narrowing even more. "Why are you asking me all these questions?"

"We'll get to that in a moment," Joanna said tonelessly. "Now tell me, is your tray all set up beforehand?"

"Yes, it is," Wendy said carefully, now on guard. "Before I walk into the patient's room I check to see what blood tests have been ordered and I determine how many tubes of blood will be needed."

"Then what?"

"Then I put a tourniquet on the patient's arm and clean the antecubital area with alcohol. Once I'm certain I see a vein I push the needle in and wait for blood to come back. Then I insert the test tube in and collect the specimen."

"It's a vacuum-type system, isn't it?"

"Yes. There's a vacuum in the test tube so that blood is automatically sucked in."

"Would it be possible to inject anything through that system?" Joanna asked, watching Wendy's expression.

"Not once the test tube is attached," Wendy said evenly, but her eyelids fluttered for a moment.

"Are all the needles safety sealed?"

Wendy nodded firmly. "They're in plastic vials that you have to twist open. You can hear a little pop when it opens."

"If you didn't hear the pop, would you use the needle?"

"No way! That would mean somebody had already opened the vial."

"Who sets up your venipuncture tray?"

"I do. When I arrive in the morning I go to the clinical laboratory and stock up on needles and test tubes."

"Is that tray ever out of your sight?"

"Never."

"Do you remember when you drew blood from Lucy O'Hara and Sally Wheaton?"

"Sure," Wendy said at once. "It was just a routine—"

She stopped in mid-sentence, her eyes suddenly bulging. "You don't think I had anything to do with their deaths?"

"I didn't say that."

"Then why all these questions?"

"We're just covering all the bases, making certain nothing is overlooked."

"Like what?" Wendy raised her voice. "You think something is being injected into these patients?"

"There's no evidence for that."

"But your questions sound like you believe somebody injected those patients with something. And it sounds like you think that somebody is me."

"Nobody is accusing you of anything."

Wendy gestured in disbelief. "So this is only a friendly little chat, huh?"

"Just covering the bases," Joanna said again.

"Well, I'm not going to answer any more of your questions."

"I don't have any more. You've told me all the things I needed to know."

Wendy got to her feet. "Well, let me tell you one other thing. When I leave here I'm going to call my lawyer and tell him about this conversation. And if any of this becomes public knowledge or gets into my record, I'll sue the hell out of you and Memorial."

Joanna watched the venipuncturist leave, then picked up a lukewarm cup of coffee from her desk and sipped it. In her mind's eye she envisioned the venipuncture apparatus used on the patients and tried to think of a method to break into the system. But she was chasing straws in the wind and knew it. There was no way to inject anything into a patient with a vacuum-type system and, even if there were, whatever was injected would have shown up in the studies done on the patient's blood. And nothing did. Zilch. A big zero. She still didn't know why Lucy O'Hara and Sally Wheaton had died. As she'd told Simon Murdock thirty minutes earlier, she didn't even have a clue.

Accompanied by a security guard, Joanna rode the R and D elevator to the ninth floor of the Health First Tower. The walkie-talkie on the guard's belt crackled with static, but Joanna could still make out someone issuing a command to double-check the fire stairs. She glanced at the guard's holstered weapon and noticed that the strap across the handle was unfastened. The elevator jerked to a stop and the doors opened. Amanda Black was waiting for her next to the security station.

"Is there trouble?" Joanna asked.

Amanda shrugged indifferently. "Someone was on the fire stairs early this morning. For some reason the alarm didn't sound, but we picked him up on camera."

"Do you think he was trying to break in?"

"Maybe. But it would be damned difficult. Those fire doors are virtually tamperproof and they open only from the inside out."

Amanda turned to the guard inside the Plexiglas cage and gave him Joanna's name, identifying her as a visitor. The guard punched the information into the computer and waited for it to process her and clear her for entry.

"Are you carrying any cameras or listening devices on your person?" the guard asked, his eyes fixed on the computer screen.

"No," Joanna answered.

The guard handed her a visitor's card and watched her pin it on. "Please wear the card at all times."

The women walked through a door and into a small room with yet another door. Amanda punched a set of five numbers into a panel on the wall. As she reached for her ID card, an alarm suddenly sounded. A shrill, beeping noise filled the air. The bolts automatically locked on both doors.

"What's wrong?" Joanna asked.

"I think one of us is carrying something we shouldn't be," Amanda said evenly.

The door to the reception area opened. A guard with his hand on his holstered weapon stepped back and motioned the women out of the small room. He pointed to Joanna. "Please empty the contents of your purse on the table."

Joanna opened her purse and turned it upside down. Out came a comb, compact, lipstick, brush, Kleenex, handkerchief, address book, and a Dictaphone.

The guard picked up the small Dictaphone and held it up. "A recording device," he said hoarsely.

"It's a Dictaphone," Joanna said, annoyed. "I was dictating letters while I was driving over here."

The guard switched on the machine and listened to Joanna's recorded voice. "And this letter is to Dr. Robert Kingman at Johns Hopkins Hospital. Dear Bob, I'm sorry it took me so long to respond to your last letter but—" The guard turned the Dictaphone off, saying, "We'll keep this at the station for you. You can pick it up when you leave."

The women returned to the small room and Amanda again punched a set of numbers into the wall panel.

"Do all visitors get fluoroscoped?" Joanna asked.

"Without exception."

The door opened with a loud click. The women walked down a long corridor. Everything was silent and dead still, all doors closed. They approached the room with the sign that read HAZ-ARDOUS BIOLOGIC MATERIALS. The door suddenly opened and a laboratory technician exited. Joanna glanced in and saw a huge room, brightly lit, with rows of laboratory benches and sophisticated machinery. It took her a moment to realize that there was a glass wall separating the laboratory from the corridor. In the background she caught a glimpse of a technician opening a large incubator. He was wearing a space suit with a hood that had a darkened plastic shield. The door closed.

"What sort of toxins do they study?" Joanna asked.

"Cell toxins that are capable of paralyzing the immune system."

"Selectively? The toxins work just on the immune system?"

"So I've been told."

They came to the Electro-Cardiac Laboratory. Amanda tried the doorknob, but it was locked. She reached for her plastic card and inserted it into a slot atop the knob. The door opened with a loud hiss. Quietly they entered a darkened room. Joanna could barely make out a group of people standing by the console. The computers off to one side hummed loudly, their sound exaggerated by the stillness. Suddenly the giant video screens on the wall lit up and began flashing numbers faster than the eye could follow. The screens went blank for a moment, then turned a deep blue. Blurry white lines appeared and gradually sharpened into electro-cardiographic rhythms. Now all the screens were filled with EKG rhythms. Joanna felt as if she was watching a hundred cardiac monitors at once.

Amanda led the way over to the console where Alex Black was busily punching in numbers. His hair, usually perfectly groomed, was a little mussed, and Joanna thought he looked worried. Standing behind Alex was Robert Mariner and next to him a woman in a nurse's uniform whom Joanna didn't recognize.

"Come on, come on," Alex muttered, trying to coax the information from the computer. He punched in another code, but nothing changed on the video screens. He tried again, and again nothing changed on the screens.

Mariner shook his head disgustedly and walked over to Joanna. "I may have wasted your time. When I called you I had been told that Sally Wheaton's cardiac rhythm would be on the screen in a matter of minutes. That was two hours ago."

"Are you saying that you don't have her heart rhythm recorded?"

"Oh, we have it all right. But we're having problems retrieving the data."

Joanna watched the giant screen in front of her. The EKG lines were racing across the screen faster and faster. "I'm not sure I follow you. You have the patient's name and number and you have the serial number of the pacemaker. Surely that's enough identification for the computer to work with."

"Ordinarily it is. But the amount of information we're dealing with is so immense that we had to develop a new storage system. The system is so microminiaturized that the entire Bible can be stored on a disk the size of a matchbook cover. Unfortunately, it's still in the developmental stages and it has a very complicated code." Mariner took a deep breath and exhaled loudly. "It was invented by one of our very best scientists, who died in a boating accident last month. He was the only person who really knew every aspect of the system. The man was a genius."

"A real genius," Amanda said. "If Bob Cipro was alive and in this room, we'd have that data on Sally Wheaton up in five minutes."

"Or less," Mariner said. "I'm afraid that when it comes to this particular system, we're all rank amateurs."

Joanna turned her attention to the giant video screen. The EKG readings continued to run rapidly across the screen. All rhythms were normal. A number suddenly flashed up—208B. "What does that number signify?"

"It's the number of the pacemaker that the recording comes from," Mariner explained. "You may remember that the number of Sally Wheaton's pacemaker was one-four-oh-eight *B*. That means we've got to go through twelve hundred more pacemaker recordings before we get to hers."

"Can't you bypass all the recordings in between and go directly to one-four-oh-eight?"

"That's what we're trying to do, but the computer won't let us."

"If we had the goddamn code we could," Alex growled.

Mariner was about to say something, but decided not to. Instead he turned to the woman in the nurse's uniform. "Forgive me for not introducing you. Dr. Joanna Blalock meet Kate Phillips. Kate is our transplant coordinator at Health First."

Joanna extended her hand and Kate shook it firmly. Too firmly, Joanna thought. "How do you do?"

"Fine, thank you."

Mariner said, "I asked Kate to be here because she knows our prospective transplant patients so well. You may have questions that she can answer better than anyone."

"The deaths were so tragic, so tragic," Kate said, her voice surprisingly soft for such a big woman. She was tall and muscular with broad shoulders and blond hair that was very short and swept back in a unisex cut. "They were so close to having the only procedure that could have saved their lives."

"Were they worried about anything as far as you could tell?" Joanna asked.

Kate thought for a moment. "The usual. They were concerned that they might not survive the transplant or that the transplant might not work. But that's very common in these patients." She squinted her eyes, thinking back. "And Sally was worried about her pacemaker. She was having dreams in which the pacemaker suddenly stopped functioning."

"But she never had problems with her pacemaker," Mariner quickly interjected.

"Never," Kate agreed. "She just didn't like the idea of her heart being controlled by an electrical device."

"Did they have any thoughts of impending doom or death?" Joanna asked.

Kate shook her head firmly. "If anything, they were looking forward to life. They seemed very hopeful to me. Those three women were anxious to get on with their lives."

"You mean, these *two* women were anxious to get on with their lives," Joanna corrected her.

"No. There were three transplant patients who died recently," Kate said.

Mariner stared at her in disbelief. "A third patient died? When?"

"Four months ago," Kate said evenly. "Surely you remember her. Karen Butler, the young nurse with rheumatoid arthritis and aplastic anemia."

Mariner strummed his fingers against the desktop, concentrating. "I don't remember her. Who was her primary doctor at Health First?"

"I'm not sure," Kate said and reached into her pocket for a

stack of index cards. She began flipping through them. "Let me check."

Three transplant patients dead, Joanna was thinking. She wondered if the first had also died suddenly and mysteriously. And at Memorial Hospital. Jesus! Three identical deaths could never be blamed on happenstance or coincidence. It would have to be murder.

"Dr. Kohler was her physician," Kate said at last.

"Arnold Kohler?" Joanna asked quickly.

"Yes."

Joanna kept her expression even, but her mind was racing as pieces of the puzzle began to fit together. Kohler had been the primary physician for Sally Wheaton and Karen Butler. That was two out of three. She wondered if he'd had any association with Lucy O'Hara. "Do you have any clinical information on Karen Butler?"

Kate glanced down at an index card. "She was a young nurse with rheumatoid arthritis who had been treated with gold shots. She had a wonderful response but developed aplastic anemia from the gold. That's when we referred her to Memorial for a bone marrow transplant."

"Did Dr. Kohler administer the gold shots?"

Kate shrugged. "You'll have to ask Dr. Kohler."

I plan to, Joanna said to herself, now wondering if Kohler had been foolish enough to administer the gold injections himself. Gold was an effective form of therapy for rheumatoid arthritis, but it carried with it the risk of significant toxicity and had to be administered by an experienced rheumatologist. Otherwise catastrophies could occur, like the aplastic anemia in Karen Butler. "Did the patient receive the transplant?"

"No. She died before it could be set up."

"Did she die at Memorial?" Joanna asked.

"In their parking lot," Kate said.

"Had she been seen in the hospital on the day she died?" Joanna asked.

Kate looked at her index card again. "I'm not sure. Is that important?"

"It might be," Joanna told her. "Please check it out for me."

Kate jotted down a note to herself.

Mariner said, "I'm surprised Memorial didn't call and notify us of her death."

"If they found her in the parking lot she may have been a coroner's case," Joanna suggested.

Amanda raised her hand. "I think I remember her now. They found her dead in her car. We received a call because they wanted to know if we could sign a death certificate and give the cause of her sudden death. We couldn't, and she became a coroner's case."

Mariner asked, "Was an autopsy done?"

"I assume so," Amanda said.

"I'm not interested in assumptions, goddamn it," Mariner snapped. "I want facts."

Amanda was obviously stunned by Mariner's outburst. She stared at him for a moment, her face losing color, then she looked away.

"I think an autopsy was done," Kate said. "I remember seeing a report from the coroner's office that stated they found amphetamines in her blood."

"Was she into drugs?" Joanna asked at once.

"As a teenager," Kate said. "But she had supposedly been clean for years."

"Do you recall the level of amphetamines in her blood?"

"Not offhand, but I can find out."

Mariner reached over and gently squeezed Kate's forearm. "And don't forget to find out if an autopsy was done. And if one was done, get the report for me."

"No problem," Kate said, her voice a little lower than normal.

Joanna watched the interchange, her gaze still on Mariner's hand, which only now was letting go of Kate's forearm. That touch was more than just a gesture, Joanna thought. And then there was the change in Kate's voice when Mariner touched her. Joanna glanced over at Amanda, who was staring unhappily at the blond nurse. If Amanda had been a cat her claws would have been extended. "By any chance, did the last patient have a pump in place or a pacemaker?"

Kate shrugged. "You'll have to ask Dr. Kohler."

"Now there are three dead," Mariner said disgustedly. "Three women died and the only thing they had in common was that they were being set up for bone marrow transplants. What the hell is happening at Memorial?"

Amanda said, "You don't think that—?"

"I don't think anything," Mariner cut her off. "All I know is that three of our patients died suddenly for no good reason."

Kate looked at him strangely. "You don't think that somebody is doing this intentionally?"

"There are more than a few people who would like to see Health First fail," Mariner said darkly.

Joanna made a mental note to check and see if an autopsy had been done on the third patient. And if so, to talk with the coroner who performed it.

Alex pushed his chair back and called out excitedly, "We're at fourteen hundred."

Everybody looked up at the giant video screen. The EKG lines were still running and the number "1400" was flashing. The screen went black for a moment, and then the EKG lines returned. Now the number "1401" was flashing.

"Great!" Mariner patted Alex on the back. "How did you do it?"

"I punched in the patient's name and the number fourteen hundred. You see, Bob Cipro programmed the computer so that it would only respond if you punched in a serial number that was divisible by one hundred. It'll respond to fourteen hundred, but not fourteen-oh-one or fourteen-oh-eight."

"Why did he do it that way?"

"To make it difficult as hell to get into the program. Nobody would ever punch in numbers that were divisible by one hundred because there are no pacemakers with those serial numbers. Those particular numbers were skipped. For example, we have pacemakers numbered one-two-nine-nine and one-three-oh-one and one-three-nine-nine and one-four-oh-one, but not thirteen hundred or fourteen hundred. Brilliant, huh?"

"How did Bob arrange for the factory to skip those numbers?" Mariner asked.

Alex shrugged. "Probably with a phone call."

Mariner smiled to himself. He could envision Bob doing that. Just picking up the phone and telling them to do it and not giving them a reason. Bob had believed that a secret remained a secret as long as only one person knew about it. Bob Cipro had been brilliant, but he had also been paranoid and secretive, sharing his thoughts with others only when he had to. Mariner couldn't help but wonder how many great ideas Cipro took with him to his grave. "Cipro could do magic with a computer," Mariner said, turning to Joanna and smiling thinly. "He could even design a program that would reconstruct a face if you punched in the measurements of isolated pieces of facial bones."

Joanna's jaw dropped. "I'm using his program?"

Mariner nodded. "Bob designed it for Bio-Synthetics, which is a subsidiary of Health First. And of course, Phil Weideman is one of our consultants. When he asked permission to use the program to reconstruct your dead man's face, I gave it without hesitation."

"I saw you on that TV program, Dr. Blalock," Kate said admiringly. "God! That was fascinating. Are you really going to be able to put a face on that guy?"

"With time, yes."

"I'm not sure I understand why the police didn't want you to describe the tattoo on the dead man's buttocks," Kate said.

"They didn't give a reason," Joanna lied easily. "They just asked me not to."

"What kind of tattoo?" Alex asked, suddenly interested.

"Just a tattoo," Joanna said. "I'm afraid that's all I can say right now."

Alex asked, "What type of television program was this?"

Kate eagerly described the television news program to Alex Black, giving him all the details.

"Sorry I missed it," Alex said. "I really enjoy forensic investigations."

"I've got it recorded on my VCR if you'd like to borrow it," Kate offered.

"I'd really appreciate that."

"One-four-oh-eight!" Mariner shouted out.

Everybody turned to the screen and stretched their necks forward. The number "1408" was flashing. The EKG rhythm was normal, the rate seventy-two per minute.

Alex quickly punched in a new set of numbers and the date

and time of the recording appeared in the upper right quadrant of the screen.

"That's the day she died," Mariner said, his eyes fixed on the screen. "And it's eleven-forty-two a.m. What was the approximate time of her death?"

"Between eleven-forty-five and eleven-fifty," Joanna said.

Everyone stood still, watching and waiting. There was an eerie silence in the room. The ventilation system went on and Joanna felt the air stirring, but the room still seemed close and muggy. "11:44 A.M." flashed on the screen.

"Her heart rate is increasing," Mariner said, breaking the silence.

Sally Wheaton's heart rate jumped to ninety beats per minute, then one hundred. The rhythm remained normal.

"Something is causing a tachycardia," Joanna commented.

"She's up to one-twenty," Mariner said. "Now one-forty . . ."

The EKG suddenly became jumbled, then turned into broad, undulating waves. Agonal beats. The last seconds of life. Now the screen showed only flat lines.

The time "11:46 A.M." continued to flash on the screen.

The computer was telling them the exact time Sally Wheaton had died.

It did not tell them why.

12

"You'll have to sign in, sir," the receptionist said.

The man hesitated. He almost wrote "Will Patterson," the name he had been born with, the name he had when he was reportedly killed in Vietnam. He covered his hesitation by examining the ballpoint pen for a moment. Then he signed in as Karl Rimer, the name they had given him, the name he used in his offshore bank account, which didn't require that he provide a Social Security number. Karl Rimer didn't have one.

Rimer walked into the main lobby of Memorial Hospital. It was just after eight p.m. and visitors were sitting in chairs or milling around waiting for someone. Rimer passed by two old men staring aimlessly into space and a tired woman with a sleeping child on her lap. All had sad faces.

Ahead he saw a security guard, unarmed, a walkie-talkie on his belt. An old retired cop, Rimer guessed, working at night to supplement a pension that wasn't enough to get by on. Rimer nodded to the guard and the guard nodded back, then turned his back to the wall so he could secretly scratch his piles.

Rimer reached the elevators and pushed the down button. Next to him was a patient in a wheelchair, a thick bandage around his head. An old man who looked more dead than alive. A young woman stood behind the wheelchair and spoke softly to the man. He showed no signs that he heard what she was saying. Rimer moved away. He hated sick people and he hated hospitals even

more. He'd never been a patient in a hospital and never would
be. Fuck that. People died in hospitals.

The elevator door opened. Rimer looked up and saw that the
car was going down. He waited, making sure the patient in the
wheelchair wasn't going to get on, then entered the elevator. He
pressed the button for the B level and watched the door close. As
the car began to descend, Rimer took out his Beretta and attached
a silencer to it. The elevator came to a stop and Rimer placed his
weapon into the oversized pocket of his trench coat, then put on
a pair of latex gloves.

He stepped out of the elevator hesitantly, trying to look like
someone who had lost his way. Just in case he ran into somebody.
The corridor was quiet and empty. He could smell the heavy odor
of disinfectant on the tile floor and that told him that the cleaning
crew had already come and gone.

Rimer turned left toward the forensic laboratory. He had
checked it out earlier, posing as a newspaper reporter who was
doing a story on forensic pathology. They couldn't have been
more helpful. He was given an in-depth tour of the forensic facility
by Emily Ryan, the chief resident. A bright girl, Rimer thought,
and she was a talker, eager to impress. She'd told him everything
he wanted to know.

At the end of the corridor, Rimer came to the forensic laboratory. The overhead fluorescent light was out, darkening the
area. Rimer looked down at the bottom of the door and saw no
light coming from within. He pressed his ear to the door, concentrating his hearing, listening for sounds in the laboratory. Everything was quiet. He tried the doorknob, but it wouldn't turn.
Quickly he took out a set of picks and selected a long, slender
one and inserted it into the lock.

On the second try the door opened and he was inside the laboratory. He closed the door behind him and locked it. The laboratory was pitch-black. Rimer took out a flashlight and pointed
the beam around the room, rapidly orienting himself. Off to the
right were the workbenches and incubators, to the left the centri-
fuges and heavy equipment. There was a door by the incubators
and Rimer moved toward it. He had asked Emily Ryan about that
the day before.

"What's in there?" Rimer had asked.

Emily Ryan hesitated, her eyes blinking. "We do special studies in there."

"Such as?"

"Police work, that kind of stuff."

"Can we take a look?"

"I'm afraid not."

And that told Rimer where Joanna was reconstructing the dead man's face. He opened the second door and walked into another dark room. Now the smell was different. Before it had been bland, now it had a faint odor of decay and Rimer wondered what the source was. He moved his flashlight around the room and saw a desk, workbenches, equipment he couldn't identify, and then another door.

He walked over and opened it. A walk-in closet and storage area. Again he scanned the laboratory with his flashlight. Cabinets on the wall. A computer. A tray with small fragments of white bone. Then he saw it. The dead man's head with pieces of bone dangling from it.

Rimer had a sudden flashback to Vietnam. Heads on spikes. American heads. At the Vietnam-Cambodia border. A squad of Special Forces had entered Cambodia and been captured by the Khymer Rouge. The Rouge had cut off the Americans' heads and put them up on spikes, right at the border crossing. A warning. Stay the fuck out.

Rimer slowly approached the head, studying it carefully. He was close enough to touch it when he realized that the head was a replica. *Jesus Christ!* It had looked so real from a distance, particularly the hair. The hair was perfectly matched to the victim's. He took off a glove and rubbed the hair between his fingers. The texture was so natural. Rimer touched the face and felt the stickiness. He gently tugged at an attached piece of bone and it began to give. Rimer let go and left it in place.

Not much of a face, Rimer thought, now counting the pieces of bone attached. Seven. Rimer was surprised that they had found seven recognizable pieces of bone. He had left the man's face crushed, totally destroyed. The first blow with a baseball bat had split the man's forehead wide open. Rimer could still remember the sound of bone cracking. The man had dropped to the sand like a deadweight. Then twenty more blows, bone and blood flying everywhere. There was no face remaining. None.

Rimer studied the face at length and saw nothing that even remotely resembled the man he'd killed. He looked down at the tray holding the small bones. Carefully he picked up one of the fragments with his gloved hand and studied it. How the hell would they know where to put this piece? They'd have to guess. There was no way they were going to put this asshole's face back together. No way.

He put the fragment down on the table and smashed it with the butt of his gun. It broke into splinters and tiny chips. He picked up the crushed pieces and placed them back in the tray.

Rimer turned his attention to the computer on the nearby table. He didn't understand computers, didn't like them, didn't trust them. A small green light was on and he didn't know why. He punched at the keyboard aimlessly and nothing happened. He did it again with both hands and a finger hit the On button.

The computer screen suddenly lit up. Outlines of faces appeared, then pieces of bone began attaching themselves to the faces. Rimer's eyes went from the screen to the replica of the head and back to the screen. Son of a bitch! The goddamn computer was telling them where to put the pieces. The computer was going to reconstruct the face for them. Destroy the head and the bones, he told himself, and get the hell out of here. And also put a half dozen nine-millimeter bullets into the computer. That should screw it up good.

Rimer suddenly froze. He heard the sound of a door opening. All went quiet. Seconds passed. Now Rimer heard footsteps, high heels clicking on linoleum, and female voices. Quickly he looked down at the keyboard and searched for the Off button. He couldn't find it. Out of desperation he began to punch buttons at random. The computer didn't respond. The screen remained lit. Quickly he found the electric cord from the computer and pulled it out of the wall socket. The screen went dead.

The footsteps were coming closer and closer. He took out his Beretta and considered killing them. Better not. There might be others around. People could be waiting for them in the corridor.

Rimer darted across the room and entered the storage closet, silently closing the door behind him. He turned off his flashlight and made certain the safety was off on his weapon. He listened intently in the darkness. Rimer felt his heart pounding. His senses were sharpening, but weren't nearly as sharp as he'd like them to be. He reached into his pocket and took out two amphetamine pills, five milligrams each. That would do it, he thought, particularly when added to the hit he'd taken just before entering the hospital. He quickly chewed the pills before swallowing, knowing that the ground-up drug acted a lot faster than the whole pill. Almost immediately he began to feel the effect. His pulse started to race, his senses rapidly peaking. He thought again about killing the intruders. They'd be dead before they knew it, their brains oozing onto the floor. Only if I have to, he reminded himself. But the amphetamine level in his blood was going higher and higher, and now Rimer found himself hoping that the intruders would make a wrong move.

He heard the door open, then two female voices. One belonged to Emily Ryan. He didn't recognize the other.

"We just need to fit in one more piece of frontal bone," Joanna was saying, "and I think the computer will be able to project what his left forehead looked like."

"Half of the forehead isn't much of a face," Emily said.

"But a whole forehead is. Remember that for all intents and purposes opposite sides of a face are nearly identical. So if we can construct the left side of his face, the computer will tell us what the right side looked like and we'll end up with a complete forehead."

"I'd rather have the lower part of his face. You know, his cheeks, his chin, his jaw—stuff like that."

"So would I. But to get that we're going to have to find some pretty good-sized pieces of maxillary and mandibular bone."

Emily suddenly snapped her fingers. "I almost forgot. I got a phone call from Dental Pathology this afternoon. Dr. Bailey wanted us to send her any fragments of bone that might be from the maxillary or mandibular region. She's particularly interested in any piece that has dental sockets—with or without teeth."

"We need those pieces ourselves. That's the area we're working on now."

"That's what I told her. But she's persistent as hell. I agreed to let her make casts of the pieces she wants. Is that okay?"

"Fine. Did Dr. Bailey have anything new to tell us?"

"Just that she's now sure the dead man had a modest overbite." Emily squinted an eye, thinking back. There was something else, something about the mouth. "Oh, yeah, she thinks—underline the word *think*—that the guy had a big mouth. And you know what they say about men with big mouths."

Both women chuckled softly.

Joanna asked, "Were those Dr. Bailey's exact words—'a big mouth'?"

Emily thought for a moment. "No. I believe she said 'large.' Yes, she said he had a very large mouth."

"That's important. Very important."

"Why?"

"Because Caucasians with very large mouths almost invariably have thin lips."

Emily nodded slowly. "So our man has a modest overbite, a big mouth and thin lips."

"And brown eyes," Joanna added.

Son of a bitch, Rimer cursed to himself, angry at himself for having done a half-assed job of destroying the man's face. The dead man did have an overbite and a big mouth and thin lips. And brown eyes. Rimer could still see those lifeless eyes staring up at him. But he had smashed them into smithereens with the baseball bat. Over and over again until there were no eyes left. Or so he'd thought. Son of a bitch! Rimer pressed his ear against the door and listened.

"I've got a confession to make, Dr. Blalock," Emily said. "When we first started this project I thought you'd bitten off more than you could chew. I thought we had no chance at all of reconstructing this man's face. Now I'm certain we will. I have absolutely no doubts."

"Nor do I. Now show me that unusual piece of facial bone."

Emily opened a drawer and took out a small envelope. "Here's the fragment. It's different than the others. It's got a peculiar indentation on it."

"Let's put it under the magnifier."

They moved to the other side of the room.

Rimer heard them moving and now their voices sounded muffled. He listened intently, not wanting to miss a word. All was quiet. The only thing he heard was his own breathing. So the other woman was Joanna Blalock, he told himself, remembering her from the television program. Young—maybe thirty-five—and pretty. Because of her youthful appearance and attractiveness, he hadn't thought much of her talents, believing she was mostly talk. But now as he listened to her, he realized how bright and insightful she was. He also realized that she could cause him big trouble.

"See the small indentation," Emily said, adjusting the magnifying glass and focusing the light on the bone fragment.

The device they were using was a simple magnifying machine. It had an adjustable magnifying glass and a strong beam of light that came from a bulb located at the base of the device. The magnifying glass was off to one side, so that the strong light wouldn't shine directly into the viewer's eyes.

"I think this fragment is part of the mandibular ramus," Joanna said. "The indentation is a groove where the masseter muscle attaches."

"Is it usually that pronounced?"

"It can be," Joanna said. "But I think the indentation has been exaggerated because of the way the bone was fractured. If you turn the fragment on its side, you'll see—" The light on the device blinked a few times, then went out. "Damn it! The bulb burned out."

"There's plenty of new bulbs in the storage closet," Emily said. "I'll get one."

Rimer quickly moved to the back of the closet, a little over four feet from the door. He assumed a firing position, knees slightly bent, arms extended in front of him, his Beretta pointed straight ahead. A head shot, he was thinking, and she'll go down without a sound. Then out into the laboratory and terminate Joanna Blalock. The distance between them would be short, ten feet at most. Another head shot. Then cover the purpose of the murders. Sexually mutilate the bodies, trash the lab, maybe set a fire.

The doorknob turned and the door began to open.

Rimer steadied his weapon, his finger now firmly on the trigger.

"Don't bother, Emily," Joanna called out. "The bulb was just loose. It's working fine now."

The door closed.

Rimer slowly lowered his weapon, relieved he didn't have to kill them. Too risky. Too many things could have gone wrong. And besides, if he could do what he had to do without killing more people, better yet. Murder here would attract too much attention. Bashing in some asshole's head with a baseball bat was one thing, killing two doctors at Memorial was another.

"I'm fairly confident it's from the mandible," Joanna said. "Dr. Bailey will probably want to make a cast from it."

"I'll give it to her first thing in the morning." Emily glanced up at the replica of the dead man's head. She placed the small fragment of bone at the angle of the jaw, uncertain if it was a fit or not. "Do you think they'll ever catch the maniac who committed this murder?"

"Maybe. But first the police will have to know who the victim was."

"I hope they catch the bastard and I hope they tell him how we put this poor man's face back together again." Emily reached up and retrieved the piece of mandible from the replica. "Our killer may not be nearly as smart as he thinks he is, huh?"

"Don't underestimate him," Joanna said.

Rimer nodded to himself. You bet your ass, lady. He could still remember the four Viet Cong who had captured him and put him in a bamboo cage. While they slept, he got out. He killed all four with a rifle butt. They had underestimated him.

Rimer heard a drawer being opened and closed. Now the women were talking in muffled voices and he could make out only bits and pieces of their conversation. Something about a woman called Sally Wheaton and her cardiac problems.

"Do you want to do any more work on the face tonight?" Emily asked.

"No. Let's call it a day."

Rimer listened to their footsteps. The door to the laboratory opened and closed. Then more footsteps, fainter now. Another door opened and closed. Rimer remained inside the closet for a full five minutes, just in case the women decided to return for something they'd forgotten.

The closet became stuffy, the air stale. But it didn't bother Rimer. As usual, he was wearing a very strongly scented aftershave lotion and that was all he smelled. It covered up every odor, including the one he hated most. The smell of decay. It was in his nostrils all the time, ever since Vietnam. In 'Nam, everything stank like a sewer and it was a hundred times worse in the jungle where Rimer had spent most of his time. The smell. The awful smell of death and decay. He wondered if it would ever disappear from his nose and his memory. Probably not.

He pressed his ear against the door and listened for another minute. Quickly he put his latex glove back on and cleaned the doorknobs with a handkerchief, removing any fingerprints.

He stepped out into the laboratory and shined the beam of his flashlight at the replica of the dead man's head. Rimer's mind flashed back to Vietnam. Heads. American heads on spikes. Viet Cong heads squashed by a rifle butt, brains oozing out. He still dreamed about it sometimes. But not as much as before. Fuck it and fuck Vietnam, Rimer thought as he took the head down and placed it on the floor, face up. With great force, he stomped the heel of his shoe down on it. The head splintered like the shell of an egg, bits and pieces flying off in all directions.

Quickly he went over to the tray holding the bone fragments. Using the butt of his pistol, he began smashing the pieces into little chips, but then he stopped because of the noise he was making. Too much noise.

He found a thick mat close by and placed the bone fragments on it and began smashing them again. Patiently he pounded each piece into splinters and powder. Let them glue this mess back together, Rimer thought, now turning his attention to the computer.

He switched the safety off on his Beretta and fired four shots into the machine. The glass screen exploded with a loud pop and white smoke began to seep out. Wires inside the computer started to spark and more smoke appeared.

Rimer headed for the door. It was almost nine p.m. He had to hurry. Visiting hours at Memorial were almost over.

Simon Murdock gazed down at the debris littering the floor. "Have the police been called?"

"About three hours ago," Joanna said.

"And?"

"And they haven't gotten here yet," Joanna said, taking him by the arm and guiding him around a fragment of bone on the floor. "Apparently illegal entry and destruction of private property don't rate very high on their list of crimes."

"Did you tell them about the connection to the murder victim?"

"Of course. But they didn't sound very impressed."

Joanna took a deep breath and again surveyed the destruction in the forensic laboratory. The replica of the dead man's head was smashed to pieces. Even its wig was torn apart. Tiny fragments of bone were scattered everywhere, some pieces as far as ten feet away from the tray that once held them. The computer was barely recognizable. Its screen was gone, its innards a burned-out mess. "Whoever did this did a good job of it."

"Is anything salvageable?"

Joanna shrugged. "Probably not."

"Well, if need be, you could have the victim's body exhumed and make another cast of the head," Murdock suggested.

"That's not the problem," Joanna told him. "We still have the mold that the original head was made from. The problem is that

I can find only three pieces of the bone that we attached to the head. Four large pieces are gone and there's no way of telling what they looked like or where they fit on the face."

"Perhaps the computer could help."

"Only God could put this computer back together again."

Murdock leaned over and looked into the machine. He saw shards of glass and twisted metal and charred wires that smelled as if they were still burning. He reached out to touch the keyboard and Joanna quickly grabbed his arm.

"Better not touch it," she said. "They might be able to find fingerprints on the keys."

Murdock nodded and stepped back. "Nothing is sacrosanct anymore," he said disgustedly. "Not churches, not hospitals, not even research laboratories."

"They never were," Joanna said glumly, "except in the movies."

Joanna moved away from the desk and over to the workbench, Murdock just behind her. She walked on tiptoes and tried to avoid bone fragments, but she still felt as if she was stepping on sand and grit. Her foot came down on a small fragment and crushed it into powder. Joanna cursed under her breath and wondered for the hundredth time why she hadn't put the pieces of bone in the wall safe where she kept valuable documents.

"It's still difficult to believe," Murdock said hoarsely. "A man just walks into Memorial, goes down to Pathology and into the forensic laboratory and destroys your work. How did he find his way down here?"

"Easy. All he had to do was ask for directions at the Information Desk."

Murdock rubbed his chin pensively. "But how did he learn that you were reconstructing the dead man's face?"

"From the television program I was on. Remember? He probably was watching it."

Murdock nodded slowly. "Maybe going on television wasn't such a good idea after all."

"I knew there was a risk involved, that the killer might see the program."

Murdock looked at her oddly. "And knowing that, you still went on television?"

"It was risky, but it was the right move, Simon. Somebody out there knows our man. Somebody misses him."

The door opened and Phil Weideman entered the laboratory. He hurried over to Joanna and took her hands in his, wanting to hug her but resisting the urge. "Are you all right?"

"I'm fine," Joanna said, looking into his eyes and again thinking they were the bluest she'd ever seen. She smiled at him, touched by his concern. "Really. I'm fine."

Murdock watched, now certain that something was going on between Joanna and Weideman. Their looks were lingering too long, their touches holding on too long to be just friendly in nature. Murdock's gaze went to Weideman's ring finger. No ring. Maybe his marriage was over.

Weideman finally let go of Joanna's hands, but he still felt her warmth. He turned to Murdock and nodded. "Hell of a thing, huh, Simon?"

"Just part of our chaotic society," Murdock grumbled. "Criminals are everywhere, doing exactly as they please."

Weideman walked over to the computer, carefully avoiding the larger bone fragments on the floor. He leaned over and peered into the machine. "Jesus! What did he use, a bomb?"

"Bullets." Joanna went to the back of the computer and pointed to three jagged holes where the bullets had exited. She stuck a finger in one of the holes, thinking it had to be a large-caliber weapon. A .38 or maybe a .44. "Is there any chance we can retrieve the information stored in the computer?"

Weideman shrugged weakly. "Maybe, but I wouldn't be too hopeful. It looks as if he did a pretty thorough job of destroying it."

Weideman took a pocket flashlight and pointed the beam into the computer. He thought he saw something shining inside the computer and reached for it.

Joanna grabbed his hand. "We probably shouldn't touch anything until the police get here."

Weideman stared at her hand on his, then looked into her eyes and smiled.

Joanna felt herself blushing and quickly released her grasp. As she turned away, her shoulder inadvertently brushed against his. He felt the electricity and had to resist the urge to touch her back.

Weideman went over to the empty tray that had once held the bone fragments. He looked down at the thick mat and the crushed pieces of bone atop it. "Don't tell me that's all that remains of the bones from the dead man's face."

"That's it," Joanna said gloomily. "Every piece powdered and splintered and totally unidentifiable."

"The guy who did this really knew what he was doing," Weideman commented. "He made sure he got everything—the head, the fragments, the computer."

Joanna nodded. "A professional hit man."

"Too bad we don't have security guards on every floor at night," Weideman said. "That might have deterred him."

"And exactly where would the money for those guards come from?" Murdock asked defensively.

"It wouldn't have mattered a damn," Joanna said. "An old security guard wouldn't be much of an obstacle for a professional killer."

A tall blond technician stuck her head through the doorway and said, "Dr. Blalock, the police are here."

"Show them in," Joanna said.

The technician stepped aside and Jake Sinclair walked into the laboratory.

Joanna stared at Jake, caught off guard by his appearance. He looked tired and drawn, his face thinner. She felt the urge to rush over to him but pushed it aside. "When did you get back?"

"A few hours ago."

"Are you all right?"

"Yeah, I'm fine," Jake said, sensing the coolness in her voice and manner. He now wished he had waited until later to see her. Not that it would have mattered much.

Murdock stepped back, giving the detective room to pass by. For a big man, Sinclair walked softly, his footsteps almost silent. And he was much more agile than Murdock would have guessed. He moved easily amid the debris, avoiding the fragments.

Now Sinclair was bending down, studying the dead man's wig and scattered pieces of bone. He glanced over at the destroyed computer. "What happened down here?"

"We had a break-in." Joanna told him in detail about the dead man with no face and no fingertips, about her attempt to reconstruct the victim's face using bone fragments and a computer, and about her appearance on the television program. She kept her voice clinical and detached and she paid more attention to the fragments on the floor than she did to Jake. "The killer must have seen the program and gotten worried. So he came here last night and destroyed any chance we had of putting the victim's face back together. I called the police but they haven't come yet."

Murdock said to Sinclair, "Perhaps you could use your influence to have them respond a bit quicker."

"I'll see what I can do."

Joanna took Jake's arm briefly. "I'm sorry. Let me introduce you. You remember Simon Murdock, the dean at Memorial?"

"Of course," Jake said.

Murdock didn't offer his hand. He nodded.

Jake nodded back, disliking Murdock even more than usual. He knew that people like Murdock considered the police several steps below, like tradesmen. They deserved nods, not handshakes. Unless Murdock's balls were in a vise and he was screaming bloody murder and needed a cop to save his arrogant ass. That might merit a handshake.

"And this is Dr. Phil Weideman," Joanna went on. "He's a plastic surgeon who's helping me reconstruct the dead man's face. Phil, meet Jake Sinclair."

The men stared at each other for a moment, each measuring the other. Weideman nodded formally and Jake nodded back, now aware of how close together Joanna and Weideman were standing. Their elbows were almost touching. And there was something in the way she'd said the surgeon's name. Jake wondered if Weideman was the man Joanna was seeing or thinking about seeing. Or sleeping with. Goddamn it!

Jake went back to the wig on the floor, turning it over with his pen. "Was the victim's whole skull mashed in?"

"Just his face," Joanna said.

"So you figure it was done with a hand-held weapon?"

"Almost surely. But I don't know what the killer used." Joanna watched Jake as he tried to fit two bone fragments on the floor together. "Why was it so important that the killer destroy the victim's face?"

Jake shrugged. "A lot of possibilities."

"That's very helpful," Joanna said tonelessly.

Jake glanced up and caught Weideman trying to suppress a grin. Fuck you, Jake said silently, then turned his attention back to Joanna. There were a lot of reasons why someone would want the victim's face destroyed. But only one would hold water. He decided to let Joanna work for the answer. Let her strain a little. "You're the forensic pathologist. You tell me the most likely reason."

Joanna detected the edge in Jake's voice. Too bad. If he'd expected to walk in here and have everything go back to the way it was—well, he was in for a big disappointment. "Was it a gang-type thing? A Mafia hit?"

"Come on. You can do better than that," Jake said, smiling thinly.

"Well, it could be," Joanna persisted.

"Naw. They usually kill for power or revenge or to send a message. They want everybody to know who the victim was and what happened to him." Jake walked over to the computer and peeked into it. He went to the back of the machine and saw the holes where the bullets had exited. "Large caliber, huh?"

"At least a thirty-eight," Joanna said and placed a thick ballpoint pen into one of the holes. "He knew what he was doing."

"Did you find the slugs?"

"They're embedded in the wall."

Jake went to the wall behind the computer and began prying one of the bullets out with his pocketknife.

Weideman kept watching Jake Sinclair, trying to measure the man. Weideman was over six feet tall and weighed 190 pounds. He considered himself big. But not when compared to Jake Sinclair. Sinclair was only an inch or so taller, but he had wide shoulders and a big trunk and seemed to take up a lot of space. The detective had rugged good looks with high-set cheekbones, gray-blue eyes. Across Sinclair's chin was a well-healed jagged scar. Poor surgical technique, Weideman thought to himself, knowing that he could revise the scar and make it difficult to see. But he suspected that Sinclair liked the scar. It gave him a look of toughness, a hardness that could intimidate people. Weideman had heard from an OR nurse that Joanna was dating a homicide detective. Weideman had imagined that the cop would be like a modern-day Sherlock Holmes. Refined, cerebral, detached. He saw none of these qualities in Jake Sinclair.

Jake finally pried the bullet out and examined it carefully. It was flattened and misshapen, but he could still tell it was large caliber. He handled the slug with a handkerchief, careful not to touch it. The guy used a silencer, Jake thought. Otherwise it would have made too much noise.

Joanna broke into his thoughts. "Have you ever seen a case where the killer destroyed the victim's face and cut off the fingertips?"

"Once," Jake said, his mind going back a dozen years to a decomposed body in a ravine off Mulholland Drive. "The victim was a young hooker who was blackmailing one of her customers. The guy was a wealthy Bel Air businessman who was into kinky stuff and she had some photographs."

Joanna squinted an eye, confused. "But why did he have to destroy the face? I mean, dead is dead. Once the hooker was dead the blackmail stopped. Right?"

"Yeah. But the guy was being very careful. He figured that if we could identify the corpse we might find out she was blackmailing someone. And if we found out who she was blackmailing he would become the prime suspect."

Joanna slowly nodded. "So the killer not only wanted to destroy the victim, he also wanted to destroy the victim's past."

"Right," Jake said at once. "An unidentified corpse has no name, no history, no past. They bury the body in some field in an unmarked grave."

"And all of his secrets are buried with him."

"You got it." Jake dropped the slug into an empty glass beaker on the benchtop. "The general idea is to kill the guy and make damn sure nobody finds out why he was killed."

"You think the victim I'm studying was a blackmailer?"

"Maybe, maybe not. But he must have known something that was threatening as hell to somebody."

"Oh, come on, Lieutenant," Weideman said, his tone mocking. "That's just a guess and you know it."

"Right," Jake said, disliking Weideman more and more. "I guess all the time. Now if I was a doctor I wouldn't have to guess because I'd know everything."

Joanna gave Jake a sharp look. Then she glanced over at Wei-deman, staring at him for a moment. Jake watched the nonverbal interchange between Joanna and the plastic surgeon. He tried to read their faces and their eyes, but couldn't.

Joanna turned back to Jake. "The Bel Air killer you were just talking about—he wasn't a professional, was he?"

"No."

"Then the person who killed the faceless man may not be a pro either."

"Oh, no," Jake quickly corrected her. "This guy is a pro." He pointed to the debris on the floor and the burned-out computer. "This wasn't amateur night down here. The guy knew exactly how and what to do. He planned it. And this wasn't the first time he'd been here either."

Murdock looked at Jake skeptically. "What makes you so sure? He could have gotten directions from the Information Desk, come down to Pathology and broken into Joanna's laboratory."

"No, I don't think so," Jake said evenly, hiding his dislike for Murdock. "The guy had to get a layout of this department, had to find out where the victim's face was being reconstructed, had to check and see what kind of locks were on the doors, had to learn when the staff usually left for the day. There were a hundred different things he needed to know. You see, the idea was not only to get the job done, but to get it done and get out unnoticed. And that's what he did. Chances are he carefully planned it."

"I'm still not convinced of that," Murdock said.

Jake took a deep breath and tried to hold his temper in check. He felt like dropping the conversation and walking away and let-ting the burglary squad deal with this arrogant asshole. But he knew that Joanna wanted the information and that it might turn out to be helpful to her. He looked over at Joanna. "What time did you leave here last night?"

Joanna hesitated, thinking back. "I went out for a bite to eat at seven-thirty p.m. and came back to the laboratory at eight-fifteen p.m. or so. I left for the evening just after eight-thirty p.m."

"Were you the last person to leave?"

"Yes."

"And you locked the doors?"

"The front one, yes."

"Was the lock broken when you arrived this morning?"

"No. I needed a key to get in."

"So," Jake said, turning back to Murdock, "somebody had to pick the lock to get in. Can you pick a lock, Doctor?"

"No, but—"

"There are no *buts,*" Jake cut him off, now losing patience. "A guy comes down here, picks a lock and then methodically destroys every piece of evidence that has anything to do with the victim he killed. He gets in and gets out without anybody seeing him. Believe me, it was a pro who did this job."

"Just because this fellow could pick a lock doesn't make him a professional," Murdock said pointedly.

"That's right. But a guy who can pick locks and kill usually is." Jake turned his back to Murdock and let his gaze wander around the room. He'd been in the forensic laboratory on a number of occasions and had a good idea of where everything was and should be. None of the drawers or any of the cabinets were open. The glassware was neatly stacked and in place. Jake looked at the open closet door at the rear of the room. "What's in the closet?"

"It's a storage closet," Joanna said.

"Was the door open when you left last night?"

"No. It was closed."

"Did anyone come into the lab after you left?"

"No. It was after eight-thirty p.m. when I left, so the cleaning crew would have already come and gone. I arrived just before eight this morning and I was the first one here."

"And the closet door was open when you got here?"

"Yes, it—" Joanna's jaw suddenly dropped as she realized what Jake was thinking. She stared at him at length and then swallowed. "You think the killer was in the closet while I was in the lab?"

"Probably."

Weideman uttered a sound of disbelief. "That's a totally unfounded suggestion, Lieutenant. There's absolutely nothing to back it up. And I think you're frightening Joanna unnecessarily."

Jake scratched at his ear, wondering why he was arguing with an amateur. A pain-in-the-ass amateur. "Joanna was the last person to leave last night and the first to arrive here this morning. When she left the closet door was closed, when she came back in this morning it was opened. Now, who do you think opened it?"

"The person who broke in," Weideman conceded, "but that doesn't mean he was in the closet when Joanna was in the lab. He could have opened that door any time after she'd left. Like at twelve midnight."

"Yeah. Maybe," Jake said, but he believed otherwise. He figured the pro would have made his move sometime between eight p.m. and nine p.m., near the end of visiting hours. The staff would have left for the day, the cleaning crew come and gone. And there'd still be people in the corridors. Not a lot of people, but enough for the pro to blend in and not be noticed.

Jake walked over to the closet and looked inside. It was lined with shelves and was at least six feet deep—plenty of room for the killer to hide comfortably. Jake studied the inside doorknob and the inside of the door itself. For an instant he thought he detected a sweet odor, but then it faded. He placed his nose closer to the door and the aroma returned. Sweet. Cheap sweet. A cologne or maybe aftershave lotion. But only at one spot on the door, at about the level of Jake's nose. Jake backed off and sniffed the air at the rear of the closet. Neutral. Maybe a little stale. He walked back into the laboratory. "I think the killer was in the closet."

"Still guessing, huh?" Weideman asked.

"These sorts of guesses are of no help," Murdock added. "They only serve to frighten our staff."

Weideman nodded his agreement. "I think we should hold all speculation until the burglary experts have gone over everything."

"Good idea," Jake said hoarsely. "I might not be here when they arrive, so be sure to tell them our suspect is about six-feet-one and wears very cheap aftershave lotion. And make sure they dust the closet carefully for prints. Our guy spent a lot of time in there."

Weideman stared at Jake, his brow wrinkled in disbelief. "How do you know that?"

Jake smiled thinly and said nothing.

Joanna came over to Jake. "Tell me how you determined his height."

Jake took her arm and guided her over to the closet door. He pointed to an area of the door near the hinges. "Stand on your tiptoes and smell the wood here."

Joanna stood on her toes and tilted her head back, nose next to the door. She took several deep sniffs. "I don't smell any-thing."

Jake pointed to an area high above the doorknob. "Try this spot."

As Joanna moved in, her shoulder pressed up against Jake. She quickly pulled it away. She wanted Jake to understand that the touch had been accidental and meant nothing.

Jake's lips parted slightly, almost grinning. She couldn't tell if he was hurt or laughing at her. "Where was that other spot?" Joanna asked.

"Here." Jake showed her.

Joanna again got up on her tiptoes and smelled the wood. "Like a cheap perfume."

"It's aftershave lotion, I think," Jake said. "He had his cheek against the door here, probably pressing his ear to the wood so he could hear when you left."

"Emily Ryan was here with me," Joanna said quietly. "He was probably listening to our conversation."

"Jesus H. Christ," Weideman muttered under his breath. "The killer was in the closet. Suppose Joanna had opened the closet door for some reason."

Joanna swallowed hard, now remembering the malfunctioning light bulb and how Emily Ryan had almost opened the closet door. *My God! Both of us would have been killed.* "The killer probably broke into the lab during visiting hours at Memorial."

"Probably," Jake agreed. "That would be the smart move. There would still be people around. Professionals like to work in crowds."

Murdock said, "If he came during visiting hours, he'd have to sign in at the front entrance."

"Unless he came in a side door," Jake said.

"Those doors are locked after six p.m."

Jake smiled faintly. "Our guy picks locks, remember?"

"But the visitors' log should still be checked, don't you agree?"

"It should. But don't get your hopes up. Even if he came in the front entrance and signed the log, he would have used a phony name." Jake slowly turned away, now studying the debris littering the floor. "Don't expect him to make stupid mistakes. I've got a feeling that this guy is very careful."

Weideman remarked, "Well, he sure as hell destroyed every piece of bone we had."

"Maybe not," Joanna said, her mind flashing back to the night before, when she and Emily had studied the peculiar piece of mandible. Emily had stored the fragment away in the desk drawer. Joanna hurried over to the desk.

Jake watched her open the drawer and take out a small manila envelope. She turned the envelope upside down and shook it. Out came a few tiny chips and a puff of white powder.

"He didn't miss anything," Joanna said dismally.

Jake nodded to himself. "Like I said, he's a very careful guy."

14

Alex Black stood at the window in the psychiatrist's office and closed his eyes. And the dream came. Always the same dream.

He was way up on a ledge, so high that the people below looked like ants. A stiff wind was blowing and he struggled to maintain his balance. Suddenly he was falling, tumbling head over heels. Faster and faster. A free fall. The ground came up to meet him and he hit with a loud thud. He lay there, mangled, seeing the world for the last time. Passersby glanced down at him and walked on. Nobody cared.

Alex opened his eyes and the daydream ended. Now he was standing so close to the window that it was misting up. He slowly wiped it clear with a hand and watched giant raindrops pelt against the glass.

His gaze went to the street below. People were hurrying along their way, trying to reach home before darkness fell, before the full force of the winter storm hit Los Angeles.

Behind him the psychiatrist struck a match and sucked on his pipe. "You've become very quiet, Alex. Is something bothering you?"

"I keep having this peculiar dream."

"Tell me about it."

Alex described the dream in a flat monotone. There was no emotion, no fright, even when he was describing his fall and certain death.

"What do you think it means?"

"I'm not sure. Maybe . . ." Alex's voice trailed off as the wind outside howled and a sudden squall rattled the window.

The psychiatrist puffed on his pipe and waited for Alex to go on. He wondered if Alex Black was so impaired that he couldn't grasp what his subconscious mind was telling him. Or maybe he did grasp it but chose to ignore it. "Have you had any thoughts of suicide?"

"Not really." That was a half-truth. The thoughts still came to him, but now he was able to push them aside. Before he would dwell on them for hours.

"And the demons are still with you?"

Alex shrugged and wiped at the window again. The answer was yes and no. The demons came in the night. They went to bed with him, slept with him, awoke with him. They sometimes came in the daytime too, but they were worse at night. Much worse. "Not all the time."

Outside there was a violent clap of thunder. The whole building seemed to shake. For a brief instant Alex thought it was God's displeasure with him for not telling the truth. As a child that was what he believed. "The demons are there most of the time," he admitted.

"Do you still think it's necessary to refer to your symptoms as demons?"

Alex turned toward the psychiatrist and smiled. A thin, humorless smile. He knew the psychiatrist disliked the word *demons*. It had no clinical meaning, it wasn't used in his textbooks and journals. The psychiatrist preferred terms like *depression, hopelessness, despair*. But *demons* was a more descriptive word, Alex thought, and he would continue to use it.

"Are you taking your antidepressant drug regularly?" The psychiatrist watched Alex begin to play with his hair, making small ringlets by his ear. For a moment he seemed like a little boy. "Well?"

"They made me feel drowsy. I couldn't function."

"So you haven't been taking them?"

"Not regularly."

"That's not very wise," the psychiatrist said, keeping his voice even but thinking that doctors were the worst patients, impossible to manage. "You shouldn't be adjusting your medication without discussing it with me first."

"I know."

The psychiatrist reached for a prescription pad. "Let's try Prozac. Supposedly it has less—"

"Let's try it without any drugs," Alex interrupted him.

"I don't think that's a good idea, Alex. Not at this stage of your illness."

"Why don't we see how it goes? Just for a few days."

The psychiatrist hesitated, strumming his fingers on the desk. Then he nodded reluctantly. "Only for a few days. I want to see you again on Thursday."

Alex looked at his watch. The forty-five minutes were up, the session over.

He walked across the office to a coatrack and reached for his long white coat. He put it on, carefully adjusting the stethoscope in the side pocket, making certain it was prominently displayed. If anyone saw him leaving the psychiatrist's office, they would think he was a colleague or perhaps a visiting friend, not a patient. "Don't worry, I won't do anything foolish. I'll see you on Thursday."

The psychiatrist wondered if he should call Alex's wife, who was also a physician. That way at least someone would be keeping an eye on him.

The psychiatrist waited for Alex to leave, then quickly flipped through his Rolodex and dialed Amanda Black's number. Eight rings. No answer. He tried again. Still no answer. Where the hell was the answering service?

He started to dial again but saw the small red light flashing on the edge of his desk. His next patient had arrived and was waiting. The psychiatrist placed the phone down and wrote himself a memo to call Amanda Black first thing in the morning.

Ten stories below, Karl Rimer leaned against the side wall of the kiosk adjacent to the bus stop. The collar of his trench coat was pulled up to his ears on the sides, to his chin in front. A floppy rain cap came well down on his forehead. Anyone looking at him saw only thin lips and gray-green eyes. And a hearing aid, which was really a remote listening device.

Rimer pushed the receiver deeper into his auditory canal and listened intently. Moments earlier he had heard Alex Black say, "I'll see you Thursday," and then the sound of the door being closed. He wondered if Black was going to come back to the office, as he had done several times before, to tell the shrink something he'd lied about or forgotten to mention. All was quiet. A little static. Then quiet again. Now he heard a brief grunt or burp and water splashing. Rimer thought for a moment, concentrating, picturing the office. Then he nodded to himself. The psychiatrist was taking a leak.

The tiny microphone had been perfectly placed behind a painting that hung on a wall midway between the psychiatrist's desk and the couch. It was well away from the shrink's private bathroom, but it easily picked up the sound of the doctor relieving himself. And it damn well should have. The listening device had cost over a grand. When the business was done he would retrieve it.

He looked at his watch. Alex Black would be down in four minutes. Rimer had timed the doctor over and over again and could predict within thirty seconds when he would appear on the glass-enclosed bridge that connected the twin towers at their second floors. Once the doctor had taken too long to make the trip. Six minutes too long. Rimer had checked around and learned that the elevators were not working properly, so Alex Black had to take the stairs down. Other than that, he was totally predictable, always on time. Rimer glanced up at the bridge and saw a team of doctors dressed in surgical garb hurrying across. They were pushing or pulling something. He strained to see what. It was a patient on a gurney, IV running.

The rain suddenly intensified, hammering down and splashing against the cement. People under the kiosk hunched up in their hats and coats and turned away from the downpour. Rimer didn't move. He kept his eyes fixed on the glass-enclosed bridge. Now the wind was swirling and blowing rain against his face. He smiled, loving it. It was the perfect camouflage. Nobody remembered anyone or anything when it rained. All they recalled was the rain. The heavier the deluge, the better.

He had loved the rain most when he was in Vietnam. He had been a LURP, a member of the elite Long Range Reconnaissance

Patrol units. They were the hunter-killers, the men who went into the jungle for months on end to savagely butcher as many Viet Cong as possible. And he'd butchered a lot. Hell, at least a hundred. Probably twice that number if he counted the maybes. Like the time he dynamited a maze of underground tunnels that Charlie lived in. Big boom! Then a cave-in that killed God knows how many of the little sons of bitches. He got no joy or thrill out of the killing. It was just a job he'd been trained to do. No, the killings did nothing for him. But the chase, the hunt—oh, God, how he missed that! And the hunt was always best when it was raining. A heavy rain was his ally, his friend. It made him invisible and covered his smell and drowned out any sound he made inadvertently. Rain was good for the hunter, bad for the prey.

Rimer checked his watch once more. Ninety seconds to go. He moved out of the kiosk and hurried toward the lobby of the medical tower nearest him. The rain was pounding down, the sky darkening by the minute. Again the wind swirled, picking up a cardboard box and lifting it high into the air before slamming it back down. Rimer darted around the box, now thinking about Alex Black's recurring dream of falling from a great height.

Jesus Christ! For a doctor, Rimer thought, this guy was kind of stupid. Any idiot could interpret that goddamn dream. It was a death wish. Rimer had seen it before, plenty of times in Vietnam. He remembered a quiet, careful kid from Tennessee who had decided to make like Rambo and chase Charlie into deep jungle. Alone. He ended up deader than hell, his throat cut from ear to ear. And then there was Crazy Earl, the best of the LURPs, who carried around a BB gun in addition to his M16. One day Crazy Earl attacked a Viet Cong machine gun post—*with his BB gun*. God knows why. He just did it. And laughed at Charlie as the machine gun slugs tore into his chest. Yeah, the doctor had a death wish, just like Crazy Earl.

Rimer dashed into the lobby and went to the fire stairs, glancing at his watch. Forty-five seconds to go. He ran up the steps to the second floor and hurried to the elevators. No one was there. All cars were coming down. Perfect.

Rimer took out two amphetamine pills and chewed them thoroughly before swallowing. The effect of the drug would start shortly and would peak in about five minutes or so. Just right.

Rimer waited patiently, his pulse beginning to race, his muscles rippling nicely. Water dripped from his cap and coat onto the tiled floor, forming a small puddle. He wiped at it with his foot. The Muzak system was playing "Spanish Eyes." He knew the next song would be "Granada." He had heard the Muzak sound track on his listening device a dozen times. Karl Rimer was very careful and paid attention to all details, even the smallest ones. He was a man who valued rehearsal.

In his peripheral vision he saw Alex Black coming through the automatic doors. He quickly pushed the up button and stepped back, looking straight ahead. A moment later he saw the doctor's reflection in the mirrored panel next to the elevator. Alex Black was even shorter than Rimer had thought. No more than five two with little feet and hands and probably weak as hell. Rimer glanced at Alex Black's face. Good-looking little son of a bitch. But his face was lined and his eyes were dark and tired with deeply etched crow's-feet at their corners. He was in his late thirties, but appeared at least five years older. Rimer looked away, thinking that the doctor's premature aging was probably the result of his emotional turmoil. He'd seen that happen before. Plenty of times. In Vietnam.

The elevator door opened and Rimer quickly stepped forward, holding the door for Alex Black and following him into the car. He pushed the button for the eighth floor.

"Which floor are you going to?" Rimer asked, finger still on the floor selector.

"Eight," Alex said.

Rimer nodded and stepped back, moving to the side wall and giving Alex plenty of room. The men stared out in different directions, avoiding each other's eyes. Rimer looked up at the floor indicator, Alex down at his shoes.

The car stopped at the fifth floor, but no one got on. As the door closed, Alex brought a handkerchief up to his nose, now bothered by the intense fragrance of the aftershave lotion that filled the air. Alex wondered if the man in the trench coat had some medical problem that emitted a foul odor.

The elevator stopped at the eighth floor. Rimer allowed Alex Black to exit first. Then Rimer quickly walked ahead, hurrying down the corridor to the office that was directly across from Alex

Black's. He strode with even steps, never hesitating, not looking side to side at closed doors. He appeared to be going to a place he knew and had been to many times before.

Rimer stopped in front of the office of William Shaw, M.D. He tried the door. It was locked, as he knew it would be. He knocked loudly. There was no answer. He tried the door again.

"I'm afraid they've gone home," Alex said. "They usually close at six p.m."

Rimer turned around, a worried look on his face. "But I had an appointment at six-thirty p.m."

"Are you sure?"

"Positive. I talked with his office yesterday." Rimer took off his floppy cap and twisted it nervously in his hands. Water dripped down to the carpet and he quickly put the cap in his pocket. "I've had late appointments before and there was never any problem."

"Perhaps you should call Dr. Shaw's exchange."

Rimer sighed loudly, shaking his head, feigning fatigue and resignation. It was one of his better performances. He could now see sympathy in Alex Black's face. "Is there a phone close by?"

"Not really. I think there are public phones in the lobby."

He sighed again, a beaten man. "They're out of order. I tried to make a call on my way up."

Alex hesitated briefly and studied Rimer's face, trying to make a quick judgment. The man was tall and lean with an angular face and sharp, chiseled features. His hair was reddish blond, curling at the edges, and his eyes were gray-green and seemed a little sad. "If you'd like you can use the phone in my office."

"I'd be most grateful."

Alex opened the door and led the way across the reception area. They went through another door and entered the front office. One wall was lined with charts, the other with file cabinets, a copier and a water cooler. Rimer removed his hand from the pocket of his trench coat. An amphetamine pill came out and dropped to the floor. He didn't see it fall.

Rimer studied the phone on the wall, just above the copier. All of its lights were blinking, on hold. The staff was gone for the day, as Rimer had anticipated. He walked toward the phone, now seeing the volume-control knob for the Muzak system just above it.

"Use the oh-two line," Alex said.

"Thanks again," Rimer said, gratitude in his voice.

As Alex looked away, Rimer quickly reached for the control knob and turned it up to full volume. A loud blast of "Granada" suddenly filled the room. Alex spun around, startled. Some deep-seated instinct told him to run. But it was too late.

Rimer had an arm around Alex's neck, a gun at his temple.

An instant before Rimer pulled the trigger, Alex had his recurring dream. He was falling through space, faster and faster, the ground coming up to meet him.

He heard a loud thud.

His body slamming into the earth.

A bullet slamming into his brain.

15

Joanna was taking off her makeup when the doorbell rang. She dabbed on some lipstick, wondering who it could be. It was almost midnight and outside the weather was foul with wind and rain. The doorbell rang again. She hurried into the living room and looked through the peephole. Jake was standing in the rain, dripping wet with no raincoat.

Joanna quickly opened the door. "You could have called."

"I did, but your line was busy."

Joanna nodded. "Hospital business."

"For two hours."

"It was a lot of business," Joanna said and stepped aside. "Come in before you catch pneumonia."

Jake went directly to the fireplace and stood close to the flames. "Christ, it's shitty weather out there."

"Particularly for people stupid enough to stand out in it."

"We're going to have that type of evening, huh?"

"You'd better get those clothes off and hang them up."

Jake smiled broadly. "Right."

"Don't get the wrong idea," Joanna said at once. "You're not going to spend the night here. You have a warm-up suit in the closet. You can wear that when you leave."

Joanna watched him go into the bedroom, then went over to a small wet bar and poured two brandies. Briefly she studied herself in the mirrored wall. She looked awful. Her hair was a mess, her lipstick uneven. And the lines on her forehead were showing through. She quickly patted her hair in place and thought about making up her face. To hell with it. She wasn't going to primp for him. Not anymore.

Jake strolled back into the living room wearing a blue-and-gold UCLA warm-up outfit. He was barefoot and his hair was still dripping water.

Joanna handed him a snifter of brandy and they sat on a couch in front of the fireplace quietly sipping their drinks. The logs were blazing and red-hot. Outside the rain was pouring down, pounding against the side of the apartment building. The silence in the room was broken by a log crackling loudly.

"I still think you're overreacting," Jake said.

"To what?"

"You know damn well."

"Oh," Joanna said, nodding, "you mean to your running back to Greece for an ex-wife."

"She died, goddamn it," Jake blurted out.

"A lot of things died that day," Joanna said slowly, "and they'll never go back to the way they were."

Jake reached over and touched Joanna's hair. "You shouldn't be jealous of a dead person."

Joanna shook her head. "I'm not jealous. I'm just facing up to the truth. And the truth is something happened to us that night and we'll never be the same again."

Jake gently stroked Joanna's hair, taking a long strand and twirling it. She didn't respond, but she didn't move away either. Jake still didn't understand what he'd done wrong. Christ! Someone dies and you go to their funeral. Wife, ex-wife, friend. You go and pay respects. It was the right thing to do. "I guess we just think differently."

"I guess."

Jake pulled her a little closer. "You weren't serious about us seeing other people, were you?"

"Oh, yes, I was," Joanna said promptly. "One of these nights I'm going to have dinner with Phil Weideman."

"You mean he hasn't asked you yet?"

"No, but he will."

Jake smiled to himself. And maybe Weideman won't. "Well, in this age of the liberated woman, why don't you ask him out?"

Joanna's brow went up. "Do you think I should?"

"Hell, no! You've already got your man."

"Really?" Joanna's eyes looked into his and held them. "Where is he?"

"Right here." Jake suddenly pulled her close and kissed her firmly on the lips.

"No, goddamn it!" Joanna tried to push herself away.

"Yes, goddamn it!" Jake held her tightly and kissed her again. She resisted, but not as much, and then he felt her lips kissing him back and her arms around his neck. Their lips met once more, opening, tongues touching, flicking in and out.

They never made it to the bedroom. Their clothes were everywhere—shirt on the couch, pants on the chair, bra on the floor, panties on the coffee table.

They were still on the floor, Joanna's head on Jake's chest. Outside the rain was still coming down, less than before, but now the wind had picked up and was whistling through the trees outside Joanna's living room.

"This really doesn't change anything," Joanna said softly. "I'm still going to see other people."

"Jesus," Jake groaned, "doesn't being together like this mean anything to you?"

"Sure. It means we're physically attracted to each other and probably always will be. But there's more to a relationship than that."

"You figure things are going to be better with Phil Weideman, huh?"

"Maybe."

Jake squinted an eye. "I hope you don't expect me to compete for you against this Weideman guy."

"I don't expect anything from you, Jake. From now on there won't be any demands or conditions."

Goddamn it, Jake growled to himself, she does want me to compete. Like some high school kid. Screw it! He was too old for that. Or was he?

Joanna stood and put on her shirt, then wriggled into her jeans.

She sat on an overstuffed chair, crossing her legs under her. "How's your drink?"

"Fine," Jake said distantly.

"Do you want to talk about some people who died suddenly without apparent cause?"

"Sure. It would probably have a lot more warmth than the conversation we're having."

Joanna smiled to herself. He was pissed off. Good. He deserved it. She poured herself another brandy before telling him about the deaths of Lucy O'Hara, Sally Wheaton and Karen Butler. As she related the details of each case, she watched Jake pacing the living room floor, now in his UCLA outfit. It was one of Jake's peculiarities. He thought better on the move. Even after she finished he continued to pace, head down, hands clasped behind his back. "Well, what do you think?"

"It's murder," Jake said.

"You're convinced that those three patients from Health First were murdered, huh? Convinced beyond a reasonable doubt?"

"It sure as hell smells like it, doesn't it?" Jake reached for a Greek cigarette. He was starting his third pack of the day and his throat was irritated and raspy from all the smoke. For the past year he had managed to cut down to ten cigarettes per day, but then he went to Greece for Eleni's funeral and was surrounded by Greeks who smoked like chimneys. Within a few days he was up to three packs. He was killing himself and he knew it. He promised himself he would cut back again. Soon.

"But there's absolutely no proof that they were murdered," Joanna said, breaking into his thoughts. "And they had nothing in common except that they were female patients at Health First who were referred to Memorial for bone marrow transplants."

"Somebody wanted them dead," Jake said.

"I'm convinced of that too. But tell me why and who."

"Who benefits from their deaths?"

Joanna shrugged. "Nobody that I can think of."

"No suspects at all?"

"Well, maybe one," she said slowly. "There's a doctor named Arnold Kohler at Health First who bothers me some."

"How so?"

"I don't have anything solid. He's a creepy little guy, the type who never looks at you when he talks. He was the doctor for two of the three patients who died. And he's a bad doctor, Jake."

"There's no law against that."

"There is if he's killing people."

"But what's his motive?"

Joanna shrugged again. "Maybe he's covering up something. Maybe these patients threatened him with malpractice suits."

"Have you talked with him?"

"That's another thing. I've phoned his office three times. I think he's ducking my calls."

Jake stared into space, trying to fit the pieces of information together. "But how could this Dr. Kohler arrange to have his patients killed at Memorial?"

"That I don't know."

Jake started pacing again. "Somebody at Memorial has got to be involved. After all, that's where the deaths occurred. Who at Memorial might benefit from these deaths?"

"Nobody really. Memorial has got too many empty beds now. They need all the patients they can get."

"What about Health First? Do they gain anything from these deaths?"

"They lose. Big time. Health First is the model for managed care in the future. They pride themselves on delivering excellent care at a reasonable cost. If word got out that their patients were dying as soon as they came in with anything more serious than a cold—well, you can imagine the effect it would have on their reputation and their enrollment numbers."

"What do you mean by 'managed care'?"

Joanna took his cigarette and puffed briefly, then handed it back. "It's really cost containment. At the present, doctors can charge patients whatever they wish. In a managed care situation, the doctor has to deliver his services at a set price."

"Give me an example."

"Let's say you have a sore throat. You go to the doctor and he examines you and does a laboratory test. The bill is sixty-five dollars. But if you are a member of an HMO and that doctor has a contract with that HMO, the bill would be only thirty dollars regardless of what tests were done. In other words, the contract limits the amount that can be charged."

Jake let the information sink in before he spoke. "So the doctors can't be too happy about that."

"They're howling like stuck pigs."

Jake grinned slightly. "And I'll bet your surgeon friend, Phil Weideman, is screaming the loudest."

"He's an outstanding surgeon and he does wonderful work," Joanna said, an edge to her voice.

"Well, he can continue doing great work. He'll just get paid less for doing it." Jake went over to the wet bar and poured himself another brandy. He brought the bottle over to Joanna and refilled her snifter. Their hands touched lightly. She pulled her hand away, turning a shoulder to Jake. He exhaled loudly and started pacing again. "Do you think people would kill to destroy managed care in this country?"

Joanna forced a big laugh. "You're talking about an eight-hundred-billion-dollar-a-year industry. That's eight hundred billion with a big *B*. You're talking about one seventh of the Gross National Product."

"So some doctor could be doing it."

"But who? And how? I've reviewed the charts of the dead women over and over again. They were looked after in different clinics by different doctors at Memorial."

"Were they given any shots or medicines?"

"Not in the clinics. I even checked to determine if they had their blood drawn on the day of their deaths. Two did. Lucy O'Hara and Sally Wheaton. The other patient didn't. Just to cover all the bases, I talked with the venipuncturist at length. She struck me as being tough and easy to dislike. And she became defensive as hell when I started asking her questions about the dead patients. But she had all the right answers and, besides, what motive would she have to kill? Unless she was a cuckoo." Joanna slowly sipped her brandy, holding it on her tongue for a moment before swallowing. "*Sudden* and *death* are the words that keep going through my mind. Sudden death. That's the key here. But there was nothing on autopsy to account for it. No strokes or heart attacks or blood clots or hemorrhages. Nothing."

"What about poisons?"

"We've checked their body fluids with the most sensitive tests available and found nothing. A big zilch. I've even sent pieces of their livers to colleagues in San Francisco to see if they can extract anything unusual from the tissue."

"It sounds like you're really up against it."

"Tell me about it."

There was a sudden loud thumping sound from the ceiling. The whole room seemed to shake.

"What the hell is that?" Jake asked.

"It's two guys who just moved in above me. I think they play for some college football team. God, they're noisy!"

Another loud thud. A small piece of plaster came off the cottage-cheese ceiling and floated down.

Jake looked up. "Have you asked them to quiet it down?"

"About a dozen times."

Now the stereo came on. Loud. The bass vibrating.

"Hey!" Joanna shouted up at the ceiling. "How about turning it down?"

"Fuck off!" a voice yelled back.

Jake spun around angrily and started for the door.

"They're just kids, Jake," Joanna said, grabbing his arm.

"They've got big mouths, don't they?"

"Just kids," Joanna said and pulled him back. Two more years, she thought, and all of her bank loans would be paid off. Then she'd start looking for a house to buy.

Outside the rain picked up again and beat against the side of the building. There was a distant crack of lightning, then a boom of thunder. Joanna nestled her head against the back of her chair and stared into the fire.

The phone rang. Joanna stared at it, wishing that she had unplugged it. She wasn't on call at the hospital and wanted an evening of peace and quiet. Not tonight. On the fifth ring she picked up the phone. It was Jake's partner, Lou Farelli. She handed Jake the phone and watched him stoke the fire while he spoke. His conversation consisted of "Right," "Yeah," and "Good."

"Anything wrong?" Joanna asked as he put the phone down.

"Naw," Jake said and lit another cigarette. "I had Farelli talk with the officers who found your man with no face."

"Did they have anything to add?"

"Not much. They found the body nude in a shallow grave that was covered with a few rocks. The killer left nothing behind. The cops searched the area looking for the weapon he used to bash in the victim's face. *Nada.* Nothing. Our guy is real careful."

"But why did he dig such a shallow grave? Why didn't he make it six feet deep? That way the body would never have been found."

Jake smiled at her. "Have you ever tried to dig a hole six feet deep and three feet wide?"

Joanna shook her head.

"It would take a lot of time for one man to do it. Hours and hours." Jake put his arm around Joanna and drew her close. "Too many things could go wrong. A hiker or a camper might have spotted him. Maybe a forest ranger. No, it would have been too risky. It was better to make the grave shallow, get the hell out of there and take your chances."

Joanna nodded at the logic. Jake was so good at putting the pieces of a crime together. So good. Too bad he wasn't as talented when it came to relationships. "And the reason he only put a few rocks atop the grave was that a pile of rocks might have drawn the attention of a passerby."

"Right. And a few good-sized rocks would stop the rain from washing the ground away and would probably discourage coyotes if they detected the scent of the corpse. But even if the coyotes nudged the rocks aside, all they'd do is eat the remains and that would be fine with the killer too."

"Christ." Joanna winced, her stomach turning briefly. "The killer thought of everything, didn't he?"

"That's what pros do." Jake started to light another cigarette but resisted the urge. "But there's something not right here. Something is out of place."

"What?"

"I'm not sure," Jake said, his voice raspy. "It's on the tip of my tongue, but I can't reach it. My mind is working in slow motion right now."

"Maybe it's the jet lag after your trip back from Greece."

"Maybe." And the word *Greece* brought a picture of Eleni back into his mind. They were in a taverna that overlooked a magnificent harbor just outside Athens. Eleni was dancing by herself, running her hands through her hair, beckoning to Jake to come and join her. It was the last time they were in Athens together. Until her funeral.

Joanna was watching his face, seeing the faraway look in his eyes and knowing what he was thinking about. Jake was doing his best to hide his sadness, but it still showed. She wondered why men went to such great lengths to conceal their grief. It accomplished nothing except to increase the pain. "Do you want to talk about Eleni?"

"There's really not that much to talk about."

"Yes, there is."

Jake exhaled loudly. "I once loved her and now she's dead. And it hurts like hell."

"Maybe deep down you still love her, Jake."

"Naw, it's over."

"Well, if it's over, why did you fly all the way back to Greece for her funeral?"

Jake hesitated, wanting to be very careful with his answer. He had the feeling of a man about to walk through a minefield. "It was the right thing to do."

Bullshit, Joanna thought, keeping her expression even. "It was more than that."

Jake felt his blood pressure rising. "You just can't accept the truth, can you? You have to turn this whole thing into some kind of melodrama."

"Is that what you think this is? A melodrama?"

"Damned right."

"Let me tell you about a real melodrama," Joanna seethed. "It's about a stupid cop who flies back to Greece looking for a lost love that died years ago. And he can't seem to remember that this great love of his threw him out and divorced him and went on with her own life, never once looking back. Now, how does that sound to you?"

"It sounds like something a real jealous bitch would say."

"I'm way past the point of being jealous," Joanna said stonily. "But I'll tell you what I'm very close to."

"What's that?"

"Not giving a damn about you or your past."

Jake waved a hand disgustedly. "I knew I shouldn't have come here tonight."

"Nobody invited you."

The stereo in the apartment above suddenly blasted. The bass was so strong that everything began to vibrate. Then came a loud thumping noise. People jumping up and down dancing.

Jake jumped atop a footstool and pounded on the ceiling with a closed fist. "Hey up there! Hold down the racket!"

The music blasted on, the thumping noise even louder.

Jake pounded on the ceiling again. "Hey, goddamn it! It's almost midnight."

"That's too bad. And if you knock on the ceiling again, I'm going to come downstairs and we're going to have a little talk. Asshole!"

Jake grinned down at Joanna. Then he banged the ceiling with powerful blows over and over again. He heard footsteps racing across the floor above. A door opened. Now they were on the stairs coming down.

Jake hurried into the bedroom and came out holding his .38-caliber police special, checking the chamber, making certain it was loaded. He moved toward the apartment door. Joanna grabbed at his arm, trying to restrain him. "No, Jake! They're only kids."

There was a forceful knock on the front door. Then an angry voice said, "Open up, asshole, or I'll knock this door down."

Jake opened the door and assumed the firing position, arms extended and holding the weapon in front of him. He pointed the .38 special at the head of a huge man in his mid-twenties with crew-cut blond hair and a square jaw. The man had to weigh 250 pounds and was at least six five.

"You wanted to talk to me," Jake said hoarsely. "Now's your chance."

The big man stared at the gun, his eyes bulging. His mouth came open, but he couldn't form words. Just behind him was another huge man, every bit as big, with long, shaggy hair that fell to his shoulders. Both were heavily muscled, wearing T-shirts and jeans. Off to the side a young blond woman was watching, more fascinated than frightened. She had on short-shorts and an opened shirt, its ends tied in a bow across her midriff. She was showing plenty of breasts that were too big and too well formed. Implants, Jake thought, his gaze now on the cigarette she was smoking. It had the characteristic sweet odor of marijuana. In the other hand, she held a can of beer.

"Can't talk, huh?" Jake took a step out into the light rain. The man quickly backed up. "Well then, I'll do the talking. First, I'm licensed to carry this weapon because I'm a cop. Secondly, I spend a lot of nights here and I'm a light sleeper. Thirdly, if you ever piss me off again it's going to be the worst day of your life. Am I coming across?"

The man in front of Jake nodded rapidly and said in a quiet voice, "We'll keep it down."

"You'd goddamn well better."

"Wait a minute," the cute blonde blurted out, "they pay rent here too. You can't just order—"

"Yes, I can," Jake cut her off, now staring at her marijuana cigarette. "And I can also call my buddies on the narc squad and have them come over and check out your apartment. How does that sound?"

"There's no need for that," the huge man said quickly. "We'll keep it down. I promise you."

"I don't want to hear another sound, not even a peep," Jake said hoarsely. "Now get the hell upstairs and be real quiet."

The rain started pouring down again with big drops. There was a flash of lightning and the sky turned blue. Jake and Joanna hurried back into the living room.

Joanna slammed the door and glared at Jake. "Goddamn it, Jake! Are you crazy? Pulling a gun like that."

Jake's eyes narrowed, not believing what he was hearing. "He was going to kick your door in, for Chrissakes!"

"They're just kids, trying to act tough. You could have talked to them rather than pull your gun."

"Sometimes you can be so damn dumb," Jake growled, trying to control his rage. "Suppose that son of a bitch had a gun when I opened the door. We would both be dead, quicker than you can blink."

"People in this building don't have guns, and if they did they wouldn't aim them at one another."

"Yeah, and people in this building don't kick down doors, do they?" Jake hissed, his neck veins bulging. "You just don't get it, do you?"

"No, you don't get it," Joanna hissed back. "Now everyone in this building will think they'd better not knock on my door or they'll end up looking down the barrel of a gun."

"That's crap and you know it. Why do you keep overreacting to everything?"

Joanna clenched her jaw. "That's the second time I've heard that word tonight. I didn't like it the first time and I like it even less now."

"It's a simple fact," Jake said coldly.

"Well, let me give you another simple fact. You're going to get your clothes and get the hell out of here. Now!"

Jake stared at her, his face coloring.

"And don't come back unless you're invited."

"Fine!" Jake spun around and stomped into the bedroom, cursing under his breath. He came out carrying his still-wet clothes and hurried past her without a word.

Jake stepped outside, then turned to say something. But before he could, the door slammed in his face.

16

Joanna gave the nurse a sharp look. "You tell Dr. Kohler he either sees me now or I'll have him subpoenaed."

"What?" the nurse said, taken aback. "I—I'm not sure I understand."

"Listen carefully because this is the exact message I want you to give to Dr. Kohler." Joanna kept her voice down so the patients in the waiting room couldn't hear her. "I need to talk with him about some of his patients who died suddenly. These patients are coroner's cases, and since I performed the autopsies I represent the coroner's office. If he refuses to talk with me, I'll have him subpoenaed. If he ignores the subpoena, a bench warrant will be issued for his arrest. They'll come in here, handcuff him and drag him out. It will not be a pleasant scene."

"Let me talk with Dr. Kohler again," the nurse said quickly.

Joanna watched the woman hurry down the corridor. As the nurse was turning to enter a room, Arnold Kohler stepped out. The nurse nodded toward Joanna, then spoke to Kohler in a very animated fashion. Joanna tried to read Kohler's expression but she could see only his profile.

Kohler handed a chart to the nurse and rapidly came over to Joanna. "I'm sorry, Dr. Blalock. I didn't know it was you. The nurse mispronounced your name at first."

"I see," Joanna said, not believing him for a moment. "Didn't you receive a call from Dr. Mariner's office telling you that I was coming here?"

"I get so many messages," Kohler said evasively. "One says do this, another says do the opposite. It's difficult to keep up."

"Where can we talk?"

"In my office."

Joanna followed Kohler down a corridor and into a cluttered office. The room was small and windowless, the air stale with the smell of old cigarette smoke. As she sat down, Joanna glanced over at an antiquated examining table with its leather straps. Next to it was a big, bulky EKG machine that was at least twenty years old. Even the stethoscope around Kohler's neck was outdated with its oversized bell and long tubing. Joanna rearranged her chair so that she was facing Kohler. In the corner by his desk she saw a withered plant, its leaves yellowed and dying.

"It's tragic, very tragic. These patients were so close to being given a new lease on life." Kohler gestured with his hands and shrugged. "What can you do?"

"We can find out what killed them," Joanna said.

"Your autopsies haven't turned up anything yet?"

"Not so far." Joanna took out a stack of index cards and flipped through them. "Before we get to your patients, I want to talk to you about Lucy O'Hara."

"Who?" Kohler's forehead furrowed.

"Lucy O'Hara."

"I don't know her."

"Are you sure?"

"Positive," Kohler said, but he scratched at his ear nervously. "I've never seen her."

"I think you have." Joanna looked down at an index card and studied it briefly. "Six months ago you hospitalized her."

"You must be mistaken. It must—"

"There's no mistake," Joanna cut him off. "You were listed as her primary physician in her hospital chart. She was a young woman with acute leukemia and a raging pneumonia."

Kohler stared out into space at length, then slowly nodded. "Oh, yes. I remember now. She was Amanda Black's patient.

Amanda was on vacation and I was covering for her. The patient was terribly ill.''

"You didn't think so at first. According to a consultant's note, when Lucy's father called you and described her symptoms, you told him you thought it was the flu.''

"That was one possibility,'' Kohler said defensively.

"With a temperature of a hundred and four degrees?''

Kohler squirmed in his chair. "In my experience, the flu can on occasion—''

Joanna flicked her wrist dismissively. "Even her father knew better. That's why he rushed her to the ER.''

Kohler started to say something, but held his tongue.

Joanna remembered that Lucy's father was a lawyer and decided to take a stab in the dark. "Is that when he threatened you with a malpractice suit?''

"Nothing ever came of that. He was just upset over his daughter's illness.''

And over your stupidity, Joanna thought. She glanced down at the index cards on Lucy O'Hara, Sally Wheaton and Karen Butler. All now dead. All looked after by Arnold Kohler. "Let's talk about Karen Butler.''

Kohler exhaled through puffed cheeks, relieved to be changing topics. "She was a young nurse with rheumatoid arthritis that didn't respond to any of the usual medication. That's why she was placed on gold shots.''

"Who decided that she should receive gold?''

"A consulting rheumatologist here at Health First.''

"Who actually gave the shots?''

"My nurse.''

"And who checked Karen's blood counts before each gold shot?''

Kohler hesitated. "I don't know.''

"Are you telling me you allowed this patient to receive gold shots without making certain her blood counts were adequate?''

Kohler's face hardened. "Look, I'm not a specialist in this disease. You want to know how, when and what about gold shots, you ask the rheumatologist.''

"But she was your patient and it was your nurse who administered the shots."

"Look, she got gold and she had a bad reaction. It wiped out her bone marrow. It's unfortunate, but it happened."

And it just might not have happened, Joanna was thinking, if someone had been keeping a close eye on things. She studied Kohler for a moment, wondering if Karen Butler had also considered filing a malpractice suit against him. She also wondered to what ends Kohler would go to cover up his incompetence. "Did you know that Karen Butler was taking amphetamines?"

Kohler's eyelids twitched briefly. "How do you know that?"

"We found it in her blood. And she had a high level too, suggesting she was a chronic user."

"How does the blood level tell you she'd been taking amphetamines for a long time?"

"Chronic users develop a tolerance to the drug, so they have to take more and more to get the same effect."

"How do you know she wasn't shooting the stuff IV? That would also cause a high blood level."

"Because at autopsy she didn't have multiple venipuncture marks and she didn't have any tracks." Joanna smiled thinly. "And if they had been present, you would have detected them when you examined her. Right?"

"Of course, of course," Kohler said quickly, wishing he hadn't asked the question, wishing even more that Joanna Blalock would finish up and get the hell out.

"Where do you think she got the amphetamines?"

"Anywhere and everywhere. Kids today can get drugs as easily as they can buy chewing gum. It's available on just about every corner. Sellers are everywhere." Kohler smiled slightly. "Hell, they're like drugstores."

The intercom on Kohler's desk buzzed.

"Dr. Kohler, Mr. Cook is having an allergic reaction. His lips and tongue are starting to swell."

Kohler jumped up. "We are going to have to cut this interview short. If you need any more information, just give me a call."

Joanna watched him dash from the room, stethoscope swinging in the air. Something Kohler had just said was sticking in her mind, but she couldn't put her finger on it. And he smiled inappropriately a moment before he said it. What was it? Drugs? IV shooting? Street corners? Damn! What was it?

Joanna's gaze went to the prescription pad atop Kohler's desk. Her eyes suddenly brightened. Drugstore! That was the word he'd said. Drugstore!

Joanna tore a blank prescription slip from the pad and quickly left the room.

17

"Who found the body?" Jake asked, talking above the sound of the Muzak.

"The secretary," Sergeant Lou Farelli said. "She came in a little earlier than usual to do some typing. It's around eight-thirty a.m. when she walks in and sees her boss with his brains blown across the room. She screams and vomits." Farelli pointed to a small puddle of vomitus on the carpet. "Watch where you step."

Jake looked down at the puddle and felt a twinge of nausea. His stomach was still on edge from the tequila and beer chasers he'd consumed after leaving Joanna's apartment the night before. He still couldn't understand why she was being so unreasonable. And feisty. Christ! She hadn't even given him a chance to smooth things over. Well, to hell with it. If that was the way she wanted things—fine.

"Is there something unusual about the vomit?" Farelli asked.

"Naw," Jake said, quickly clearing his mind. "So, you think it's a straightforward suicide?"

"It looks that way." Farelli was a short, stocky man with a round face and thinning black hair. "The doc sits down at the receptionist's desk, takes out a street-bought thirty-two, and pulls the trigger."

"How do you know the gun was bought on the street?"

"The serial number has been filed off."

Jake walked over to the corpse of Alex Black. The body was

seated, head hyperextended back, mouth agape, lifeless eyes staring at the ceiling. There was a star-shaped hole in the skull, blood
and brain oozing out. It was an exit wound, and from the angle
of the head Jake guessed that the bullet would have ended up in
the far wall.

"Did you find the slug?" Jake asked.

"Not yet," Farelli said. "It ain't in the ceiling or wall or on the
floor. We think it's in there." He pointed to the wall that was
lined with shelves of charts. "We'll start digging for it as soon as
the medical examiner gives us the okay."

"Where is he?"

"In the back looking for a thermometer. He dropped his on
the floor and broke it." Farelli looked to the door leading to an
inner office and lowered his voice. "The examiner is that Indian
guy, Gupta."

"Don't underestimate him," Jake said, his throat raspy from too
many cigarettes.

"It's not that," Farelli said. "He looks sick, Jake. And he's got
a funny pale color. Hell, he looks worse than the corpse over
there."

"He's getting over a bad pneumonia." Jake remembered back
to his conversation with Joanna about a strange type of pneumonia
that had decimated the coroner's office. Foreign Legionnaires'
disease, something like that. "Is he going to be able to get the job
done?"

"He's trying his best."

The Muzak was now blasting out "Spanish Eyes." Jake looked
over at the corpse with its dark beady eyes staring into nothingness. "Why is the music so loud in here?"

"That's how we found it when we got here."

"You think the doc was trying to cover the sound of the gunshot?"

"Probably," Farelli replied, not totally convinced. "But why
would he bother to do that? Once he's blown his brains out it
really doesn't matter who finds him or when."

"Keep in mind he was a doctor. Maybe he thought he might
not die right away and the last thing he wanted was to be found
alive and rushed to some ICU and kept alive with tubes and
machines."

"Creepy business," Farelli said and shook his head. "We got a doctor in a plush office making really big bucks and he blows his goddamn brains out. Everything he worked for all his life is gone in a split second. Go figure."

"Maybe something was bothering him."

"Well, it ain't bothering him anymore."

Jake glanced around the spacious room. Nothing was out of place, no evidence of a struggle. The receptionist's area was bland and colorless. Charts and files, copying machine, coffeemaker, water cooler. His gaze went to the receptionist's desk. Atop it was a framed photograph of a woman holding a young boy, both smiling and happy. On the wall was a calendar showing a tranquil ocean with a slogan written on it: TODAY IS THE FIRST DAY OF THE REST OF YOUR LIFE. Jake wondered who wrote shit like that and how much they got paid to do it.

"Hello, Lieutenant," Girish Gupta said as he walked into the room.

"Hello, Doc," Jake said.

Gupta nodded rather than shake hands. He was wearing latex gloves and holding a disposable thermometer. Kneeling down, he unzipped the corpse's pants and managed to insert the thermometer rectally without disturbing the position of the body. "We'll see what time he actually died."

What a way to end up, Jake was thinking. Dead with your pants half off and a thermometer stuck up your ass. And brain oozing out of your skull.

"Nasty business, nasty business," Gupta said, his accent clipped and British. "It always seems more tragic when a doctor does it, and more of a waste."

"You think it's suicide, huh?"

"Everything points to that. No signs of a struggle, no break-in. The weapon, the wound. Everything says the gunshot was self-inflicted."

"Where's the suicide note?" Jake asked.

Gupta gestured with his hands. "A note is not always found."

"Yeah, but this guy planned it. He bought a gun off the street, waited until his office was empty and everyone had gone home, even turned up the Muzak volume to cover the noise of the gunshot. He was a real careful guy. That type usually leaves a note.''

"Perhaps,'' Gupta conceded. "But on the other hand, he may have just been giving the matter thought. And then he suddenly decided to do it.''

"It just came to him, huh?''

Gupta nodded firmly. "Exactly. On the spur of the moment, you see.''

Jake tried not to grin at the way the medical examiner had said ''on the spur of the moment.'' He made it sound like the corpse had been thinking about catching a late movie.

Gupta went on, "You mentioned that the weapon he used was bought on the street. Why didn't he simply go to a gun shop? He was not a criminal. He could have legally purchased a gun with no difficulty.''

"Maybe he was in a hurry,'' Farelli answered. "In California there's a fourteen-day waiting period when you go to buy a gun.''

"Ahh,'' Gupta said, nodding. He began to reach for the thermometer, then decided to give it a little more time. "But tell me, how would a respectable doctor know where to buy a gun on the street? I wouldn't know where to go or whom to approach.''

"Everything in the world is for sale,'' Jake told the young coroner. "I can name a dozen street corners in Los Angeles where you can buy anything you want. Women, drugs, guns. Any goddamn thing.''

"I assume Alex Black knew something about guns. He had to ask for the right-size weapon.''

Jake shrugged. "Not necessarily. All he had to do was ask for a medium-size weapon that he could handle. That usually means a thirty-two or a thirty-eight. And you don't have to be a rocket scientist to load a gun and point it at your head and pull the trigger.''

"What a waste!'' Gupta knelt down and extracted the thermometer from Alex Black's anus. He squinted his eyes, reading it in the poor light. As he stood up his knees suddenly buckled and he began to waver.

Jake and Farelli rushed over and grabbed his arms, supporting him. The thermometer dropped from his hands and bounced off the floor, breaking in two.

"Are you okay?" Jake asked.

"Just a little shaky," Gupta said weakly. "Perhaps I should sit down for a moment."

Jake helped him to a nearby chair and watched as Gupta sat down heavily and swallowed air several times. The medical examiner looked very pale under the fluorescent lights and beads of perspiration were forming on his forehead. "Do you want to lie down for a little bit?" Jake asked him.

"No, no," Gupta said quickly. "It's my first day back from my siege with pneumonia and I'm not yet up to full strength. But I'll be fine. Just let me rest for a minute or two."

"If you're really under the weather, let's get somebody else from the coroner's office."

"There is no one else. Only a few of us were well enough to return to work and I was the healthiest of all, if you can believe it."

Farelli got a cup of water from the water cooler and brought it over. Gupta sipped it slowly, taking deep breaths between swallows. He loosened his tie and leaned his head back.

Jake could see that Gupta was getting weaker by the moment, his face even more drawn than before. There was no way he could continue and they needed a forensic expert here and now at the crime scene. But who? None of the coroners were available, according to Gupta. Jake resisted the idea of asking Joanna, but the more he thought about it the more he liked it. She'd be perfect for the job, if she'd do it. And it would give him a chance to talk with her and maybe patch things up. "Would you object if I called in a consultant?" he asked.

Gupta's eyes narrowed. "Who?"

"A colleague of yours, Joanna Blalock."

Gupta nodded. "A fine choice."

Jake turned to Farelli. "Is there some place for the doc to lie down?"

"There's a couch in the doctor's office."

Jake signaled to a big uniformed cop near the door. "Help the medical examiner to the couch in the doctor's office."

"Really, that's not necessary," Gupta protested and tried to get to his feet. He had no strength in his legs. He fell back into the chair.

Jake gestured with his head to the uniformed cop, who came over and helped Gupta up, supporting him and walking him to the rear of the medical suite.

"I know what that's like," Farelli said sympathetically. "Remember when I had that bad case of bronchitis and tried to work? Hell, I couldn't even think straight."

"Uh-huh," Jake said absently.

Farelli looked up at Jake, trying to read his eyes and thoughts. "Do you think the doc overlooked something?"

"No, he's just not paying enough attention to the things that are obvious."

"Like what?"

"Like no suicide note."

"Sometimes they don't leave them. Particularly the real nut cases."

"Yeah, but look at this guy." Jake moved over to the corpse and began to point. "His hair is perfectly groomed, nails manicured, tie perfectly knotted and centered, shoes highly polished. This was a very neat man, and neat people don't leave loose ends. They want everything nice and tidy. They leave notes."

"Maybe," Farelli said dubiously. "But that's kind of weak evidence to say this is not suicide. I think you're grabbing at straws."

Jake shrugged. "I do that all the time."

The elevator door opened and Joanna Blalock stepped out. A uniformed policeman held his hand up, blocking her way.

"Sorry, ma'am, no one is allowed on this floor," he said.

"I'm with the coroner's office," Joanna said.

The policeman smiled thinly, wondering if the young, attractive woman was a TV reporter. He knew that the medical examiner was already with the corpse. "You got some ID to prove it?"

A flash of irritation crossed Joanna's face. "Look, I'm here because—"

"Either produce the ID or move out," the cop said firmly.

Joanna looked past the policeman and down the corridor. She spotted Lou Farelli and waved. The cop turned and saw Farelli waving back. He quickly stepped aside and mumbled something that sounded like "Sorry."

Joanna walked down the corridor, passing opened doors.

Nurses and secretaries peeked out, following Joanna with their eyes, whispering to one another as she went past. The Muzak system was playing "People Who Need People."

"Hi ya, Doc," Farelli said genially.

"Hello, Sergeant," Joanna said, liking the man and thinking for the hundredth time that he looked more like a waiter in an Italian restaurant than a homicide detective. "How have you been?"

"Never better."

They entered the office together, Farelli guiding her around the small puddle of vomitus. Joanna saw Girish Gupta and walked over to him. He seemed much thinner than when she saw him last and his face appeared drawn and tired. "I'm sorry you're not feeling well."

"Oh, not to worry," Gupta said lightly. "I'm slowly getting my sea legs back."

"Perhaps you came back to work too soon."

"I'm afraid you're correct."

Joanna turned to Jake, her expression firm. "I'm way behind in my work at Memorial. I can only give you an hour of my time."

"Fine," Jake said, sensing the coolness in her voice.

"And regardless of what I find, you'll have to get somebody else to do the autopsy."

Jake felt like telling her to go to hell, but he needed her and wanted a reason to be around her. "I thought you'd be more interested. After all, this guy did work at Health First."

"That's my main reason for being here."

"And you figure it's only worth an hour of your time, huh?"

"Look," Joanna said stonily, "I'm already so far behind in my work I'll never catch up. Yet I've managed to free up an hour for you. Now if that's not good enough, find somebody else."

Jake studied her for a moment. His neck veins bulged as he fought to control his temper. "I don't care how long it takes you. Just do the job right."

Joanna moved over to the corpse that was sprawled out on the swivel chair. Her gaze went to his outstretched hand, the gun and the pool of blood on the floor. "Want to fill me in?"

Jake quickly gave her all the details, including who found the corpse and how, the turned-up volume of the Muzak system, the particulars of the weapon used. "And he didn't leave a suicide note," Jake concluded.

Joanna snapped on a pair of latex gloves and examined the head of Alex Black. She saw the entrance wound just below the right temple, its edges blackened and burned. The exit wound on the left upper parietal area was bigger and more ragged. She stepped back, tilting her head to one side and imagining the path of the bullet once it exited. Her gaze went to the far wall where the charts were. Then she turned her attention back to Alex Black's head. The entrance wound was anterior, almost to the frontal area. She made her hand into a gun and pointed her index finger at the anterior edge of her own temple. It felt awkward and she had to strain to squeeze an imaginary trigger. She glanced down at the weapon on the floor. A .32. Alex Black's outstretched hand was almost touching it. "Have you found the slug?"

"Not yet," Jake said. "Farelli figures it's somewhere in the wall lined with files and folders."

"Probably," Joanna agreed. "But sometimes bullets that go through skulls don't travel that far. You'd better check the carpet carefully."

"We already did," Farelli told her. "All we found was some kind of pill."

"May I see it?"

"Sure." Farelli took out a plastic envelope and emptied it onto the receptionist's desk.

Joanna studied the triangular-shaped orange pill with her magnifying glass. On it she saw the letters SKF and the number E19. She went over to a bookshelf and took down a volume of *Physician's Desk Reference.* Quickly she flipped through the pages until she came to the product identification section that showed photographs of pills. "It's Dexedrine, a form of amphetamine."

"Speed?" Jake asked.

Joanna nodded. "But probably bought at a drugstore. It's made by a very reputable pharmaceutical company—Smith, Kline and French."

"Maybe the doc was using it in some kind of experiment." Farelli suggested.

"No," Joanna said at once. "It's a controlled substance and besides Alex Black didn't do any research in this office."

"Well, someone in this office was using it," Jake said.

"Yes," Joanna said, smiling thinly, "someone was."

Jake tried to read the expression on her face, but couldn't.

Joanna leaned over and examined the corpse's neck and throat, looking for bruises. There weren't any. With her magnifying glass she checked for skin and blood under his fingernails. Nothing. His hands were clean, the knuckles free of cuts or abrasions. There was no evidence that Alex Black had fought or struggled before he died.

Jake broke the silence. "Does the absence of a suicide note bother you?"

"Not really," Joanna said, still lost in her thoughts.

"Most of the upper-class suicides I've seen left notes," Jake argued.

"Right," Joanna said, slowly circling the corpse.

"How well did you know Dr. Black?"

"Like I told you on the phone, I met with him and his wife on two occasions to discuss the deaths of the Health First patients."

"So you didn't know him socially?"

"Not at all."

Jake rubbed at his nose, now smelling the stale odor of the vomitus on the floor. "I'm still bothered by the absence of a suicide note. It should have been there."

"Maybe," Joanna said as she measured the size of the exit wound with a small ruler. "But I think you should know that Alex Black disliked his wife. There was no love lost between them. I think he disliked her enough not to leave a suicide note."

Jake smiled to himself. Only a woman would think of that. It was the best type of revenge. Kill yourself and don't leave a note. Your wife—no matter that she no longer cares for you—will always wonder if she drove you to it. Guilt! Imagined guilt! Always there, eating away at the wife. Son of a bitch! He must have really hated her.

"I'm going to turn the lights off for a moment. I can visualize better in darkness." Joanna walked to the door and switched off the lights. The room went dark and quiet. Joanna waited a moment, then let her mind go back to the night before. She envisioned Alex Black returning to his office. He switches the light on. Joanna switched the light on. He walks to the receptionist's desk and sits. Joanna walked over to the desk and sat beside the corpse. He takes out his gun and— No! No! The weapon wouldn't be in the receptionist's desk. He would have gone to his office to get it. Unless he carried it in with him.

Joanna turned to Gupta. "What time did he die last night?"

"Between six p.m. and seven p.m.," Gupta answered promptly.

Joanna asked, "Do we know where Alex Black was between five p.m. and six p.m.?"

Farelli took out his notepad and flipped through the pages. "According to his secretary, he had an appointment with Dr. Brian Hummer at five p.m."

"Who is Brian Hummer?"

Farelli shrugged. "We're checking that out now."

So, Joanna reasoned, Alex Black met with a doctor at five p.m. and was probably wearing the long white coat that he had on when he died. The coat had no place in which to conceal a weapon. And he wouldn't have been carrying one around with him anyhow. So he came back to the suite and went into his private office, got the gun and then returned to the receptionist's desk, where he— Joanna shook her head. That can't be right. Why return to the receptionist's desk?

"Peculiar, peculiar," Joanna said, more to herself than to the others.

Jake's ears pricked up. "What?"

"Little things that aren't right. Little things that bother me."

"Like what?"

"Like the location of the bullet wound where Alex Black supposedly shot himself."

Jake gestured with his hands. "It was in the temple. That's where most people blow their brains out."

Farelli nodded firmly. "Everyone I've ever seen."

"Everyone but doctors," Joanna said. "Doctors know better than to aim for the temple. Your hand might slip, you may be an inch or so off. And what happens then? Well, you destroy the frontal lobe of your brain and instead of dying you become a vegetable. Doctors who commit suicide with a gun always place the gun in their mouths, pointing it straight back to the midbrain.

That way the bullet hits the vital brain centers and you die. Most doctors would do it that way, and a bright one like Alex Black almost certainly would.''

"How many doctor-gunshot-suicides have you seen?" Jake asked.

"Six."

"And how many of them put the gun in their mouths and pulled the trigger?"

"All six." Joanna pointed to the site of the entrance wound on Alex's head. "And look where he supposedly shot himself. At the anteriormost aspect of his temple. Empty your gun and point it at the very front edge of your temple."

Farelli removed the shells from his revolver and aimed it at his temple.

"Even more forward," Joanna told him.

Farelli had to twist his head awkwardly to get the correct position.

"How does it feel?" Joanna asked.

"Clumsy as hell," Farelli said. "I'd have trouble pulling the trigger."

"If this is murder," Joanna said slowly, "our killer made an obvious mistake. He shot Alex Black in the wrong place."

"Maybe he came in looking for drugs," Farelli thought out loud.

Jake shook his head. "Naw. If that was the case the office would have been trashed."

"Well, how do you figure the amphetamine pill got on the floor?" Farelli asked.

Jake thought for a moment, then shrugged.

"Maybe the killer brought it in with him," Joanna said carefully. "Maybe he was popping pills just before he did the job and maybe one fell to the floor."

Jake nodded. "That works. And it would also explain why he did some things so sloppily."

Farelli made a face. "It's hard to make a case for murder just because the doc got shot in the wrong place."

Joanna watched Farelli reload his weapon and holster it. "There are other things too. Like the area of the office where he shot himself. At the receptionist's desk. Why? That makes no sense. He had an appointment with some doctor at five p.m. and returns here, say, at six p.m. He's not carrying his gun with him, so he goes to his private office, where he's got the weapon hidden. Why didn't he shoot himself in the private office? Why come back to the receptionist's desk? It doesn't make sense."

"And then there's the absence of the suicide note," Jake added.

"And it may have been the killer who turned up the volume on the Muzak system to cover the noise of the gunshot."

Jake thought for a moment, tapping his finger against the copying machine. "There's a lot of things wrong here. Little things, but nothing substantial."

"I think there's some reasonable doubt about this being a suicide," Joanna said.

"Would it hold up at a coroner's inquest?"

"It's hard to say."

Jake strummed his fingers against the machine again, deliberating, then looked over at Farelli. "Call the Crime Scene Unit."

Farelli took out a handkerchief and reached over the corpse for the telephone on the receptionist's desk. His elbow hit the chair, rocking it, and the corpse slid off, going to the floor in a sitting position.

Farelli and Jake lifted the body up by its arms. Alex Black's long white coat came up to his waist and his unzipped pants slipped down to his knees.

Joanna stared at the corpse's buttocks. "Hold him! Hold him right there!"

Jake and Farelli had to strain to hold the corpse up. Alex Black didn't weigh all that much, but now he was dead weight.

Joanna took out a magnifying glass and carefully studied the figure on Alex Black's buttock.

"What is it?" Jake asked.

"A tattoo. A tattoo of a bluebird."

"So?"

"My man with no face. He also had a tattoo on his butt."

"Of a bluebird?"

"A butterfly. But the colors are the same. Blue and gold. And the design is very similar with oversized eyes and little feet."

"You figure the guy and the faceless stiff are somehow connected?"

Joanna shrugged. "Maybe, maybe not. But I'll bet dollars to doughnuts that whoever did this tattoo also did the one on the faceless man."

Jake nodded, now grasping her line of thought. "So, if you can find out who did this guy's tattoo, maybe the artist will remember doing the butterfly on the other stiff."

"You got it."

"And he might just come up with a name."

"He just might." Joanna placed the magnifying glass in her purse and started for the door.

Jake came over and took her arm. "If the Crime Scene Unit comes up with anything, I'll give you a call."

"Fine, but only at my office." Joanna abruptly pulled her arm away and left the room.

18

Amanda Black looked more shocked than saddened. She stared straight ahead without blinking and spoke in a monotone. "Are you saying that my husband did not take his own life?"

"We're just investigating his death," Jake said.

"Your question made it sound . . ." Amanda's voice trailed off. She brought a cigarette up to her lips and puffed on it absently. She had a faraway look on her face, her mind obviously elsewhere.

"Do you feel up to answering more questions?" Jake asked.

Amanda nodded briefly. "I'm fine."

But Jake could see she wasn't. She was obviously trying to be calm and collected, but he could sense that she was straining to hold herself together. He felt for her, his mind flashing back to Eleni's funeral and the awful emptiness that had consumed him. But he knew that now was the time to ask the widow questions. Her answers would be more honest, less guarded. "Can you think of any reason why your husband would kill himself?"

Amanda nodded slowly. "My husband suffered from depression. At times, severe depression."

Jake leaned forward. "How long had he had this depression?"

"Off and on for years. But it had gotten much worse recently."

"Was he seeing a psychiatrist?"

Amanda nodded.

"Could we have his name?"

"Brian Hummer."

Jake took out his notepad and flipped pages until he came to Brian Hummer's name. Alex Black had seen the psychiatrist at five p.m., an hour or so before his death. So maybe it was suicide after all, Jake thought. A nutty doctor who blew his brains out for God knows what reason. And maybe that was why he didn't leave a note behind. Like Farelli said, the real nut cases usually didn't bother with suicide notes.

The phone rang. Amanda glanced at it briefly and let it ring. She looked away and stared blankly into space.

They were sitting in the conference room on the tenth floor of the Health First Tower. The drapes were open, the day outside gray and gloomy, another storm threatening. The heat in the room was turned up and it felt muggy and close.

Amanda puffed on her cigarette and a shower of ashes fell onto her white coat. She studied them for a moment, then slowly brushed them off. While Amanda was distracted, Jake glanced over at Joanna and signaled with his head for her to pick up the questioning.

"How severe was your husband's depression?" Joanna asked.

"At times it was totally incapacitating."

"Had he ever attempted suicide?"

"No."

"Did he talk about suicide?"

"Not to me."

"Were there any suicide gestures?"

Jake scribbled down the term "suicide gestures" and underlined it.

Amanda gave the question thought. "Once in medical school, I think. He swallowed a handful of Valium tablets, then had second thoughts and called the paramedics."

"Was your husband taking any antidepressant medications?"

"For a while, but I don't think he took them regularly. He complained that they made him feel drugged and dopey and interfered with his thinking. He hated that."

And that might have cost him his life, Joanna was thinking. So stupid to try to regulate the dose of drug you're taking. But she knew that when doctors were patients they did it frequently. So stupid. "Did Alex own a gun?"

"God no!" Amanda blurted out, her voice showing emotion for the first time. "He didn't even want to be around them."

Jake quickly leaned forward. "Was he frightened of them?"

Amanda shook her head. "No, it wasn't that. When he was a boy he used to hunt with his father. One day his father shot at a deer—or what he thought was a deer. It turned out to be another hunter. The man lost a leg because of the gunshot wound. From that day on, Alex never touched a rifle or gun again."

"But he was familiar with firearms?"

"Oh, yes. I'm certain of that."

Jake leaned back and Joanna resumed the questioning. "Did you know that your husband had a tattoo?"

A hint of a smile crossed Amanda's face and rapidly faded. "No, I didn't. That must be new."

Shit, Joanna grumbled to herself. She had hoped that Amanda could tell her the name and location of the shop where Alex had gotten his tattoo. "Forgive me for asking, but when was the last time you and your husband shared the same bed?"

Amanda's eyes narrowed noticeably. "Is that really important?"

"Yes, it is."

Jake smiled inwardly. Of course, it's important. Tell us when you screwed him last and we'll know when you saw his ass last. And we'll know that the tattoo was done after that.

"Almost a year," Amanda said softly, as if she was conceding defeat. "It was no secret that our marriage was over and that we were going our separate ways. But we still cared for each other."

"Why not divorce?" Joanna asked.

"I think we were reaching that point."

"Do you think the prospect of a divorce might have tipped your husband over the edge?"

"I don't know," Amanda said quietly, but her face lost color. She began to say something else, but decided not to.

"Was Alex dating anyone?" Joanna asked.

Amanda hesitated, her eyelids fluttering for a moment. "Not that I know of."

Jake saw the fluttering lids and knew from experience that that was a sure sign the person was either lying or holding back information. But why? What difference would it make now? "Would anyone benefit from your husband's death?"

"You mean, financially?"

"Yes."

"No one really. He was not a wealthy man. His largest asset, to my knowledge was the shares of stock he had in Health First."

"How much was that worth?"

"I would guess somewhere around a hundred thousand dollars."

"And you would inherit?"

Amanda nodded. "Unless he changed his will during the past year."

Jake wrote himself a note. "Check the will." See if he'd changed it and made a bequest to some little honey he was fucking. Maybe she persuaded him to get the tattoo. Older men do stupid things when they're screwing young women. "Let's go back to your husband's social life this past year. When there were social affairs at the hospital, did he bring a date?"

"He never showed up for those types of gatherings. He thought that doctors as a whole were very boring people."

"When he was away from the hospital, did he go to clubs or bars?"

"Occasionally he went to clubs in Santa Monica and in Hollywood. Although he was not a social person, he was a very good dancer, Lieutenant. A very, very good dancer."

"I see," Jake said, thinking about Hollywood. Not the Hollywood of movie stars and bright lights that no longer existed. But the Hollywood of today. A small area in the middle of Los Angeles that was filled with crime and whores and pimps and drugs. A sleazy piece-of-shit area where everything and everybody was for sale. "Did he mention any clubs he went to by name?"

"Not that I recall."

"Did he go to these clubs often?"

Amanda shrugged and her eyelids fluttered briefly. "I wouldn't know."

Oh, yes, you would, Jake was thinking. You know where and who and for some reason you don't want to talk about it. He wondered if she was trying to protect her dead husband's name. But from what? What was she trying to hide?

Joanna asked, "Did he go to these clubs with someone?"

"He never mentioned anyone."

"What type of music did he enjoy dancing to?"

Without hesitation, Amanda said, "Country and western. For some reason he liked the line dances, which, of course, you can do without a partner."

"You dance country and western as well?" Joanna asked.

"Oh, no," Amanda said promptly. "Alex just told me about it once."

Jake hummed to himself, pleased. Good questions, better answers. So old Alex liked country and western, huh? Liked to do the two-step and the Tush-Push. Well, that's just fine because there was only one country and western club in Santa Monica and only one in Hollywood. It would be easy to check them out. And Jake knew that tattoos were frequently found among the crowd that went to country and western bars. All sorts of tattoos.

The door to the conference room opened and Robert Mariner entered. He rushed over to Amanda, who was now standing, and warmly embraced her in a bear hug.

"I flew back as soon as I heard the news," Mariner said.

"Th—" Amanda's voice broke and she buried her face in Mariner's shoulder. Her whole body seemed to shake with silent sobs.

Joanna watched the couple, wondering again what their relationship really was, and again sensing that it was far more than just friendship. She focused in on Mariner, who was now handing Amanda a handkerchief to wipe away the tears. Joanna couldn't help but be impressed with him. The man just took center stage naturally, as if it belonged to him. Most people wouldn't have dared enter a room where the police were questioning someone —not without knocking first. But not Mariner. He simply barged in, never giving it a second thought. People of power acted that way, Joanna knew. They moved whenever and wherever they wished, and you either moved with them or moved out of their way.

Mariner helped Amanda to her seat and nodded to Joanna. He studied Jake for a moment, then extended his hand. "I don't believe we've met. I'm Dr. Robert Mariner."

"I'm Lieutenant Sinclair from Homicide," Jake said, shaking the doctor's hand.

Mariner squinted his eyes as he sat. "From Homicide? Is there some question about the cause of Alex's death?"

"Not really," Jake said. "We're just trying to tie up some loose ends."

"Such as?" Mariner asked.

"Well, we're a little concerned about the place where Dr. Black shot himself. He put the gun to his temple. According to Dr. Blalock, most doctor-suicides put the gun in their mouths. Less chance of an error that way."

"Ordinarily that's true," Mariner said, his voice now clinical. "But Alex may have remembered a colleague of ours named Joseph Mann."

Amanda sucked air through her teeth, a pained expression on her face.

"Joseph Mann," Mariner went on, "was a research physician at Harvard when we were all on the staff there. He attempted suicide by placing the gun in his mouth and pulling the trigger. The gun must have slipped, because the bullet went straight up and blew out both of his eyes and the front of his brain. He's now a vegetable in some chronic-care facility with tubes in every orifice in his body."

Jake asked, "And Alex Black knew Joseph Mann pretty well, huh?"

"They were roommates in medical school," Amanda said.

Jake nodded. "Well, that would explain why he put the gun to his temple."

Not necessarily, Joanna said to herself, now thinking back to something Amanda had mentioned earlier. She reached for a scratchpad on the table and scribbled down the word *Hunter.*

Mariner was shaking his head. "I still don't understand how this could have happened. We knew about Alex's depression and he was under the care of a very fine psychiatrist. What in the world went wrong?"

The phone rang. Mariner reached over and jerked it up. "This is Mariner. Hold all calls." He listened for a moment, then said, "I don't give a damn who it is. Hold all calls." He put the phone down and turned back to Jake and Joanna. "Alex was seeing a psychiatrist two to three times a week. He was being carefully monitored. His depression was supposedly under control."

Joanna said, "Amanda mentioned that Alex might not have been taking his medication regularly."

Mariner looked at Amanda. "Is that right?"

Amanda nodded.

"So bright and so stupid at the same time," Mariner said disgustedly.

Jake studied Mariner, thinking that his response to Alex's death was more one of anger than sadness. "Were you and Alex Black close friends?"

"Not even good friends," Mariner said promptly. He explained how he had met Alex in Boston and offered him the position as director of research and development for the newly formed HMO, which would later be called Health First. Their relationship was that of employer to employee. "Like most brilliant people, Alex disliked the idea of having a boss, of having someone who could dictate to him."

"And did you dictate to him?" Jake asked.

"I tried, but Alex usually did exactly what he wanted to do."

"You allowed that, huh?" Jake asked, not believing it.

"Of course. Alex was a genius and far and away the most important person at Health First." Mariner watched Amanda light a cigarette and waved a hand to push away the smoke coming toward him. "You see, Alex Black was an idea man. Most researchers get an original idea maybe once every month or so. Alex could get a dozen in a day. And every one of them could end up having a practical use. He was very, very important to us. If one wanted to destroy Health First, one would start by destroying Alex Black."

"Can you think of anyone who would want to destroy Health First?" Jake asked.

"Most of the doctors, hospitals and insurance companies in America, for starters." Mariner forced a weak laugh. "They're so naive. They still think they can block the reform of medicine. They think the train is still at the station."

"And it's not, huh?"

"Not only has the train left the station, Lieutenant, it's now traveling at full speed. The old days of medicine are over, gone forever. There are exciting days ahead."

Not for Alex Black, Jake thought. He had a few more questions he wanted to ask Amanda Black about Alex's private life, but decided to do it later, when Mariner wasn't around. He pushed his chair back and stood. "We appreciate your time. Thanks for helping us clear up matters."

"Will an autopsy be done?" Mariner asked.

"Oh, yes," Joanna said firmly.

"We would like to be informed of the findings."

"Of course."

Jake and Joanna took the elevator down to the lobby and walked out into a dreary day. The sky was now packed with dark clouds, the air heavy and still.

"What do you think?" Jake asked.

"About what?" Joanna said.

"Alex Black's death. It's looking more and more like suicide, isn't it?"

"Not really."

"Well, I think he had a pretty damn good reason for not putting that gun in his mouth."

"You're forgetting something, Jake," she said, taking his arm as they walked. "Alex Black had once been a hunter. He knew all about rifles and shotguns. If he wanted to be really sure, all he had to do was put a twelve-gauge shotgun in his mouth and pull the trigger."

"It's kind of hard to sneak a shotgun into a medical office," Jake said. "I mean, hell, he'd want to keep it concealed."

"Easy as pie. All he had to do was put it in a box."

Jake nodded hesitantly, still not convinced.

"And he killed himself in the receptionist's area," Joanna went on. "That just doesn't work. It doesn't fit. There are too many things off the mark here, Jake."

They came to a street vendor selling thick hot pretzels and coffee. The aroma was delicious, causing their mouths to water. Jake guided Joanna over and he bought two orders. The pretzels were so hot they had to hold them with napkins. They leaned against Jake's car as they ate.

Joanna slowly chewed on her food, thinking back to other times when she and Jake had eaten hot pretzels. Usually on a park bench, sometimes on the sidewalk. It was always great fun and they seemed so close. And now it felt so ordinary. Something between them was missing. "What do you think about Amanda and Mariner? Do you think they're lovers?"

"Maybe," Jake said carefully. "They're more than just good friends, I'll tell you that."

Joanna bit off a large piece of pretzel and chewed on it for a while. "I think Amanda is holding back. She's not telling us all she knows about Alex."

"You picked that up, huh?"

"Yeah," Joanna said, washing down the pretzel with coffee. She thought she felt a drop of rain and held out her hand, feeling for more. "I wonder what it is about Alex that Amanda is holding back."

Jake shrugged. "We're going to have to do some digging to find out the answer to that one."

"Where should we start?"

"At either country and western bars or tattoo shops. Take your pick."

Joanna hesitated as she wiped her hands with a napkin. "This is going to be strictly professional. No ifs, ands or buts."

"Strictly professional," he agreed.

"Let's do country and western."

19

"I still can't believe that Alex Black killed himself," Phil Weideman said as he paced around the forensic laboratory. "He just didn't seem to be the type."

"What type is that?" Joanna asked.

"Well, you know, he was never moody or down or depressed."

"Did you see him often?"

"At least once a week. Sometimes more."

"And he seemed fine, huh?"

"Always." Weideman stopped in front of the new replica of the faceless man's head and studied it. The wig was in place, but there were no facial bones attached. "Are all the news reports about Alex's death accurate?"

"They've tended to sensationalize it," Joanna said evasively.

"What a waste," Weideman said sadly. "Not only was he brilliant, but he was also a very nice person. His wife must be devastated by this."

Joanna stared at Weideman briefly, now realizing how little he really knew about Alex Black. "I'm certain she was."

"A waste," Weideman said again.

Emily Ryan looked up from the magnifying device she was using in an attempt to piece together tiny fragments of facial bone. Who the hell cares? she wanted to ask aloud. A nutty researcher blows his brains out and the whole world is supposed to go into mourning? Get real. Emily felt nothing for people who committed suicide. Nothing at all. She'd seen too many young patients die of awful diseases, all of them trying desperately to survive, some going through hellish forms of therapy just for a chance to live a little longer. And this nutty researcher, who probably could have lived to be a hundred, kills himself, blows his head off. Throws his life away. A waste, huh? Emily couldn't have cared less about Alex Black.

"Are we having any luck with those bone fragments?" Weideman asked, glancing at the table, then at Joanna.

"Not much. They've all been crushed." Joanna studied Phil Weideman as he paced. He wasn't wearing his usual surgical garb, but rather a blue blazer, tan slacks, white shirt and pink tie. He looked so handsome he looked like a model for *Esquire.* "Maybe we'll have to concentrate on the maxillary bones."

The maxillary bones were the only intact fragments remaining. The killer hadn't destroyed those pieces because they hadn't been in the laboratory when he broke in. They had been in the Department of Dental Surgery being studied by Dr. Mary Bailey. She had determined that the faceless man had a slight overbite, but little more.

"There's no way anybody is going to put these bits of frontal bone back together again," Emily said gloomily.

"Keep trying," Joanna urged. "Without a forehead we can't reconstruct his face."

Shit, Emily grumbled to herself, and went back to the impossible task.

Joanna walked over to her new computer and punched at the keyboard. An outline of the dead man's head appeared on the screen. The face was featureless with slits for the eyes, nose and mouth. She pushed another key and now the faceless man had hair. She gave him a triangular-shaped face, gray-brown eyes and a slight overbite. Then she added a section of forehead, based on the measurements from detailed photographs taken of the victim's face at autopsy. But it didn't help much. The face was still incomplete and impossible to identify.

Weideman looked over Joanna's shoulder and tried to give the impression he was studying the screen, but he was really watching her. She was wearing her hair loose, down to her shoulders, and as she leaned forward it covered the side of her face, giving her an incredibly sexy look. She had on a silk blouse and a tight tweed skirt. Her waist seemed so small that Weideman was certain he could encircle it with his hands.

He envisioned Joanna sitting on the side of his bed and unbuttoning her silk blouse, slowly, ever so slowly, one button at a time. He felt himself stirring and looked away. Weideman planned to take her out. And soon. Maybe dinner at a small, cozy Italian restaurant. No, no. Don't rush it. Start off with lunch at an outdoor café for an hour or so. That way there would be no pressure. But one way or another they would go out, and one way or another they would end up in bed together. He was sure of that.

"It's no good," Joanna said disgustedly. "We've got no face without a forehead."

"Maybe this will help." Weideman reached into the inside pocket of his blazer and took out a manila envelope. As he handed it to Joanna, their fingers touched and he felt the electricity. And he was certain she did too. To hell with lunch, Weideman thought. We'll have dinner at a quiet, out-of-the-way place. "It's a new program I got from Alex Black. According to the people at Bio-Synthetics, it can make projections of shape and size from very small pieces of facial bone."

Joanna opened the envelope and looked at the program inside. Weideman was standing close to her, too close, and she should have moved away but she didn't. She glanced down at his left hand. No ring. She had heard a rumor that Weideman's marriage was in trouble. She forced her mind back to business. "When did you see Alex last?"

"Last week."

"And he seemed fine, huh?"

Weideman gestured with his hands. "He seemed in good spirits. We talked about the new program he had devised and he told me there was an even better one on the way. But we spent most of the time talking about opera."

Joanna's brow went up. "Alex liked opera?"

"Oh, yeah. And he had tickets for *Tosca* with Placido Domingo. But he was going out of town to some research meeting, so he offered me the tickets."

"Did you take them?"

"Of course. Wouldn't you?"

Joanna sighed loudly. "Placido singing *Tosca.* I know people who would kill for those tickets."

"Well, if you'd like, you could be my guest," Weideman said easily.

Joanna hesitated. *Say no, goddamn it. He's married—separated but still married. Say no.* "I'd like that."

Emily looked up from the magnifying device and smiled broadly. The older generation, she was thinking, so damned uptight about everything. Why not just go out and have steaks and wine and then go home and jump under the sheets? That's where they were going to end up anyway.

Joanna said, "You and Alex must have gotten along well."

"I've known him for a long time."

"How long?"

Weideman thought for a moment. "About ten years. We were all in training together back in Boston. Alex, Amanda and I. They were in internal medicine, I was a resident in surgery."

"Did you know Mariner then?"

"I knew him," Weideman said tightly.

Joanna nodded. "So that's how you came to work for Health First."

Weideman looked at her stonily. "I don't work for Health First. I'm a consultant for Bio-Synthetics. Nothing more."

And Bio-Synthetics is owned by Health First, Joanna said to herself, but she decided not to argue the point. "From the tone of your voice I take it that you're not a big fan of Robert Mariner."

Weideman shrugged indifferently. "He has his views, I have mine."

"There are a lot of people who believe strongly in Robert Mariner."

"Of course," Weideman said with mock sincerity. "He's the Messiah, the Second Coming. He's going to part the waters and show us the way."

"So you don't believe in managed care?"

"Not when it's filled with deceit and false promises."

It was Phil Weideman's deepest conviction that the health care reforms now under way in America were fundamentally flawed and a prescription for disaster. The politicians were selling snake oil and making promises they could never keep. They promised that costs would go down, that quality of care would go up. And that, of course, was absolute nonsense. Anyone with sense knew that the only way to cut costs was to ration or eliminate services. Just like they had done and were still doing in England. They made patients go to general practitioners rather than specialists. They made the elderly wait months for a simple cataract extraction, a year or more for a total hip replacement. They denied hemodialysis to people over sixty, gave cardiac patients a bottle of pills rather than the needed coronary bypass surgery. And that's probably what would happen in America. Costs would come down and within a few years America would be exactly like England, with a mediocre, antiquated health care system.

"Second-rate care," Weideman said, thinking aloud. "Everybody will receive second-rate care."

"Because of HMOs?" Joanna asked.

Weideman nodded firmly. "And because of liberals like Robert Mariner who want to micromanage medicine. These folks are perfectly willing to destroy the best medical system in the world—as long as they can substitute their own system in its place."

Joanna gestured with her head, not convinced. "But the people at Health First get good care, don't they?"

"Ask that of the families of the patients who died as they were being referred here for treatment."

"You don't blame Health First for those deaths, do you?"

"You're goddamned right I do," Weideman said in a tight, angry voice. "They want to take the credit when things go well, then let them take the blame when things go badly."

"I don't think that's fair, Phil. You really don't know anything about those patients."

"I know more than you think," Weideman said promptly. "Lucy O'Hara's mother was once a patient of mine. And Lucy herself was almost a patient."

"How does one almost become a patient?" Joanna asked.

"It's a long story."

"I've got time."

Emily Ryan listened intently, latching on to every word. Like Weideman, she hated the health care reforms now under way in America. They were destroying everything she'd dreamed about and worked so hard for.

"A few years back," Weideman began, "Lucy's mother asked me to take a look at Lucy. In high school, Lucy's nose was broken by a volleyball and she was left with a small but definite depression just below the bridge. It was a straightforward case and I agreed to do it. They came back to see me at least four times with questions and concerns before she was finally put on the OR schedule. Then we had to postpone the surgery because Lucy caught the flu, and when she finally recovered I was preparing to go on vacation. I suggested we do the surgery when I returned. Well, her father called and suggested we do it as soon as possible, and knowing that he had important friends at Memorial, I changed my schedule to accommodate them. A couple of days before the operation, they decided to delay the surgery without giving me any reason. When I returned from my vacation, I had my secretary call Lucy's mother to set a new date for the rhinoplasty. My secretary was told that my services would not be required."

Joanna thought back to the autopsy on Lucy O'Hara. "I don't recall seeing any deformity of Lucy's nose. Somebody must have fixed it."

"There's more to the story," Weideman went on. "Whenever this sort of thing happens, I always call the patient to find out if something went wrong or if something I did upset them. So I called Lucy's mother and she told me that they had joined Health First and that the surgery would be done over there. I wished them well and hung up. The next day Michael O'Hara called Murdock and told him I tried to pressure them into having the surgery done by me at Memorial. And Murdock calls me in and politely reads me the riot act. Of course, it was all crap and I tried to downplay it."

Weideman took a deep breath, keeping his temper under control with effort. "But goddamn it, it hurt. Here I was, trying to be the good doctor, and I get accused of pressuring the patient, of trying to drum up business. Can you imagine how I felt?"

Joanna nodded, feeling for him. "Did Lucy ever get her nose done?"

"Twice."

Joanna looked at Weideman strangely. "Twice."

"Uh-huh. The plastic surgeon who was under contract with Health First is a guy named Anthony Title. He's the liposuction king of Beverly Hills. He botched the first attempt on Lucy's nose. It seems he left it a little bit off center.''

''Jesus.'' Joanna winced.

Weideman's jaw tightened and a vein bulged on his forehead. ''All for money. All so Lucy's family could save a few thousand dollars.''

''I thought Michael O'Hara was a wealthy man.''

''He is. I read somewhere that his income is over a million a year. But the wealthy are funny when it comes to money.'' Weideman shook his head slowly. ''To save a few bucks, he subjected his daughter to a mediocre surgeon.''

''And to the risk of general anesthesia twice,'' Joanna added.

Weideman nodded. ''People!'' he said sourly, as if that explained everything.

''Hey!'' Emily called out. ''I think I've got a match here.''

Joanna went over and studied the two small fragments of bone atop the desk. One piece was shaped like a tiny quarter moon, the other sliver had a rounded surface. Joanna carefully moved the two pieces together. A perfect fit.

''What do you think?'' Emily asked.

''Good job,'' Joanna said and patted Emily's shoulder. ''Now do that a few dozen times and we're back in business.''

''I might be able to accomplish that sometime in the next hundred years or so.''

''I know it's a tough job, but it's our only hope,'' Joanna said. ''Let's put those two fragments in a separate envelope.''

Emily opened the desk drawer and began rummaging through it. Out came a comb, lipstick, Kleenex, then small slips of paper with numbers written on them. She found an envelope and carefully put the matching bone fragments in it.

Joanna's gaze stayed on the slips of paper with numbers written on them. ''What are these?''

''Just pieces of scratch paper,'' Emily replied.

''I know. But what are these numbers?'' Joanna asked quickly, hoping against hope.

Emily picked up a scrap of paper and studied it for a moment. ''Oh, these,'' she said, now recalling. ''Remember when we were measuring those pieces of bone? I did the measurements in triplicate and wrote them down before I determined the average of the three numbers. Then I—'' Emily stopped in mid-sentence, suddenly understanding. "Oh, Jesus! These are the measurements of the frontal bones that were destroyed."

"Take these numbers and give me an average." Joanna walked over to the computer and waited patiently for Emily to average the numbers. Emily did the calculations, wrote down the averages and handed them over.

Joanna punched the information into the computer and waited. A figure of a bone fragment appeared on the screen. She punched in another set of commands and the computer placed the fragment of bone in the left upper forehead of the face on the screen. "How many scraps of paper do you have with numbers written on them?"

Emily emptied the drawer and quickly sorted through the mess. Carefully she picked out all of the scraps of paper and studied each one. "I've got six slips of—no, check that. Here's another scrap hiding in the back of the drawer. I've got all seven."

"We're back in business," Joanna said, rubbing her hands together. "We're going to give our man a forehead after all."

Weideman said, "You can use the new program to reconstruct the forehead. It'll work even better than the old one."

"Will do."

"And don't forget to lock it up at night. That program is very, very valuable."

Joanna pointed to a big framed watercolor on the wall. "It'll go in the wall safe every night before I leave."

"Good." Weideman glanced down at his watch. "I've got to run. I've got a rhinoplasty in thirty minutes."

Weideman waved as he left the laboratory and hurried down the corridor. Before he went to the OR he had to make an important phone call. And he had to instruct his secretary to beat the bushes and come up with two good tickets to *Tosca.*

Weideman grinned broadly, now thinking about the nurse he was sleeping with, the one who loved opera and happened to mention that Joanna was a real opera buff.

At the elevator, Weideman almost bumped into a very attractive secretary. She had long blond hair and deep brown eyes. She stared at him for a moment, then smiled.

Weideman smiled back. Women were so easy, he thought, so damn easy. Even the bright ones, like Joanna Blalock.

20

The Boot 'N Scoot in Santa Monica was not what Joanna had expected. She had anticipated seeing rough cowboys, cheap women and sawdust on the floor. Instead she saw trim, good-looking men wearing jeans and boots and large silver buckles. And young, attractive women with cowgirl boots and short skirts and bodies that wouldn't stop.

"I think we should have worn our hats and jeans," Joanna said.

"Not really," Jake told her. "This is all camouflage. They're just regular folks who have regular jobs in the real world."

Jake took her hand and led the way in. They had to walk sideways to wedge through the crowded nightclub. To her left Joanna saw pool tables and a small bar used mostly by the waitresses. On the right was a large hardwood dance floor filled with people dancing to music that came from a small disc jockey's booth. And beyond that was a huge oval-shaped bar where people were packed in three deep.

They passed a giant bay window that overlooked the street, then came to a string of small tables. One of the tables was empty.

"Sit here a minute," Jake said. "I'll be right back."

Joanna watched Jake walk over to a big, broad-shouldered man wearing jeans and a cowboy shirt with a sheriff's badge pinned to it. Her gaze drifted to the dance floor, where couples were doing the two-step to a song that kept repeating the phrase "I'm up to my ears in tears." At first glance, the dance seemed difficult, with complicated twists and turns and spins. But Joanna could see that there was only one basic step to the dance. Right foot back, then left foot back, then both together. One. Two. One-two. Easy. She tried it standing in place, keeping rhythm with the music. One. Two. One-two. One. Two. One-two. She felt a hand on her shoulder and turned.

A young, handsome cowboy smiled down at her. "Want to dance?"

"I—I don't know how," Joanna said, now studying his eyes. They were deep blue, like Phil Weideman's, and they had the same hint of mischief in them.

"I'll teach you."

"I'm here with someone."

"Would he mind?"

"Yes, I think so."

"Well, maybe another time."

Joanna gave him a big smile. "I'd like that."

She kept her eyes on him as he walked away. Big and tall and good-looking. And young. Late twenties at the most. At least ten years younger than she was. She loved it when she attracted younger men. Joanna knew that it was just stupid female vanity, but it still felt great. Nearby, the young cowboy found a cute blond partner and headed for the dance floor. He looked over his shoulder at Joanna and gave her a big wink and an even bigger smile.

Joanna smiled back, thinking that the cowboy's mannerisms also reminded her of Phil Weideman. She wondered how Phil would look in a cowboy outfit with boots and buckle and hat. Probably sexy as hell.

"You make friends fast, don't you?" Jake asked, coming up to her side.

"I sure do," Joanna said, her eyes still on the cowboy.

"He's kind of young for you, isn't he?" Jake teased.

"Not really. We're just about right for each other."

"Then why did he leave so fast?"

"You scared him away."

Jake grinned. "Did you tell him I was your date?"

Joanna grinned back. "No, I told him you were my father."

"Jesus." Jake groaned, wondering if she was just kidding. Hell, he didn't look that old. Or did he?

Joanna pointed to the broad-shouldered man wearing a sheriff's badge. "Who was that fellow you were talking to?"

"The bouncer. I needed to know which bartenders worked the most frequently over the past six months or so."

"Did you find out which?"

"Sure did, partner."

Jake took her arm and guided her through the crowd. They squeezed their way between other couples until they reached the bar. A young, broad-shouldered bartender with blond locks covering his ears and neck was feverishly mixing drinks. His cowboy hat was tilted back on his head.

The bartender glanced over at Jake and Joanna. "What will you have, folks?"

"Are you Johnnie?" Jake asked.

"I must be." Johnnie grinned. "That's what the badge on my chest says."

"Give us a couple of Bud Lights," Jake said, handing over a ten-dollar bill. "I'm also going to need some information."

"Like what?" Johnnie produced the beers and snatched up the ten in one quick move.

"Like, do you know this guy?" Jake took out a snapshot of Alex Black.

Johnnie studied the picture at length. "He looks a lot different wearing a coat and tie."

"Hey, Johnnie!" a voice down the bar yelled out. "We need a Coors and a Miller's Genuine and a couple of hooters."

"Be right back," Johnnie said, reaching into the cooler for the beers.

Joanna sipped her beer and scanned the bar, focusing in on the faces. Like everything else in life, they all looked better at a distance. Directly across from her were two old men, in their late sixties at least, hunched over their drinks with expressions on their faces that looked as if they were waiting for the world to come to an end. Next to them was a woman who seemed to be aging right before Joanna's eyes. The woman's hair was dyed pitch-black to cover all the gray and her face was falling apart and sagging everywhere and the excessive makeup she wore to cover the damage only made it seem more obvious. Joanna wondered if the bar was the woman's only social outlet and if every night the woman went home alone to some dreary apartment where she had a cat and a TV set to keep her company.

The bartender returned and Jake asked, "So you knew him, huh?"

"Not really," Johnnie said. "I saw him in here a lot, but we never talked. He was kind of a loner, kept to himself."

"Did he dance?" Joanna asked.

Johnnie thought for a moment. "Some, I guess. Usually with the older women."

Joanna looked across the bar at the woman with the badly sagging features. Now she was laughing and it made her face seem even more wrinkled. "You get quite an age range in here, don't you?"

Johnnie nodded. "Everything between twenty-one and death."

Jake flicked at the snapshot of Alex Black with an index finger. "So he was a loner for the most part."

"Yeah," Johnnie said.

"Did he talk with anyone?" Jake asked.

"He didn't have any friends in here," Johnnie said. "You know, nobody who gave a damn about him. But he used to talk some with Stacey and Glen."

"Are they here?"

Johnnie stood on his tiptoes and looked over the crowd. "Yeah, there they are. They're coming off the dance floor now." Johnnie waved to the couple and motioned them over.

"What's up?" Glen asked.

"These people are looking for that doctor guy you two used to talk with," Johnnie said.

Jake held out the snapshot and Stacey snatched it. She studied it briefly and made a face. "He's kind of freaky."

"How do you mean?"

"He was a control freak," Stacey said without hesitation. "He needed to be in control, to be smarter than you. The first time I met him he told me that I was going to be intimidated by his brains."

"Were you?" Joanna asked.

"Hell, no!" Stacey picked up her beer from the bar and took

a long swallow. "I graduated from Stanford with honors and I'm a second-year law student at UCLA. You don't get where I am by being stupid."

"Did you tell him that?" Joanna asked.

"Sure did."

"And what was his response to that?"

"Suddenly it became a contest to see who was brighter."

"Who won?"

"It was a draw," Stacey said. "I didn't know much about medicine and he knew even less about the law."

Joanna couldn't help but like the young law student. She was obviously bright and open and pretty. Very, very pretty with black hair, flawless skin and pale blue eyes. "Did you ever dance with him?"

"Once," Stacey said. "He wasn't a very good dancer, although he thought he was."

"So he never tried to hit on you, huh?" Joanna asked.

Stacey shook her head. "I'm usually here with Glen and I think old Alex was intimidated by Glen."

Joanna turned to Glen. He was tall and slender with light brown hair and deep brown eyes. "What was it about you that bothered Alex?"

"The fact that I was a doctor," Glen said, his accent soft and southern with a hint of Bostonian. "He didn't seem to like that very much."

"What he really didn't like was when I told him that Glen was a professor of medicine and had published over a hundred and fifty scientific manuscripts," Stacey interjected. "That bothered old Alex."

"What's your area of research?" Joanna asked.

"The immune mechanisms in rheumatoid arthritis," Glen said easily.

"Which research group are you with?"

"I'm in Paulson's unit."

Joanna nodded knowingly. Paulson's group was based at a nearby university. It was probably the best division of rheumatology in the world. All of the staff were excellent clinicians and even better researchers. Turning back to Stacey, Joanna asked, "Did you ever see Alex dance with other women?"

Stacey pondered the question. "I think he danced some with the Chief."

"Who is she?"

Stacey pointed out to the dance floor to a tall, dark-complected woman with very sharp features.

"Is she American Indian?"

"Half Cherokee."

"Did they dance together a lot?" Joanna asked.

"I guess," Stacey said with a shrug. "I didn't keep score."

"Did she ever leave the club with him?"

"A couple of times," Stacey said. "Maybe more. Like I said, I didn't keep score."

The disc jockey's voice come over the loudspeaker. "Okay, folks, let's rise and shine. We're going to do a Slapping Leather and a Walking Wazzy."

Stacey took Glen's arm. "Let's go kick it out."

"I'm ready, darlin'," Glen said and quickly finished his beer.

Stacey looked over at Jake and Joanna. "Want to do a little line dancing?"

"Maybe later," Jake said, now closer to Joanna, their arms touching.

"Yes, maybe later," Joanna said and moved her arm away.

The dance floor became crowded and disorganized with people wandering about and chatting with one another. Then, as if by some silent command, the dancers lined up in long, even rows. The music started, loud and snappy, and the dancers moved in perfect rhythm, as if they'd rehearsed the dance a hundred times. Stacey was in the front row with Glen on one side and the handsome cowboy who had asked Joanna to dance on the other.

"It looks like real fun," Joanna said.

"It is," Jake said, his gaze still on Stacey, who had a body most women would kill for.

"Do you know how to do these dances?"

"Some of them."

"How did you learn?"

"I used to go to a club out in the valley," Jake said, his mind flashing back to Eleni and to the times when she'd dress up in her cowgirl outfit and they'd go drink beer and hoot and holler with everyone else. She had been such a remarkable woman, he thought, missing her more now than ever and knowing that a part of him would always love her. With effort he pushed her image out of his mind. "What do you think about our good buddy, Alex Black?"

"It doesn't sound as if he was very popular."

"Are you saying he was a horse's ass socially?"

"Something like that."

They pushed their way through the crowd at the bar and walked over to the woman called the Chief. She was standing by the railing next to the disc jockey's booth. Beside her was a short, heavily muscled man with a thick mustache, old acne scars, and long hair held together in a ponytail. His hair looked greasy, as if it hadn't been washed for weeks.

"I need a few minutes of your time," Jake said to the woman. He showed her the snapshot of Alex Black. "Do you know this man?"

The woman studied the photo briefly. "Maybe."

"Yes or no?"

"I danced with him some," she said.

"Do you remember his name?"

"Alex. I'm not sure about his last name."

"When did you see him last?"

"Let's see now," she said, rolling her eyes upward in thought. "I saw him about—"

The stocky man next to her nudged her with an elbow and gave her a hard stare.

"I can talk if I want to," she said. "I can talk about—" She fell silent as the man elbowed her again, harder this time.

Jake glared down at the man with the pockmarked face. "Have you got a problem?"

"Yes," the man hissed. "Have you?"

"Yes," Jake hissed back. "It's the stupid piece of shit standing in front of me."

It took a moment for the man to realize that Jake was a cop. Initially he'd thought Jake was a private investigator or just some asshole asking questions. But Jake was a cop—the man was now certain of it—and he hated Jake because of it. "She doesn't have to answer your questions."

"Yeah, she does," Jake said hoarsely and flashed his badge. "Now, we can do it here or we can go down to the station. Take your pick."

"I'll do it here," the woman said promptly.

Jake said to the man with the ponytail, "If you touch her again with your elbow, I'm going to get upset. I might even get pissed."

The man hesitated for a moment, then took a quick step away from the woman.

"Did you dance with Alex a lot?" Jake asked the Chief.

"Yeah. A lot."

"You ever leave the club with him?"

"No. Never."

Jake took out a Greek cigarette and lit it, slowly inhaling and exhaling but never taking his eyes off the woman. "You lie to me again and I'm going to run your ass in for interfering with the investigation of a murder case."

The Chief's eyes bulged and she swallowed hard. "Who got murdered?"

"Just answer the question."

The Chief hesitated, caught in a dilemma, not wanting to lie to the cop but frightened of telling the truth in front of her boyfriend. "He walked me to my car a couple of times," she admitted.

"That's not what I heard."

The Chief glanced quickly at her boyfriend, then down at the floor. "He took me to a fast-food place a couple of blocks from here. We ate and talked. That's all we did."

"Right." Jake studied the woman at length, watching her squirm. She was a sensuous woman with dark skin and very high-set cheekbones. Her cowgirl hat was pulled down over her forehead almost to the level of her very, very dark eyes. She had a heavy layer of makeup on, particularly around her eyes. In the poor light, Jake thought he saw a bruise on her upper cheek. But all in all she was attractive as hell, and he wondered why she was screwing the ugly bastard next to her. Women! Try to figure them and you'll go crazy. "What did you and Alex Black talk about?"

"His wife, who he didn't like and who treated him like shit," she said.

"Did you go to his place?" Jake asked.

"Never," she said firmly. "And that's the truth. I swear it."

Jake knew instantly that she was lying. The "I swear it" was a sure sign. "He said you did."

"Then he's lying," the Chief said, and suddenly her mouth dropped open. "Is he using me as an alibi? Is that what that little schmuck is doing?"

Jake just looked at her, said nothing.

"It's my word against his."

"Yeah," Jake said, drawing deeply on his cigarette. "Did you ever see his tattoo?"

"I never saw him with his clothes off," the Chief said, and immediately realized her mistake.

"How did you know where his tattoo was located?" Jake asked.

"He—ah—he told me about it," the Chief stammered, trying to cover her lie.

The ugly man suddenly became interested. "That little butt-head had a tattoo?"

"That's right," Jake said.

"Was it a good one?" the man asked. "You know, with nice colors and details?"

Jake shrugged. "You know tattoos?"

"Damned right." The man rolled up his sleeve and exposed an intricate tattoo over the deltoid area. It was a screaming eagle, wings spread, landing on a bed of red and blue flowers.

"Nice," Jake said and meant it. "Who did it for you?"

"Old Sam," the man said proudly. "A true master. The last of his kind."

"Where's his shop?"

"He doesn't have one anymore," the man said. "His eyesight is going."

"Too bad," Jake said, knowing that Sam was the person he wanted to speak with. "I'd like to talk to him about a tattoo."

The man shook his head, thinking that Jake wanted to have a tattoo done. "He won't do tattoos anymore. If he can't be perfect, he won't do it."

"I'd still like to talk to him."

"All you've got to do is walk to the other side of the bar." The man pointed to two old men hunched over their drinks. "He's the one that the old woman ain't hanging on to."

Jake and Joanna headed for the other side of the bar. The dancers on the floor were now doing the Walking Wazzy, a fast, high-
kicking dance that moved right to left, then left to right. The
music was so loud that Jake almost had to yell to Joanna to make
himself heard.

"Do you think that Alex and the Chief were banging each
other?" he asked.

Joanna gestured with her head noncommittally. "There was
something strange going on there. If it was sex, then it wasn't sex
in the conventional fashion."

"Kinky maybe?"

"Oh, I'd give it more than a maybe."

"Why?"

"Because I think the Chief and her ugly boyfriend play very
kinky games. I'd guess at S and M if that bruise under her eye is
any indication. She probably likes it rough and demands it. So,
find out what games she and Mr. Ugly play and you'll have a good
idea of what she and Alex did."

Jake smiled. He had missed that, but it all fit together. Mr. Ugly
looked mean as hell, and that was probably what turned the
woman on. And her hat was pulled way down. Too far down. The
hat was probably concealing a bruise or a knot. And then there
was the heavy makeup covering the bruise under her eye. Jake
wondered what games Alex and the Chief had played and whether
Mr. Ugly had also been involved. Maybe they had been a threesome. No, Jake quickly decided, if they had been a threesome, Mr.
Ugly would have known about Alex's tattoo, and he hadn't.

They came to the two old men, now staring down at their
drinks. The old woman moved aside as Jake leaned in next to Sam.

"I hear you do tattoos," Jake said.

"Used to," Sam said, his voice a croak from too many cigarettes
and too much alcohol.

"I need some information."

"Then dial 411." Sam picked up a shot glass and emptied it
with a quick swallow. He chased it with a gulp of beer.

"What are you drinking?"

"Wild Turkey."

Jake motioned to the bartender, who promptly refilled Sam's
shot glass. "I need to know about a tattoo."

"Don't do them anymore," Sam said. "My eyesight's gone to shit. Cataracts, you know."

Joanna said, "That can be corrected surgically."

Sam squinted up at her. "You a doctor?"

"Yes."

"Well, Doc, they did my left eye and fucked it up. I bled after the surgery." Sam shrugged his shoulders resignedly. "It didn't work out."

Jake asked, "Who does tattoos of birds and butterflies with beautiful shades of blue and gold?"

"At least a dozen people," Sam replied.

"With oversized eyes and small feet?" Joanna added.

"Oh, that's Steely Dan's trademark."

Joanna smiled. "Like Steely Dan, the band?"

"Lady, Steely Dan was doing tattoos before the people in that band were born."

"Has Steely Dan got a shop?" Jake asked.

"Yeah. On the walkway down in Venice."

"You wouldn't happen to know where?"

"Across from that goddamn park where all the asshole hippies hang out."

"Thanks," Jake said and signaled to the bartender to pour Sam another round.

"You going to see him, huh?" Sam asked.

"Yeah."

"You'd better hurry."

"Why?"

"Because last I heard, Steely Dan was sick as hell with lung cancer. And that was back three or four months ago."

21

Arnold Kohler stormed into his office and glared at Jake and Joanna. "You just can't come in here unannounced any time you want."

"Sure we can," Jake said and flashed his shield. He studied Kohler for a moment, disliking him instantly.

"What the hell is this all about?" Kohler asked, his eyes darting back and forth between Joanna and Jake.

"It seems you've been writing a lot of prescriptions for controlled drugs," Jake said.

"An awful lot," Joanna added, unfolding the computer printout on her lap. "You've prescribed a huge amount of amphetamines and Percodans, haven't you?"

Kohler sat down behind his desk, gathering himself. "I have a lot of patients who need these drugs."

"I'll bet," Jake said sarcastically.

"There were definite medical indications for those drugs." Kohler took out a handkerchief and mopped his brow.

"Like what?" Joanna asked quickly.

"Amphetamines for weight loss and narcolepsy, Percodan for chronic pain syndromes."

Joanna looked down at the computer printout. At the top of the page was Kohler's California medical license number and his DEA number. She had obtained the numbers from the prescription slip she'd taken from Kohler's office and had given them to

Jake to check out. "What about Karen Butler? Why so much amphetamines for her? She wasn't obese and she didn't have narcolepsy."

"I used the drug to pick up her spirits," Kohler said at once. "She was quite depressed over her illness."

"Depression is not an indication for amphetamines and you know it," Joanna snapped. "And you prescribed so much of it you had to be aware that she was addicted."

Kohler gestured with his hands and said nothing, wondering if he should call his lawyer. No, better not. That would be like an admission of guilt. And besides, all they had on him was overprescribed drugs. That wasn't even a felony.

"Why did you lie to me before when I asked about the source of Karen Butler's drugs?"

Kohler gestured again. "It wasn't intentional. It just slipped my mind."

Bullshit, Joanna thought, detesting Kohler and his lies.

"And then there's this fellow Rimer." Jake got to his feet and walked over to the withered plant in the corner. He tested the dirt with his finger. It was dry as sawdust. "This guy must have been chewing amphetamines like they were candy."

"He has severe narcolepsy," Kohler said evenly, but sweat was pouring down his back.

Jake looked over to Joanna. "What the hell is this narcolepsy he's talking about?"

"It's a disorder in which the patient keeps falling asleep during the day," Joanna told him.

"Is it treated with big doses of amphetamines?"

"Sometimes," Joanna had to admit, thinking that Kohler was a bad doctor but he wasn't stupid. He was the type who caused a lot of harm but somehow always managed to cover it up. "But these doses would be huge even for severe narcolepsy."

Jake went over to the sink and turned on the faucet, filling up a large glass. He came back to the potted plant, sprinkled its leaves and poured the rest of the water into the soil. "Dr. Kohler, buzz your nurse and have her bring in Mr. Rimer's chart."

Kohler stiffened for a moment, but quickly recovered. "His medical records are confidential."

"I can get a search warrant," Jake said easily. "And we'll just sit here and wait for it to arrive."

Kohler exhaled heavily. "He's not a patient at Health First."

Jake's face hardened. "Then who the hell is he?"

"He was a patient of mine when I was in private practice some years ago," Kohler explained. "I've continued to write his prescriptions for him."

"So where's his old chart?"

"In storage somewhere."

"Well, you'd better dig it out, because in the very near future the DEA boys are going to pay you a visit. And they're going to go through everything you've got with a fine-tooth comb."

"I've done nothing wrong."

"We'll see," Jake said, sensing that he'd only scratched the surface of Dr. Arnold Kohler.

There was a long, awkward silence. No one moved. Overhead the air-conditioning system noisily went on.

Kohler pushed his chair back. "I think I've answered enough of your questions."

"For now," Jake said. "But we'll be back."

Kohler got to his feet. "Well, the next time you barge in here, I'm going to call a lawyer."

"I don't blame you," Jake said as he helped Joanna from her chair. "And if I were you I'd get a real good one."

Kohler watched them leave, then dropped back down into his chair. His legs began to shake, dancing off the floor. He had to grab them to make them stop.

22

Karl Rimer followed the detective and the doctor at a distance of thirty yards. It was eight-thirty p.m. and a dense fog was rolling onto the Venice boardwalk, rapidly reducing the visibility. That didn't bother Rimer. He liked the fog. It provided excellent cover.

The couple began walking faster and Rimer increased his pace, moving past some panhandlers and joining a small group of German tourists. He blended in perfectly. Just another face.

A cool breeze came in from the ocean and the fog lifted briefly. Ahead he saw the couple slow down as they passed a string of stores, most of them closed. Rimer slowed, keeping the distance at thirty yards, playing it safe. But he really wasn't worried about being detected. A pro might spot him, but not these two amateurs.

Rimer reached for two amphetamine pills and chewed them quickly before swallowing. He kept his eyes on the detective, watching his gait and movements. The cop was big—really big—and powerfully built. Rimer could easily envision the detective in-timidating Kohler and scaring the shit out of him. A few hours earlier Rimer had visited Kohler's office to pick up a new prescrip-tion and had found Kohler coming apart at the seams. The doc-tor's hands had been shaking so much he could barely hold a pen to write. And he was popping Valium pills like they were aspirin. Stupid. So stupid. All Kohler had to do was stonewall. If they really had anything on him they would have arrested him.

Rimer watched the detective take Joanna Blalock's arm and he knew they were about to turn and come back toward him. Quickly he ducked into a T-shirt shop. It was more of a shed than a shop, with a roof but no walls. He still had a clear view of the couple.

"Can I help you?" a young woman with bad teeth asked.

"No, thanks. I'm just looking," Rimer said.

"Those," she said, pointing to a nearby rack, "are on sale."

"Thanks."

Rimer appeared to be examining a T-shirt, but he could still see the street in his peripheral vision. He buried his face in the shirt as the couple passed by. Rimer was having difficulty figuring out their movements. They continued to walk back and forth, slowing as they passed a string of closed stores. At first, Rimer thought the couple might be worried about being followed and were using a delaying technique in an effort to expose the tail. But they kept doing the same thing over and over again. No sudden or random moves, like one would expect from an expert. No, it wasn't a tail they were concerned with. It was something else.

Rimer replaced the T-shirt and went back onto the street. Although the night was cool, he was wearing only a shirt opened at the collar. No coat or tie. He concentrated on the couple again, now thinking back to the evening before, when he'd followed them into the Boot 'N Scoot. A piece-of-shit cowboy bar. Why were they questioning all those people? Rimer asked himself. What did they hope to find? He had memorized the faces of those questioned. He would return to the bar later and find out what the questions had been.

Rimer passed a clogged-up sewer and quickly moved away from the foul odor. It reminded him of the stench of rotting jungle. He took out a bottle of strong cologne and splashed some on his face. The odor of decay subsided, but it didn't go away altogether. It never did.

The goddamn jungle smell stayed with him and he hated it. But damn, he had been good in the jungle. So good that the Agency offered him a job while he was still a LURP. Rimer told them he'd think about it. Maybe later. Later came real soon. Two Marines bullied him in a bar in Saigon. Rimer tried to walk away. They wouldn't let him. He killed both of them with a chair. Rimer was arrested and faced a court-martial for murder. That's when the Agency offered him the deal. Instead of having him tried and almost surely sent to jail, they would arrange to have him reported as killed in action. They would give him a new name, but he would have no identity. Karl Rimer was a fictitious name that would exist only as long as Rimer lived. Rimer didn't give a shit about losing his identity. He had no family, no home to go back to. He agreed to become an operative for the Agency. Without their knowledge or consent he did contracts on the side.

Up ahead he saw the couple suddenly turn and walk toward one of the shops. Rimer picked up his pace, hurrying now. He almost bumped into a young woman walking a big Doberman. He nodded at her, his eyes still on the shop. Then the neon sign above the store went on. STEELY DAN'S TATTOO PARLOR. Suddenly, all of the pieces fell into place. Goddamn it! Rimer cursed silently, remembering the tattoo of the butterfly on the dead man's ass. They're tracking the faceless man by his tattoo. That must be it. Goddamn it!

Joanna looked over her shoulder as she entered the tattoo shop. She saw a tall, middle-aged man passing by. He had no coat on, his shirt opened despite the chilly night.

"Did you see something?" Jake asked.

"Just a stupid tourist who's going to catch pneumonia," Joanna said.

A bell tinkled as Jake closed the door. The shop was tiny and stank from stale cigarette smoke. It was divided into a front and back by a tattered curtain. An emaciated man, small and grizzled, looked up from his stool.

"What can I do for you?" he asked.

"Are you Steely Dan?" Jake asked.

"That's right." Steely studied them suspiciously. They weren't looking for tattoos, he was damn sure of that. The big guy had cop written all over him. "You a cop?"

"Yeah," Jake said. "Does that bother you?"

"Naw." Steely grinned and exposed a nearly toothless mouth. "Just as long as you're not one of those assholes from the Health Department that come to check on my needles."

"They give you a hard time, huh?" Jake asked.

"They're full of shit." Steely reached for a pack of unfiltered cigarettes and lit one. He inhaled deeply, his eyes on Joanna. "Are you a cop too?"

"No," she said, now seeing the distended veins in his neck and the deep-red color in his face. "I'm with the coroner's office."

Steely took another drag on his cigarette and started coughing. A deep, raspy cough. Phlegm rattled in his chest, but he couldn't get it up. His face turned purple. He held up a hand to excuse himself and hurried behind the curtain.

Jake heard water running out of a faucet, the man still coughing his guts out. "Jesus! Did you see the color of his face?" he asked quietly.

"That's caused by a superior vena cava syndrome," Joanna told him. "The tumor in his lungs is blocking off the big veins that carry blood from his head to his heart. That's why his face is so red."

Jake shook his head. "And he's still smoking."

"It doesn't matter now," Joanna said matter-of-factly. "He's a dead man."

"I've got to stop smoking."

"You'd damn well better or you could end up just like Steely."

The sound of running water stopped. A moment later, the curtain parted and Steely came back to his stool and sat down heavily. He took a few deep breaths, as if he was checking his airway, then lit another cigarette. He didn't cough this time. "Now, what can I do for you folks?"

Jake said, "Sam told us that you were the only one that did birds and butterflies in blue and gold with little feet and big eyes."

Steely nodded. "How's Sam?"

"Not so good," Jake told him. "His eyesight is going."

"I heard, I heard," Steely said sadly.

"How many of those birds and butterflies have you done?"

"Hundreds and hundreds. Maybe a thousand."

Shit, Jake grumbled to himself. He had hoped the number would be smaller. "That many, huh?"

"It's what I'm known for," Steely said.

Joanna asked, "Did you do all of them in blue and that lovely gold?"

Steely smiled. "You like that gold, huh?"

"It's beautiful," Joanna said sincerely.

"A Chinaman showed me how to make that color," Steely said,

puffing away on his cigarette. "Hell, those Chinamen are the best when it comes to colors. The best."

Jake's eyes narrowed. "Are you saying there's a Chinese man in Los Angeles who also does butterflies and birds?"

"No, no." Steely waved off the question. "He was in Hong Kong. After the war, around 1946, I joined the Merchant Marines and sailed the China Sea. We ran into a bitch of a typhoon, meaner than hell with winds up to a hundred and fifty knots." Steely leaned back, eyes half closed, remembering, almost reliving it. "Waves so big they came over the hull and onto the deck. Jesus Christ! I thought we were dead. But somehow we limped into Hong Kong Harbor and we had to stay for four months while they fixed the ship. That's when I learned to do tattoos and colors."

"Are all your butterflies and birds done with the gold?" Joanna asked.

"Naw," Steely said. "Only about a hundred or so. Gold is tough to work with and takes a lot more time. I got to charge more for it."

Jake took out the snapshot of Alex Black and showed it to Steely Dan. "Do you remember doing him?"

Steely squinted at the photo, his nose almost up against it. "Let me get my glasses," he said and disappeared behind the curtain.

Jake glanced around the shop, now seeing the framed photographs on the wall. He studied a picture of two young men in their World War II sailor uniforms. Smiling, happy. It was a photo of Sam and Steely Dan. It had to go back fifty years. Another picture showed Steely sitting in a rickshaw, a beautiful oriental woman next to him. An inscription read "HONG KONG 1948."

Steely returned with his reading glasses. "Let's see that snapshot again." He looked at it briefly and handed it back to Jake. "Yeah, I did him. So what?"

"Do you remember his name?" Jake asked.

"No."

"Do you take credit cards or give receipts?"

"No."

"What does the IRS say?"

"Fuck 'em," Steely said, unconcerned. "I pay enough taxes."

"How long ago did you do this guy's tattoo?" Jake asked.

"About six or seven months ago."

"And where did you put the tattoo?"

"On his ass," Steely said promptly. "You can tell social class by where the tattoo is, you know. Working people put them on their arms and chests. The upper class likes them to be hidden, like on their ass."

Jake decided to see just how good the old man's memory really was. "So you put a butterfly on his ass?"

"Nope. I gave him a bird. I put the butterfly on his boyfriend's ass."

Joanna's jaw dropped. "His boyfriend?"

Steely grinned, enjoying the startled looks on their faces. "That's right, lady."

"Are you sure?"

Steely puffed on his cigarette. "You didn't know, huh?"

"Are you sure he was gay?" Joanna asked again.

"Gay!" Steely said the word derisively and forced a laugh. "The goddamn words they come up with today. Of course they were gay, or queer or whatever word you want to use."

Jake had his notepad out. "Do you remember what his friend looked like?"

Steely shrugged. "Tall, sandy brown hair. Like a surfer, you know. Maybe thirty years old or so."

"Can you describe his facial features?"

Steely thought for a moment. "No, not really. I spent most of the time looking at his ass."

"You've got to do better than that," Jake pushed.

"I ain't got to do anything except smoke cigarettes and die of lung cancer."

"Shit," Jake said disgustedly and closed his notepad. "Do you think they lived around here?"

"Probably. But I can't be sure." Steely puffed on his cigarette and stifled a cough. "I saw them a couple of times on the boardwalk, once over at the big convenience store on Main next to the gas station."

"They could have been visiting."

"Could have," Steely agreed.

"But you don't think so."

"Hell, I don't know," Steely said, now tiring of the conversation. "But they had suntans and looked like they spent time on the beach, particularly the one who got the butterfly."

Jake took out a card and handed it to Steely. "If you see either of the two again, call this number night or day."

Jake and Joanna walked out into the chilly night air. The fog was thick now, blurring the streetlights. All of the tourists and panhandlers were gone.

Joanna said, "I don't understand why you asked Steely to be on the lookout for two dead men."

"Alex Black is dead, but his companion may not be."

Joanna looked at him strangely. "His companion is the guy with no face."

"Maybe, maybe not."

"But everything fits," she argued. "The faceless man was tall, in his thirties, with sandy brown hair and a tattoo of a butterfly on his butt."

"You could probably find a dozen guys with that description."

"Probably," Joanna conceded, "but deep down you know I'm right, don't you?"

"Yeah. But we need proof, solid proof."

"So what do we do next?"

Jake lit a cigarette and blew smoke into the night air. "We find out where the happy couple lived."

23

Lou Farelli was having no luck tracking down Alex Black and his companion. So far he'd covered a ten-square-block area, beginning at the convenience store where Steely Dan had seen the pair a few times. Nobody there remembered anything or anybody. Nor did the people at the gas station, supermarket, hardware store, ice cream parlor, restaurant, cleaners, hairdressers, or video shop. A blank. Nobody remembered seeing Alex Black.

Farelli was leaning against his car, watching the tourists walk down Main Street in Venice. It was a warm, muggy day and most of the people were dressed in T-shirts, tank tops and shorts. They looked so seedy to Farelli, just like the beachside community itself. He remembered back twenty years to a time when Venice had been a pleasant place to bring the family on the weekend. Now it was congested and filled with crime and gangs. It was turning into a piece of shit, and although there were some nice stores and restaurants on the main street, a block away the town resembled a ghetto.

Farelli heard skates on the sidewalk and turned. He saw a young kid on roller blades zooming toward him.

"Why the hell aren't you in school?" Farelli yelled at him.

"Because school ain't fun and this is, asshole!" The roller-blader gave Farelli the finger as he whizzed by.

"Our future leaders," Farelli grumbled to himself. He pushed away from his car and headed across the street to the supermarket.

He'd get an ice-cold Coke and start again. This time around he'd do his tracking off the main thoroughfare. There were still plenty of smaller shops and stores and markets to check out. Too many, he thought, still not convinced that Alex Black and his pal had lived in Venice. Hell, they could have been visiting or passing through. Or maybe they just shopped here occasionally but lived in a nearby, more affluent city such as Santa Monica or Marina Del Rey. Alex Black had been a doctor and had plenty of money. Why would he live in a shithole like Venice?

Farelli entered the supermarket and opened his coat wide, letting the cool air get to his shirt. A woman nearby smiled at his antics, then saw his holstered weapon. The smile quickly faded from her face. Farelli went to the cold drink section and popped open a Diet Coke. He sipped it absently, wondering if there were any shortcuts he could take. Too bad there wasn't a goddamn gay bar close by. That would have been perfect. And too easy. Life never worked out that way for Farelli.

He went to the express line and noted that the checker had changed since he'd been in the market earlier. She was tall and thin, in her early thirties, with bleached blond hair. The tag on her uniform stated that her name was Sherry.

"Is that all?" Sherry asked.

"Yeah," Farelli said. "I'm on a diet."

"Aren't we all?"

Farelli reached into his coat pocket. "I'm looking for a guy."

Sherry smiled. "Me too. They're in short supply these days."

Farelli showed her the photo of Alex Black and waited while she studied it. "You ever seen him?"

"Are you a cop?"

Farelli nodded. "Well?"

Sherry looked at the photo again. "Yes. He's shopped here before."

"How many times?"

"A lot. At least a dozen times."

A man behind Farelli cleared his throat and said, "I thought this was the express checkout line."

"It's closed," Farelli said hoarsely. "Find another counter."

"It looks open to me," the man said, not budging.

Farelli flashed his shield and the man moved out quickly. Customers in a nearby line also saw the badge and they looked away, but they concentrated, trying to overhear.

Farelli lowered his voice and asked the checker, "Do you usually work days?"

"Almost never," Sherry said. "I go to Santa Monica City College during the day and usually work evenings. But the girl working the express line got sick and they called me in."

"No school today?"

"I'm missing two classes," she said, unhappy about it. "But I need the money."

Farelli put down his Diet Coke and took out his notepad. "What time did he usually come in?"

"Like seven or seven-thirty p.m. Sometimes a little later."

"Was he alone?"

She shook her head. "He was always here with his friend."

"And what did his friend look like?"

Sherry wrinkled her brow, thinking back. "He was tall with light blond hair. Kind of good-looking."

"Did he try to hit on you?"

Sherry looked at him strangely. "Get real."

Farelli grinned. "They were a pair, huh?"

"They weren't the overtly faggy type, but yeah—they danced together."

"You ever get their names?"

"No."

"Know where they live?"

"No."

"Ever see them outside the market?"

"No."

Farelli glanced over to a nearby counter and saw a young mother holding her baby in one arm and pushing a grocery cart with the other. He turned back to Sherry. "How much groceries did they buy?"

Sherry thought for a moment. "A fair amount. At least two bags' worth."

"Not just doughnuts and potato chips?"

"No way. Those guys ate pretty good. Steaks, veal, shrimp, lot of fresh fruit."

"Did somebody help them carry the bags to their car?"

Sherry shrugged. "I'm not sure. Maybe Charlie helped them."

"Can I talk with him?"

Sherry stood on her tiptoes and looked around the counters until she saw a short, well-built young man with brown hair that was crew-cut. She waved him over.

"What can I do for you, beautiful?" Charlie asked.

Sherry said, "Charlie, this is a policeman and he needs some information on one of our customers."

Charlie came to attention. "May I know your name, sir?"

"Sergeant Farelli," Farelli told him.

Charlie nodded formally. "My name is Charles P. Miller. I'm an Explorer."

Farelli nodded back. The Explorers were a group of young men in their late teens and early twenties who were interested in becoming police officers. They wore uniforms, rode with cops in patrol cars, learned what being an officer was really about. They were very serious young men and most ended up becoming good cops.

Farelli showed Charlie the photo. "Have you ever seen this man?"

Charlie studied the photo carefully. "Yes, sir."

"How many times?"

"A half dozen or so. He was always with another man."

"You know their names?"

"No, sir."

"Did you ever carry their groceries to their car?"

"No, sir. They preferred to carry their own groceries. And they usually didn't have a car."

"How do you know that?"

"A couple of times I saw them walk out and down the sidewalk carrying their bags. They didn't go to or through the parking lot."

"Maybe they parked on the street. You know, maybe the parking lot was filled."

"Naw," Charlie said promptly. "There are plenty of parking spaces at seven-thirty at night."

"You know where they live?"

"South of here," Charlie said. "No more than a couple of blocks away."

"How do you know that?"

"Because they walked south when they left here."

"Why only a couple of blocks away?"

Charlie smiled. "Have you ever tried to carry a big bag of groceries more than a few blocks?"

"You've got good eyes," Farelli told the young man. "And an even better memory."

"Thank you, sir."

"Do you ride out of the West L.A. station?"

"No, sir. I ride with Officer Heyward in the Santa Monica Police Department." Charlie hesitated for a moment, then went on. "If you run into Officer Heyward, you might tell him I was of some help to you in your investigation. It'd look good in my file."

"I'll take care of it."

Farelli walked out of the market, thinking that Charles P. Miller was going to make a fine cop someday.

The sun was even brighter now and the day warmer. Farelli walked southward, sipping his Diet Coke and mumbling to himself about the strange string of events that was going to lead him to the place where Alex Black lived. Had Farelli not gotten thirsty he wouldn't have gone back to the supermarket, and had he not gone back to the supermarket he wouldn't have talked to Sherry, the checkout girl, and had he not talked with Sherry he wouldn't have talked with Charles, the bag boy, who turned out to be an Explorer with a damn good set of eyes. Hell, maybe it was all luck, he thought. But that was okay too. He'd take all the luck he could get.

Farelli spotted a mailman on the opposite side of the street and crossed over. "Hey! How are you doing?" Farelli called out.

"Just fine." The mailman was a tall African-American with light skin and prematurely gray hair. "Can I help you with something?"

"Yeah." Farelli took out the snapshot of Alex Black and held it up. "Have you ever seen this guy?"

The mailman nodded. "I saw him a few times. A real cold fish. He was the type that looked right through you and said nothing. Not even a hello."

"You ever deliver mail to him?"

"Nope."

"So you don't know where he lives?"

"I didn't say that." The letterman shifted the large mailbag on his shoulder and pointed to a large white building across the street. "I saw him coming out of the White Sands a few times. I guess he lives there."

"You know his name?"

The mailman shook his head. "Like I said, I never delivered any mail to him."

Farelli crossed the street again and walked up the steps of the White Sands Apartments. It was a white stucco building, two stories, with a center courtyard that had a swimming pool and a leaning palm tree. An old man with wire-rimmed glasses was watering a bed of flowers near the mailboxes.

"Are you the manager?" Farelli asked.

"That's right," the old man said and turned off the hose.

Farelli showed him the snapshot. "Do you know him?"

"Who wants to know?"

Farelli showed the manager his badge. "You know him?"

The manager nodded. "He lives in one-oh-six. His name is Brown."

Farelli smiled to himself. Brown, huh? "I'll bet his first name is Alex."

"That's right."

"And I'll bet he paid his rent with a money order or cash."

"Wrong." The manager grinned. "He used traveler's checks."

"And what did his roommate use?"

"The roommate doesn't pay the rent. Mr. Brown does."

"What does the roommate look like?"

"Tall, light brown hair. Nice-looking fellow. Why?" The manager squinted his eyes suspiciously. "Did they do something wrong?"

Farelli ignored the question. "Where's your phone?"

24

"We'll call you if we need you," Jake told the manager and guided the old man to the door, closing it behind him.

Jake quickly scanned the living room in Alex Black's apartment. It was neat and clean and sparsely furnished. A Naugahyde couch, coffee table, one beanbag chair. On the wall was a framed poster for the movie *Casablanca* with Humphrey Bogart in a trench coat, collar pulled up.

"They didn't spend a lot of time here, did they?" Jake commented.

"It doesn't even look lived in," Joanna said.

They went into a small kitchen that had a range and refrigerator on one side, a tiled counter and sink on the other. The cabinets were empty except for a jar of instant coffee, an open box of tea bags and some bouillon cubes. In the refrigerator were beer, soft drinks and a nearly full bottle of chardonnay. The freezer contained some TV dinners and two rock-hard pork chops.

"They probably just used this place on the weekends," Jake said and walked over to a small dinette table. Atop it was a two-week-old Sunday edition of the *Los Angeles Times* and a letter from the manager informing the tenants that the pool would be emptied while repairs were done. The letter was addressed to Mr. Brown and Mr. Smith.

They walked across the soft carpet and into the bedroom, which seemed larger than the living room. There was a built-in closet, a dresser, a king-size bed, a lamp table and a TV set on a stand.

Jake started with the pillows, patting them down and making sure nothing was concealed in them. He lifted one corner of the mattress and flipped it onto the floor. Nothing. He picked the box spring up, looking beneath it, and dropped it back. Again nothing. Jake moved to the dresser. The top was bare except for a thin layer of dust. Jake saw no fingerprints. He used a handkerchief to open the upper drawer. There were socks and underwear neatly arranged. A pack of condoms, a porno video movie. Beneath the video Jake found a folded letter and opened it. The letterhead read "HIQ SPERM BANK."

"You ever hear of the HIQ Sperm Bank?" Jake asked.

Joanna nodded. "It's a nonprofit group of pseudoscientists who believe that intelligence is genetically transmitted. If you can prove you're a genius or have an IQ above one-forty they'll let you be a sperm donor. And, of course, there are plenty of crazy women who buy that nonsense and can't wait to be impregnated with those sperm."

"Well, now, our lover boys decided to pass their brains on to future generations," Jake said lightly. "And guess what? They used their real names. The sperm donors were Alex Black and Bob Cipro."

Joanna's jaw dropped. "What was that last name?"

"Cipro. C-I-P-R-O. Why?" Jake asked, now seeing the stunned expression on Joanna's face.

"Bob Cipro was a scientist at Health First," she said slowly. "He was director of their research program."

"So?"

"Bob Cipro was killed in a boating accident last month," Joanna said, her mind racing and putting all the pieces in place.

"So what?"

"So plenty." Joanna opened her purse and thumbed through a small black book until she found the number she wanted. She went to the phone, picked it up with a handkerchief and dialed. She was put through immediately to Amanda Black. They spoke briefly and only about Bob Cipro. Alex Black's name was never mentioned. Joanna put the phone down slowly and turned to

Jake. "Something awful is going on. It's brutal and it's murder."

"Whoa!" Jake said, holding his palms up. "You're going too fast for me. Slow down."

Joanna took a deep breath, arranging her thoughts. "Let's go through this point by point."

"Fire away."

"Bob Cipro was Alex Black's lover."

"Right."

"Bob Cipro worked at Health First as a senior scientist. He was killed a month ago in a boating accident. Cipro was an expert kayaker, so good he could kayak in the ocean. They found his boat up on the beach, smashed to pieces, and presumed he'd drowned. They never found his body."

"So?"

"So I think Bob Cipro had a tattoo of a butterfly on his butt, put there by Steely Dan."

Jake's eyes suddenly widened. "Jesus Christ!"

"You got it," Joanna said grimly. "Bob Cipro is the faceless man. Somebody killed him on the beach, then destroyed his face and buried him in the forest. When his damaged boat was found but no body was discovered, everyone assumed that he had been killed accidentally and that his corpse had washed out to sea. The killer cut off Cipro's fingertips just in case the body was found. That way the corpse would never be identified and Cipro's death would continue to be listed as accidental."

"But why?"

Joanna shrugged. "All I know is somebody wanted him dead. Accidentally dead. Just like somebody wanted Alex Black dead and tried to make it look like suicide."

Jake began pacing the floor, head down, concentrating. "You may be right, but we've got one problem. We're not sure that the faceless man is Bob Cipro. And there's no way to prove it."

"Oh, yes, there is."

"How?"

"DNA fingerprinting," Joanna said and held up the letter from HIQ Sperm Bank. "I'll take tissue from the faceless man and match it up against the DNA from Bob Cipro's sperm."

Jake scratched at his ear. "You can do that with tissue from a dead man?"

"It's been done on Egyptian mummies four thousand years old."

"We'll need a court order to get those sperm," Jake said, walking over to the dresser.

"Will that be a problem?"

"Not in a murder case."

Jake emptied the top drawer onto the box spring and sorted through the contents. He found nothing new. He pulled out the lower drawer and rummaged through it. Jockey shorts, T-shirts, socks. A bar of perfumed soap. Jake was about to close the drawer, but instead he removed it from the dresser and emptied it. His gaze went to the back of the drawer. A piece of black tape was stuck to it.

"What the hell is this?" Jake scratched at the tape with a finger, carefully removing it. It was a segment of microfilm attached with Scotch tape. He held the microfilm up to the light, squinting at the tiny images. "It looks like some kind of mechanical design."

Joanna reached into her purse and took out a magnifying glass. While Jake held the film up, she studied it. "It's an X ray of some electrical device. I can see wires and coils and what I think is a battery."

Jake took the magnifying glass and looked at the film. "Yeah, I see what you mean. But what's that white line running down the middle of it?"

Joanna shrugged. "I'm not sure."

"Looks like cement."

"Whatever it is, it's radio-opaque."

"What does that mean?"

"That X rays can't penetrate it."

Jake studied the film again. "You got any idea what this thing is?"

"No. But if you'd like I can show it to the people in Bioengineering at Memorial. They're pretty good with these kinds of devices."

Jake handed her the microfilm and she wrapped it carefully in Kleenex, then placed it in her purse.

Joanna asked, "Do you think this film belonged to Alex or Cipro?"

Jake looked down at the contents of the lower drawer, now

spread out on the box spring. The Jockey shorts had the initials "B.C." stenciled on them near the label. "I'd say it belonged to Cipro."

They heard the door to the apartment open and footsteps stomping across the living room. Farelli walked into the bedroom, shaking his head.

"I just heard the damnedest thing," Farelli said. "You ain't going to believe it."

"Try me," Jake said, still thinking about the film and wondering what it was.

"Well, I just got a call over the car radio," Farelli went on. "Remember when somebody broke into the doc's lab and smashed everything to hell and back? And you told the crime scene boys to see if they could lift some fingerprints from the inside of the closet door?"

"Yeah. I remember," Jake said, ears pricked up.

"Well, they got a damn good set of prints off that door and they ID'd the guy."

"What's his name?"

"Will Patterson."

"Has he got a record?"

"Nope."

"Shit," Jake muttered, now wondering if the prints really belonged to the pro. "Have we got anything on this Will Patterson?"

"Yeah. A military file," Farelli said and started shaking his head again.

"And what does it say?"

"It says he was killed twenty years ago in Vietnam."

25

The moment Joanna walked into her laboratory she knew there was trouble. Simon Murdock was leaning against a benchtop, arms folded across his chest. Next to him was a tall, slender man with chiseled features and carefully groomed gray hair. He was wearing a tweed sport coat and a bow tie. He looked Ivy League.

"Ah, Joanna," Murdock said, pushing away from the benchtop. "I'd like you to meet our new consultant, Dr. David Portman from Harvard. He's here to help us with the Lucy O'Hara case."

"How do you do?" Joanna said formally, trying to keep her voice down.

Portman nodded back. A disinterested half nod.

"Lucy O'Hara's father insisted on an outside consultant," Murdock went on, "and I, of course, agreed. I've asked Dr. Portman to also review the charts of the other two patients who died so mysteriously and he has consented to do so."

Joanna stared at Murdock, detesting him and his underhandedness. He hadn't even given her the courtesy of telling her that an outside consultant was definitely being brought in. She felt her face flushing and looked away.

"He'll need space to work in," Murdock continued, "and I thought your laboratory would be an ideal location."

"Fine," Joanna said curtly. "He can work in the back of the laboratory, near the spectrophotometer."

"Will that be enough space?" Murdock asked Portman.

"For now," Portman said.

Emily Ryan hunched over her desk and played with the bone fragments, hearing every word and feeling bad for Joanna. Murdock was such a bastard and he seemed to go out of his way to put Joanna down. Probably because he couldn't stand to see a woman in a position of authority. He was a real chauvinistic pig, Emily thought, and an asshole to boot.

"If you need more space, just let me know," Murdock said.

Portman took a brief tour around the laboratory, stopping in front of the replica of the faceless man's head. He studied it carefully, then glanced over at the bone fragments on Emily's desk. "Reconstructing a face, huh?"

"That's right," Joanna said.

"Would you like to tell me about it?"

"Not particularly."

"Oh, come on, Joanna, the story is fascinating," Murdock said, and he began to expound on the gruesome details of the case of the faceless man. Portman was all ears, his head constantly moving from the replica to the bone fragments to the computer.

Joanna couldn't believe what she was hearing. Murdock made it sound as if he was intimately involved in the project. He was so superficial, Joanna thought, and wondered if he really believed the bullshit he was now spouting. Probably not, but it sounded good. Murdock was all front and no back, and lies and misinformation never bothered him as long as they served his purpose.

Joanna glanced to the back of the laboratory and decided it would be enough space for Portman, at least to begin with. He could use the microscope room to study the tissue slides, the computer in her office to recall any data he wanted. Her gaze stopped at the door to the storage cabinet and she made a mental note to check and make certain there were adequate supplies in case Portman wanted to do his own experiments. She continued to stare at the door, now thinking about the man who had broken into her laboratory and smashed all the bone fragments, the man who had been killed twenty years ago in Vietnam. Jesus! As if the case wasn't tough enough already. Now there were people returning from the dead.

"Joanna," Murdock said, breaking into her thoughts, "I would like you to sit down with Dr. Portman and go over each case in detail with him. Take as much time as you need."

Joanna shook her head. "I'll provide him with all the charts, records, slides and laboratory data and he can review them by himself."

"I would like *you* to get him started," Murdock insisted.

"Let Emily do it," Joanna said tersely. "She's a good starter. Just show her which button to push."

Joanna stomped out of the room and into the outer laboratory. A metal trash can was in her way and she kicked it with all of her might and sent it flying. It hit the far wall with a loud bang and rattled around on the floor. A startled technician jerked her head around. Joanna hurried past the technician and out into the corridor, cursing under her breath, hating Simon Murdock for belittling and embarrassing her and hating herself for putting up with him.

But no more. Enough was enough. She would begin making plans to leave Memorial and find a position elsewhere. There were a dozen openings across America and any of them were hers for the asking. She had no reservations about leaving Los Angeles. It was a crumbling city, filled with crime and violence, decaying from the inside out. The air was foul, the water contaminated, and that was not to mention the earthquakes, fires and riots. Soon it would be unbearable. But on the other hand, it was one of the murder capitals of the world and a wonderful place for a forensic pathologist. Maybe she should become an independent consultant and open her own office, free from Simon Murdock and Memorial and its bureaucracy. And if Memorial still wanted her services, they could pay her a consultant's fee. The more Joanna thought about the idea, the more she liked it.

She turned down another corridor and came to a door with a sign that read BIO-ENGINEERING LABORATORY. NO ADMITTANCE. Joanna knocked briefly on the door and walked in. There were no laboratory-type workbenches, just tables with sophisticated equipment atop them. Complicated diagrams and mathematical equations were written in chalk on the blackboards that covered most of the walls.

"Over here," a voice called out.

Joanna went to the far corner of the laboratory where Henry Benson sat. He was hunched over a table watching a metal ball suspended on a wire move back and forth like a pendulum. He pushed a button and the ball stopped and remained motionless. He pushed the button again and the ball began to move and make figure eights. "Electromagnetism is wonderful stuff," he said, eyes following the ball.

"I don't understand it," Joanna said.

"Nobody else does either. It's kind of like gravity. We talk a lot about it, but nobody really knows what the hell it is."

Joanna reached into her pocket for an envelope and took out the microfilm. "I want you to tell me what this is."

Benson held the film up to the light and squinted at it, unable to make out the details. "Let's put it up on the screen."

Benson pushed himself up from the chair and ambled across the laboratory. He was a huge man, six four and at least 275 pounds, with an unkempt gray beard and a large belly that lapped over his belt. He had been head of Bioengineering for twenty-two years. In general he didn't care much for the doctors at Memorial, believing them to be mediocre scientists with overblown opinions of themselves. But Joanna Blalock was different. She had a keen mind and was tenacious as hell. He admired these qualities, particularly in women.

He pulled down a screen on the wall, shut off the lights and placed the microfilm on a magnifying projector. The image that flashed on the screen was blurred and Benson carefully focused it. "Oh, yes," he said.

"Do you know what it is?"

"Sure. It's a cardiac pacemaker."

"Are you positive?"

"No doubt about it." He pointed with a pencil. "Here you can see the wires and microchips and here's the battery."

"What about the white line that runs down the center?"

Benson shrugged. "It's not part of a pacemaker, I can tell you that."

"Then what is it?"

Benson stroked his beard, concentrating. "Don't know."

"Maybe a glue of some type," Joanna suggested.

"Why a glue?"

"Let's say the device cracked and someone tried to glue it back together."

"No way. If that represented a crack, then the white line wouldn't be so straight and even. There would be irregular margins."

Joanna threw her hands up. "Why in the world would someone put a radio-opaque material into a pacemaker?"

"I can take a guess, if you'd like."

"I'm listening."

"I suspect it was done as a test. You see, sometimes these devices develop tiny microfractures that you can't pick up, even with an X ray. So you push some radio-opaque dye under pressure into the space and if there's even a little fracture some of the dye leaks out and you can see it."

Joanna stared at the screen. "I don't see any leaks."

"Right. It's intact."

"So your best guess is that someone was looking for a defect, right?"

Benson shrugged again. "That would be my explanation, but remember it's only a guess." He magnified some small print near the bottom of the device. It read "MPI." "This gadget was made by Medical Products and Instruments. You might show it to them and see what they say. I'll bet they can tell you why that dye is in the pacemaker."

Benson returned the microfilm to Joanna, shut off the projector and switched on the lights. He walked with her to the door. "I'm sorry I couldn't be of more help."

"I appreciate your time, Henry."

"Well, all I can say is that the device looks fine."

But it's not, Joanna thought as she left the laboratory. Something was wrong with that pacemaker. Otherwise Bob Cipro wouldn't have hidden the microfilm.

26

"Would you like another martini?" Phil Weideman asked.

"No, thanks. I'm fine," Joanna said.

"Are you absolutely sure?"

"Positive."

Joanna watched Weideman leave the terrace and go over to a mirrored wet bar. He poured a large amount of vodka into a shaker, added ice and gently swirled it.

"You're double sure, huh?" Weideman called out.

"Absolutely."

Joanna was beginning to feel uncomfortable. This was Weideman's third drink within the past hour and he was starting to slur his words and talk too much. She wondered if he was an alcoholic. No, she quickly decided. At least not a full-blown one. Maybe he was just nervous on their first date. Or maybe he was trying to build up his courage.

Joanna walked along the terrace and gazed out at the twinkling lights of West Los Angeles. She was in the Bel Air home of Gary Goldin, an orthopedic surgeon at Memorial. At lunch she had seen Phil and Gary sitting in the cafeteria and had joined them. The three of them had hit it off immediately with interesting conversation and quick humor. Gary had invited her to a small dinner party he was having that evening and she'd accepted, thinking it would be great fun. And it would give her a chance to see Phil

Weideman away from the hospital. When she arrived at the house, Gary was on the way out. His girlfriend's car had broken down and he was going to help her. That had been over an hour ago.

"How's your drink holding up?" Phil asked. He walked out onto the terrace carrying his glass in one hand, a shaker of martinis in the other.

"I'm okay."

"You'd better have a refill," Weideman said and began pouring before she could withdraw her glass. Some of the martini splattered onto Joanna's arm, spotting her linen jacket. Weideman appeared not to notice. He raised his drink in a toast and took a big swallow. "Old Gary has quite a house, doesn't he? Just look at that living room for starters."

"It's very impressive," Joanna agreed, looking into the immense room with its cathedral-type ceiling and marble fireplace. The chairs and couches were French antiques upholstered in a royal blue silklike fabric. One set of glass doors led onto the terrace, another set opened into a lovely garden with a swimming pool.

"Gary was very smart. He got a divorce before he made the big bucks." Weideman took another swallow from his glass. "That way his wife didn't end up with everything."

"How long was he married?"

"Let's see, they got married while he was in medical school and they divorced just after he finished his residency." Weideman counted on his fingers. "They were married for about eight years."

Joanna remembered that at lunch Gary had mentioned that his ex-wife was a nurse. "So his wife worked and supported him through medical school and his residency, then he dropped her, huh?"

"She ended up all right," Weideman said.

"But old Gary ended up with most of the wealth, didn't he?"

"Well, he was the one who worked for it."

There was a sudden flash of lightning, followed by a clap of thunder. A moment later the deluge started, catching them before they got off the terrace. Weideman quickly closed the sliding glass door and locked it. The rain pounded against the glass, causing it to rattle.

"You want to get out of those wet clothes?" Weideman grinned, eyeing the outline of her thighs against her wet skirt.

"No, thanks," Joanna said. "I'll just stand by the fire."

Outside the weather was worsening. The wind had picked up and was driving the rain down in horizontal sheets. There was a loud boom of thunder and the lights in the room dimmed for a moment, then came back.

Weideman went over to the bar and pushed a button controlling the stereo system. An old Johnny Mathis song came on.

"Let's dance," he said, taking Joanna's arm.

They danced to the slow music, Weideman holding her close, too close. And every time she tried to pull away, he held her tighter.

Joanna managed to slip her right hand between her body and Weideman, and that gave her a little room. But Weideman misunderstood her move and thought she wanted to touch his chest. He started stroking her neck and back.

Joanna wished the song would end. She wished even more that Gary Goldin would return so she could have dinner and leave. The evening was turning into a disaster and Weideman into a big bore. Now he was humming in her ear. She hated that.

Joanna used her right hand to put a little more distance between them, but again Weideman misunderstood. He began to rub his pubis up against her. He dropped his hands down to her buttocks and squeezed hard.

Joanna pushed him away. "Back off, damn it!"

Weideman stared at her, stunned. "What the hell is wrong?"

"I don't go that fast. It's not my style."

"Don't give me that hard-to-get crap," Weideman snapped. "You know damn well why you came up here."

"For a dinner party. Nothing more."

"Bullshit! You came up here to jump in bed with me and you know it."

Joanna went for her purse. "I'd better leave."

Weideman grabbed for her and tried to pull her back. "You know you want to."

Joanna swung her purse at Weideman and hit him on the side of his face. "Leave me alone!"

"Bitch!" Weideman spat as a trickle of blood came from his lower lip. "Get out! And find somebody else to take you to the goddamn opera."

"You and the opera can go straight to hell," Joanna said and stormed out.

27

Rain drummed on the roof of Joanna's car. She was driving very carefully along Mulholland Drive, a winding road atop the mountains separating West Los Angeles from the San Fernando Valley. To her left she could see the lights of the valley sparkling in the misty darkness a thousand feet below. A patchy fog was now setting in, reducing visibility on the road even further. In the rearview mirror Joanna saw a pair of headlights and slowed down, hoping the car behind her would pass so she could follow its red taillights around the tight curves.

The car behind slowed down too. He was no fool, Joanna thought. If she went over the side or ran into a big rock that had rolled onto the road, he'd see it and have plenty of time to stop. She leaned across the steering wheel, her eyes glued to the center dividing line.

Joanna hated Mulholland Drive at night, and every time she took it she wished she had taken the freeway instead. But Mulholland was the quickest route from Bel Air to Jake's bungalow in Studio City. And she had to talk with Jake about a lot of things. But most of all about getting back together again. Damn! She'd been a fool. So Jake wasn't perfect. So he didn't always understand a woman's feelings. But what man did? And Jake was fun and clever and a lot brighter than he wanted people to know. And he was a thousand times more of a man than that arrogant lout Phil Weideman.

She clenched her teeth together as she thought about Weideman and the way he had groped at her. What a monumental bore! And so damn superficial. Her mind returned to Jake and she tried to think how best to get their relationship back on track. She could start by apologizing, but then Jake really deserved most of what he'd gotten. And besides, Jake didn't like words. He preferred action. She smiled to herself. The easiest and best way was just to grab him and . . .

Her car ran onto the rocky shoulder and the fender scraped against something. Joanna jerked the steering wheel and pulled her car back to the center of the road. Pay attention, damn it! Otherwise you're going to kill yourself.

Ahead she saw traffic lights through the rain and mist and breathed a sigh of relief. The Laurel Canyon turnoff. Almost there. She used her blinker to signal a left turn. In the rearview mirror she saw the car behind moving closer, now also signaling for a left turn. A flash of fear surged through her. There were so many nuts and crazies in this city, she was thinking, and they particularly liked dark places and defenseless women.

She quickly made certain all the doors were locked, all windows up. The traffic light was yellow. She went through it and completed the turn on a red light. The car behind her also made the turn. Joanna speeded up. The street was wider now and better lit. And Jake's house was less than a mile away. Joanna planned to pull into the driveway and keep her motor running. She figured Jake was home because it was Monday night and he never missed the pro football game on television. If the creep followed her into the driveway she'd blow the hell out of the horn. Jake would be out of his house in a second and the man who had followed her would wish to God he hadn't.

Joanna slowed as she approached Jake's bungalow and switched on the blinker. The car behind her closed in. Joanna turned into the driveway, her hand ready to push down on the horn. The car behind her whizzed by, its driver looking straight ahead. Quickly she got out of the car and ran through a light rain to the door of the bungalow. She rang the doorbell repeatedly, but there was no answer.

Joanna looked around the neighborhood before reaching down into a potted plant for the key. She opened the door and glanced over her shoulder, then returned the key to the plant holder. She didn't see the car with its lights off pull up to the curb a half block away.

The bungalow was dark except for a lamp burning in the living room. Joanna stopped briefly in the kitchen, poured herself a glass of chilled chardonnay and went into the bedroom. She turned on the television set with a remote control and began switching channels aimlessly. She came to a cable channel that was showing a documentary on the Pyramids. A team of British archaeologists was studying the Pyramids in the Valley of the Kings. Joanna sat on the edge of the bed and turned up the sound.

A bearded archaeologist was talking about the incredible weight of each block of stone used to construct a pharaoh's tomb. In the background was a magnificent Pyramid. When viewed from a distance the surfaces of the Pyramid looked smooth. Joanna knew they weren't. In fact, the huge blocks of stone jutted out several feet and a person could walk up them, like steps, to the very top. Joanna had done it on a visit to Egypt. It was a very long climb, but it was worth it. When she'd reached the pinnacle, she stared out across the desert, mesmerized by its vastness. She had thought she was looking at eternity.

Now the archaeologist was talking about the various safeguards that went into protecting the pharaoh's tomb and the riches contained within. False passageways were common. They led to dead ends. Even the true way in was made to look like a false passage. The architects of the Pyramid had been very shrewd, the archaeologist was saying, and by means of ropes and pulleys had been able to place one final block of stone at the end of the true passageway, making it seem a dead end.

Joanna watched intently as a diagram of the Pyramid came up on the television screen. Blue lines pointed out the false passages, a red line depicted the true way in. Now the diagram showed the red line pulsating against the final block of stone that obstructed the way. Suddenly the final block exploded and the red line flowed into the pharaoh's tomb.

Joanna stared at the screen, her eyes bulging. "Oh, my God!"

She bounced off the bed and over to her purse on the dresser. Holding the microfilm up to the light, she carefully studied it with a magnifying glass. Jesus! It had been there all the time, right in front of her nose, and she'd missed it. So clever, so very clever. But not as clever as Bob Cipro, who had left a message on the microfilm.

She ran into the kitchen and scribbled a note to Jake, leaving it on the refrigerator door. It read:

I KNOW HOW. MAYBE WHO. GOING BACK TO MEMO-RIAL FOR ONE MORE TEST.

JOANNA

Joanna slammed the front door and jumped into her car. She speeded up Laurel Canyon and through a fog that seemed much denser than before. The streetlights were a blur, the air so heavy with humidity that drops were forming on the windshield. But the higher Joanna went the better the visibility became, and when she turned onto Mulholland Drive the night was crystal clear.

She pushed down on the accelerator and took the sharp turns nicely, but her tires began to squeal so she forced herself to slow down. So simple, she kept saying to herself, and right in front of our faces. And so easy to prove. Just get an X ray of Sally Wheaton's pacemaker. The Department of Radiology at Memorial would be closed now, but there was an X-ray unit in the ER. One X ray and she'd have the answer.

Glancing at the rearview mirror Joanna saw a set of headlights closing in fast. She slowed down even more and pulled over to the right a little to let the driver pass. She couldn't pull over very much because there was only a narrow shoulder to the road and beyond that there was a steep cliff that dropped a thousand feet to the valley below.

The headlights were almost upon her now, the bright beams shining in the rearview mirror and blinding her for a moment. The car behind slammed into her rear, propelling her car toward the narrow shoulder. She jerked at the steering wheel, trying to bring the car back to the center of the road. The car behind separated briefly and then slammed into her again, moving her back to the shoulder.

Fear flooded through Joanna as she realized what was happening. She fought to keep her car on the road, but now their bumpers were somehow locked and he was pushing her toward the edge. She stood on the brake pedal but it made no difference. Slowly the car behind pushed Joanna's car across the shoulder. The nose of her car tilted over the edge and she saw the sparkling lights of the valley a thousand feet below.

She pulled at the door handle. Locked! Frantically she tried to open the door. The car behind her backed up, paused for a moment, then slammed into Joanna's car and pushed it out into the blackness. Joanna felt as if she was suspended in space. Everything seemed to be happening very slowly. She had plenty of time to scream before her car smashed into the rocks below and the windshield shattered in her face.

28

Jake quickly went through the file on Will Patterson. It was thin and offered little insight into the man. Patterson had been born in a small town in Indiana that no longer existed and had been raised by grandparents who were now dead. His military record in Vietnam was undistinguished. He had served two tours, received no medals or decorations. "There's nothing much here."

"There is if you read between the lines," said William Buck, director of a sensitive intelligence unit in the Los Angeles Police Department.

"How do you mean?"

"Well, let's start with the group he was assigned to in Vietnam. He was a member of the Long Range Reconnaissance Patrol Units. It sounds nice and benign, doesn't it?"

Farelli chewed on a toothpick and rocked back in his chair. "Like a scout, huh?"

Buck forced a laugh. "Calling him a scout would be like calling a Bengal tiger a kitty. These men were known as LURPs. They were highly trained, cold-blooded killers. Meaner than hell and twice as vicious. They were the crazies and anyone with any sense stayed out of their way."

Jake listened intently as Buck described the LURPs. They were like psychotic pit bulls who could kill quickly and effortlessly, almost by instinct. They usually fought in units, but some of the craziest were independent agents who were set loose in the jungle to kill whoever they could find. Buck knew about the LURPs first-hand. He had been an intelligence officer in Vietnam for five years, stationed in I Corps.

"So our guy is really a pro, huh?" Jake asked.

"And some," Buck said.

"What else do you see in the guy's file?"

"I see that it's been sanitized."

"How so?"

Buck flicked an index finger against the file. "Look what it says about this guy. He was born in a town that no longer exists, raised by grandparents who are now dead. Hell, it's like he's got no past."

"Do you think the information is false?"

Buck shrugged. "Maybe, maybe not. But even if it is true, what difference would it make? Everything and everybody associated with this guy is scattered to the wind."

Outside there was a flash of lightning, then a clap of thunder. The lights in the conference room at the police station dimmed for a moment before coming back. Now the rain was pelting against the window. Jake lit a cigarette and glanced at the wall clock. It was nine-thirty p.m. "Well, I know one thing in this guy's file that's an out-and-out lie. He sure as hell wasn't killed in Vietnam twenty years ago."

"That's for certain," Buck agreed.

"What do you think really happened?"

"There are three possibilities," Buck said slowly. "First, it could have been an honest mistake. Maybe somebody thought they saw Patterson getting killed or saw his body and reported it. But that idea doesn't work because Patterson would have eventually showed up and there's nothing the military likes to do more than change a soldier's status from killed in action to alive and well. Sort of like a reverse body count, you know. The second possibility is that Patterson decided to desert and leave the army. To cover his tracks he arranges to have himself reported as killed in action, goes to Saigon and catches a plane to God knows where. Maybe he joined the Foreign Legion or went to Rhodesia to fight the terrorists. But this is a very unlikely scenario. According to his file, he had only two months left on his last tour in Vietnam. He could have finished that in a snap, collected his separation pay and gone along his way. No, the first two explanations just don't work."

"What's the third?" Jake asked.

Buck stared at the detectives for several seconds, hesitating. "What I'm about to tell you is a guess, nothing more. But I think it's as close to the truth as you'll ever get. I would prefer that what I'm about to tell you goes no further than this room."

Jake and Farelli nodded and leaned in closer.

"This man had some rather unique talents and there are agencies in our government who place a high value on these talents. The agencies are particularly interested in such a man if he has no past, no face, no identity."

Jake crushed out his cigarette and reached for his notepad. "Give me a profile on this guy."

Buck smiled thinly. "They have no profile, Jake. They don't look mean or sinister or menacing. Hell, they look like everyone else and they know how to blend into any background. You see them, but you don't. They're like chameleons. Let me give you an example. You're walking down the street and see a tall, middle-aged man coming toward you. His shoulders are slumped and he's staring at the ground. He looks beaten, like he's carrying the weight of the world on his back. You might even feel a little sorry for him. You pass each other. Suddenly you feel a knife go deep into your back. You drop to the sidewalk, dying. He goes to the corner and waits for the light to change so he can cross the street safely."

"You never see him coming, huh?"

"Or going."

"They always work alone?"

"Always."

Jake rubbed at the stubble on his chin. "Chances are this guy is going to be a real loner."

"Oh, yeah. He eats alone, lives alone, has no family or friends, no credit cards or bank accounts, pays for everything in cash. So what? There's a million other guys who fit that profile."

"So we've got nothing to go on," Jake said sourly.

"I didn't say that." Buck reached into his coat pocket and took out a photograph. "I came up with a military photo of your man. It's a little blurred, but it'll do."

Jake studied the photograph. It showed a young man with an angular face, thin lips and light hair. His eyes were blanks, devoid of any emotion. "He looks like the type who'd go to the top of the Texas Tower with a high-powered rifle and start popping off people."

"That's only because you know his history," Buck said. "Otherwise you'd think he was just a kid staring into a camera."

No, I wouldn't, Jake thought, still studying the photo.

"Of course, this picture is twenty years old," Buck went on. "He probably looks different now."

"Maybe he had his face changed."

Buck shook his head. "Why bother? Nobody knows him or his past."

Jake handed the photo back. "Could you have your people age his face twenty years or so?"

"It's being done at this very moment," Buck said. "I'll have it for you tomorrow."

Jake and Farelli stood. Buck stayed in his wheelchair, a blanket over his thighs. Both of his legs had been blown off by a Viet Cong mine in 1972.

"I really appreciate your help," Jake said, shaking Buck's hand.

"Want some advice?" Buck asked.

"Sure."

"Don't take on this fellow alone."

"Why not?"

"Because you'll lose."

Jake and Farelli walked out of the station and across the parking lot. It was still raining lightly, but the sky was beginning to clear.

"Did I ever tell you the story I heard about Buck?" Farelli asked.

"What story?"

"When the mine exploded and blew off his legs, he was thrown about twenty feet. Next thing he knows he's looking at a stump where his leg used to be. And right beside him he sees his blown-off leg with a shoe still on it. He grabs it and tries to reattach it, to push it back on. Over and over he tries but the damn thing keeps falling off." Farelli shook his head sadly. "Can you imagine that?"

"Can anybody?" Jake lit another cigarette and blew smoke into the cool night air, glad he hadn't been forced to fight in that goddamned, senseless war. "Do you have anything new on Cipro?"

"I got his sperm from that sperm bank."

"Did they squawk?"

"Oh, yeah. They bitched and moaned and told me all about their constitutional rights. But they came across when I showed them the search-and-seize warrant. That's the good news."

"What's the bad?"

"That it's going to take two months to get back the DNA results."

Jake winced. "Why so long?"

"It's a complicated test. And worse yet, the test results aren't always clear-cut. Sometimes it's kind of like comparing smudged fingerprints. Sometimes you can't be certain it's a good match."

"Shit," Jake muttered. "What else have you got?"

"Neither Cipro nor Black had a safety-deposit box. Black lived at home with his wife, so I hesitated trying to get a search warrant for the place. It might be better to wait on that one, don't you think?"

Jake nodded. "What about Cipro's apartment?"

"He used to live in Westwood. He moved out two months ago."

Jake thought back to Alex's and Cipro's apartment in Venice. There were sparse furnishings, hardly any clothing. The place barely looked lived in. Where the hell had Cipro put all of his things? Jake took a final drag on his cigarette and flicked it away. "Check all the storage companies in the area. See if they have anything under Cipro's name."

"Right."

"You got anything else?"

Farelli hesitated for a moment, thinking. "Oh, yeah, they found Steely Dan dead in his tattoo shop this morning."

"How did he die?"

"With a bullet in his head," Farelli said. "The Venice police think it was burglary. Maybe an addict looking for cash."

"Or maybe a professional killer tidying up loose ends," Jake said grimly.

"Maybe," Farelli said dubiously. "But how would the pro know that Steely Dan had put the tattoo on Cipro's butt? And there's no way the pro could have known that Steely Dan had talked to you."

There was one way, Jake thought, remembering back to the night he and Joanna had visited Steely Dan's shop. The pro could have followed them. "Get the bullet from Steely Dan's head and compare it to the slug from Joanna's laboratory."

Farelli looked puzzled. "What slug?"

"Remember the break-in at the doc's lab and the bullet that went through the computer and into the wall?"

Farelli slapped his forehead with an open palm. "I swear to God, my brain is going."

"It's late and we're both tired." Jake reached for the door of his car. "We'll start early tomorrow morning. Eight sharp."

Farelli started to walk away, then turned back. "One more thing. Why does Buck want us to keep all the information on this Patterson guy under wraps?"

"Because Buck is part of the intelligence community and those fellows try not to step on each other's toes."

"The games those bastards play," Farelli grumbled and headed for his car.

Jake took the San Diego Freeway north and exited at Mulholland Drive. The rain had stopped, but the air was still misty and heavy with humidity. The police radio in his car was on and the dispatcher was issuing an all-points bulletin for a suspected rapist in the mid-Wilshire area.

Jake switched off the radio and concentrated his thoughts on the killer. A pro. A real professional who would be difficult as hell to track and even harder to catch. But at least they now had a picture of him. And Buck would have his people age the pro's face by twenty years and they'd have a pretty fair idea what the guy looked like now.

Jake wondered what he should do with the photo. He decided not to plaster it all over television and the newspapers. Not now. All that would do would be to make the pro run or use a disguise. Dye his hair, wear glasses, grow a mustache. And nobody would recognize him. No, better to wait.

Jake heard the siren of a fire engine coming up behind him and pulled over to the side of the road. The truck whizzed by, its horn and siren deafening. Jake moved back onto the road and went around a wide curve. Ahead he saw a black-and-white patrol car, lights flashing, blocking Mulholland. A police officer was directing traffic to a side street. Overhead there was the loud putt-putt noise of a helicopter and Jake could see its floodlights streaking through the misty night air. Immediately he knew what was happening. Somebody had been driving too fast on the rain-slicked road and had gone over the side, plunging a thousand feet down. Mulholland at night was a beautiful drive, but when it rained and the driver was speeding it became a death trap.

Jake turned off of Mulholland and onto Woodcliff. It would take him out of his way, but he was in no hurry. He wanted to think more about the pro he was after.

29

The paramedics rappelled down the side of the mountain. Giant floodlights from the fire truck and the helicopter overhead illuminated their way and pinpointed the location of the wreck. From a distance the car appeared to be wedged between two boulders, but as the paramedics got closer they could see that the car wasn't wedged in at all. It was sitting between the two boulders, having crashed into one before careening into the other. The car was now resting on a small ledge, its nose pointed downward. A rock jammed under the axle was the only thing holding it in place.

Nick Owens, the lead paramedic, approached the car on the driver's side. He was careful not to touch it, since the car's position was so precarious and unstable that even a slight jolt might send it tumbling down the final eight hundred feet of mountain. Nick called over to the paramedic on the other side of the car. "Can this thing be stabilized, Red?"

"No way in hell. Not even with a two-ton crane. And it's not going to stay in this position much longer, either." Red Murphy lowered himself down a little farther and peered into the shattered side window. "I can't see anybody in there. Can you?"

Nick shined his flashlight in and saw the steering wheel and an inflated air bag. Slowly he tried to open the door. It was locked. He swung around to the windshield, partially blown out on the driver's side. Taking out his knife, he reached in and punctured the air bag, then waited for it to deflate. Nick carefully pushed the air bag aside. He saw sandy blond hair and a bloody forehead. "A woman!"

"Alive?"

"Not sure." Nick stretched his arm out and tried to reach her neck and feel for a carotid pulse. He was inches short. "Can you hear me? Can you hear me?" he yelled in.

There was no answer.

As Nick moved away from the windshield his body bumped against the hood. The car moved, its nose pointing down even more severely. There was a grinding sound of metal against stone before the car came to rest again.

"Careful, man! Careful!" Red shouted.

Nick went back to the driver's side window. It was intact and down a few inches. He tried to get his hand through, but there wasn't enough room. Nick placed his mouth at the opening and yelled, "Can you hear me?"

Joanna's head moved slightly. "I hear you," she said, her voice barely audible.

"She's alive!" Nick hollered out.

His voice carried up to the firemen and other rescue workers at the top of the cliff. They yelled and clapped and shouted down encouragement.

"Okay, sweetheart," Nick told her, "you just stay calm and we'll have you out of there in a snap."

Joanna's head was spinning and she had difficulty focusing her eyes. But she could see the blackness in front of her and the twinkling lights far below. She wasn't certain where she was. Maybe in an airplane, way up, flying over a city.

"Are you in pain?" Nick asked.

"My head hurts," Joanna said weakly.

"Can you move your fingers and hands?"

Joanna clenched and unclenched her fists. "Yes."

"Now try to move your arms and elbows."

"Where am I?" Joanna asked.

"In a car and I'm going to get you out. But you'll have to do exactly as I say. Now, try to move your arms and elbows."

Joanna did as she was told. "They're fine."

"Can you move your toes and feet?"

Joanna wiggled her toes and ankles. They felt stiff and cramped, but they moved. "I can move them."

At least her spinal cord was intact, Nick thought to himself. But he knew she could still have a fractured cervical vertebra and, if that were the case, one sudden move and her spinal cord would be severed and she'd end up a quadriplegic. The correct procedure now would be to immobilize her neck, but Nick knew there was no way to accomplish that, not under these circumstances.

A blue streak of lightning cracked in the sky and Nick froze. The gas tank in the wrecked car had ruptured and Nick could smell gasoline everywhere. One spark and he and Red and the woman would be incinerated. Now the rain started again and Nick cursed at it. The hills were already saturated with water and it wouldn't take much more to start the mud sliding.

"What happened to me?" Joanna asked, fear now in her voice.

"You were in a car accident," Nick said calmly. "Now no more conversation. Do exactly as I tell you and do it as quickly as you can. First, reach down with your right hand and release your safety belt."

Joanna groped for the button and found it. The belt released and self-retracted.

"Good," Nick encouraged her, wiping rain from his eyes. "Next I want you to reach down with your left hand and push the automatic door lock button."

Joanna pushed on a button with her left hand. Nothing happened.

"You probably pushed the window lock button," Nick said, knowing the panel layout because he also owned a Toyota. "Move your hand over to the next button."

Joanna pressed the next button and all doors immediately unlocked with a chorus of clicks.

Nick carefully began to open the door and as he did Joanna slumped against it like a deadweight. Nick had to strain to keep the door from opening any farther. "Red! I need some help over here."

Red hoisted himself up and swung over the top of the car, careful not to touch it. "What have you got?"

"She's leaning against the door and as soon as I open it she's going to tumble out."

"Then you'd better not open it, partner."

"Move your ass over here and help me hold the door shut. When I say so, hold the door for a second longer, then swing it wide open."

The paramedics slowly positioned themselves. Red was just above the door, Nick at the level of the door handle. They held the door closed with the palms of their hands.

"On the count of three," Nick yelled out. "One! Two! Three!"

Nick released his hold. Red held his for a second more, then swung the door open. Joanna tumbled out onto Nick's shoulder. He gripped her tightly, his left arm around her waist. "I've got her!"

"Pull us up!" Red shouted at the top of his lungs.

Joanna wasn't certain what was happening. She saw only darkness and twinkling lights below. The man had told her she'd been in a car accident, but she couldn't remember it. Her head started to spin again and she squeezed her eyes shut, trying to stop the vertigo. *Where am I?* she asked herself, wondering if this was all a bad dream. She opened her eyes and focused in on the lights below. Her mind began to flash back. She was driving somewhere, around sharp turns, her tires squealing as . . .

"We're almost there," Nick told her. "Hold on tight."

Joanna felt stiff and sore and her head was throbbing. Suddenly there was a bright light in her eyes, blinding her, and her headache got even worse. Gentle hands grabbed her and lifted her up. There were men's voices close by. She tried to make out their faces, but saw only shadows. The rain was coming down harder and giant drops were splashing against her forehead.

"Want to take her to Memorial or to Saint Luke's?" Red asked.

"Let's go to Saint Luke's," Nick said. "It's closer and there's a great doughnut shop across the street."

"Right on."

Joanna was secured onto a stretcher and placed in the paramedics' ambulance. She kept her eyes closed because it made her head feel better. She heard the static of a two-way radio and heard a man telling the ER at Saint Luke's Hospital what his estimated time of arrival would be. The ambulance began to move, its siren wailing in the night.

Nick took the woman's pulse. One hundred beats per minute.

A little fast, but not bad considering what she'd been through. He put a blood pressure cuff on her arm, pumped it up and slowly released it. "Ninety-five over sixty," Nick called out. "She's a little hypotensive."

"No, I'm not," Joanna said. "My systolic pressure usually runs between ninety and a hundred."

Nick smiled. "Are you a nurse?"

Joanna moved her head and said nothing.

Nick reached over and picked out a few slivers of glass from Joanna's bloody forehead. There were a dozen small cuts, none now bleeding, none requiring any sutures. He gently cleaned her forehead with a peroxide solution. Nick hadn't realized how pretty the woman was. But the style of her hair and her clothes and jewelry told him she was expensive too. Way out of his league.

"What really happened to me?" Joanna asked, still dazed and having trouble concentrating.

"You drove off a road and down a mountain. You almost got yourself killed."

"How did I get out?"

"I came down and got you," Nick said matter-of-factly. "Remember?"

Joanna nodded, but she didn't recall it. "I should thank you," she said slowly. "I guess I owe you."

"I'll tell you what. When you're all well, we'll go out and I'll let you buy the hamburgers."

Joanna grinned slightly. "I'm a chili dog girl myself."

Nick was instantly in love. "What's your name?"

Joanna hesitated and knotted her brow in thought. "I'm—I'm not sure."

"Don't worry about it," Nick said lightly. "It happens all the time. You get a hit on the head and you don't know who you are or where you're at. But it's usually temporary. I've seen it plenty of times."

The ambulance turned onto Sunset Boulevard and headed east. The rain was pouring down, drumming against the roof. Joanna listened to the sound of the rain and her mind again flashed back. She was driving somewhere, the rain beating down on her car. There was a fog and she couldn't see well. Then she saw the tiny lights again.

"Damn," Nick grumbled, breaking into her thoughts. "I forgot to start an IV. That's bad form."

"Is that really necessary?"

"I'm afraid so." Nick reached up for an IV setup and a plastic bag of fluid. "Let's try a little saline."

"I'd prefer five percent D and W," Joanna said without thinking.

Nick grinned. She had to be a nurse. "Five percent D and W" meant five percent dextrose in water. It was medical parlance, used only by those in the profession. And she was right too. All he'd wanted to do was get an IV line started, just in case she became shocky. Five percent D and W was a better choice than saline. He swabbed her forearm with alcohol and found a vein on the first try.

"That didn't hurt, did it?" Nick asked, hanging up the bag of solution.

"Hardly at all."

The ambulance made a sharp turn and pulled up to the emergency entrance at Saint Luke's Hospital. The doors of the ambulance opened and Joanna felt herself being lifted and placed on a gurney. She kept her eyes closed and wished that her head would stop hurting.

A black orderly pushed Joanna's gurney through a set of automatic doors and down a wide corridor. Nick ran alongside holding up the IV bag. Joanna felt as if she was having a bad dream and kept wishing that she'd wake up. In her subconscious mind Joanna now saw the Pyramids. She was back in Egypt, out on some vast desert. *I must be dreaming. I must be.*

They came to the triage area, where a tall, red-headed charge nurse was waiting. "What have you got, Nick?" Judy Travers asked.

"An automobile accident. Vital signs are stable, no major injuries," Nick said evenly. "But she has a pretty good concussion. She can't remember who she is or what happened."

The nurse took out a penlight and shined it into Joanna's eyes. Both pupils were round and regular and reacted well to light. "Let's put her in room three," she said, setting the gurney in motion.

"I thought one was the trauma room," Nick said.

"It is, but it's in use. A drunk driver got on the freeway going the wrong way and crashed head-on into another car."

"What happened to him?"

"He's dead."

Good, Nick thought to himself, hating drunk drivers and the carnage they caused. "What about the victims?"

"They're fighting for their lives in room one," the nurse said, then lowered her voice. "A mother and her young daughter returning from a recital."

"Shit," Nick muttered.

"Yeah."

They wheeled Joanna into room 3, a rectangular area divided into halves by a ceiling-to-floor curtain. The nurse took Joanna's vital signs and jotted them down.

Nick said, "She told me that her systolic usually runs a little low."

"Is she a nurse?" Judy Travers asked.

Nick shrugged. "She can't remember."

The nurse patted the patient's hand, admiring for a moment the gold necklace and earrings Joanna was wearing. "Do you remember what happened to you tonight?"

"I was told I was in an automobile accident," Joanna said slowly.

"But you don't remember it, huh?"

"No, I don't remember."

"Do you know what day it is?"

"I—I'm not sure."

"What's your name?"

Joanna involuntarily pursed her lips and tried to form a word. No sound came forth.

"It looked like you tried to say something that started with a G," the nurse coaxed her. "Does your name start with a G?"

Joanna tried to concentrate, but her mind stayed blank. "I don't know."

The nurse patted the patient's hand again, now seeing the bruise on Joanna's temple and wondering if there was a fracture beneath it.

"Why can't I remember my name?" Joanna asked anxiously.

"Because you've had a concussion."

A dirty hand pulled back the curtain that divided the room and a middle-aged woman in a wheelchair looked in. She had an unwashed face, leathery skin from too much sun, and stringy, unkempt hair. "Don't you serve any food in this hospital?" she demanded.

The nurse stared disdainfully at the homeless woman. "Not in the emergency room we don't."

"Well, I'm starving. I haven't eaten all day." The homeless woman coughed loudly, phlegm rattling in her throat. "Can't you get me a sandwich or a candy bar?"

"No, I can't," the nurse said tersely. "Now you just hold still and keep quiet. We'll get your X rays read in a little bit and you can be on your way."

"What's taking them so long to read my X rays?"

"Because there are other people here who are a lot sicker than you are. And they come first." The nurse stared at the woman, hoping she wouldn't leave body lice behind in the ER as some of the homeless did.

"Shit," the woman grumbled and began mumbling to herself.

The nurse turned her attention back to Joanna. "I'm going to have the doctor take a look at you. Okay?"

Joanna nodded and watched as the nurse and paramedic left the room. She looked around the area, now seeing an otoscope and an ophthalmoscope attached to the wall and next to them the blood pressure cuff and manometer. In the corner was an EKG machine, its leads dangling. It all seemed so familiar to Joanna. She felt as if she'd been here before.

"What did they bring you in for?" the homeless woman asked.

"I was in an auto accident," Joanna said.

"You know what they brought me in for? A police car ran over my foot. Can you believe that?"

Joanna looked up at the ceiling and said nothing. She really didn't want to talk to the woman.

"What's your name?" the homeless woman asked.

"I—I don't know," Joanna said slowly.

"It doesn't matter. Names aren't that important anyway. Take me, for example. My name is Emma Stanley. But nobody really knows who I am." Emma scratched vigorously at an armpit. "Did you see how that nurse treated me? Like dirt. She thinks I'm dirt. She thinks that about all homeless people."

Emma scratched her armpit again, this time putting her fingers inside the sleeve of her dress. "Did you know I was a school-teacher? That's right. I was a schoolteacher with a good car and a nice apartment. Then they laid me off and I couldn't find an-other job. I couldn't make the payments on my car and they took it away. Then they shut off my phone and utilities. And then they threw me out of my apartment because I couldn't come up with the rent. I had no one to turn to, no one to help me. That's how I ended up on the street."

Everything Emma had said was true. But she omitted the fact that she had been laid off when she was diagnosed as being a paranoid schizophrenic and that she had refused to keep her ap-pointments with the psychiatrist or take the medicines he pre-scribed because she thought he was trying to poison her.

The door to the room opened and the nurse walked in, an oriental doctor just behind her.

"Hey, Doc," Emma called out, "can I get a sandwich? Maybe a candy bar?"

The doctor ignored the homeless woman and went over to Joanna. "I'm Dr. Chang. How are you feeling?"

"A little better," Joanna said. "My head hurts less."

"Good." Chang was middle-aged and pudgy and wore wire-rimmed glasses. "Do you know where you are?"

"A hospital," Joanna said promptly.

"Good. Do you remember what happened to you tonight?"

"Not really."

"Do you know what day it is?"

Joanna hesitated. "I'm not sure."

"Can you tell me your name?"

Joanna concentrated, trying to remember. She slowly shook her head.

Chang did a quick neurologic examination. Joanna's reflexes were bilaterally equal, her motor and sensory functions unim-paired. All of her cranial nerves were intact. Other than her am-nesia, she had no neurological deficits. "I'm going to call in a specialist. He'll want to do some tests on you and will probably admit you to the hospital."

"Don't let them put you in the hospital!" Emma blurted out. "Don't let them do it! They put one of my friends in the hospital and he never came out. They killed him."

Chang whirled around and stared icily at the woman. "Close that curtain and keep your mouth shut!"

Emma stared back defiantly for a moment, then did as she was told. But she left the curtain cracked so she could see what was going on.

Chang and Judy Travers walked out of the room and down the corridor. The ER was overflowing. All of the rooms and suites were occupied. Patients in wheelchairs and on gurneys lined every wall. A hum of conversations filled the air. Mostly English. Some Spanish. A Chinese dialect Chang didn't recognize. "Who is the neurologist on call?" he asked.

"Dr. Payne."

"Good. If you can't get him, call Kanter." A patient in a wheelchair retched and brought up a small amount of vomitus that went onto the floor. Chang ignored it. "I'll be in room one if you need me."

Judy hurried toward the nurses' station, where the phone numbers of the consultants were kept. She now wished she hadn't agreed to work a double shift even though she needed the money badly. She was so tired and her feet were sore and her back was killing her. And she still had ten hours to go. Approaching the nurses' desk she saw a young nurse having an animated conversation with a visitor, a tall man wearing a trench coat and a floppy rain cap.

"Is there a problem, Karen?" Judy asked.

"This man wants information on the patient in room three," Karen said.

Judy studied the visitor briefly, her gaze going to his reddish blond hair that was curling around the edges. "We can only give out patient information to family."

"I am family," Karl Rimer said, thinking quickly and putting a worried expression on his face. "I'm her uncle. I was driving behind her when she went off the road and down the mountain."

"Could you tell me her name?" Judy asked.

"Don't you know?" Rimer said evasively.

"I'm afraid she struck her head and is suffering from amnesia."

"Oh, my goodness!" Rimer shook his head sadly, but inwardly he was delighted. It was going to make his task even easier. "Is that serious?"

"They usually come back, but it takes time," Judy said, seeing the sadness on the man's face and feeling for him. "Perhaps if we call her by her name it will help jog her memory."

"Of course, of course," Rimer said, thinking quickly again. "Her name is Jane Blackwell. And I'm her Uncle Will. Would it be possible for me to see her?"

"Yes. But only for a few minutes."

"That would be fine," Rimer said gratefully. "Then I'll be able to report to the rest of the family, who are very worried."

Judy led the way back down the corridor, passing patients in wheelchairs and on gurneys. Rimer tried to stay as far away from them and their body odors as he could. They smelled like death and decay and it reminded Rimer of Vietnam. He took out a small bottle of cologne and applied some to his face.

Judy held the door to room 3 as Rimer entered. She picked up the strong scent of his aftershave lotion and wondered if he was aware of how awful it smelled.

"Jane, your Uncle Will is here to see you," Judy said softly, leaning over Joanna.

"Janie, how are you feeling?" Rimer asked, very concerned.

"Better," Joanna said, looking up at the man and studying his face.

Judy asked, "Do you recognize your Uncle Will?"

"I don't think so," Joanna said.

The door opened and a young nurse looked in. "Judy, we need you in room one. The little girl is becoming more agitated."

Judy nodded and turned to Rimer. "I'll be back in a few minutes. If she gets tired, please leave."

"Of course. And thank you for your kindness." Rimer waited for the nurse to leave, then moved quickly. He came in closer to Joanna and placed his left hand under her neck, lifting it up slightly and exposing her larynx. One karate chop and her larynx would be crushed, her airway blocked. She'd be dead in less than sixty seconds. Rimer had killed a dozen Viet Cong using this method and all had gone quickly and quietly, their only sound a soft gurgle. Rimer flattened his right hand, fingers extended, and brought it up high over his head.

Joanna saw the raised hand and realized what was about to happen. She tried to scream, but her voice only made a squeak. She attempted to turn away but she was strapped onto the gurney.

"He's going to kill her!" Emma yelled out at the top of her lungs. *"He's going to kill her! Murder! Murder!"*

Rimer spun around, startled. He saw a dirty hag peering out from behind the curtain and instantly reached for his Beretta. But he heard voices outside the door and footsteps approaching. He covered his weapon with his trench coat.

The door opened and Dr. Chang ran in. He stared over at Emma. Crazy Emma. "What's wrong?"

"He tried to kill her." Emma pointed a finger at Rimer.

"That's nonsense," Rimer said, acting offended. "I was leaning over to kiss my niece's forehead and this lunatic started screaming."

"Your niece?" Chang asked.

"Yes. I'm her Uncle Will," Rimer said. "Your nurse was kind enough to let me spend a few minutes with Janie."

"Good, good." Chang nodded to himself, pleased. "Having a family member present might help a great deal."

"Anything to help Janie," Rimer said.

"You're right about Crazy Emma being a lunatic," Chang said to Rimer. "But she'll be out of here as soon as her X rays have been read." He took Rimer's arm and guided him to the door. "We'll have this room cleaned in a few minutes and then you can spend some quality time with your niece."

"Thank you." Rimer hated being touched by another man but resisted the urge to pull his arm away from the doctor. He had had an open shot at Joanna Blalock and had missed because of a lunatic hag. Rimer felt the Beretta beneath his trench coat and fingered the silencer. He wouldn't miss the next time.

Emma waited for the door to close, then jumped out of her wheelchair and hurried over to Joanna. "He was going to kill you! Did you see that? The man was going to kill you."

"Why?" Joanna asked, confused and frightened.

"I don't know, but you'd better get out of here before he comes back," Emma urged.

Joanna hesitated, unsure of what to do. "I'm—I'm . . ."

"You saw him trying to kill you, didn't you? He had his goddamn hand up like a karate expert."

Joanna nodded quickly. "He was aiming for my throat."

"Damn right he was. You'd have been real dead." Emma loosened the straps on Joanna's gurney and slapped the IV needle out of her arm. She noticed the gold necklace and earrings Joanna was wearing and wondered what they'd bring on the street. At least a hundred dollars. She helped Joanna up to a sitting position.

Joanna's head began to swim. "Maybe we should wait."

"For what? For him to come back and kill you?" Emma lifted Joanna off the gurney and held on to her until Joanna seemed steady. "Try to walk."

Joanna took a few choppy steps. Her legs felt like jelly, like they wouldn't support her. But they did. Her next steps were stronger, but still unsteady. "Why would he want to kill me?" Joanna asked again.

"You'll have to ask your uncle that. Maybe you've got a lot of money that he will inherit." Emma handed Joanna a small spray can. It was badly rusted, nearly corroded through in places. "If he comes at you again, squirt him with this Mace."

"The container is so old. Does it still work?"

"I don't know. I never tried it." Emma put her arm around Joanna's waist, giving her support. "Lean on me. I'll show you the way out."

They walked into the corridor, which was even more crowded now. Doctors and nurses and orderlies were jammed in among the patients in wheelchairs and on gurneys. The noise level was intense, people yelling above it to make themselves heard. All Joanna saw was a sea of heads.

The women approached a lounge, its door open. On a coat rack Emma saw two long white coats. She grabbed them, handing one to Joanna. "Put this on and keep your head down."

They went back into the corridor and headed for the front entrance. They walked past the nurses' station, then past a small laboratory. Joanna was getting stronger with each step, but Emma still gave her an arm to lean on. They were almost to the reception area when the door to room 1 opened and Judy Travers walked out. She almost ran into the two women. "Hey! Where do you think you're going?"

"Run!" Emma yelled, grabbing Joanna's arm and pulling her along.

"Stop those two!" Judy shouted and ran after them.

Everyone in the reception area stood up to see what the commotion was about. Rimer jumped to his feet and looked over the heads of the crowd. He saw the red-haired nurse giving chase. Then he spotted Joanna and the crazy hag running for the automatic doors.

Rimer pushed people aside, trying to make his way through the crowd. He bumped hard into a man who gave him a mean stare and angrily drew back a clenched fist. Rimer fractured the man's clavicle with a single blow. Rimer bulldozed through the crowd, knocking people off their feet. Finally he was at the doors, then outside.

The night air was misty, making it difficult to see. A municipal bus went by and began braking as it approached the bus stop on the corner. The mist lifted for a moment and Rimer saw two women in white coats getting on the bus. He ran as fast as he could for the corner, but he had trouble getting traction on the wet concrete. He slipped and almost fell and had to struggle to regain his balance. The bus pulled away as Rimer reached the corner. He screamed at it, but the bus kept going.

Quickly, Rimer reached into his pocket and took out a small, collapsing telescope. He opened it and focused in on the rear of the bus, getting its number and memorizing it. Then he ran for his car.

30

"Her uncle!" Jake spat the words out. "She doesn't have an uncle!"

"How the hell was I supposed to know that?" Judy Travers snapped back.

"Don't you people ask for ID down here?"

"What good would that have done?" Judy asked, unintimidated by the detective. She was tired and irritable and wanted to get out of the ER and go home to a nice bed. "Last night this place was a madhouse. It was filled with sick people, some of them critically ill. Then your woman came in. She'd been in an auto accident, had stable vital signs and no major injuries. She was intact except she couldn't remember who she was. And we have no way to identify her. Then a man comes in and tells us he's her uncle. Now tell me, what should I have done? Call the FBI and have him checked out?"

Jake took a deep breath and tried to calm himself. "Didn't you think it was a little unusual that this guy just suddenly showed up?"

The nurse shrugged. "Not really. He said he was driving behind her when she went off the road."

Jake looked over at Farelli and the men exchanged nods. The killer had been right behind Joanna, moments before he'd pushed her off the mountain road. The rear of Joanna's car was smashed in and the Crime Scene Unit thought it had been hit by another car or truck. "The guy said he was her uncle, huh?"

"That's right."

"Did he give any other name?"

Judy thought for a moment. "I think he said he was her Uncle Will."

"Jesus." Jake groaned aloud. Good old Uncle Will Patterson. "Do you remember what he looked like?"

Judy shrugged again. "Not really."

"Try."

Judy concentrated, thinking back. "He was wearing a trench coat and a floppy rain cap. He was kind of tall and middle-aged, maybe in his late forties."

"What about his face?"

Judy tried to recall the man, then slowly shook her head. "It was so busy last night. I wasn't with him more than a minute or two."

"Did he ever take his cap off?"

"No."

Smart, Jake thought. Pull the collar of a trench coat up and pull the rain cap down and fifty percent of his face is obscured. Jake remembered back to what William Buck had said about the LURPs. They blended into the background like chameleons. You didn't see them coming or going.

"There was one thing about him," Judy said, wrinkling up her nose. "He had on the worst-smelling cologne I've ever encountered."

Jake turned to Dr. Chang, who was sitting on a stool in the consultation suite. He had his shoes off, his legs stretched out. "Can you tell us anything about this guy?"

"No more than what Judy has already said. He was tall and middle-aged, a little stoop-shouldered."

"Do you recall any of his facial features?"

Chang tilted his head back and stared up at the ceiling. He tried to think about the man, but his mind kept drifting back to the mother and daughter who had been critically injured in the car wreck the night before. The mother had multiple fractures, the daughter a subdural hematoma that had been evacuated. They now looked as if they were going to pull through. But it had been close. Too close. "Naw, I hardly saw the guy. I do remember that it was about ten-thirty p.m., if that's of any help."

"What about the guy's cologne?"

Chang shook his head. "I've got a bad head cold. Right now I couldn't smell horseradish."

Jake took out his notepad. "Tell me about her amnesia."

"It was global."

"What do you mean, 'global'?"

"Amnesia is fairly common after head trauma," Chang said, now sounding clinical. "Usually the person is disoriented to time and place. It's rare for them to forget who they are. But she did. So she had no recollection of time, place or person. That's global amnesia."

"How long does it last?"

"Days to weeks, sometimes longer." Chang reached for a handkerchief and sneezed into it.

"Is it ever permanent?"

"It can happen."

Jake asked, "Do you take any precautions with patients who have amnesia?"

"There's no need for that," Chang told the detective. "These patients aren't dangerous."

"Yeah, but they just might walk the hell out of here, like Joanna did," Jake said bitterly.

"She was strapped onto a gurney," Chang said, wondering why the cop was so emotional about a missing person. "And besides, it didn't happen that way."

"How did it happen?"

Chang sneezed again. "Judy knows more about it than I do."

"After she was brought in by the paramedics," Judy told the detectives, "I put her in room three and made sure her vital signs were stable. Then I left the room to attend to other matters and ran into the patient's uncle. He wanted to see her, so I took him to room three and left him there."

"That's when all hell broke loose," Chang said, picking up the story. "I heard someone screaming out at the top of their lungs in room three. 'He's going to kill her! He's going to kill her!' I ran into the room and saw a middle-aged man standing next to the patient. He identified himself as the patient's uncle. Crazy Emma kept screaming that he was trying to kill the patient."

"Wait a minute," Jake said quickly. "Who is Crazy Emma and what was she doing in the room?"

"Most of the rooms are divided into two by a curtain," Chang explained. "Your woman was on one side, Crazy Emma was on the other with an injured foot. Emma is a paranoid schizophrenic who visits the ER as frequently as she can."

"You left a patient who doesn't know who she is or where she's at with a crazy nut?" Jake asked incredulously.

"Emma is harmless," Chang said calmly. "Crazy, but harmless."

"Bullshit!" Jake hissed. "Don't tell me about paranoid schizo-phrenics' being harmless. I saw one throw a man fifteen feet across a room once."

"Well, I guess that could happen if they were threatened," Chang conceded. "But Emma wasn't that kind of crazy. She was the type who didn't want an X ray because the rays were going to penetrate her brain and cause it to explode. I didn't consider her violent."

"Ah-huh," Jake said, not believing a word Chang was saying. "So, when you ran into the room you actually thought Emma was going through one of her paranoid episodes."

"Exactly," Chang said. "I thought she had imagined the whole thing. So I escorted the uncle out and asked him to wait in the reception area for a few minutes until we could clear the room. A couple of minutes later I heard Judy yelling in the corridor."

"I had just walked out of room one," Judy said, continuing the story, "when I saw the patient and Emma dressed in long white coats. I yelled for them to stop, but they ran for the door. Then all hell broke loose again. People in the waiting room jumped up to see what was happening and started pushing one another. And then a fight broke out. One poor guy ended up with a badly frac-tured clavicle. He was waiting for his grandmother to be seen. It was a goddamn riot down here."

"And the two patients walked right out the door, didn't they?" Jake asked.

"Yes."

"And I'll bet old Uncle Will didn't come back to inquire about his niece, did he?"

"No," Judy said sheepishly. "He didn't come back."

Jake reached into his coat pocket and took out a picture of Will

Patterson. It was the military photo, aged twenty years. "Is this the patient's uncle?"

Chang studied the picture at length and shrugged.

"I can't be sure," Judy said. "He had on that damn hat."

Jake pocketed the picture and asked, "Can you remember anything unusual about the patient? Was she wearing anything unusual?"

Judy said, "She had on a lovely gold necklace and earrings. They were plain and simple, but really elegant."

"Do you think Crazy Emma saw the jewelry?" Jake asked.

"Maybe."

Jake gave them each a card and said, "If you can remember anything else, give me a call at this number—day or night." Jake turned to walk out, then turned back. "What was Emma's last name?"

"Stanley," Chang said at once.

"You wouldn't happen to have an address for her, would you?"

"She's homeless."

Jake and Farelli walked out of the ER and into bright sunlight. The morning air was clear and cool and free of smog. Traffic on Sunset Boulevard was heavy.

"Give Buck a call," Jake told Farelli, "and ask him to have his people redo the photo on Will Patterson. Tell him we want one made that has him wearing a floppy rain cap."

"Right." Farelli took out his notepad and started scribbling.

"Then get as many men as you need and start combing this area. Check out the all-night restaurants, doughnut shops and convenience stores—anything that might have been open between ten and eleven p.m. Show them pictures of our guy and of Joanna. See if anybody remembers anything."

"Got you."

"Then call all the cab companies in the area and see if there were any pick-ups in this vicinity. Tell them we're looking for two women wearing white coats." Jake took out a cigarette and lit it absently. "Also check out any buses that were on Sunset Boulevard between ten and eleven p.m."

Farelli hesitated. "Those are real long shots, Jake. The doc didn't have her purse and the homeless broad probably didn't have two nickels to rub together."

Jake shook his head, disagreeing. "The homeless always have loose change on them—from begging. And most of them have got a ten- or twenty-dollar bill stashed away in a shoe or someplace safe for emergencies. They may be filthy, but they sure as hell know how to survive on the street."

Farelli said, "You figure the doc is still alive, huh?"

"Maybe," Jake said, hoping against hope. "If the killer had caught them last night he would have killed them on the spot and made no effort to hide the bodies. A homeless hag and an amnesiac. Who would give a damn? Yeah, if they were murdered we would have found their bodies by now."

They're dead, Farelli thought to himself. A hag and an amnesiac up against a pro. There was no way they were going to get away. "You figure the doc ran because she saw the guy trying to ice her?"

"I doubt it," Jake said. "Remember, Joanna was strapped on a gurney. Somebody had to loosen those straps. It had to be the crazy nut who did that."

"Why would she help the doc?"

"I can think of at least two reasons. Maybe she was really trying to help. Or maybe she saw Joanna's jewelry."

"Which do you think it was?"

"The jewelry."

Farelli nodded. "I'd better check out all the pawnshops. Do you know what the jewelry looked like?"

Jake thought back to the morning before, when he'd stopped by Joanna's lab to get a follow-up on the microfilm. "The necklace is plain gold, no links. The earrings were shaped like tiny leaves." Jake threw his cigarette down and angrily crushed it out. "She's got no chance, no chance at all."

"Hell, Jake, you never know. The doc might get lucky."

Jake slowly shook his head. "I talked with Buck this morning and told him what had happened in the ER. Then I asked him one question. Is our pro as good a tracker in the city as he was in the jungle?"

"What'd Buck say?"

"The pro would be better in the city. The tracks are easier to follow."

31

Robert Mariner was suddenly awake. He bolted upright in bed as the doorbell rang again. "Who the hell is that?"

"What time is it?" Amanda asked, half asleep under the blankets.

"Seven a.m."

"Jesus Christ!"

The doorbell rang once more and Mariner went to the intercom on the bedroom wall. "Yes?"

"This is Rimer. We've got to talk."

Mariner stared at the intercom, sensing trouble. "Go around the side and meet me on the deck."

Mariner and Amanda quickly put on their bathrobes and hurried down the stairs of the two-story beach house. Amanda stopped in the kitchen for a large bottle of orange juice and glasses and followed Mariner out onto the deck. The beach at Malibu was deserted, the ocean pale blue and calm as a lake.

Rimer trudged through the sand and came up the steps. "The woman got away."

"What!" Mariner said, taken aback. "What the hell happened?"

Rimer carefully detailed the events from the evening before, paying particular attention to Joanna's escape from the hospital. "But it's temporary. It's only a matter of time before I find her."

"We don't have time," Mariner snapped. "You are supposed to be a pro. How did you let her get away?"

"It wasn't anything she did intentionally. It was all luck," Rimer said calmly, thinking back to the homeless hag who had helped Joanna Blalock. He would kill the hag too. For the inconvenience she'd caused. "Her luck will run out very soon."

"It damn well better," Mariner said, now pacing the deck.

"We've paid you a lot already," Amanda said, wondering if Rimer was just trying to get more money out of them. "But as an incentive we'll give you a ten-thousand-dollar bonus if she's dead within twenty-four hours."

Rimer nodded, disliking the woman even more than usual, but the ten-thousand-dollar bonus appealed to him.

Mariner considered bringing in another professional to do the job, but there wasn't enough time. "And I want proof of her death. Pictures, photographs, whatever. And for your extra ten thousand dollars you'll perform one other task. I want you to search Blalock and if necessary her laboratory. You'll be looking for a cardiac pacemaker."

Rimer listened to Mariner describe what the pacemaker looked like, then asked, "You want me to destroy it?"

"No. I want it back."

"You'll have it by tomorrow morning," Rimer said.

Mariner watched Rimer walk down the steps and around the side of the house. Then he started pacing again. "Goddamn it! We need Blalock dead and we need that pacemaker back."

"But if Joanna Blalock is dead we won't have to worry about the pacemaker. The intricacies of the pacemaker will die with her."

"Don't bet on it. Maybe she's already discussed it with somebody else. Hell, she may have even sent it to another lab for further study."

"But if she's not around, nobody is going to follow up—"

"That big cop will," Mariner cut her off. "And it's not going to take a genius to put everything together."

Amanda lit a cigarette, her hand shaking noticeably. "How do you know she sent the pacemaker out?"

"I don't know for sure. But every time I asked Blalock to let us have a look at Sally Wheaton's pacemaker, she said it was still being studied. Now, what would you make of that?"

"Oh, shit," Amanda muttered, nodding to herself. "We have to get that pacemaker back."

"And quick," Mariner said, "before somebody connects that pacemaker to Bob Cipro's death."

Amanda nodded again, thinking about the phone call she'd received from Joanna Blalock. The one in which she'd asked for the details of Cipro's death, in particular whether his body was ever found. They knew that Cipro was the faceless man. Goddamn it! Everything was coming apart. Amanda tried to swallow, but her throat was bone dry. "What do we do now?"

"We start covering up our tracks."

"Maybe that won't be necessary. Suppose Rimer gets Blalock and the pacemaker."

"Suppose he doesn't," Mariner said and went back into the house.

32

Joanna awoke in a room flooded with sunlight. The light was blinding and everything was blurred. It took her a few moments to clear her head and focus her eyes. She was in a bare room with wooden floors and broken windows. In the distance she heard a mixture of sounds. People talking, birds squawking, and another noise she couldn't recognize.

"How are you feeling, Janie?" Emma asked.

Joanna stared at the dirty woman at length before remembering her. "Where are we?"

"At the beach."

"But where?"

"In a deserted apartment building in Santa Monica." Emma cackled loudly. "With an ocean view, mind you."

"How did I get here?" Joanna asked, still confused.

"On a city bus," Emma said and looked at Joanna strangely. "Don't you remember last night? Don't you remember what happened in the emergency room?"

Joanna thought back, recalling the ER and the nurse and the oriental doctor. And the man standing over her, arm raised and ready to strike. "The man," she said softly.

"You're goddamn right, the man," Emma said hoarsely. "He was going to kill you with a karate chop. You should have seen it, Teddy. It was the damnedest thing."

"Why did he want to do that?" Teddy asked.

"Who knows?" Emma picked at her teeth with her fingers. "All he said was that he was her uncle."

"Maybe he wanted her money," Teddy suggested.

"Could be."

Teddy studied Joanna, not liking her. He didn't like any new-comers because that meant another face to feed and there wasn't enough to go around as it was. And he didn't like Joanna because she really wasn't one of them. Teddy could tell she'd lived the good life. Her skin was soft and smooth and her hair was clean and fashionably cut. And she smelled good. He wondered what it would be like to screw her.

"Wish they'd get back with the food already," Emma said.

"Yeah, me too." Teddy was now studying Joanna's neck and ears, where the jewelry had been. The earrings had brought fifty dollars and Emma had given him ten dollars. But where the hell had Emma hidden the necklace? It was worth a lot, Teddy knew for sure. Emma was probably keeping it all for herself. He trusted Emma, but not when it came to money. Teddy didn't trust anyone when it came to money. His gaze drifted to Joanna's leg, now uncovered halfway up her thigh. Nice and smooth with no hair. He reached over and touched it.

Joanna quickly pulled her leg away, disgusted by the man's appearance. He was a short, wiry man, unshaven, with sores on his forehead that were covered with scabs.

"What's wrong?" Teddy asked.

"I don't like to be touched," Joanna said at once.

Emma smiled to herself, thinking that Janie was going to be touched by a lot of men in a lot of places. And soon too. But not until Emma made sure that Janie had no more jewelry or money or anything else of value hidden away.

They heard footsteps coming up the stairs. Emma hurried to the far corner of the room. Teddy took out a switchblade knife and opened it, then went to the wall beside the door and waited.

"What—?" Joanna said.

"Shhh!" Emma shushed her and whispered, "Keep quiet."

The footsteps drew closer and closer, then stopped. The door opened and a man and woman walked in. They were both tall and skinny, in their thirties, with strawberry-blond hair and unwashed faces. They wore filthy jeans and layers of sweaters that had gaping holes in them.

"What the hell took you so long?" Emma demanded.

The tall woman said, "We went by the Free Clinic to have them take a look at Timmie's leg, but they were closed for lunch." She turned and looked down at Joanna. "How are you, Janie? Is your head still hurting?"

"No, it's fine," Joanna said, trying to place the woman.

"You probably don't remember us from last night," the woman said softly. "I'm Bertie and this is my brother, Timmie."

"Did you bring the damn food?" Emma growled impatiently.

"Sure," Bertie said and put a brown paper bag on the floor. "Here it is."

Emma grabbed the bag and removed a package of cinnamon buns wrapped in cellophane. She stripped off the wrapping and the homeless group tore into the buns, ripping off large pieces and filling their mouths. They reminded Joanna of a pack of hyenas tearing apart a gazelle carcass.

"Got anything to drink?" Teddy asked, his mouth stuffed with food.

"Yeah," Bertie said and reached into the bag for a bottle of water.

Emma glared at her. "You wasted money on goddamn bottled water?"

Bertie shook her head quickly. "I found it in a trash can. I guess somebody just took a swallow or two and threw it away."

"Good," Emma said approvingly and removed the cap. She took a long swallow and passed the bottle around to the others.

Joanna stared at the window, her mind now flashing back to the night before. She began to remember events that had preceded her arrival in the ER. An ambulance, somebody placing an IV in her arm. Then there were lights, bright lights, and she was being carried upward on someone's shoulder. He was talking to her, telling her everything was going to be all right.

"My leg is getting worse," Timmie complained, "and it hurts like hell."

"Let's see it," Emma said.

Timmie pulled his pant leg up and extended his leg. On the

outer side of the calf was a red, angry-appearing sore. "The damn thing is getting bigger all the time."

"Maybe it's cancer," Teddy suggested.

Joanna looked down at the lesion and said, "It's a carbuncle."

"A what?" Emma asked.

"A carbuncle," Joanna said again. "It's a boil filled with pus."

"Do you know how to treat it?" Bertie asked.

"Sure," Joanna said easily. "You just I-and-D it. You incise it and you drain it."

"How do you do that?" Timmie asked, fear now in his voice.

"With a knife," Joanna told him.

"Oh, no!" Timmie pulled his pant leg down and backed away. "No way! Nobody is sticking a knife in me."

Emma grabbed Timmie's sweater and pulled him back. "Keep still and do as you're told." She turned to Joanna. "Do you need a special knife to do it?"

"No," Joanna said. "Any knife will do, as long as it has a sharp point."

"How about a switchblade?" Emma asked.

"That would do fine."

Teddy shook his head firmly. "You're not using my knife. You're not going to get pus all over my knife."

Emma held out her hand to Teddy and waited. He hesitated, then unhappily gave her his switchblade. Emma looked over at Joanna. "You've done these I and D's before, huh?"

"Lots of times."

Bertie asked excitedly, "Are you a nurse, Janie?"

Joanna shrugged. "I don't know what I am."

"Do you need anything else to do this I and D?" Emma asked.

"Just some gauze and a bottle of alcohol," Joanna said.

"We'll get those at the drugstore," Emma said and led the way out.

They walked down a flight of stairs, then went through a side door into the alley. They made certain the door stayed unlocked and strolled out to the walkway in front of the old apartment building. Before them was the ocean, deep blue and calm as a lake. It was midday and the sun was bright and warm. People were lying on the sand, tanning themselves. Overhead seagulls were swooping down and picking up scraps of food from the beach.

They headed north along the cement boardwalk, stopping only to peer into trash cans to see if anything was salvageable. They passed building after building, all of them boarded up and deserted.

"Why are all the buildings closed?" Joanna asked.

"They're like the building we live in," Emma said. "Condemned because of damage caused by the earthquake."

Joanna nodded, but she couldn't remember the earthquake and wondered when it had happened.

Ahead Emma saw a group of either German or Scandinavian tourists with cameras around their necks. She figured that Bertie, with her blond hair and waiflike face, would do the best with them. "Bertie, do your thing."

Bertie darted out in front and approached the tourists, hand out. "Could you spare some change for the homeless?"

The tourists began reaching into their pockets.

"What is she doing?" Joanna asked.

"She's begging," Emma said simply. "That's how we get money to live."

The walkway widened and was becoming more populated now. On the right were people gathered around tables watching chess matches. On the left were park benches with men sleeping on them. Joanna stared at the men lying motionless, shirts off, mouths agape. Her mind started to flash back and she saw a large tiled room with stainless steel tables and dead bodies on them. The bodies were split wide open, eviscerated. "Corpses," Joanna said quietly.

"Naw," Emma said. "They're just sleeping."

Moments later they came to a small drugstore. Emma reached into her pocket and felt the loose change, mainly nickels and dimes. Beneath the coins was the thirty-five dollars remaining from the sale of the earrings. And beneath that was the gold necklace. It was worth at least a hundred dollars, Emma thought happily, maybe even more. "Okay, everybody wait out here while Janie and I go in to get the things we need."

The women walked into the store and down an aisle where bandages and antiseptics were displayed. The store owner was a step behind them.

Emma saw the man behind them and wondered if he had been

sent by the government to spy on her, now that she had money. Those government bastards were everywhere. She fingered the switchblade knife in her pocket, ready to defend herself.

"Is there something I can help you with?" the owner asked, keeping his distance and hoping the pair wouldn't bring fleas into his store.

"We need a small bottle of alcohol, a roll of tape and some gauze," Joanna said.

"What type of gauze?"

"Two-inch," Joanna ordered. "Preferably something impregnated with a bactericidal agent."

The owner was taken aback by Joanna's demeanor and use of medical terminology. "What kind of bactericidal agent?"

"Polymyxin will do."

The owner quickly collected a bottle of ethyl alcohol, a roll of tape, gauze and a tube of polymyxin sulfate. "You got the money to pay for all this?"

Emma asked, "What does the polymyxin cost?"

"Eleven ninety-five," the owner said.

"We'll do without it," Emma said promptly.

The owner smirked and replaced the tube. "Anything else?"

"That'll be all," Emma said, waiting for the man to turn before she quickly reached back to the shelf.

They paid at the front counter and walked outside. The sun seemed brighter and hotter now and there were even more people on the boardwalk.

"Do we have to go back to the apartment to do this I and D?" Emma asked Joanna.

"No. We can do it on a park bench."

"Good."

The homeless group gathered around a bench outside the drugstore. Timmie laid his head back on Bertie's lap and stretched out his leg. He squeezed his eyes tightly shut and clenched his jaw.

"Jesus," Emma hissed at him. "You're acting like a big baby."

"It's going to hurt," Timmie moaned as Bertie stroked his head.

"No, it won't," Joanna assured him, then turned to Emma. "Get me a napkin and a cube of ice."

Emma hustled over to a nearby vendor and talked him out of some crushed ice and a paper napkin, then hurried back. "What the hell is the ice for?"

"Anesthesia." Joanna poured alcohol over the carbuncle and gently cleansed the area with the napkin. Then she poured more alcohol on the sore and placed crushed ice atop it.

"It stings," Timmie whined.

"Tell me when it stings a whole lot." Joanna looked over to Emma. "Open the knife, strike a match and put the tip of the blade into the flame."

Emma quickly performed the task and handed the knife to Joanna. Timmie was bitching louder and louder, tears streaking his cheeks. Bertie continued to stroke his forehead.

Joanna removed the ice and rapidly incised the frozen skin over the carbuncle. Thick yellow pus spurted out. She gently pressed down at the edges of the sore and more pus came out, thicker yet and foul-smelling. Joanna now saw something thin and brown protruding from the incision. She pulled it out and examined it. "A foreign body," Joanna said to herself.

"A what?" Emma asked.

"A sliver of wood," Joanna replied. "A splinter that probably started the infection."

Emma reached into her pocket. "I've got a surprise for you."

"What?" Joanna asked.

Emma took out a tube of polymyxin. "I lifted it from the drugstore."

"Christ." Joanna groaned, wondering what would have happened if they'd been caught. She carefully rubbed the antibiotic ointment into a strip of gauze and then packed the gauze into the now-drained carbuncle. She took several long pieces of tape and strapped them around Timmie's calf, bandaging the wound. "We're done."

"You're done?" Timmie asked, opening his eyes. "I hardly felt anything."

"Good," Joanna said, pleased.

Emma patted Joanna's shoulder. "You're pretty cool, you know?"

"She's great," Bertie chimed in and leaned over to kiss Joanna's cheek. "I'm so glad you're with us."

Timmie stood and walked around the park bench. "My leg feels great. All the pain is gone."

"Then you ought to thank Janie," Bertie said.

"I do thank you," Timmie said gratefully.

"I think I'll make Janie my top assistant," Emma said importantly.

Bertie and Timmie applauded loudly, happy with Emma's decision.

Teddy cleaned his knife with alcohol and kept his expression even, although inwardly he was seething. He had disliked Janie from the beginning and now he hated her. She was taking his place as the number-two person in the crowd, the person closest to Emma, the one who gave the orders when she wasn't around. Now he would be like Bertie and Timmie, who just sat on their asses and waited to be told what to do and when to do it. Like slaves. Teddy wasn't going to stand for that. He tested the sharpness of the blade with a finger, his eyes fixed on Janie's neck.

"How do you know about antibiotics and all that stuff?" Emma asked Joanna. "Are you a nurse?"

"I don't know."

"Do you have any idea where you live?"

"I'm not sure," Joanna said slowly. "I keep trying to remember."

Try harder, Emma wanted to say, believing that Janie was a nurse. And Emma knew that nurses made a lot of money and lived in nice apartments where they kept cash and jewelry and other valuable things hidden away.

The group moved northward along the boardwalk, now approaching an amusement park with a merry-go-round and a small ferris wheel. Beyond that was the Santa Monica Pier.

"I think we should work the pier," Emma said. "There's a lot of tourists out today."

"I'm going over to the Third Street Promenade," Teddy said.

"There won't be many tourists there," Emma warned him.

"Maybe. But there's a new dinosaur movie that just opened," Teddy said. "Those things usually draw a nice turnout."

"Okay," Emma said, not trusting him and planning to search his clothes later. "We'll meet back at the apartment."

Teddy walked up a steep overpass and crossed Ocean Avenue.

A motorist honked his horn at Teddy because he was crossing on a red light. Teddy gave the motorist the finger and kept walking. On the other side of the avenue the atmosphere changed and became much more expensive. Teddy passed by two trendy restaurants and watched the people leisurely eating lunch and sipping wine. He wondered what that would be like. To eat as much as you wanted whenever you wanted and to be waited on while you did it. Maybe have some coffee and dessert too. Teddy spat on the sidewalk, knowing he'd never be able to afford that. Not in a million years. He was lucky if he could afford to eat at McDonald's.

Teddy passed an appliance store that had one of its television sets turned on in the front window. He suddenly jerked his head around and stared at the picture on the screen. They were showing Janie's face. It was Janie, surer than hell. A younger Janie, but still her. Now her picture was gone and the television reporter was talking. So they're looking for Janie, Teddy told himself, and she's important enough to be on TV.

But was it the police or her uncle who was looking for her? That was important. The police usually didn't give any rewards, but relatives did. Teddy tried to concentrate on his problem and how to deal with it. Maybe he could call the television station and see who was looking for Janie. Yeah. But what station and how would he get the number? Emma would know. Yeah, maybe discuss it with Emma. But then Teddy thought again. If the reward was big money, Emma would take most of it, giving him only a little, like she did when they pawned the earrings. Maybe it was big money. Really big. Like a thousand dollars. Teddy's heart pounded at the thought of such a huge sum. And it could be all his too. But how to go about it? How?

Teddy spotted a liquor store across the street and hurried toward it. He'd get a bottle of wine. A big bottle. Teddy always thought better with wine.

33

It was late afternoon and the crowd on the Third Street Promenade in Santa Monica was starting to thin out. Karl Rimer chewed on a hot dog purchased from a street vendor and watched the people passing by. He paid particular attention to the faces of the homeless. He'd already questioned a dozen of them and none knew Crazy Emma, or if they did they weren't talking about it. But that didn't bother Rimer. He was certain that Joanna Blalock and the homeless hag were in the area. All of his instincts told him so.

Rimer thought back to the night before. Tracking the two women had been a lot easier than he'd anticipated. The only difficult part was tracking the first bus they had boarded. It had taken Rimer nearly twenty minutes to locate the bus and when he had the pair wasn't on board. And the driver—a big, black, surly son of a bitch—wasn't talking. But for a hundred dollars the driver suddenly remembered the homeless hag and her companion. And for another hundred dollars he recalled giving them a transfer for their final destination in Santa Monica. And for another hundred dollars the driver took out a book and told Rimer the exact route the bus in Santa Monica would take. Most of the stops would be on a street called Lincoln.

Rimer had driven like a wild man down Sunset, hoping to get to Santa Monica before the women did. But when he reached Lincoln, the street was deserted, traffic sparse, no homeless in sight. The next morning he had breakfast at a local coffee shop and talked with a group of rednecks at the counter. After agreeing with them that the country was going to hell because of the influx of foreigners, they told Rimer all about the homeless, whom they also despised. The homeless lived mainly in vacated houses and buildings near the beach. There were hundreds and hundreds of these places. Far too many for one man to search through. They also told him that most of the homeless did their begging on the Third Street Promenade.

Rimer licked the mustard from his fingers and moved along the promenade. He glanced into the windows of several stores, checking the reflections and seeing if anyone was watching him. Then he went into a bookshop and browsed leisurely.

Coming out of the store, he walked in the direction of the street vendor before suddenly turning and heading southward again. All the while he looked for familiar faces or people trying to cover their presence. He was looking for tails. He knew there weren't any, having checked a half dozen times already, but he double-checked again. Rimer was a very careful man.

Rimer passed a movie complex with a long line of people waiting to enter. The promenade was more crowded now, the homeless more obvious. To his right Rimer saw a homeless beggar sitting on the sidewalk and playing a harmonica badly off tune. A sign on his lap read MUSIC IS MY LIFE. Beside him a woman with a vacant stare stroked a cat with one hand and begged with the other.

Rimer wasn't interested in those types of homeless. They were the shy and harmless ones. All they wanted was something to eat and to be left alone. Rimer was looking for a special kind of homeless person. He wanted to find a down-and-out hustler, someone who lived by his wits and knowledge of the street, someone who was willing to sell anything or anybody.

Rimer crossed to the other side of the promenade and came onto a sidewalk show. A young Caucasian man was pedaling a unicycle, his small daughter up on his shoulders. The crowd— mainly Hispanics and Orientals—were applauding and throwing loose change to the cyclist. America was turning into shit, Rimer thought disgustedly and glared at the crowd. Foreigners. All goddamn foreigners.

Rimer stopped at the corner and glanced over his shoulder, again checking for a tail. That's when he saw his man. The homeless man was leaning against a building, hands in his pockets. He had a ferretlike face with slicked-down black hair and dark eyes that moved continually. Rimer slowly approached the man.

The homeless man was instantly on guard. He studied Rimer carefully, ready to run at a moment's notice.

"I need some information," Rimer said.

"You a cop?"

Rimer ignored the question and took out a roll of bills. "And I'm willing to pay for it."

"How much?"

"That depends on the quality of the information." Rimer peeled off a twenty-dollar bill and handed it to the man. "You know a homeless hag named Emma?"

"Could be," the man said vaguely, his eyes still on the thick roll of bills.

Rimer peeled off another twenty and held it out. "I need to find her. How do I do that?"

"That's a real tough question," the man said, smiling thinly.

Rimer gave the man the second twenty. "Now you've got forty dollars and for that you're going to tell me all about Emma. If you lie or give me bad information, I'll come back and break both of your legs and you'll never walk again."

The homeless man signaled with a finger and turned, then walked up the promenade in the direction Rimer had just come from. Rimer stayed a few steps behind and kept his eyes on the homeless man's feet. The feet would give the first sign that the man was going to split and run. And if the man did make a break for it, Rimer knew that he'd have to catch him in the first few seconds. Otherwise the man would melt into the crowd and disappear.

They passed the sideshow, where the unicyclist was now on his knees picking up the dimes and quarters thrown to him. His little daughter was helping him retrieve the coins. A street child, Rimer thought, remembering the street children in Vietnam. She'd be a thief and a whore by the time she was twelve.

As they approached the movie complex, the homeless man

stopped and bent down to retie his shoelaces. He didn't look at Rimer as he spoke.

"See the guy hustling the line of moviegoers?"

Rimer glanced over quickly. "You mean the guy with sores on his forehead?"

The homeless man nodded. "He lives with Emma. Follow him and you'll find her."

"How did you know to check the pawnshops in Venice?" Jake asked.

"I didn't," Farelli said. "I just put out the word to cover all the pawnshops in the whole city."

"That's a pretty big area."

"It's a pretty important person I'm looking for," Farelli said and chewed vigorously on his gum.

"Yeah," Jake said quietly, but inwardly he was cursing his slip-shoddiness. When he had spoken with Farelli last night about covering all the pawnshops, he'd thought they were talking about pawnshops in the vicinity of the hospital. And that was stupid. Of course you had to cover every pawnshop in the whole damn city because the homeless roamed everywhere. It was an oversight on Jake's part, but luckily Farelli knew how to handle these types of investigations. Jake was aware that he was making little mistakes because he was emotionally involved with Joanna, and he knew that he should take himself off the case. But he couldn't. He just couldn't.

They exited the Santa Monica Freeway and turned south on Lincoln Boulevard. It was five-thirty p.m. and traffic was still heavy and moving at a snail's pace. Farelli took out a red light and placed it on the roof of the car, then switched on the siren. Traffic immediately parted and they sped the final six blocks to the pawnshop. A black-and-white patrol car was outside the shop, the two officers inside.

The older of the officers, a middle-aged man with a paunch and gray-brown hair, gave the detectives a quick summary. At ten-forty-five a.m. a homeless woman brought in a pair of gold, leaflike earrings and hocked them for fifty dollars. She said her name was Mary Smith and gave a Redondo Beach address. The pawnshop owner called the police at three-twenty p.m., five minutes after receiving the police bulletin to be on the lookout for the gold earrings.

"You check the Redondo Beach address?" Jake asked the cop.

"It doesn't exist."

Jake walked over to the owner of the pawnshop. "Let's see the earrings."

The owner placed the earrings on a black velvet cloth and stepped back.

Jake examined them briefly. They looked like Joanna's but he couldn't be positive. "Did you ask the homeless woman how she happened to have gold earrings?"

"I sure did." Mo Green was short and stout with a ruddy complexion. "She said she found them on the beach."

"And you believed that crock of shit?"

Green shrugged. "It happens."

"Did she mention any other jewelry?"

Green wrinkled his forehead, thinking back. "She didn't, but her companion did."

"Describe her companion," Jake said quickly.

"A thin guy, unshaven, maybe forty or so."

Shit. Jake groaned to himself and sighed wearily. "How tall was the guy?"

"Maybe five-foot-eight."

"How much did he weigh?"

"He was really thin," Green said. "He couldn't have weighed more than one-forty."

"Did he have any physical features that really stood out?"

"Yeah," Green said, making a face. "He had these sores all over his forehead. They were covered with scabs and he kept picking at them." He shook his head disgustedly. "He'd pick a scab off and examine it."

"This other piece of jewelry that the companion mentioned— did he say what it was?"

"A necklace, I think. But they never showed it to me."

Jake asked, "Had you ever seen this Mary Smith before this morning?"

"A couple of times," Green replied. "She'd bring in little trinkets that were worthless, but I'd still give her a few bucks and send her on her way."

"Do you think she lives in this area?"

Green gestured with his hands, palms out. "Who knows? But if you want me to guess, I'd say yes, she lives around here."

"Why?"

"Because of her skin," Green said at once. "It was rough and sunburned. You know, like the beach people."

Jake and Farelli walked out of the pawnshop and past a small group of curious onlookers. The sun was setting now and a chilly wind was coming in from the ocean.

Jake handed Farelli a small envelope containing the gold earrings. "See if you can get some prints off these."

"Right." Farelli pocketed the envelope and spat out his gum. "Why in the hell didn't they hock the necklace too?"

"Maybe they were saving it for a rainy day."

"Or maybe they ain't got it yet. Maybe it's still around Joanna's neck."

Jake shook his head. "If they can get her earrings, they could get her necklace."

"I guess so," Farelli said and absently scratched at his piles. "You figure the pawnbroker is right? You figure the old hag lives in this area?"

"Probably," Jake said. "But it's still a damn big area. We're talking about all of Santa Monica and Venice and the beaches around them."

"It's going to take a busload of cops to cover it all."

"Take as many as you need."

"If there was only some way to narrow down the possibilities."

"Yeah, if only . . ." Jake's voice was drowned out by a huge, sixteen-wheel truck that rumbled by, shaking the sidewalk. Then a municipal bus whizzed by and the ground shook again. Jake followed the bus with his eyes, watching it stop at the corner and let passengers on. "Maybe there is a way to narrow it down."

"How?"

"How did Crazy Emma and Joanna get here last night?"

"Maybe they didn't come last night," Farelli said thoughtfully. "Maybe they waited until morning."

"No way," Jake said quickly. "There was a killer after them and they knew it. They'd want to get the hell out of there fast."

"Well, they sure didn't have a car," Farelli said.

"And they didn't hitchhike because nobody would have stopped and given them a ride. Not at ten-thirty at night. And the taxis are too expensive."

"That leaves the buses," Farelli said and reached for his notepad.

"You got it," Jake said, now thinking how to cover all the buses. "Double-check all the buses that were on Sunset Boulevard between ten and eleven last night. See if the drivers remember Crazy Emma or Joanna. See if they were given transfers for Santa Monica. Also check the schedules and find out what Santa Monica bus they would have ended up on and the exact route that bus would take."

Farelli was writing down the instructions as fast as he could. "And maybe the Santa Monica bus driver will remember where he dropped them off. I'll show him the doc's picture."

Jake reached into his pocket for a photograph and handed it over to Farelli. "Show him this photo too. See if he's been around asking the driver questions about Joanna and Emma."

Farelli studied the photo. It was the military photograph of Will Patterson, aged twenty years. Now he was wearing a floppy rain cap.

34

"It's going to look suspicious as hell if we just start destroying pacemakers," Amanda said.

"Not if we do it right," Mariner told her. "We'll say we're doing a random quality check and select out the special pacemakers."

"But you still have to destroy them."

Mariner shrugged. "They'll mysteriously disappear. Nobody will know the difference."

"What about the other special devices?"

"We'll do the same thing."

"It's going to seem peculiar," Amanda said dubiously. "Somebody might catch on."

"Have you got a better idea?" Mariner snapped.

Amanda hesitated, thinking. "I just don't want us to rush and do something stupid."

"Sure, let's take our time," Mariner said loudly. "Let's wait until this place is crawling with cops."

"Keep your voice down," Amanda said sharply. "Unless you want everybody in the building to hear you."

They were standing at the rear of a large laboratory on the tenth floor of the new Health First Tower. It was lunchtime and the room was deserted, but the door was half open. Mariner hurried over to the door and closed it, then came back.

"You don't seem to understand," he said, keeping his voice

down. "Without those implantable devices there's no evidence against us."

"Why are you in such a hurry to destroy all of our work and all of our plans?"

"Because it could send us to jail for life or worse."

"I can see it now," Amanda said, an edge to her voice. "You destroy everything and a moment later Rimer calls and tells us Blalock has been taken care of. How does that sound to you?"

Mariner looked at the wall clock. It was nearly one p.m., six hours since they'd last heard from Rimer. "Are you willing to trust your life to that son of a bitch?"

"He's supposedly very good at what he does."

"If he's so good, why is Joanna Blalock still walking the streets of Los Angeles?"

The PA system clicked on and a female voice said, "Dr. Mariner, call on line two. Dr. Mariner, line two please."

"Maybe it's good news," Amanda said.

"Maybe."

She watched Mariner hurry over to the phone and talk briefly. There was no expression on his face and his voice was even, but his hand kept balling up into a tight fist. Joanna Blalock had gotten away again, Amanda was thinking, or maybe even worse. Maybe the police had found her and she'd regained her memory.

Mariner placed the phone down and walked back slowly, a stunned expression on his face.

"What is it?"

"The call was from a Dr. Benson at Memorial," Mariner said tonelessly. "He's head of their Bioengineering Department. He told me that last week Joanna Blalock showed him a microfilm of an MPI pacemaker. They couldn't determine what the opaque material inside it was. And his curiosity just got the best of him. That's why he called."

"Oh, Jesus!" Amanda went pale and slumped down into a chair. "What did you tell him?"

"That I'd look into it."

"She's got the microfilm," Amanda said weakly and tried to light a cigarette with shaking hands. "We're as good as dead."

"Like hell we are!"

Amanda tried to light her cigarette again, but her hands were trembling badly. She threw the cigarette down as tears welled up in her eyes. "We're dead."

Mariner picked her up from her chair and shook her roughly. "Pull yourself together, goddamn it!"

"We're going to jail."

"Not if we use our heads. There's always a way out if you're smart enough to find it."

"But the microfilm—"

"Screw the microfilm! If we can get the pacemaker back and destroy the others, we'll be fine."

Amanda gathered herself. "Have you got the serial numbers of the devices that we have to destroy?"

"In my wall safe." Mariner took her arm as they walked to the door. "Are you going to hold up all right?"

"I think so."

"Good." But Mariner could see that she was still pale and shaky, and he knew she would crack under the least bit of pressure. He would have to watch her closely. If she started to crack, she would become a huge problem. But it was a problem that Mariner could fix and maybe even turn to his advantage. In the back of his mind Mariner saw the outline of a plan in which all the blame would be placed on Amanda. And Rimer would make certain she could never defend herself or point the finger at Mariner.

"You'll think of a way out, won't you?" Amanda asked.

"I already have," Mariner said and smiled to himself.

35

Rimer watched the man with scabs on his face open the side door to the apartment building. The homeless man paused for a moment and began to fiddle with the lock. Rimer quickly took out his pocket-sized telescope and saw that the man was making certain the door remained unlocked. That told Rimer that the side entrance was in all likelihood the only way in or out. But he'd have to double-check.

Rimer waited for the door to close and slowly circled the apartment house. Like the surrounding buildings, it was three stories tall, deserted and boarded up. Rimer carefully tested another door, then moved on to the ground-floor windows. All were nailed shut.

Rimer walked back onto the boardwalk and glanced out at the water. Daylight was fading fast, a big red sun sinking into the sea. No one was on the beach. He studied the area for a few seconds longer, then turned back to the apartment building just as light appeared in a second-floor window. There was no electricity—Rimer was sure of that—so it had to be either candles or a lantern. He hoped it was a lantern. It was easy to start a fire with one of those.

Rimer wondered how many people were in the apartment. The guy with scabs on his face and Emma for certain, and probably others too. But how many? Five? Ten? A dozen? Who the hell knew? The smart move would be to keep the building under surveillance and get an accurate count so he'd know what he was dealing with. But there wasn't time for that. Joanna Blalock's face was in the newspapers and on television and every cop in Los Angeles was looking for her. No, there wasn't time. And watching the apartment and keeping himself concealed would also be a problem. There was no good cover, only a wide boardwalk and an open strand of beach. Rimer decided to work from the inside.

He checked the safety on his Beretta, keeping the gun under his trench coat, and went into the alley where the side entrance was located. The door suddenly opened. Rimer turned around abruptly and stepped back onto the boardwalk. He walked slowly down the way, gazing up at the stars, a man on a leisurely stroll. He heard footsteps behind him and slowed down even more. The man with scabs on his face hurried by.

Rimer waited until the man was out of sight, then turned and headed back to the apartment building. The light was still on in the second-floor window. A figure passed in front of the window and was gone. Rimer was certain it was a female and he thought she had long hair. Quickly he moved into the alley and went to the side entrance. Pressing his ear to the door, he listened and heard nothing. He took out his Beretta, switched the safety off, and entered.

The lobby was dark except for a beam of light coming down the staircase. Rimer remained stationary and waited for his eyes to accommodate to the dimness. To his left was a rusty elevator. The old type, built like a cage. Next to it was a closed door. Rimer moved to the staircase and slowly walked up on his tiptoes. The steps were old and wooden and despite his best efforts they creaked with each step he took. Rimer stopped and listened for movement or voices. There was total silence. He started up the stairs again. His foot almost went through a rotten step. The wood cracked loudly.

"Is someone there?" a female voice called out.

"Ah-huh," Rimer muttered.

"Teddy, is that—?"

Rimer was through the door and in the apartment. He pointed his gun at the head of a tall woman sitting on the floor. She was skinny and dirty with strawberry-blond hair. Rimer quickly scanned the room, his weapon held out in the firing position.

"Who are you?" Rimer asked.

"I—I'm Bertie," the woman said, her voice trembling.

"You live here alone?"

"No," Bertie said and stared at the gun, her eyes big as saucers. "My friends also stay here."

"I'm looking for Emma. Where is she?"

Bertie shook her head. "I don't know."

"You've got ten seconds to give me an answer," Rimer said coldly.

"Please, mister," Bertie pleaded. "They don't always tell me."

"You've got five seconds."

"It's the truth, I swear it," Bertie cried, holding up a hand.

Bertie heard a soft thumplike sound and immediately felt a terrible pain in her hand. She looked at it and saw blood spurting out. She opened her mouth to scream, but Rimer stuck his weapon into it.

"Now where are your friends?" he asked.

She garbled an answer and he removed the gun from her mouth.

"Where are they?" he asked again and stepped back.

"I don't know." Bertie's voice was a squeal. "I really don't."

"You've got one last chance."

"Don't! Please don't!"

The bullet went in between Bertie's eyes. She slumped against the wall, her eyes still open.

Emma and Joanna were halfway up the stairs when they heard Bertie cry out. They stopped in their tracks.

"What's wrong with Bertie?" Joanna asked, too loud.

"Shhh!" Emma quieted her and took Joanna's hand, then began to slowly back down the stairs.

"Maybe Bertie needs our help," Joanna said softly, but her voice still carried.

"Keep your mouth shut and do as you're told," Emma hissed.

Joanna's foot went through a rotten step and she tumbled backward, still holding on to Emma and pulling the homeless woman down the stairs with her. The women landed hard, but unhurt.

The light at the top of the stairs suddenly dimmed and when the women looked up they saw a silhouette of a tall man wearing a trench coat and a floppy rain cap.

"Run!" Emma yelled and jerked Joanna up by her collar.

Joanna started to run, but tripped and fell, skinning her knees. Emma jerked her up again as the man bounded down the stairs.

He'd catch us in the alley, Emma decided in a fraction of a second and ran for the door next to the elevator, pulling Joanna along with her. They went through the door and down the stairs into pitch blackness.

Rimer was right behind them. He came to the door and looked down into the darkness. He wondered if it was a basement or another floor or perhaps just a storage area. It was so dark he had no feel for its size. Slowly Rimer took a step down, then another before he changed his mind. He ran back up the stairs for the lantern.

"Did you see him?" Joanna asked breathlessly. "Did you see him?"

"Damn right I did," Emma said in a whisper. "He's the son of a bitch who tried to kill you."

"Why?" Joanna asked, fighting her panic. "Why is he trying to kill me?"

Emma shrugged. "Ask him. He's *your* uncle."

Joanna reached down to rub her throbbing knees and felt the abraded skin and warm, sticky blood. "Where are we?"

"In the basement."

"Let's get out of here."

"How?"

"Isn't there another way out?"

"Not that I know of," Emma said, realizing their predicament, but still believing she'd made the right decision. He would have caught them in the alley and killed them there and then. At least they had a chance in the basement. A small chance.

Joanna's heart was pounding. Now everything was worse. They were cornered, imprisoned like in a container, with no way out except the door where the man was. "My God! We're trapped."

"Everybody is trapped," Emma said philosophically. "We're all trapped in cages constructed by our own emotions."

"What?" Joanna looked at Emma oddly.

"It's just something I once heard." From a patient who was in the room next to Emma's at the UCLA Psychiatric Hospital. What the hell was her name?

"We've got to find a place to hide."

"Yeah." Emma took out a disposable cigarette lighter and flicked it on. The basement was featureless with cement walls that had no air vents. The only light fixture had a broken bulb. There was human excreta on the ground.

Joanna saw several corridors that led into blackness. "Which way do we go?"

"Just follow me," Emma said and turned the lighter off. "There are some low-hanging beams in this place, so keep your head down. And don't talk unless you have to. Remember, the bastard can't see us, but he can hear us."

"Suppose he has a flashlight."

"Then we're in big trouble."

Suddenly there was a light at the top of the stairs. The man was coming down, holding a lantern in front of him.

"Oh, shit!" Emma said, grabbing Joanna's hand and pulling her down a darkened corridor.

Rimer heard muffled sounds in the distance, but he couldn't identify them or tell the direction they were coming from. The basement was cavernous, much larger than he'd thought, and all noises tended to make echoes. He concentrated his hearing, but picked up no other sounds. Holding the lantern high, Rimer saw that he was standing in the center of the basement and that there were four corridors leading away. He decided to start with the one that pointed directly north.

Joanna and Emma were huddled together in an alcove, hiding behind a big cardboard box. The floor was damp and cold, the blackness so complete they couldn't see their hands in front of their faces.

Faintly, above the sound of her breathing, Joanna heard the sound of footsteps. "Is he coming?"

"I don't know," Emma said quietly. "But you'll see his light before you hear him. Keep looking for the light."

"And what do we do when we see it?"

"Go to the left," Emma said, clearing her throat as softly as she could. "Remember, go to the left. You got that?"

Joanna nodded quickly. "Go left."

"Now you stay put. I've got to do something." Emma pushed the box aside and slipped away in the darkness.

Joanna fought the fear flooding through her. She felt so alone in the darkness and so vulnerable. Quickly she reached for the cardboard box and pulled it close to her. Christ! She didn't like the thought of the bastard catching her alone in the deserted basement. God knew what he'd do to her before he killed her. Joanna huddled up in a ball and started to tremble. The cardboard box she was holding onto also shook and scraped softly against the floor.

Rimer returned to the center of the basement after finding nothing in the first corridor he'd searched. He was about to go to the next when he heard a sound coming from the corridor directly behind him. It was a soft, rustling sound. Something was rubbing against something. Rimer moved toward the sound.

Joanna heard someone coming. She tensed up and brought her legs back, ready to kick out at the attacker. Then she'd go left. That's what Emma had told her. Go left. The sounds were closer now.

Oh, God, I'm going to die! Joanna sensed that someone was very near, almost on top of her. But she saw no light. No lantern!

"Emma, is that you?" Joanna asked softly.

There was no answer.

Joanna froze and thought how stupid she'd been to speak and give away her position. She knew she was dead.

"I'm back," Emma whispered.

"Where have you been?" Joanna asked, angry that Emma had left her alone but relieved she was back.

"I had to pee." Emma shifted around on the floor and placed an object next to her. "Be careful of my bucket. It's half filled."

"With what?"

"My pee."

Oh, Jesus, Joanna groaned to herself, we're being tracked by a killer and this crazy woman is carrying around a bucket of urine. We're dead, she thought, we're as good as dead. Joanna hoped that it would all be over with quickly and that there would be no pain.

Both women suddenly tensed. Now there was a stream of light coming down the corridor. They heard footsteps approaching, slow and deliberate. The man was in no rush.

Emma got to her feet, pulling Joanna up, and reached for her bucket. "Just hang on to me and remember we go left."

But he's got the lantern, Joanna was thinking, and he can follow us everywhere we go. The damn lantern. She touched Emma's arm and whispered. "Give me the bucket."

"No," Emma hissed back. "I might have to pee again."

"Give me the goddamn bucket," Joanna growled under her breath.

Reluctantly, Emma handed the bucket over. "I want it back when you're finished."

The footsteps were louder now, the light brighter. The man was only a few yards away. Joanna held her breath. He was so close that she could hear him breathing. She slowly raised the bucket.

Rimer saw the flash of the metal bucket and started to react, but it was too late. A pint of urine landed on the hand that was holding the lantern, and the liquid doused the flame. Rimer whirled around and fired two shots into the alcove.

Joanna and Emma hurried down the corridor, feeling their way along the wall. They went to the left, then to the right. There was no light, not even a ray, the blackness so complete it was disorienting. Joanna held on tightly to Emma's skirt.

Somewhere behind them they heard the man cursing and mumbling. And they heard his footsteps coming.

Emma crouched down, pulling Joanna along and feeling for a large hole in the wall. It had to be close, had to. But she couldn't be sure in the intense darkness. She thought about flicking on her lighter, just for a second, but decided against it. The last thing she wanted to do was to give the bastard their exact location. She moved down the corridor and crouched even more, remembering that this was the area of the basement with the low-hanging beams. She neglected to remind Joanna about the beams as she picked up the pace.

Joanna thought she heard a sound just behind her and raised up to look back. The top of her forehead collided with a wooden beam and she dropped like a deadweight. Emma heard the dull thud and sensed Joanna falling. Immediately Emma knew what had happened. She quickly knelt down beside Joanna. "Are you okay?"

"My head," Joanna groaned, too loud.

"Keep quiet." Emma felt the lump on Joanna's forehead, but there was no blood. Good. Now where the hell was that hole in the wall? Emma flicked her lighter on, just for a moment, but the light it gave off seemed intense in the darkness. Directly across from them she saw the hole in the wall. It was a tunnel, three and a half feet in diameter and ten feet deep, built as part of some flood control drainage system but never completed. Emma crawled into the tunnel and pulled Joanna in after her. Emma put her hand over Joanna's mouth to muffle any groans.

Rimer saw the flash of light. At first he thought it might have been a door opening, but he was certain there was only one door out of the basement. And besides, no door opened and closed that fast when two people were exiting. No. It was a match or a lighter. He remained motionless and listened intently. He heard only silence. The women were no longer moving.

He walked on and waved an outstretched hand in front of him, feeling for unseen obstructions. The women were near. He knew it. He sensed it. His hand touched a low-hanging beam and he stopped, tapping it to see what it was.

Emma heard the man knocking on wood. He was close, so close. She squeezed herself back into the tunnel as far as she could go. Phlegm accumulated in the back of Emma's throat and she had to resist the urge to hawk it up. The knocking sound ceased. Now there was total silence. Emma clamped her hand tightly over Joanna's mouth.

Rimer slowly walked by the opening of the tunnel and continued down the corridor. It ended in a dead end. He turned and went back, a little faster now, waving his hand in front of himself and ducking beneath the beams. The women were still down here, he was sure of that. But they had the advantage. They knew the terrain and he didn't. The darkened basement with its nooks and corridors was excellent for hiding, just like the underground tunnels Charlie had lived in in Vietnam. Rimer had known precisely how to deal with Charlie and his tunnels. He'd use the same technique here.

Emma heard the footsteps pass by and fade into the distance. She removed her hand from Joanna's mouth. "Are you okay?"

"My head is killing me." Joanna moaned. The pain was over

her eyes. It felt like someone with a jackhammer was inside her skull.

"You ran into a beam," Emma whispered. "You've got to be more careful, Janie."

"My name is not Janie," Joanna said at once.

"What is your name then?"

"Joanna. Joanna Blalock."

"Do you know where you live?" Emma asked, wondering how big Joanna's house was and how much money she kept there.

"In Los Angeles."

"Yeah, but where?"

Joanna hesitated, trying to recall.

"Do you remember the accident you had?" Emma asked.

"Somewhat," Joanna said slowly. She flashed back to a winding road. The car behind was slamming into her and pushing her off the mountain.

"Maybe you were home just before the accident. Do you remember?" Emma asked, trying to jog Joanna's memory.

"No," Joanna said without thinking. "I was at Jake's place."

"Who's Jake?"

A picture of a man with a small scar on his chin flashed into Joanna's mind, but she couldn't recall anything else about him. "I'm not sure."

The door to the basement slammed shut with a bang, startling the women.

"Do you think he's left?" Joanna asked.

"Yeah, but don't get your hopes up," Emma said. "He's probably going to get a flashlight."

"But he'd have to leave the building to get one, right?"

"Yeah, I guess so."

"Maybe this is our chance to escape," Joanna said quickly.

"Maybe," Emma said thoughtfully. "But it'll be risky. He could be waiting up there for us."

"I say we go for it. Anything is better than being trapped in this basement."

"I guess," Emma said, not at all certain they were making the right decision.

They came out of the tunnel and both women stretched their cramped muscles. Emma flicked on her lighter and led the way down the corridor. They came to a bucket sitting in a puddle of urine and Emma picked it up. The flame in her lighter died and Emma flicked it back on.

They continued down the passageway, trying to see into the darkness ahead. A rat squealed and the women froze for a moment, then walked on. Now they were in the central area of the basement. On tiptoes they moved to the bottom of the stairs. Quietly they went up.

Joanna reached for the doorknob and slowly turned it. The lock clicked open. Joanna pushed at the door but it didn't budge, not even a little.

They were still trapped.

36

Timmie limped down the boardwalk in Santa Monica, favoring the leg with the carbuncle that had been incised and drained the day before. The bandage had come off and the packing was working its way out, dangling in the air. And it was hurting more and more. *Damn! Damn!* He hoped it wasn't festering back up and needing to be cut again. Maybe Janie could just put the packing back in. Yeah, maybe that would do it.

Approaching the apartment house, Timmie looked up at the second-floor window and saw no light. Good. Bertie was still sleeping. She needed the rest. The doctor had said that would help her liver heal. A virus had caused the problem, Timmie remembered, some kind of virus that injured the liver. Maybe it was time for them to move back home to Kansas, where they still had relatives. Bertie would get better a lot faster there—he was sure of that. He'd talk with her about it tomorrow.

Timmie turned in at the alley just as the side door to the apartment building opened. A man came out. A tall man wearing a funny-shaped hat. The man ran down the alley and disappeared in the darkness. Cautiously Timmie moved to the side entrance, ready to turn if the man came back. He waited another thirty seconds to make sure the man wasn't going to return, then opened the door. A cloud of smoke enveloped him, choking him and stinging his eyes.

"Bertie! Bertie!" Timmie screamed out and tried to fight his way in and find the stairs. But the smoke was too dense and there was no light. The heat and smoke seared his lungs and forced him back into the alley. *Bertie! My God! Bertie!* He thought about wrapping himself up in a wet blanket and trying to enter again. Like he'd seen Steve McQueen do in a movie. But he had no blanket and he had no water.

Timmie ran for the boardwalk as fast as he could, his eyes tearing and burning from the smoke. He rubbed at them, clearing his vision, then raced for a fire alarm a block down the way. He pulled the alarm and leaned heavily against the telephone pole, straining to catch his breath. His lungs felt as if they were on fire, and he heard himself wheezing loudly. Then the coughing started. He coughed so hard he brought up a doughnut he'd eaten a half hour earlier.

With effort he pushed himself away from the pole and started back to the apartment building. Maybe Bertie wasn't in the apartment, Timmie tried to tell himself, maybe she'd decided to go out. Maybe she got hungry and went to find food. But deep down he knew Bertie was still in the room, waiting for him like she always did. His coughing eased and he broke into a run.

Ahead he saw a small crowd gathering in front of the apartment house. There was thick smoke coming from the alleyway and now Timmie could see a light flickering in the second-floor window. A bright light. Then he saw the flames.

37

Joseph Blake glanced down at the charred remains and quickly looked away. He had been a fireman for twenty years and a fire chief for five, but he still hadn't gotten used to the sight of burned bodies. "I wonder how old she was."

"Who knows?" Max Hollander took off his helmet and wiped at his forehead with his sleeve. "It's hard to tell when they're fried like this."

Blake forced himself to look down at the victim again. Her skin was blackened and blistered, eyes and nose gone. He hoped she'd died quickly and better yet in her sleep. "And you found two hot spots, huh?"

"And maybe a third."

"So now we've got arson and murder, don't we?"

"Looks that way."

Both firemen knew that finding more than one hot spot was a sure sign of arson. A hot spot was an area where the flames and heat had been the most intense and usually indicated the place where a fire had started. In most accidental fires there was only a single hot spot, such as where an electrical outlet or burning mattress might have been. Two hot spots almost always meant that the fire had been deliberately set. And the burned body meant murder, regardless of whether or not the arsonist had known the victim was in the structure.

They walked down the stairs to the central lobby area. The ceilings and walls had been extensively damaged and the floors were badly scorched but still intact. Water was dripping down from above and forming large puddles. They came to the open door beside the elevator.

"What's in there?" Blake asked.

"It leads down to the basement," Hollander said.

"Did you check it out?"

"It's clear and bare. No sparks, but a fair amount of smoke. I guess it seeped through the cracks in the door."

"The door was closed when you got here?"

"More than closed," Hollander told him. "Somebody had jammed a board between the doorknob and the floor. And I mean really jammed. We had to cut through the damn board with an ax."

"Why do you think it was boarded up that way?"

Hollander shrugged. "I don't know. Maybe to keep anyone from going down there."

Blake nodded slowly. "You did check the basement out, though?"

"Oh, yeah. It's all cement and bare as hell. Nobody lives down there."

Blake stared at the door and studied it. Something about it was bothering him. Something was wrong.

A fireman came down the stairs and hurried over to them. "Chief, you might want to take a look at this."

"What have you got?" Blake asked, his concentration broken.

The fireman held up two long white coats. "We found these in a metal lockbox upstairs."

Blake immediately knew what the coats were. He'd seen them plenty of times when he worked as a paramedic. Doctors' coats. He reached into a side pocket of one coat and found a stethoscope and a reflex hammer. Above the left breast pocket was embroidered: "Dr. Lewis Chang, ER—Saint Luke's Hospital."

"After you've shown this to the arson boys, give Saint Luke's a call," Blake told the fireman. "Tell them we've found their coats."

"Somebody is going to be real happy," Hollander said. "That equipment in the pocket costs a bundle."

"I wonder how the coats got here," the fireman said.

Hollander smiled thinly. "They sure as hell didn't walk in by themselves, did they now?"

Blake turned back to the open door beside the elevator. Something about the door kept gnawing at him, but he couldn't put his finger on it. Maybe it would come to him later.

It was noon and Rimer was back on the Third Street Promenade in Santa Monica. He was looking for the homeless hustler so he could kill him. The hustler had seen him up close and was the only person who could connect Rimer to the homeless people who had died in the fire.

The day was bright and warm, the sky cloudless. Rimer had his trench coat off and over his arm, but he was still wearing his floppy rain cap. He had the cap pulled down over his forehead so that it obscured most of his face. He knew that people would think he was just trying to protect his fair skin from the sun.

Rimer moved down the promenade, looking from side to side like a tourist there for the first time. He went past the movie complex and a string of crowded outdoor restaurants. A panhandler came up to Rimer and begged for money. The beggar smelled like urine. Rimer waved him away disgustedly and walked on.

Near the corner he saw his man. The hustler was leaning against the wall of a bank building, eyeing the passersby and searching for an easy mark. Rimer approached the hustler slowly.

"Do you remember me?" Rimer asked.

"Yeah, I remember," the hustler said, chewing his gum loudly.

"Well, we need to talk again."

The hustler didn't move from his leaning position. "Don't blame me because you fucked up."

"I—I don't understand," Rimer said, caught off guard.

"You wanted to snuff Emma, right?"

"I didn't say that."

"Cut the bullshit," the hustler said evenly. "You set their building on fire last night."

"How do you know that?"

"I hear things on the street."

"It wasn't me," Rimer said firmly. "I didn't set any fire."

"Ah-huh," the hustler said, knowing the man was lying. "Well, whoever did sure fucked up."

"Why?"

"Because I saw Emma and her friend about an hour ago."

"Where did you see them?" Rimer asked at once.

The hustler smiled thinly and held out a hand. "I'm trying to remember."

Rimer glanced around and saw a policeman coming toward them on a bicycle. He waited for the cop to pass and handed the hustler a twenty-dollar bill. "Where?"

"Over in the park at Arizona and Ocean."

"What did Emma's friend look like?" Rimer asked and saw the hustler hold out his hand again. He gave the hustler another twenty, hating the man and looking forward to killing him.

"A younger woman, kind of pretty with light brown hair." The hustler watched Rimer turn and walk away, then called after him. "But you won't find them at Arizona and Ocean now. They're long gone."

Rimer came back, straining to control his temper. "Where are they?"

"I don't know," the hustler said, "but I know where they'll be tonight."

"Where?"

"It'll cost you a hundred."

Rimer peeled off five twenty-dollar bills. "I'm listening."

The hustler snatched and pocketed the bills in a single motion. "There's a restaurant at the corner of Wilshire and Seward. On Thursday night at around ten o'clock the guy who owns the restaurant gives the leftovers to the homeless."

"They must have a big turnout."

"Not really. He'll only feed Emma and her friends. Don't ask me why."

"He feeds them outside, right?"

"Yeah. In the back off to the side of the parking lot."

"What's behind the parking lot?"

The hustler squinted his eyes, thinking. "An alleyway and an apartment building. But by ten p.m. it's pretty quiet around there."

"Good." Rimer considered luring the hustler to a side street and killing him but decided not to. He might need the hustler again. "I may require your help in finding another homeless person," Rimer lied easily.

"Oh?"

"A man. I'll know more about him tomorrow."

"It's going to cost you."

"Let's make it a hundred even."

The hustler nodded eagerly. "I'll be here tomorrow. Same time, same place. It's my lucky spot."

It won't be lucky tomorrow, Rimer thought and walked away.

"Have they identified the body?" Jake asked.

"Not yet," Farelli said. "All they're saying is that it's a young female, burned beyond recognition."

They walked through a set of swinging doors and Jake said, "Tell me about the sequence of events again."

Farelli began with the telephone call he'd received from Judy Travers, the nurse in the ER at Saint Luke's Hospital. She'd told him about the fireman's finding the white coats in a building in Santa Monica that had been deliberately set on fire. The same white coats Emma and Joanna were wearing when they ran from the ER. Farelli then talked with the firemen who had put out the blaze and learned they had found a badly burned female corpse.

"Was the victim wearing any jewelry?" Jake asked, thinking about Joanna's necklace.

"They didn't say."

They went down a long, deserted corridor in the Los Angeles County Morgue. It was very quiet. The only sounds they heard were the clicks of their shoes against the tiled linoleum.

Jake stared straight ahead, thinking about the numerous times he'd come to the morgue to look at dead bodies. Bodies he didn't give a damn about. Bodies that were someone else's grief and heartache. But now the sadness was going to be Jake's. He dreaded the moment when he would learn that the burned body was Joanna. And he dreaded what would come after. The pain. The sleepless nights. Seeing someone on the street and believing it was her for a moment, then finding out it wasn't. He'd gone through the same things when Eleni had died. And now he would have to go through it again.

They entered a large autopsy room with ten stainless steel dissecting tables. Everything was clean and scrubbed down except for a table at the far end, where Girish Gupta was standing. He was dressed in surgical garb and a long black apron. His expression was somber.

Jake slowly approached the table, his gaze fixed on the burned corpse. It was charred and blackened and only up close did it seem to have human features.

"The sergeant asked me to wait for you before beginning the autopsy," Gupta said, "but I took the liberty of doing some preliminary observations."

Jake swallowed hard. "Do you think it's Joanna?"

Gupta looked at him strangely. "Dr. Blalock? Dr. Joanna Blalock?"

"Yes," Jake said softly.

"No way!" Gupta shook his head emphatically. "Absolutely no way! This corpse was six feet in length. Now Dr. Blalock may be tall, but she's not that tall. And then there's the color of the hair. Although the hair of the corpse was badly singed, I can tell you she was a natural blonde, which of course Dr. Blalock isn't." Gupta waved a finger at Jake. "No, no, Lieutenant. This most definitely is not Joanna Blalock."

Jake breathed a deep sigh of relief and looked up, offering a brief prayer of thanks. Out of habit he reached for his notepad.

"And I think the corpse was considerably younger than Dr. Blalock," Gupta added. "On X ray, the bone density of the victim was that of a twenty-year-old."

"So we've got a young woman, probably homeless, who burned to death," Jake said calmly, but inside he was still shaking.

"She didn't die by burning," Gupta said with certainty. "This woman was killed by a bullet wound to the head."

The detectives moved in closer as Gupta pointed to the round entrance wound in the middle of the forehead. "There was no exit wound, so the slug is still in her skull."

Jake turned to Farelli. "We'll want to compare that bullet with the one I dug out of the wall in Joanna's laboratory."

"Right," Farelli said and scribbled a note to himself.

Gupta's eyebrows went up. "You know who the murderer is?"

"We've got a pretty good idea," Farelli said.

"Why in the hell did he kill her?" Jake wondered.

"Maybe she got in the way," Farelli guessed.

Jake looked down at the charred corpse again. "Well, we've got a murder victim and we're never going to know who she was."

"I'm not so sure of that," Gupta said. "About an hour ago someone came here to claim the body."

Jake jerked his head up. "Who?"

Gupta shrugged. "Some young fellow. I didn't actually see him, but according to my secretary he identified himself as being her brother."

"Is he still here?"

"I don't think so, but you'll have to ask my secretary. She's in the big office down the hall."

Jake and Farelli left the autopsy room and walked quickly down the corridor to the assistant coroner's office. A plump, middle-aged secretary with curly brown hair was hunched over a type-writer, busily punching keys.

Margie Wilson looked over at the detectives. "Farelli, you're putting on too much weight."

"You should talk," Farelli snapped back good-naturedly.

Jake said, "Gupta told us that someone came to claim the burned body."

"That's right," Margie said. "He came in around four p.m."

"Is he still here?"

"Nope."

"Tell me about him."

Margie reached for a legal pad and read from her notes. "He gave his name as Timmie Sanders. No address. He claimed that the victim was his sister Bertie. I told him he had to come up with a definite ID before we could release the body."

"What did he say to that?" Jake asked.

The secretary shrugged. "Hell, he was a young kid. He couldn't

have been more than twenty. I explained that we'd need something like fingerprints or a dental record to definitely identify the
body. And he said he'd get her dental records.''

"Shit," Farelli scoffed. "Where the hell is a homeless kid going
to get dental records from?"

"The Free Clinic," Margie said at once. "There's a Free Clinic
in Venice and another one in the mid-Wilshire area."

"How do you know that?" Jake asked.

"Because I work with the homeless," Margie said.

Jake looked over at Farelli. "You take the mid-Wilshire clinic
and I'll cover the one in Venice."

"Maybe we should get some black-and-whites over there
pronto," Farelli said, glancing at the wall clock. It was four-forty-
five p.m.

"No," Jake said promptly. "The homeless are frightened of
cops, and if he sees them he might run. We don't want to lose
this guy. Maybe—just maybe—he'll lead us to Joanna."

Farelli shook his head dubiously. "That's a big maybe. Hell,
we're not even sure this guy knows Joanna."

"Oh, yes, we are," Jake said. "His sister died in the same apartment where they found the white coats that Emma and Joanna
were wearing. They're probably all living together, like a family."

Farelli thought for a moment, then nodded in agreement.
"Yeah, I'll buy that."

"Now we've got to call those clinics and tell them not to give
out any dental records on Bertie Sanders. If Timmie does show
up, they're to stall him. Tell him they're having trouble finding
the records."

"We'd better hope he hasn't already gotten to the clinic and
picked up those records," Farelli said.

Jake turned quickly to the secretary. "Where can we get the
phone numbers to these dental clinics?"

"From me," the secretary said and reached for her phone
book.

39

"Are you sure you're a doctor?" Emma asked.

"I'm sure," Joanna said.

"What kind of doctor?"

"I think I'm a pathologist," Joanna said slowly. "I think I do autopsies."

"You mean, like on dead people?"

"Yes."

"How much money do you make?"

"I'm not certain." Joanna didn't know how much her income was or where she worked or even the city she worked in. She knew she was in Los Angeles and that was probably where she worked. But her mind kept flashing back to Baltimore and some hospital there. An old, gray hospital. She couldn't remember its name.

"You probably live in a real expensive house," Emma said. "Most doctors do."

Joanna tried to recall where she lived. In her mind's eye she saw a small bungalow. Jake's house—whoever Jake was. And she remembered driving away from the house and onto a mountain road. And a car behind her pushing her off the road. And the emergency room where a man tried to kill her. Why was he after her? Why?

"Maybe I should go to the police," Joanna said at last.

"Oh, yeah, that's a great idea," Emma said derisively. "Then they can call your uncle and he can come down and finish you off for good."

"He's not my uncle," Joanna said, now remembering her sister Kate and her mother.

"Well, whoever he is, he sure as hell means to kill you, doesn't he?" Emma took Joanna's arm and guided her off of Lincoln Boulevard and onto Wilshire. It was nine-forty-five p.m. and traffic was light. "He goddamn near got both of us in that basement, huh?"

Joanna shuddered, recalling how they had been locked in the basement and how the smoke had started coming down, choking them. They had crawled back into the tunnel and, using cardboard boxes and rags, had sealed themselves in. It had helped, but some smoke had still seeped through. Her lungs still felt as if they were on fire.

Joanna had been certain she was going to die in that basement. They had been trapped, suffocating, with no way out. Then the air had begun to clear and they'd heard male voices. They'd believed it was the man who had tried to kill them, now back with an assistant to make sure they were dead. Or maybe the voices belonged to firemen. But that was bad too, Emma had warned. The firemen would almost certainly blame the women for the fire and charge them with arson. Homeless people were always getting blamed for crimes they didn't commit. Emma had decided it was better for them to stay put and wait for everyone to leave the building.

"And remember," Emma went on, "that man found you and almost killed you when you were trying to hide. Imagine what he could do if he knows where you are. The smart move is to stay away from the cops."

Joanna nodded slowly. "You're probably right."

"Damn right I am." Emma's stomach began to rumble loudly and she patted her abdomen. "Jesus, I'm starving. I hope they make beef stew tonight. It's real tasty."

"Do they let us eat inside the restaurant?"

"No. Outside where they park the cars."

"Good."

"Why is it good?"

"Because I'm filthy and beginning to smell."

"Get used to it," Emma said flatly.

A block away Karl Rimer was waiting. He was crouched behind a wall that separated a closed mini-mart from the parking lot of the restaurant. He raised up just enough to see over the wall. He counted a half dozen cars in the parking lot. At the rear door of the restaurant he saw a waiter and the parking lot attendant smoking cigarettes and talking in Spanish. Just to his right was a giant Dumpster and beyond that the alleyway.

Rimer could see several old folding chairs near the Dumpster and he knew that the homeless would be given their food there, well away from the cars and the restaurant. The setup was perfect. He couldn't have planned it any better. The target distance would be under ten feet and there were two avenues of escape. The driveway to the restaurant and the alley. He preferred the alley. It was dark and led to a quiet street where he'd parked his car. Rimer lowered himself behind the wall and checked his weapon.

"There's the restaurant," Emma said and pointed to the neon light ahead.

"Will there be a lot of people there?" Joanna asked.

"Just our group. You know, Teddy and Timmie and Bertie." Emma picked at her nose and flicked away a piece of mucus.

"Do you think that Bertie is all right?" Joanna asked. "She sounded as if she was frightened to death."

"She's okay. That guy is interested in you, not her."

"I hope she didn't get caught in the fire."

"Not old Bertie," Emma said, unconcerned. "As soon as that man came down the stairs, she ran for the fire escape on the second floor. And kept running."

They turned in at the driveway and walked toward the rear of the restaurant. The parking lot was well lighted except in the area of the Dumpster, where there were shadows.

"We eat over there, by the garbage can," Emma said.

Joanna wrinkled her nose. "What about the smell?"

"How hungry are you?"

"I'm starving."

"Then the smell won't bother you at all."

Rimer heard the women coming, heard their conversation. Then a Spanish voice and a door closing. The kitchen helper was going to get the food for the homeless, Rimer thought, and he switched off the safety on his Beretta. Slowly he raised up and peeked over the wall. The women had stopped and were talking with the parking lot attendant. Something about beef stew. Shit! They were too far away for a clean shot. Too far. Rimer lowered himself and waited.

Timmie was hurrying down the alleyway when he saw a man's head duck behind the wall. He thought the man was wearing a funny-shaped hat, like the guy who had run from the apartment building just before the fire. But he couldn't be sure. It was too dark and the man was in the shadows. Timmie remained motionless in the alley behind the closed mini-mart. He stared at the wall and wondered if the man was still there.

Rimer heard the women approaching, still talking. He recognized Joanna's voice and decided to go for a head shot. She would be plenty close enough. Rimer raised up and, using the top of the wall to steady his arms, he assumed the firing position.

Timmie saw the man and the funny-shaped hat and the gun. An instant later, he saw Emma and Joanna walking toward the man. *"Look out, Emma! He's got a gun!"*

Rimer whirled and fired at the voice. The first shot ripped into Timmie's throat, the second shot went through his right eye. He was dead before he hit the ground.

Rimer whipped back around and aimed at the women as they dove for the safety of a parked Mercedes. He squeezed off two rounds. Emma's head exploded, blood and brain flying into the air. The shot meant for Joanna went wide and shattered the rear window of the Mercedes. The parking lot attendant ran for his life down the driveway, screaming at the top of his lungs.

Rimer hopped over the wall and moved quickly toward the parked car. He dropped down on a knee and, looking under the Mercedes, he saw Joanna's ankles on the other side.

Rimer got to his feet and closed in for the kill.

"Freeze, asshole!" Jake called out, his gun pointed at Rimer's back.

Rimer hesitated for a second and spun around, firing. Jake fired his weapon at the same moment.

Rimer went down, blood streaming from his left shoulder. He scrambled on his knees for the Dumpster, away from the alley where the shots had come from. He didn't see Jake dash across the parking lot to the other side of the Mercedes.

Joanna stared at the man next to her and suddenly all the pieces of her memory came together. "Jake!"

"Shhh!" Jake put a finger on her lips. His left arm cramped and he had trouble moving it. "Keep your voice down. That bastard is still out there."

"Jake!" Joanna said again, happy to see him, happy to have her memory back. "How did you find me?"

"I followed Timmie here."

"Where is he?" Joanna whispered.

"He's dead."

A shot rang out and another window in the Mercedes shattered loudly.

"Stay close to me behind the tire," Jake told her.

Joanna moved in closer and put her head on his shoulder. She felt something warm and sticky on her cheek. She tasted it. Blood! "Jesus, Jake, you've been hit."

Now Jake felt the pain. A deep, stinging sensation in his left arm just below the shoulder. Using his right hand, he ripped the sleeve off his coat. "Take a look and tell me how bad it is."

Joanna tore his shirtsleeve open and examined his arm. It was a through-and-through wound in the deltoid area. Blood was pouring out. "You're losing a lot of blood."

"Bandage it."

"No, Jake. We've got to get you to a hospital."

"Fuck the hospital and bandage the wound," Jake said. "We either get this guy now or you'll spend the rest of your life looking over your shoulder."

Joanna unknotted Jake's tie and removed it. She tightly bandaged his upper arm, stemming the blood flow but not stopping it altogether.

There was an eerie silence. Then Jake heard someone moving. Carefully he looked around the fender of the Mercedes.

Rimer was trying to crawl from behind the Dumpster to the alleyway, but Jake saw him and fired twice. Rimer dove back into the shadows.

"I hope he tries that again," Jake said in a whisper. "I'll blow his goddamn head off."

"Have you got him cornered?" Joanna asked.

"It looks that way, doesn't it?"

Jake heard another sound. A deep, rumbling noise. Jake slowly looked out. The Dumpster had wheels and was moving down the driveway. The assassin was pushing it from the other side and using it for cover.

"I'm going after him," Jake told Joanna. "You stay put."

"Like hell! The only place I'm staying is close to you."

Keeping low, Jake moved from the car to the back of the restaurant. Joanna was a step behind him. He edged his way to the corner of the building and peeked quickly down the driveway. He saw the Dumpster. The killer was gone.

Cautiously, Jake went down the driveway, his gaze fixed on the Dumpster. He wondered if the killer was behind it or maybe inside it, ready to spring. Jake fired two shots into the Dumpster and listened for groans or movement. He heard nothing. The top of the Dumpster was open and Jake glanced in, his weapon pointed downward. It was empty.

Jake looked down the sidewalk in both directions and saw nothing but the misty night air. "Shit! We've lost him."

"Maybe not," Joanna said and pointed to several small pools of blood on the sidewalk. "He's been hit."

"And he's dripping like a faucet too." Jake quickly reloaded his gun. "You stay behind me. Always behind me."

They followed the trail of blood east on Wilshire Boulevard. Jake moved deliberately, glancing from side to side, wondering if the assassin was going to double back and try to ambush them. That was how the bastards worked. Never face-to-face. When you finally saw them it was too late.

They crossed a side street and lost the trail briefly, but then picked it up again. If anything, the killer was bleeding less than before. The spots of blood were smaller and farther apart. Then the trail disappeared altogether. There was no blood, no sounds. Only the misty air now turning into a fog.

"Damn," Jake growled, wondering what to do next. He tried to concentrate, but his left arm was throbbing badly and starting to go numb. "My arm is killing me. Is there any way to ease the pain?"

"Put your hand inside your shirt, like Napoleon," Joanna said. "It'll act as a splint and you won't move it as much."

Jake did the maneuver and it helped. A little.

Suddenly there was the noise of tires screeching and motorists yelling obscenities. Jake looked in the direction of the sounds and saw a tall man with a floppy rain cap running through traffic across the boulevard. The man made it safely to the other side and glanced over his shoulder before dashing up the steps to a huge, glass-plated building.

"Those bastards," Joanna hissed softly.

"Well, well!" Jake said and took her arm.

They waited for traffic to clear and hurried across the street to the new Health First Tower.

The lobby was quiet and deserted, the security guard's desk empty. Jake looked up at the elevator panels. Three of the cars were stationary, the fourth was moving upward. It stopped at the ninth floor.

"What's on the ninth floor?" Jake asked.

"Research and Development," Joanna told him. "Only one car goes to that floor."

Jake pushed the elevator button and the R and D car began to descend. He glanced over at Joanna, now seeing her for the first time in bright light. She looked awful. Her hair was disheveled, her face dirty and chapped with no makeup. He wondered about the ordeal she'd been through and how much of it she would remember. "Are you doing okay?"

"Better than you," Joanna said and pointed to the floor.

Jake's arm was dripping blood again.

The door to the R and D elevator opened and he saw the security guard. He was in a sitting position propped up against the rear wall. His lifeless eyes stared straight ahead. There was a bullet hole in his chest.

Jake pressed the button for the ninth floor and checked his weapon. The car began to zoom upward. "What does the elevator open into?"

"A small lobby," Joanna said.

"Is there any place to hide?"

Joanna thought for a moment. "Not really. There's only a small Plexiglas cage for the guard in the middle of the floor."

"Is it bulletproof?"

"I don't know."

The car jerked to a stop and the doors parted.

Jake took a quick step out and, keeping down, he swept the area with his gun. The lobby was clear. He moved to the Plexiglas cage and glanced in. Empty. "Do you think there's a guard up here at night?"

Joanna shook her head. "I doubt it. Amanda Black once told me there was a very sensitive alarm system that was activated at night."

"Great," Jake said sourly and walked over to a large wooden door. He tried to turn the doorknob. It didn't budge. "Where does this lead to?"

"The research section."

"Any ideas on how to get in?"

Joanna thought back to the times when she had come to the R and D floor with Amanda. The guard had given Joanna an ID card and the women walked right through the outer door. No card slots, no panels to push. They'd just walked in. "There may be a switch in the Plexiglas cage that can open the outer door."

Jake hurried over and kicked the door to the cage off its hinges. The movement caused his arm to start throbbing again, the pain now sharp and stabbing. He took a deep breath and waited for it to ease. Entering the cage, he saw three buttons beneath the counter. They were marked "O," "F" and "N." "What do these symbols mean?"

Joanna studied them briefly. "O is probably the outer door, N the inner."

"And the F?"

"That's to activate a fluoroscope."

"What the hell does that do?"

"It X-rays people to make certain they're not sneaking things in or out."

Jake went to the outer door. "Push the O button."

Joanna pushed the button. There was an audible click from within the lock.

Jake turned the knob and the door opened. "We're in."

Joanna came over and held the door while Jake entered. A wall panel of numbers was brightly lit. Jake pointed to a horizontal slot next to the panel. "Your ID card goes here, huh?"

"Right. But you've got to punch in your numbers first."

"Well, let's see if the N button will do it for us," Jake said.

Joanna took off her shoes and placed them so that the door couldn't close. Then she returned to the cage and pressed the N button.

"Are you pushing the button?" Jake called out.

"Yes."

"Well, the damn door is still locked." Jake walked out into the small lobby. "That N button must not be for the inner door."

"I'll bet it is," Joanna said. "It's not working because we're doing something wrong."

"Like what?"

"I don't know."

"Is there another way out of here?" Jake asked.

"There's a fire escape inside."

"Christ," Jake said miserably. "Our guy could be on his way out of here right now."

Joanna's eyes went back and forth between the buttons inside the cage and the door still propped open by her shoes. Suddenly she stared at the door. *Of course, stupid! It's open!* "I think I know what's wrong."

"What?"

"My shoes."

Jake looked at her strangely. "What!"

"My shoes are keeping the outer door open," Joanna explained. "As long as the outer door is not closed there's an override system that won't allow the inner door to be opened."

"You've seen this kind of system before?"

"Once," Joanna told him. "At a place where they cut and polish diamonds in Amsterdam."

"I'm not sure you're right," Jake said dubiously, "but we'll give it a try. How do you want to work it?"

"Move my shoes out of the way and let the door close. I'll push the O button and you reopen the outer door. Then I'll push the N button and tape it in place." Joanna reached into her pocket for the spool of tape she'd used to bandage Timmie's draining carbuncle. "Then I'll run over and close the outer door and within seconds the inner door will click open."

Jake took a deep breath. "If your plan doesn't work, you know what's going to happen, don't you?"

"What?"

"We're going to be trapped in there."

Joanna watched Jake move to the door and remove her shoes. The door locked shut. "On the count of three, Jake. One . . . two . . . three!" She pushed the O button and waited for Jake to reopen the outer door. Then she pushed the N button and taped it firmly in. Then she dashed across the lobby. Jake closed the door behind her, and a moment later the lock clicked and the inner door hissed open automatically.

Jake took Joanna's shoes and positioned them so that the inner door wouldn't close. "Just in case we have to shoot our way out. It's easier to go through one door than two."

They walked slowly down the dimly lit corridor. Ahead they heard the murmur of a conversation coming from one of the laboratories. Jake held up a hand, stopping Joanna. He signaled for her to remain silent and to stay behind him. Then he tiptoed up to a half-open door that led into the Immuno-Toxins Laboratory.

They crept into the laboratory and around a clear plastic wall. Behind a row of workbenches they saw a man wearing a floppy rain cap. His trench coat was over his arm, his shirt opened and off his shoulders. He had his back to them.

"Just bandage the wound and I can be on my way," Rimer said hoarsely.

"It's not that simple," Amanda Black said. "That bullet is lodged in deeply. It's going to require surgery."

"Just dress the damn wound."

Amanda reached for a wad of cotton. "You were so stupid to come here. So stupid! Suppose you were followed?"

"I wasn't followed. There was no one behind me."

Jake moved to within ten feet of Rimer and assumed the firing position. "Oh yes there was, asshole."

Rimer started to reach for his trench coat.

"Go ahead," Jake said evenly. "We'll save the taxpayers a lot of money."

Amanda fought her panic and tried to think of a way out of her dilemma. "I don't know who this man is," she said quickly. "I never saw him before. He just broke in here and demanded that I treat his wound."

"Is that right?" Joanna asked disdainfully. "He just broke down both doors, huh?"

"The—the guard. He forced the guard to let him in," Amanda stammered.

Joanna stared at her. "You mean the guard we found dead in the elevator?"

Amanda jerked her head toward Rimer. "You killed the guard?"

Rimer reached ever so slightly, almost imperceptibly, toward his trench coat. He hoped Amanda Black would keep talking, keep them distracted.

"Why did you poison those patients?" Joanna asked.

"I don't know what you're talking about," Amanda said, regaining her composure.

"Sure you do," Joanna said easily. "You had a secret compartment built into Sally Wheaton's pacemaker."

"You can't prove that."

"Oh, yes, I can," Joanna went on. "And I can also prove there was a similar compartment in Lucy O'Hara's morphine pump and in Karen Butler's artificial hip. That was a common denominator among the three dead patients, wasn't it? They all had artificial implants. And all of the implants had secret compartments that contained some powerful toxin. What was the poison you used?"

"Ricin," a man's voice said behind them. "And I'm pointing a gun at your head, so please don't make a foolish move. Now drop your weapon, Lieutenant."

Rimer waited for Jake's gun to hit the floor, then grabbed the Beretta from his trench coat. "Too bad, you lose."

Robert Mariner laughed softly and walked over to Amanda's side. He had no gun. Instead he had his thumb and index finger extended like a toy pistol. "I always wondered if that would work." Mariner put his hand down. "Let's see. Where were we? Oh, yes, we were talking about ricin. You recall ricin, don't you, Joanna? It's the most potent toxin known to mankind. It's so potent that one molecule can kill a human cell. Imagine that. And of course you're right. We did have small compartments placed in certain implants, and these compartments contained the poison. It was a simple matter to release it. We just placed a small electrode near the tip of the compartment. An electric signal from a phone or beeper could melt an opening and allow the ricin to be released. In most cases, Amanda and I used our beepers while visiting patients at Memorial to activate the device. We didn't even have to be in the patient's room. Our beepers send their signals a considerable distance, you see."

Joanna couldn't believe what she was hearing. "My God! Ricin!"

"Yes, ricin."

"But why did you do it?"

"To spare patients from useless procedures that would only cause them misery and pain. These bone marrow transplants may sound good on the evening news, but in reality most of them don't work out well."

"That's not true," Joanna argued.

"Oh, really? Let's talk about Lucy O'Hara and the marrow transplant she was to receive from an unrelated donor. Do you know what the success rate for that is? I'll tell you. It's somewhere around ten percent. And some of those patients who do get a take end up having a terrible graft-versus-host reaction. They live, but they're sick as hell. So we're dealing with a five percent success rate. And the other ninety-five percent who have this procedure will hurt and suffer and hemorrhage and get infected and die in agony. How does that sound to you?"

"A five percent cure rate sounds better than a no percent cure rate," Joanna snapped.

"At what cost, Joanna? At what cost?"

"Ask the O'Hara family what Lucy's life was worth to them."

"You just don't understand," Mariner said calmly. "The day of medicine in America's doing everything possible for everybody is over. We're going to have to make hard choices on who gets what treatment. And treatment with bone marrow transplants will be the first thing to go."

"But autologous bone marrow transplants work in patients with breast cancer," Joanna said, trying to buy time and hoping that Jake would come up with a way out.

"Have you got the data to back that up?" Mariner asked. "Of course you don't. Because the data doesn't exist. No one has ever shown that bone marrow transplants work any better than intensive chemotherapy. The fact of the matter is that the cure rate is miserable in cancer patients who receive bone marrow transplants. Yet we continue to do them. Why? Because that's the motto of American medicine. Do something, even if it doesn't work. And if it happens to be expensive, so much the better. Crazy, isn't it?''

"You think it's preferable to give patients ricin?"

"In some instances."

"You're talking euthanasia."

"I'm talking reality. These patients are going to die of their disease regardless of what we do. But we keep doing these procedures, draining off health care dollars that are urgently needed elsewhere. Do you have any idea what a bone marrow transplant costs?''

"No, I don't," Joanna said, glancing at the floor as blood dripped from Jake's arm.

"Just for Lucy O'Hara's transplant the cost would have been two hundred thousand dollars. And her follow-up care could have been another hundred thousand. That adds up to three hundred thousand dollars for a procedure that usually doesn't work."

"Jesus," Joanna seethed, "so money was the real reason. You killed three women to save a million dollars."

Mariner smiled thinly. "We've done this to sixty terminal patients over the past two years."

"Sixty!"

Mariner nodded. "That's only a few patients each month. You must remember that Health First has over a million patients enrolled in its HMOs. So if two or three terminally ill patients suddenly die each month, it doesn't raise any suspicions. But the savings are immense. We've already saved twenty million dollars. Our savings over the next few years could be as much as . . . forty-five million dollars."

"But why kill them at Memorial?" Joanna asked, now feeling Jake leaning on her, hoping he wouldn't pass out.

"It's better when it happens in a hospital. People almost expect it to happen there. And it also shifts any blame away from Health First." Mariner gave Joanna a long look. "You would have never learned about the implants without the microfilm. Where did you find it?''

"We found it in Bob Cipro's apartment. He used a radio-opaque dye to show the compartment."

"That homosexual piece of shit," Mariner said hatefully. "He was going to blackmail us and bleed us dry."

"Was Alex in on it too?"

Amanda forced a laugh. "Alex didn't know anything until you advertised the tattoo on the faceless man's butt. Then he put two and two together and—"

"Enough talk!" Mariner said abruptly. "Now we have to attend to these two."

"I'll take them downstairs and kill them outside," Rimer said.

"No," Mariner said at once. "We'll do it up here."

"But the bodies," Rimer protested. "We'll have to move the bodies, and they'll be dead weight."

"That won't be a problem," Mariner told him. "We have a garbage chute in this laboratory that drops ten stories down into the basement. When a weight of greater than a hundred pounds hits, the garbage is automatically compacted into small blocks which are later taken away to be incinerated." Mariner looked over at Joanna almost sympathetically. "You'll feel very little. The fall will kill you."

Amanda hurried across the lab to the wall where the garbage chute was located. She opened the door to the chute. The opening was a square, three feet by three feet. It was plenty big enough to accommodate a body.

Rimer pushed the barrel of his gun into Jake's back. "Move!"

Joanna was desperately trying to think of a way out. Jake was leaning on her heavily, his color pale from the loss of blood. *Make a run for it!* she screamed to herself. *At least die trying to get away.*

Rimer prodded her with his gun. "Move faster, bitch!"

Joanna fought to control her fear. *God! I don't want to die. Not like this. And not like Emma, either, with my brains blown out.* "Poor Emma," Joanna said softly to herself.

"Don't worry about the old hag," Rimer said. "You'll be joining her soon enough."

Joanna suddenly remembered the gift from Emma. The can of Mace. She reached furtively into her pocket and flipped the top of the rusty can. *God! Let it still be functional! Please!* Without turning, she pointed the can over her shoulder and pressed on the nozzle.

Rimer was blinded, the pain terrible. He clawed at his eyes with one hand and fired the Beretta wildly with the other.

Two shots went into Amanda's neck and severed her carotid arteries. She dropped, blood spurting out into the air and onto the floor.

Rimer was spinning like a wild man, his semiautomatic weapon spitting bullets in all directions. Mariner crawled on hands and knees for the door. Jake reached out for him and knocked him into a chair.

Joanna went to the floor and grabbed Rimer's feet, trying to trip him. He kicked at her in an attempt to free himself, and this caused him to lose his balance and fall to the tiled floor. As he got back up, his shoes slipped on Amanda's blood and he again lost his balance, now tilting awkwardly.

Jake saw his chance and lunged at Rimer, his good shoulder catching Rimer in the abdomen. Rimer banged into the wall behind him, his back and buttocks now against the opened chute. Again he kicked at Joanna and she tightened her grip and jerked his legs from under him. Rimer fell backward and disappeared down the chute, screaming at the top of his lungs.

Mariner saw Jake's gun on the floor and went for it. Jake dove for Mariner, knocking him away from the weapon but landing on his wounded shoulder. A terrible pain shot into Jake's arm and elbow. He thought he was going to pass out. But he could feel the weapon under him.

Mariner scrambled to his feet as Joanna grabbed at him and clutched his long white coat. He tried to wriggle free, but she held on with all her might. Mariner twisted his body around and the buttons of his coat popped off. He pulled away, leaving Joanna holding his white coat.

Mariner ran out of the laboratory and down the corridor. He reached the door that led to the lobby. Kicking aside Joanna's shoes, he entered the area between the doors and let the inner door close behind him. He quickly punched his number into the wall panel. Above the panel an electric sign blinked:

PLEASE INSERT I.D. CARD

Mariner reached for his card.

Joanna and Jake hurried out of the laboratory and down the hallway. The door to the lobby was closed, Joanna's shoes pushed aside. They heard a loud banging coming from within. Jake aimed his gun at the door, ready to fire. Then they heard Mariner screaming to be let out.

"Looks like he got himself trapped, doesn't it?" Jake said.

Joanna held up Mariner's white coat and pointed to the attached ID card. "He forgot something."

Jake placed his weapon in its holster and adjusted the makeshift bandage on his arm. He could still smell tear gas on his clothes. "Where'd you get the Mace?"

"From a friend named Emma."

Mariner banged against the door, causing it to shake. He was yelling about his card.

"Yeah, you forgot it," Jake yelled back at him.

"He forgot something else," Joanna said.

"What?"

"The most important part of the Hippocratic oath."

"What does that say?"

"Above all, do no harm." Joanna put the tip of the ID card into its slot. "Ready?"

Jake pulled out his gun and handcuffs. "Ready."

Joanna pushed the card in and the door hissed open.

Epilogue

"Pretty good-looking couple, huh?" Jake asked.

"Not bad at all," Joanna grinned.

They were standing in front of the Dorothy Chandler Pavillion at the Music Center, studying their reflections in the glass. Joanna was wearing a black cocktail dress with a single strand of pearls, Jake was resplendent in a double-breasted tuxedo. They heard a light ripple of applause behind them and turned to see the crowd parting to make room for the mayor of Los Angeles and his party, which included Simon Murdock and his wife.

Murdock saw them and quickly came over. "Nice to see you," he said and sounded sincere. "Wonderful evening for a wonderful cause, huh?"

"Yes, indeed," Joanna agreed. The opera premiere was a benefit to fund research into Alzheimer's disease. It was expected to raise $250,000.

"Well, I hope to see you at intermission," Murdock said and hurried back to join the mayor and other dignitaries.

Joanna turned to Jake. "Did you know that Robert Mariner was supposed to have been a distinguished guest at this affair?"

"How do you know that?"

Joanna showed him the program for the gala. Mariner was listed as a distinguished sponsor. "He even donated twenty-five thousand dollars."

"Hell, it's easy to be generous when it's somebody else's money."

Joanna shrugged. "Maybe it really was his money."

"Forget it!" Jake said and carefully lit a cigarette. "Remember all that crap he told us about killing those people to save money for Health First? Well, he was saving a little for himself too. Like five million dollars. That's what they found in his Swiss bank account."

"Jesus," Joanna said softly, "all that brilliance and power and he threw it all away so he could have more success."

"And more money," Jake said. "Don't forget the money."

"It's more than money, Jake." She took his cigarette and puffed on it before giving it back. "People like Mariner need power and success. It's like a damn disease."

"Well, he's not controlling anything from jail," Jake said, then smiled thinly. "Did you know that Mariner is claiming he's innocent?"

"What!"

"Oh, yeah. He says it was all Amanda's doing and he only found out about it at the last moment."

"What about the implant devices we found in his safe? You know, the ones that were loaded with ricin."

"He says Amanda planted them in there."

"You think a jury will believe that?"

"No way. He's either going to suck cyanide gas or spend the rest of his life in prison."

Joanna shook her head slowly. "So he destroys himself and takes Health First down with him."

"Well, he got some help from your pal Arnold Kohler."

"What about Kohler?"

"The DEA boys found out he was writing a ton of prescriptions for amphetamines and narcotics. And he was selling them on the side. Rimer was one of his very best customers." Jake flipped his cigarette into a sand-filled receptacle. "They figured he was making an extra four thousand dollars a month."

"Has he been charged?"

"Better than that. The DEA boys marched into Health First this morning and arrested the little bastard. They handcuffed him right in front of everybody. And guess what? The news media was on hand to get some good pictures. I think Health First is going to go under."

"Don't bet on it," Joanna said evenly. "There's big bucks involved here, and I'm talking billions. They'll just change their name and go on with business."

"Maybe. But one thing is for damn sure. They'll be a lot more careful from here on out."

Chimes rang out in the night air. It was the first call for the audience to take their seats.

Joanna removed a piece of lint from Jake's tuxedo and patted his lapels gently. "Ready?"

"Oh, yeah," Jake said, taking her arm. "What's the name of this opera?"

"*Otello.*"

"What's it about?"

"A black hero becomes jealous and kills his white wife."

Jake's brow went up. "Are you kidding me?"

"I'm dead serious."

"It sounds like the O.J. trial."

Joanna shook her head. "The story was written by Shakespeare over three hundred years ago."

"This black fellow—what the hell is his name?"

"Otello. He's a Moor king."

"Does he go to trial?"

"Nope."

"Christ! Don't tell me he walked."

"No. He killed himself."

Jake smiled broadly. "I love happy endings."

"You're rare, Jake," Joanna said, nestling her head against his shoulder. "Very rare."

"Naw. Just honest."

"That's what makes you so rare."

AUTHOR'S NOTE

Ricin is real, very real. It is the most powerful poison known to mankind. One molecule of ricin can kill a human cell. No other poison in the world even begins to approach this level of toxicity. Interestingly, ricin may prove to have value in the treatment of cancer. A number of laboratories in the United States are currently designing "magic bullets" that can zero in on and selectively destroy malignant cells. One such magic bullet consists of ricin hooked onto an antibody that specifically reacts with a cancer cell. The antibody attaches to the cancer cell and kills it. Experimental studies have shown this form of therapy to be effective against a variety of malignancies, including leukemia, lymphoma, and carcinomas of the breast, lung and ovary.

However, ricin has also been used by assassins. Not long ago a Bulgarian defector who was employed by the BBC became deathly ill after he was poked in the buttock with the tip of an umbrella. It was believed that the umbrella was used to inject ricin into the victim. But this was never proven because the amount of ricin needed to kill a person is so small it could not be detected in the patient's blood by available methodologies.

—Leonard S. Goldberg, M.D.

REFERENCES

1. Le Maistre, C. F.; Rosen, S.; Frankel, A.; Kornfeld, S.; Saria, E.; Meneghetti, C.; Drajesk, J.; Fishwild, D.; Scanno, P.; and Byer, V. "Phase I Trial of H65-RTA Immunoconjugate in Patients with Cutaneous T-Cell Lymphoma." *Blood* 78:1173–1182, 1991.
2. Ravel, S.; Colombatti, M.; and Casellas, P. "Internalization and Intracellular Fate of Anti-CD5 Monoclonal Antibody and Anti-CD5 Ricin A-Chain Immunotoxin in Human Leukemic T-Cells." *Blood* 79:1151–1517, 1992.

3. Rodriguez, G. C.; Boente, M. P.; Berchuck, A.; Whitaker, R. S.; O'Briant, K. C.; Fengji, X.; and Bast, R. C. "The Effect of Antibodies and Immunotoxins Reactive with HER-2/neu on Growth of Ovarian and Breast Cancer Cell Lines." *Amer. J. Obstet. Gynecol.* 168:228–232, 1993.

4. Lynch, T. J. "Immunotoxin Therapy of Small Cell Lung Cancer. N901-Blocked Ricin for Relapsed Small Cell Lung Cancer." *Chest* 103:436S–439S, 1993.

5. Faquet, G. B., and Agee, J. F. "Four Ricin Chain A-Based Immunotoxins Directed Against the Common Chronic Lymphocytic Leukemia Antigen: In Vitro Characterization." *Blood* 82:536–543, 1993.

6. Amiot, P. L.; Stone, M. J.; Cunningham, D.; Fay, J.; Newman, J.; Collins, R.; May, R.; McCarthy, M.; Richardson, J.; Ghetie, V.; Ramilo, O.; Thorpe, P. E.; Uhr, J. W.; and Vitetta, E. S. "A Phase I Study of an Anti-CD22-Deglycosylated Ricin A Chain Immunotoxin in the Treatment of B-Cell Lymphomas Resistant to Conventional Therapy." *Blood* 82:2624–2633, 1993.

The typeface used in this book is a version of Baskerville, orig-
inally designed by John Baskerville (1706–1775) and considered to be one of the first "transitional" typefaces between
the "old style" of the continental humanist printers and the
"modern" style of the nineteenth century. With a determi-
nation bordering on the eccentric to produce the finest possible printing, Baskerville set out at age forty-five and with no
previous experience to become a typefounder and printer (his
first fourteen letters took him two years). Besides the letter
forms, his innovations included an improved printing press,
smoother paper, and better inks, all of which made Baskerville
decidedly uncompetitive as a businessman. Franklin, Beau-
marchais, and Bodoni were among his admirers, but his typeface had to wait for the twentieth century to achieve its due.